BREATHING YOU IN

The Courtlynd Series: Book 1

CHRISTINA MARIA

Please note, this book contains sensitive subject matter.
To view the trigger warnings, please see the end of the book.

1
CARSTEN

I PULL OUT OF HER AND ROLL OVER, PANTING." FUCK, THAT
was great." I let out a deep breath, gasping for air. Just about as good
as Tiffany or Brittany from last night whatever their names were,
that threesome was fucking awesome that's all I know. I don't give a
fuck what their names were. Twins and threesome that's all I fucking
cared about. Oh, and getting my dick sucked and licked by two
different girls at the same time. Fucking. Heaven.

"It was, wasn't it babe?" Brynn snaps me out of my thoughts,
rubbing her finger up and down my sweaty chest. I turn my head
rolling my eyes at her calling me *babe* and sigh. That's one thing I
can't stand about her, how clingy she is. But she sure knows what
she's doing and it's fucking hot. I guess I kinda did it to myself and
caused my own damn problems, I let my dick do my thinking and it
always gets me in trouble. I'm used to it.

"I love you, baby," she says, and I turn over to grab my phone.
She knows how I feel. She knows that this isn't anything serious. I
specifically told her that this was just sex when we met because I
knew she wanted more; I thought if I told her she'd just accept it and
be ok with being fuck buddies. Most girls I fuck are lucky that
they're even getting the chance to fuck me. That I'm choosing them
to please and fuck. Yeah, I'm cocky... but how can I not be? Every

girl I look at wants me, and once they hear I'm a bad boy who has been arrested three times, they're drooling even more all over my nice hard cock. That's another reason why I don't stick to the same girl; there's so many beautiful girls out there, why stick to just one when I can sample them all? Fuck, I'm such an asshole. I laugh to myself with my fucked-up thoughts. My dear Brynn here is lucky that I'm even still fucking lying here next to her. Usually, I pull out of whoever I fuck and practically run out the door like they're diseased. I don't stick around to cuddle or talk; I'm not interested in conversation. I'm only in it to fuck.

"Aren't you gonna say it back?" Pools of tears well up in her big eyes. "Don't you love me, Carsten?" She sits up getting angry this time. The look of disgust on her face. I can't blame her though, I am quite a pig, I can't help it. But at the same time, she knew what she was getting herself into, I never said I'd take her on dates, or anything more than just fuck. All of these "feelings" she's feeling she's creating with her own fucked up mind of hers.

She starts to cry now making me feel like shit, I shouldn't fucking care, this literally means nothing to me, and it will never fucking mean anything to me. Fucking ever. I already told her a few weeks ago, when I met her, that this was just to hook up. She's lucky I'm even still fucking her. I usually only hook up with a girl a few times and call it quits so they don't get attached. "I just, I thought after a couple times you'd love me–that's why I continued…"

I cut her off sick of hearing it. "This is over, I'm not doing this anymore. If you're going to cry about me not loving you, then I'm done." I pause looking at the time. "I gotta go anyway. I gotta get to work before Chase ends up opening alone." I jump up, losing my balance, stumbling trying to get my pants on, still a little hungover from last night. Usually when I hang out with Brynn, we end up shitfaced then fuck the rest of the night and barely get any sleep. I don't even bother brushing my teeth yet, I'll do it once I get to the bar. I don't want to spend any more time listening to her cry, she might even start begging. So, I'm getting my ass out of here before I'm stuck here even longer.

"Please, Carsten, I promise." She stops for a second, thinking of what to say next. "I promise I won't say it anymore. Please don't end this. I'm fine being fuck buddies." She gets up grabbing a T-shirt from the floor and starts chasing after me.

"Goodbye, Brynn." I decide to ignore her this time instead of responding, or else I'm never going to leave.

Walking out her front door I start down the porch stairs. Hearing Brynn running after me, she cuts me off and races to my car door standing in front of it. She blocks me from getting in. I pick her up from under her arms, like the child she's acting like, and move her out of the way completely. I'm not talking because I just don't have time for a conversation right now, and this could literally be a never-ending conversation that just keeps repeating itself. I'm already running late. I sit down in my car and go to shut the door but she's now standing in the doorway, one hand on my car roof, the other on the door blocking me from shutting it.

"Please, baby, stop ignoring me," she pleads with tears streaming down her face.

"Brynn, stop calling me baby. I told you, I'm not your boyfriend." I sigh aggravated.

"Carsten, please. We can't end it like this. I promise I'll chill out some." She fists her fingers through her messy hair, clearly trying to think of anything to keep me from ending this. "I'll stop calling you baby. I won't tell you I love you anymore." She lets out a breath like she's been holding it in then suddenly, she's breathing heavily while crying hysterically, and it's hard for me not to laugh with how dramatic she's being.

"Fuck, Brynn, ok fine. This is the last time though, I'm serious." I turn the key in my ignition, starting my car now, I glance at the time, again. "Fuck, dude, now I'm late. Chase is going to be pissed."

She sniffles, putting her head down. "I'm sorry. Have a good night at work, I might be stopping in with some friends, just so you know."

"Alright, see you later then, I guess." She finally backs away from my door and I slam it shut, putting my car in reverse and begin speeding down her long driveway, not even giving a fuck about turning around. I check for cars and pull out onto the main road, now checking for cops as I speed to work. I don't need another ticket or to be arrested again for something stupid. Courtlynd is a small ass town where everyone pretty much knows everyone, and everyone always wants to be in your business. Even the cops are shitty, once they pull you over or you're arrested for one thing, it's like you're always on their radar and they're always looking for reasons to pull you over again. That's why I'm checking for cops as I speed to work because I don't have time for their bullshit.

I pull into the parking lot of Black Velvet, to my brother, Chase, standing at the door with his arms crossed shaking his head.

"Fucckkk," I say to myself as I quickly put the car in park. I get out and lock the doors.

"Sorry man, I forgot I took the keys with me last night after we closed. Usually, I'm the one waiting on you when you take the keys." He laughs, shaking his head.

"It's cool man, I understand. Brynn again?" he asks, smirking.

"Fuck yeah, bro. But apparently now she loves me." It's hard to not roll my eyes as I say it out loud, the thought alone makes me cringe. Even if I was a relationship kind of guy, there would be no way Brynn would be one that I would even think about making my girlfriend. She would drive me fucking crazy.

He cuts me off, "What? She loves you? It's been what... a week, your dick must be good man." He throws his head back laughing.

"Right, I guess for her it is. I'm not bragging, but I've never had any complaints." I laugh hitting him on the back lightly. "But now she's crying because I didn't say it back and I don't want to be in a relationship. She knew in the beginning going into this that we were just going to be fuck buddies and nothing more." Sighing again I run my hands through my hair, frustrated that I even have to deal with this.

"Damn, well you better cut ties if you don't want her to turn psycho on your ass."

"I think I'll give it a little longer and see if it sinks in that we won't be anything more, the pussy is pretty good." I smile, because it's true I haven't had a pussy this good in a while, and she definitely knows what she's doing.

"That's awesome man, but don't say I didn't warn you if she turns into a psychopath." He gives me a serious look.

"Yea, yea. I'll deal with it then if she does." I walk off to the back room to finish setting things up so we can open the bar.

2

WINTER

Line dancing. Not exactly sure how *just dinner* with my best friend turned into line dancing, but here we are on a Thursday night going line dancing at our local town bar. Emerald, my best friend, told me I work too much and needed a night out to have some fun and relieve some stress. It was supposed to be just dinner and catching up, but when we drove past Black Velvet, the popular college hangout, and saw the sign, things changed very quickly.

"Holy shit, Winter, did you just see the sign at Black Velvet?" Emerald practically screams out and it's so loud she made me jump and drop my phone.

"Holy shit, Emerald. No, I didn't!" I respond in a mocking, smart-ass tone. "I was texting Chastity back, updating her on how close we are, and then you ever so rudely scared the shit out of me." I sigh, holding my hand to my chest dramatically. "Now what sign was so important you gave me a heart attack and made me drop my phone?"

"Line dancing!" Shrieking excitedly, she pulls the car over into the nearest parking lot and smiles at me. "Line dancing, Snow! Line. Dancing." She places her hands under her chin, with her fingers interlocked like she's praying and gives me a big smile.

"Hell no. Girl you know I HATE line dancing and I suck at it," I say laughing while she still smiles and now flutters her eyes at me.

"Please, Winter, this will be so much fun. Chastity would love it too. Plus, dancing will help relieve some of your stress. Line dancing is so fun and it's easy, everyone around you pretty much shows you what you're supposed to be doing anyway."

I sit there and stare out the window, not responding right away, the thought of going to the bar makes me nervous. I hate letting my dad ruin all my fun by thinking of every thought that's going to come out of his mouth if he finds out I'm at the bar. It's not that I'm too young, it's the fact he's a drunk and always assumes the worst of me.

"I know you're thinking about what your dad would say, but c'mon Snow, you can't let him ruin your fun all the time. You're twenty-two you are supposed to be going to college parties, going to bars, clubs—living your life like a normal twenty-two-year-old." She sighs, looking at me then speaks quietly. "You're not supposed to be taking care of your drunk father all the time, and I mean that as nice as a best friend could mean it."

"Fine, I'll go, but if I hate it, I'm not dancing, I'll sit and watch you guys. As soon as we are done, we're going to eat, because I'm starving," she screams in excitement, clapping her hands, then comes in for a tight hug.

"Thanks, Winter, you're going to have so much fun. Chastity loves to dance, so do I. I Promise you're going to love it too."

Before pulling back onto the road she calls Chastity to let her know our change of plans and I can hear her screech over the phone. I chuckle to myself and shake my head, I'm glad they're excited. I really am looking to let loose and keep my mind off my stress, especially the unwanted stress from my dad. So dancing, even if it is line dancing, I guess I'll have to make the best of it and try to have some fun.

A few minutes later, we walk into Black Velvet. It isn't as packed as I thought it would be, getting close to the weekend in a college town, but there's still a decent amount of people on the dance floor.

"I don't see anyone line dancing, Em," I shout into her ear from behind.

"It starts in a half hour, babe." She laughs knowing I'm trying to get out of it. "Don't worry, you didn't miss any of it, and... you're not getting out of it either."

"I know, I know. I've accepted my fate," I say, glancing around looking for Chastity.

"I don't know if Chastity is here yet, can you see her at all? I'm too short?" Em says, trying to jump up to see her through the people dancing.

"Girl, do you not remember, I'm five-five too." I shake my head at her, chuckling a little at how forgetful she is sometimes.

"Shush." She pushes me lightly on the shoulder. "Oh wow, I never thought I'd actually see him here. I never see him anywhere," she says, glancing at the bar.

"Who are you talking about, you act like there's only one person in here, Emerald."

"Ok, smart-ass. Behind the bar, the guy in the tight ripped black jeans, wife beater, full sleeve tattoos going over his chest, from what you can see, and light-brown hair and beard. His name is Carsten Hatcher. His mom, him, and his brother all own this bar, but he and his brother helped her bring it back to life. They help her run the bar; I usually don't see him here though. Usually, he's busy tattooing at one of his uncle's tattoo shops. I met him a couple of times, then it was almost like I imagined him, I never see him anywhere." Damn she sure knows a lot about this guy.

"Well damn, anything else you know? You seem to know a lot about him, you got it bad huh?" She rolls her eyes, letting out a small snort before slapping my arm playfully. "No way. I mean he's fucking fine, don't get me wrong, but he's not my type."

"Huh, doesn't seem that way." I wink obnoxiously to let her know I'm joking. "He is very sexy though," I say to her and quickly look away because I think he notices me watching him. Yep, he definitely noticed with that wink and panty dropping smile. He stands there for a second just staring at me before finally going to the back room carrying boxes with him. I turn around to see Emerald just staring at me with a big smile on her face.

"Ya know, the offer is still there for you to move in with me if ya know you wanna get to know him more." She starts laughing, grabbing my hand and pulling me to the dance floor. The bar seems to have a thing with theme nights. Tonight is country with line dancing, tomorrow is 90s hip-hop and R&B, I definitely would come for that one. Country night hasn't started yet so as we get on the dance floor Nelly's "Hot in herre" starts playing.

"Hell yeah!" Emerald shouts over the music to me. "I fucking love this song." I laugh as she starts joking around, shaking her ass at me.

"Calm down with those moves you got going on there girl." I put my hand on my chest, bending over slightly and laugh. "Might call all the nasties over in your direction, don't wanna have a bunch of men lined up to take turns letting you shake your ass for them like that." I turn around shaking my ass back at her the same way she just was. "Ha, ha, very funny bitch, you know that's not how I really dance, now get your ass over here you hoe and let's show these men what they aren't leaving here with tonight."

We start dancing the only slutty way we know how to this type of music, just like the rest of the girls in the bar, grinding on each other, when I just so happen to turn towards the bar while dancing and catch Mr. Panty Dropping Smile staring over in our direction. Not sure if he's checking Emerald out, or me. It would make more sense for it to be Emerald since he is her neighbor, but part of me hopes he's checking me out.

3

CARSTEN

LOOKING UP I JUST SO HAPPEN TO NOTICE THIS GORGEOUS fucking girl staring at me. My head is still a little groggy from last night, but next to her looks like my neighbor, Emerald. I actually haven't really talked to her much, not that she doesn't seem cool, I just kinda keep to myself and work my ass off to stay out of trouble, especially after being arrested three times last year for dumb shit. The only time I really do dumb shit is when I get shit faced hanging out with Brynn, but sometimes she's annoying so it makes it easier to handle her being fucked up. I usually have a new girl I fuck every night, no strings attached. Brynn's the first one I stuck with for longer than a few days, and I don't want anything more. I still fuck other girls besides her. She's just really fucking easy, and I don't have to work hard to get her to give it up to me. So, I've only gone to her a couple times on nights I couldn't get pussy from some other chick. Does that make me an asshole? Probably. Do I give a fuck? That's gonna be a big fuck no from me. She probably doesn't deserve it, but she keeps comin back though. She must like the way I treat her then.

But damn, this girl who I can't help but wink at while giving her my sexy smile, I end up making her blush from it, she's fucking gorgeous. She has pink and purple hair, the sexiest curves in all my favorite places, with her ripped jeans hugging her ass just right. Her tight shirt showing off her perfect tits and she has a ton of tattoos from what I can see from here, which is so fucking sexy to me. I can't help but keep staring like I've never seen a fucking girl before or something. I must look pretty stupid as she looks back at me.

"Yo, Carst, get your ass moving," my brother, Chase, yells to me. "These fucking boxes aren't gonna move themselves and I'm not gonna be the only one busting my ass moving them bro." I snap out of it and look over at him.

"Shut the hell up, I've moved more than you have dip shit." I shake my head.

"I know, I'm just busting your balls, but like really help me out man. I'm sore as shit from working out yesterday." Yesterday we both busted our asses in the gym. Another thing we do to keep ourselves busy and out of trouble.

Snapping out of my thoughts I start carrying the boxes that were delivered for inventory into the back room. My mom's out of town this week, and we promised we would have everything under control. That we wouldn't fuck anything up so she could enjoy her girl's trip with her best friend. My mom took over my uncle's bar when he retired. He figured instead of selling it he'd give it to family, since he didn't need the money. The bar was pretty much something to keep him busy when he first retired. Then he and my aunt decided to move someplace warm and leave the bar to us to take care of.

Carrying boxes back to the break room I can't help but think about that girl. I've never seen her before over at Emerald's house and I'm curious as to why I haven't. I don't even think I've seen her around town before and it's driving me crazy especially since she has tattoos. I've been working in my uncle's tattoo shop since I was eighteen and I've never seen her in there, not even while I've been getting ink done myself.

Like I said before, this is a small ass town so mostly everyone knows everyone. Sometime tonight, maybe on my break I'll get out there and dance with her or try to find a way to start a conversation with her if she comes up to get a drink, which I've noticed she hasn't done yet. For being a bar, usually that's the first thing people do when they come in is get a drink of some sort or order a round of shots.

The music finally stops, the DJ announces he's going to set up for country night, which is moms favorite, she'll be sad she missed it. Usually, the DJ doesn't play anything dance worthy while he sets everything up and we try to clear the dance floor to make sure it's clean from spilled drinks and everything else before it gets crazy again. Of course, as I'm heading to check out the dance floor I see the girl who was with Emerald head to the bar. Mother fucker. I quickly turn around and book it behind the bar to get to her before my brother does.

"Move it fucker, I'm taking her order." I push past Chase.

"Hey, what the hell man. I saw her first, she's hot." I turn and glare at him.

"I know, that's why she's mine dick cheese. Keep your hands to yourself."

He laughs. "God, you're such a man whore dude. Can't you keep your dick in your pants or keep your dick to just one woman long enough to have an actual relationship." I don't even stop to talk. I need to get to this gorgeous girl that I've been watching half the night before he gets to her. Something about her draws me in, and I need to figure out what it is. Besides the fact that she's gorgeous as hell and mmm, her fucking body man, I'd love to see her underneath of me, while fucking her until she's screaming out my name. Yep, that's the kind of guy I am, I usually go straight to thinking about sex like the man whore I've trained myself to become. But that doesn't mean I wouldn't show her a good time. Besides she seems different, there's something about her that doesn't make me want to fuck her just once and I haven't even spoken to the girl yet.

"I don't have time for this right now Chase, I got a woman to swoon." Stepping up to the bar I give her my best smile. "Hey gorgeous, what can I getcha?" I wink at her. Placing both hands on the counter, smiling at her. But I'm instantly sucked in, Fuck, she's even more gorgeous up close. I try not to stare at her pouty lips as she opens her mouth to talk and I instantly think about biting her bottom lip and sucking it into my mouth, and I regret that decision because I end up with an instant hard on just thinking about it.

"Hey there, umm-" Blushing, she smiles and pauses then looks over to her friend.

"Em, I think I'm just gonna get some water. I don't think I'm really in the mood to drink, especially since I haven't eaten anything today." Her friend pouts. This probably isn't a good idea if she drinks on an empty stomach. But I'm not going to put my nose where it doesn't belong, I'll just make sure to keep an eye on her, and if she gets too drunk, I'll get her something to eat without taking no for an answer. Especially if she tries to leave, hopefully she wasn't the one who drove.

"C'mon just one shot." Emerald pouts at her even more dramatically than she did before she started talking. I move myself closer waiting to hear her name, but her friend never says it and I don't want to look like just another creepy bartender and ask her.

"I don't know Em. Then I gotta make sure I don't get drunk, or even buzzed for that matter, or else my dad's gonna go crazy on me," she says that a little quieter this time.

I wonder how old she is if her dad gets that worked up over her drinking. Hopefully she's of age, not that I care, we get a lot of fake IDs in this bar. I just don't want her dad coming up here if he cares that much.

"Fuck your dad." She laughs. "I keep telling you, the offer is open, just one shot, it'll loosen you up before we line dance." She smiles at her friend then looks over at me. "We'll have two lemon drops please."

"I'll take a water with that as well please," the girl says to me after Emerald orders the shots.

"Comin' right up ladies." I wink and walk away doing my best to work quickly before she walks away. "Here you go." I handed the one shot to Emerald "Here you go snowflake." I smirk at the gorgeous mystery girl, and she pauses, shit I hope that wasn't too corny. But the look on her face tells me it might have been, what the fuck is wrong with me. I'm usually good with what I say to girls, but for some reason talking around her she makes me feel like I don't know how to talk, or like I don't know what I'm doing, and I don't like my sudden lack of confidence.

"Wait, why'd you just call me snowflake?" She giggles while swirling her finger around the shot glass I just sat in front of her. She looks away nervously, while the color of pink on her cheeks grows a little further from her blushing. For some reason she keeps blushing when I talk to her, and I find it very fucking attractive. What a weird thing to find attractive, but let's be honest here everything about this girl has my dick hard and all I've done is talk to her.

"Not sure really, snowflakes are beautiful and unique and you're definitely beautiful and unique, not gonna lie." I lean my arms onto the bar to get closer trying to work my charm. I usually don't have any issues getting women to want to fuck me, but with her I feel like it might be a little different, I might have to work my charm a little harder, she doesn't seem like the one-night stand type of girl.

"Holy shit," Emerald says. "Soul... mates, fucking soul mates." I look over at her, raising one eyebrow, as she looks back and forth between her friend and me, with the biggest smile on her face and I have no idea what's going on or what she just said, all I've been paying attention to is her gorgeous friend. I laugh as I look at Emerald. "What are you talking about?" Let's hope she fills me in on what she just said.

But Snowflake chimes in before she answers, "My name's Winter." Holy. Fucking. Shit. I had no idea. I've been waiting for her to tell me her name, or for her friend to at least mention her name, but neither have come up. I was serious, I love the cold, snow, and snowflakes are fucking beautiful. "My nickname is Snow, no one's ever called me snowflake before, but I like it." She nervously pushes her hair behind her ear looking at me. She blushes again, making my cock twitch from how sexy it is. Why the fuck am I finding a blush sexy, what is wrong with me? I snap back out of my perverted thoughts.

"Really? You gotta be busting my balls, there's no way you're gonna tell me that's your name after I just called you snowflake. Seriously, is that your name?"

Laughing, she holds her right hand up. "Swear to God." I can't believe I basically just guessed this girl's fucking name. Winter, what a beautiful name, to go right along with this beautiful girl right in front of me.

"Well, no shit. My name is Carsten." I hold out my hand smirking at her. I can't seem to take my eyes off her, I feel like if I look away, she'll disappear and I'm not ready for that just yet. I think about walking up to her and kissing her soft, pouty lips, slipping my tongue between them and tasting her, I bet she tastes sweet. Yet again I get lost in my perverted thoughts that I need to snap out of.

"Nice to meet you Carsten, I'm Winter." She laughs and it's almost like she's shy suddenly, but God damn, I love the sound of her laugh, I don't want her to stop. I could listen to the sound of her laugh all day and never get sick of it. What the fuck is wrong with me?

"Oh my God. I knew it. Holy shit." Emerald is staring back and forth at the two of us. I'm not exactly sure what she's talking about, but I feel like she's almost losing it, or maybe she's already started drinking before she came here and that's why she keeps rambling on about things, but for some reason every time she talks, I'm caught in staring at Winter, and having perverted thoughts about her.

"You're..." I pause for a second not really wanting to sound like a creep when I say this so I'm trying to think of how to word it. "You live next door to me, right?" I guess it sounds creepy either way, but maybe she won't think of it that way.

"Yeah, I'm Emerald, or Em. Whatever you'd like to call me." She smiles at me. But I'm too busy looking over at Winter, I can't take my eyes off her, I keep glancing back and forth at them both, not wanting to be rude like I'm ignoring Emerald, but all my attention is on Winter, she's the one my eyes keep going back to.

"Ok, I thought so. I'm not exactly home much, but I thought I'd met you before. Just didn't want to be weird and assume I knew who you were and be completely wrong." I laugh still looking back to Winter, not wanting to lose her attention to some other guy.

"Nah you're good. That's me, your crazy neighbor, just over here rambling to myself." She snorts, placing her hand to her head like she's embarrassed now.

"Oh my God, Em. Shut up with your crazy ass and let's take these shots so I can die on my empty stomach." Winter sighs, holding her stomach with an already pained look on her face like she knows how the alcohol is going to affect her, or even hurt her empty stomach.

"If you're hungry I can make you girls something, we do have a menu and the kitchen just opened." I look back and forth between them both but linger a little longer on Winter. God, I probably look like a psycho if she notices how much I've been staring at her, but I can't help it. She's a beautiful fucking magnet that won't let me pull my eyes away

"No, that's ok, we're gonna go get some food after this. I'd hate to make you do that." Winter smiles at me, holding her drink in her hand with a look on her face like she already regrets it, and she hasn't even taken the shot yet.

"Well, Snowflake-" I pause, smirking, "It is part of my job. As part owner of this bar, it's my job to make sure everyone's taken care of here." I try to give what I think is my best sexy smile, hoping all my extra charm is helping me out and not fucking me over.

"Well thank you kind sir." You can tell she's being sarcastic, but damn, calling me sir instantly makes my dick hard, I've been standing here with a half hard dick this whole time because of her, and well let's just say I might not be able to walk away from this spot anytime soon if she calls me sir again. "I'll keep that in mind if I decide to eat something before we end up leaving here."

"We can always just eat here, ya know, Snow," Emerald says to her. With a look on her face that says she doesn't want to leave anymore.

"But I gotta make sure I bring my dad home his favorite food and dessert to hopefully calm him down about me being out late, Em, especially if he smells alcohol on me. I can lie my way out of it easier, or he'll drop it if he has it." I can't help but get a weird feeling about her dad, the way she's talked about him so far, she seems almost afraid of him or something.

"Where were you guys going to get food from?" I chime in being nosey.

"We were gonna go to the diner up the street, my dad loves their food." She shifts nervously, I wanna ask more questions but I don't even know the girl and don't wanna pry.

"Well, you can always order to go and pick it up after you leave here, besides, how am I gonna let you two leave knowing you're going to eat food somewhere else and only use me for my line danc-ing?" I give my best sad look trying to make them feel bad.

"Yeah, let's go outside for some fresh air and call up Lisa and ask her to have the food made up and ready to go by one thirty, she loves you Winter, you know she won't care."

"Alright, let's do this shot and go step outside. Then, we'll just stay here."

They take their shots both making disgusted faces afterwards, I can't help but laugh. These girls are pretty entertaining. Too bad I'm working and not able to hang out with them more while they're here.

"Mind If I join you girls and take a break with you?" I glance at Emerald for a second, but I'm instantly pulled in Winter's direction, she has these gorgeous honey-brown eyes that you can get lost in, a dimple in her right cheek when she smiles the right way, and her smile–damn it's fucking beautiful.

"Of course not," they say at the same time, both getting up.

"Take your water with you, Snowflake." I wink. "I don't want anyone doing anything stupid to it while we're gone. I usually don't allow drinks outside, but I'll let it slide this time." Laughing, I hold my arm out to point them in the direction to go ahead of me.

"Chase, I'll be right back. I'm going to take a break really quick," I shout to my brother over the terrible music the DJs playing still.

We step outside and thankfully it's not as crowded as it is inside. I love the crowd but sometimes it's a lot and can be overwhelming. "So, you ladies come here just for the hell of it or specifically for the line dancing?"

"Ha, ha. Emerald over here practically begged me to come here for line dancing. If it were up to me, I'd be home already and snuggled up in my bed watching crime documentaries." Winter snickers as she looks over at me, she slowly opens her mouth a little, biting her bottom lip that I just want to bite so badly.

"Hey, Winter I'll be right back, Chastity is calling me." She walks away leaving just the two of us to talk.

"You chicks and your crime shows, you could probably solve a murder faster than the FBI."

"Hey, don't judge us with our obsession for creepy men who lure women and then kill them." Laughing I shake my head at this beautiful crazy girl telling me her obsession with crime shows, maybe I should be running but instead it draws me to her more. Emerald walks back over just in time to add to the conversation.

"Yeah, there's nothing wrong with women loving crime documentaries, there is nothing weird about us being obsessed with them," Emerald says laughing.

"If you ladies say so, then who am I to judge?" I shake my head again; these girls are awesome. I could see myself hanging out with them, and actually becoming friends with them. Although I'd like to be more than friends with Winter, I'd like to be on top of her, behind her, any way I could be inside her I'd be fine with. God what is wrong with me?

"See and if she wouldn't have dragged me here, then you never would have learned about my love for crime." Winter sighs.

"Hey, I love dancing. I can't help the fact that I dragged her here and who doesn't love some fun line dancing? There's nothing wrong with country and line dancing." Emerald crosses her arm in a defensive way, clearly joking.

"I have nothing wrong with country night as I'm the one who thought of it since my mom loves line dancing," I say to them both.

"See, there you go Winter. Now you can't hate country night when he's the one who thought of it to lure us here. Maybe he'll be like the psychos in your documentaries and kill us both next."

"Perfect, that's exactly what I'm looking for to add some excitement to my Thursday night." Man, this woman couldn't get any more perfect, if she says anything else to draw me in I might fall in love. "What did Chastity have to say?"

"Oh, unfortunately she can't make it. Her and her boyfriend got into a fight and she's going to go to his house to talk things over with him," Emerald says in a sad tone.

"Well damn, let's hope everything is ok with the two of them. I love them together." Winter looks at Emerald with a worried look on her face. Not sure why she's worried if her friend and her boyfriend are okay. This is why I don't do relationships, too much drama. Then there's always having to answer to someone else, always making plans with that person, then the fighting. That's the main reason why I stay away from relationships, besides the drama being my first reason, the fighting I'm good on all of that I don't need to fight with a girl about stupid shit, when I can just fuck her and leave. I don't have to explain myself or tell her who I'm with or where I'm at. It's a lot less stress on my end just staying single and sleeping around.

"Same girl, same." Emerald puts her phone back in her purse, with somewhat of a sad look on her face.

"Hey ladies, sorry to cut you off but I gotta head back in. Maybe one of you ladies can save me a dance later." I smile back and forth at them, but then I stop, staring at Winter, because I was too much of a pussy to ask her to save a dance for me, so hopefully my lingering look gives the hint that I want to dance with her. I don't do stuff like that, usually the girl is the one coming to me for these things. I'm not really sure how to even be like "hey save me a dance". Fuck I'm an idiot.

"Of course, Winter would love to dance with you, preferably a slow song in case you were wondering what she likes to dance to." Emerald winks at me and chuckles. Laughing, I turn my back to head inside without them. I gotta stop getting distracted and get my work done for the night before Chase chews me a new asshole.

Back at the bar we take care of our hour of non-stop drink and food orders. Having themed dance nights really does help with the drink orders. The more people dance and sweat the more alcohol they order, so we're usually pretty nonstop. I head to the back room to grab a food order and when I come back out Brynn is at the counter with her friends Colette and Daisy. They're all staring at me with googly-eyes, I'm surprised they aren't drooling yet.

"God, you're so lucky he's your boyfriend Brynn, he's so fucking sexy," her friend Colette says to her so loud I'm sure the whole bar can hear her.

"Yeah, he sure is dreamy, I'd kill to have a boyfriend that fucking hot," Daisy says, smirking at me as I start heading over to them.

"Shut up guys, I don't want him to hear you, he gets mad when I talk about that stuff," Brynn quickly says as she elbows her friends.

"Ladies," I say smiling, gotta make tips somehow even if it's from annoying girls who lie to their friends for the attention.

"Hey, handsome." Brynn winks at me and leans over the bar trying to kiss me, but I back away, which makes her friends gasp and put their hands over their mouths in shock.

"Shut up guys." She glares at them, her cheeks red from embarrassment.

"Sorry, Brynn, can't kiss on the job."

"Well, wanna hang out after work tonight?" she asks pouting.

"I'll see if I'm busy," I say, glancing at her, but searching for Winter over her shoulder, trying to find her in the crowd of dancing people.

"But, if you have to see if you're busy, doesn't that mean you're not busy?" she asks, smiling like she just called my bluff.

But that's ok because I'm about to call her out on her little lie. "Brynn, I don't have to answer to you." I smile, licking my lips, and her friend's gasp. "I'm not your boyfriend." I laugh a little. They look over at her in shock like I just told her someone died. "So, if I find plans for later, I'm going to stick to those plans, if not... sure, I'll hit you up," I say, shrugging my shoulders. I should have gotten rid of her after the first two times I fucked her, but I couldn't step away that easy, the pussy is too good. But now I'm getting so sick of Brynn and her bullshit lies, her thinking we're in a relationship and crying every time I break things off with her. I'm thinking after today if I decide to fuck her, it'll be the last time. She's got to go, this is why I stay single, I don't need relationship drama from someone I'm not even in a relationship with.

I walk away to head outside and get some fresh air for a minute since I can't find Winter. I'm hoping I run into her out here since it was the last place I saw her, but of course, Brynn and her friends come following me like dogs following their owner. Guess I can always make out with her and see if it gets me in the mood to hang out with her. But if not, I'm definitely ending things tonight. Especially now that I have a new interest.

4

WINTER

We head back in and set our drinks down by a table where we will be dancing. I'm not sure what I'm doing, but now I gotta give it my best knowing Carsten will be watching. Not gonna lie he's really fucking hot and I'm kinda hoping to impress him. They start the night off with "Boot Scootin' Boogie" and thankfully it's a dance I'm familiar with, so I don't start off dancing looking like an idiot. Although, I'm still a little nervous and unsure of how the rest of the dances will go. I'm thinking I'll sit out if I don't know any of them. I'll just act thirsty; I'm sure Emerald will understand. She knows I'm not big with line dancing, now ask me to dance like a hoochie and grind up on my best friends or some man. That's a different story. Because I just lose myself to the music when I dance that way, it's not easy to fuck up hoochie dancing, unlike line dancing where you have to pay attention to what you're doing and follow specific dance moves, I'm not good with dancing that way, but I'll give it a try for my best friend.

The next three dances I'm not sure if they're country dances, but they're definitely line dances I'm familiar with, so we're actually having a great time and I'm starting to sweat. This time I head back to the counter for a refill on water and and then head outside to cool off, so I hopefully stop sweating. Not sure where Carsten went, I saw him talking to some girls at the bar, maybe he went home with one of them or maybe he's done with his shift and just didn't say goodbye.

I step outside to find Carsten standing in front of a blonde girl. Who looks to be angry or sad. It's kind of hard to tell. Not that I really care, it's not my business. But for some reason I'm instantly hit with jealousy. Not sure why, I literally just met the guy tonight and it's not like he promised to marry me or something. Besides he's busy with what looks to be a heated conversation as the girl crosses her arms and scrunches her brows.

"Please just come home with me tonight, Carsten." I hear what sounds like yelling, as I walk to the side of the building. It sounds like the girl is getting frustrated.

"I already told you; I'm not really feeling it. Plus, I might have plans later." I hear Carsten say to her, in an already annoyed tone.

"But, baby, please I just..." then he cuts her off.

"What did I tell you? Stop calling me baby. I'm not your boyfriend," he says to her, in an angry voice.

Well that makes me feel a little better knowing he doesn't have a girlfriend, although I feel bad for her, she seems to really like him. I wonder if they have some sort of past that makes him feel the way he does about her.

I pull out my phone trying to distract myself from their conversation when I hear a man stumbling and rambling. I glance up at him then quickly back down at my phone, hoping he ignores me so I can just be left alone in peace, but my luck is always pretty shitty.

"What's a pretty girl like you doing out here all alone?" He stumbles up next to me, slurring, trying to grab a piece of my hair to twirl in his fingers but misses since he's only able to see with one eye due to how drunk he is, and he's squinting, the other eye closed.

"Just trying to get some fresh air and away from the noise for a few minutes, in peace," I say hoping he gets the hint, but obviously he doesn't. I step away a little trying to get some space, and step on his foot in the process. He closes in on me and blocks me up against the wall where I barely have any room to move. Maybe I should've just stayed in front of the bar instead of going to the side of the building, but I didn't feel like watching Carsten flirt with that girl.

"Well, that wasn't nice you rude bitch, why the hell did you do that?" he snarls, getting into my face even more. Just when I thought he couldn't get any closer, he's talking into my ear, and I can smell the whiskey on his breath.

"If you weren't so close to me maybe I wouldn't have been close enough to step on you trying to get some space, asshole." I try to shove him off me but instead he starts lifting my shirt and rubbing my stomach.

"You're gonna wish you were a lot nicer, you dumb bitch," he says while sliding his hand further up my shirt groping my boob, trying to get his fingers inside my bra as he breathes heavily in my face. His breath smells like death, like he hasn't brushed his teeth in days, with a mix of alcohol and it's making me want to puke in his face. I try to push him away, but I'm not strong enough, plus it doesn't help that I'm backed up into the wall of the building, so it doesn't give me much room to even try to push him.

"Get the fuck off of me asshole," I yell attempting to shove him again, but then he's ripped off me and the next thing I know he's falling to the ground after Carsten punches him in the face.

"What the fuck man, this bitch asked for it," the guy says, with anger in his voice as he holds his bloody nose giving Carsten a nasty look, while spit flies from his mouth from his heavy breathing. He steps forward, moving his hand away from his nose and putting them up like he's going to come swinging at Carsten to fight back. But stops as soon as Carsten steps towards him, getting loud.

"The bitch asked for it? What the fuck is your problem, no woman is ever going to ask to be groped by a drunk stranger you fucking dick. He lands another punch right on his nose making the blood gush out even more. The screams coming from the man more intense as he grips his bloody nose with both hands.

"Now I'm gonna ask you to fucking leave unless she wants me to call the police." He glances over at me, I'm shocked and shaking, literally shaking as I stand there hugging myself. Trying to fight any flashbacks that are trying to creep up in my mind, along with the panic attack that is trying to creep up on me right now, my breathing is heavy, and my chest is aching from anxiety. So, I'm a little thankful for the question to help distract myself from both the flashbacks, and panic attacks hitting me full force.

"No, I'd rather not get the police involved if that's ok with you, since you own the bar," I say to Carsten, in not quite a whisper, but a very quiet voice, almost afraid to talk from how freaked out I am.

"Perfectly fine with me, I'd rather not get them involved anyways. Now, I'm gonna ask you to fucking leave, and if I ever see you come in my bar or even come around her ever again, you're going to regret it." He steps into him seething with anger, as he leans down practically growling in his face. His breathing heavy as he balls his fists up at his sides, like he's having a hard time stopping himself from doing more. But the drunk decides to piss Carsten off more by adding more fuel to the fire like the idiot he is.

"Fine by me, this bar's shit anyways, but next time tell your whore not to throw herself at anyone." The asshole drunk smirks, as he looks up at Carsten spit still flying from his mouth as he slurs his words and breathing like he's out of breath. Carsten starts slowly walking towards him more, and I laugh a little as the guy tries scooting himself away but backs himself into the wall with nowhere to go and no room to stand up. There's something about the way that he stands up for me that makes my stomach flutter with excitement.

Carsten grabs the man by the head, pulling him down and kneeing him in the face. "Don't you ever..." he growls, "ever call her a whore again, she is the farthest from a whore. No woman ever asks to be touched by a man she doesn't give permission to." He knees him again, blood pouring from his mouth and nose. I don't even feel bad. Tears well up in my eyes as I stand there. Even this stranger thinks I'm a whore who asks to be touched.

Flashbacks from that night come blurring my vision and I fall to my knees shaking and crying. I can't even control the panic attack that's about to happen anymore. I probably look like a crazy person crying over something so little, but he has no idea about all the times my dad punishes me for being the "town whore" or the time I was almost raped for "asking for it." I can't control my sobs as he leans down next to me wrapping his arm around me.

4 YEARS AGO

I'm whipping my body back and forth trying to get him off me, but being a football player he's a lot stronger than I am. He puts his knee on my right leg and pushes my leg open, leaving his knee there to stop me from moving. He licks his way from my jaw line down my neck. "You might as well stop fighting. I know this is what you want." He's sucking on my neck now. "Whores like you love the fight, love to feel like you're innocent when really you're begging for it." He leans down licking the tears from my cheek and I start kicking my legs and hit him in the junk. "Goddamn you stupid bitch, now you're definitely going to get it." He rips my underwear off, screaming under the tape from the way it rips my skin before the fabric finally breaks.

"God, this is gonna feel so good. I can't wait to shove my cock in your tight pussy." He pushes my legs further apart and shoves two fingers into me so hard, I scream out a muted scream from behind the tape. Fresh tears start falling down my face faster this time. It feels like he ripped my skin, or his nails scratched me as he shoved his fingers into me. I wasn't wet at all, which I wasn't expecting to be, and now he's just shoving his fingers in and out of me. "Come on you whore, get your fucking pussy wet for me. Don't act like you're not enjoying this as much as I am." I feel bile rise in my throat that I struggle to swallow down, and start coughing, but it doesn't matter, the tapes still there, even if I choke on my puke he'll still continue.

"Hey, hey, it's ok I'm right here. He's gone. I'm so sorry I didn't get to you sooner. I had no idea you were out here. Did he hurt you?"

Carsten asks, concern written all over his face, as he pulls me a little closer to him, rubbing my back slowly with his right hand in a comforting way. "Shh, shhh. It's okay Snowflake, I'm right here" he says trying to soothe me with his comforting voice.

Crying, I glance up at him. "No, just lifting my shirt, touching my stomach, he started touching my boobs over my bra." I sniffle trying to take a deep breath to calm myself some. "He tried to get inside my bra too, but thankfully you pulled him off of me," I say as tears stream down my face.

"Shit, I'm so sorry, Snowflake. What do you need me to do for you?" He looks so serious, and you can tell he is really bothered by what he just stopped from happening. I've never had a man truly seem to care about how I've felt before or about what has happened to me, my whole life I've always felt alone in anything that's happened to me. So, for once this feels nice, to see and feel the concern on his face and in his voice, to actually be able to trust someone that you barely know. Feel's good.

"Can you help me find Emerald?" I hug myself tighter, finally able to breathe a little easier with his big arms wrapped around me while squatting next to me.

"Of course I will." He wastes no time lifting me into his arms, carrying me further down the side of the building into a side door I'm assuming is another entrance to the bar.

"I'm gonna take you to my office and set you on my couch," he says carrying me like I weigh nothing. "Then I'm gonna go out there and get Emerald for you, is that ok? Will you feel safe being in here?"

"Yeah, that's fine," I say, looking up at his handsome face as he sets me on his couch. "Do you need anything while I go out to get her?"

"Just something to drink please, alcohol this time." I laugh because I need something to take the edge off and calm my nerves. "Anything but pineapple or coconut please." He laughs. "Of course, should I get one for Em too?" I shake my head yeah as he's staring at me, you can see he's truly concerned about what just happened to me.

"They're on the house too, no need to worry. I'll be right back." He starts walking out the door to the bar.

"Hey, Carsten–" He stops in the doorway.

"Yes, Snowflake?" He gives me a sad smirk.

"Thank you for the drinks and thank you so much for saving me." He walks back in and squats back down in front of me, cupping his hand on my cheek.

"You're welcome, Snowflake. As long as I'm around you, you'll have nothing to worry about, you'll always be safe. He rubs my cheek softly with his thumb. "Thank you," I whisper, closing my eyes as more tears fall freely onto my cheeks.

He wipes my tears then slowly stands. "I'll be quick I promise."

Emerald rushes in about five minutes later running over to me and grabbing me by my shoulders. "Oh my god, Snow are you ok?" She pulls me in, hugging me tightly. "I'm so sorry I wasn't there with you babe, I'm so sorry."

She's so upset, she was at the party the night everything happened with Preston. Carsten stands in the doorway, concerned. You can tell he wants to ask more questions but doesn't want to be nosey. "It's ok Em, Carsten was out there and ended up getting there just in time before anything went any further than it already had."

"Oh, thank God. I thought you went out there alone, but wait, if Carsten was out there with you, how did it happen?" She looks to me, and then to Carsten.

"I was out there with a friend. I didn't see her walk out, so she was on the side of the building when I heard her yelling. I must've had my back turned when she came out so I didn't see or hear her," Carsten says looking down, you can tell he's embarrassed and doesn't want to talk about the fact that I saw him out there with another girl.

"Oh ok, but still thank God you got to her in time, what did the guy do, Snow?"

"He was pissed because I wouldn't let him touch me. He was in my face, so I tried to step away to get him away from me and stepped on his foot in the process, then he got even more pissed and pushed me into the wall lifting my shirt. He was rubbing my stomach and my boobs; he almost got inside my bra, but that's when Carsten got there and kicked his ass." I smile at the memory of him punching him and kneeing him in the face a couple times. "It was pretty bad ass the way he kicked his ass too." I laugh.

"Thanks, I'm glad I got to you, who knows what would have happened if not, and I don't want to imagine what would've happened either," he says, walking in further and pulling a chair in front of us giving us our drinks. "I wasn't exactly sure what to make so I put cherry vodka and Sprite in there for you guys."

"That's actually me and Em's favorite drink," I say, both laughing at the fact that that's what he made for us. "How funny that's twice tonight you guessed something right about me."

He smirks at me. "I don't even have anything to say to that either, I was gonna think of something funny and smooth, but I can't even do that." He puts his hand on his face shaking his head.

"Oh my god, you broke him Winter, he can't even woo you with his man charm. What is this?" Emerald starts laughing while staring at me.

"I guess I have that effect on men, I ruin their charm then they can't even flirt with girls anymore, or maybe they can with other girls, and I just ruined it to where they just can't flirt with me, cause I suck."

"No, you definitely don't suck." He looks at me with a serious look on his face. "Trust me, I'd definitely love to flirt with you." He winks standing up. "I really hate to leave you girls, but this is our busy time and my brother is gonna kill me if I don't get my ass out there, he doesn't even know what's going on in here."

"It's ok, I think we're gonna take off anyways." Emerald stands setting her empty drink down. "We need to head out to get some food so we can get Winter's dad some food too."

"Yeah, plus I don't need to be out too late either, my dad's not happy when I'm home too late," I say, looking down. That's all I need tonight after what that guy did is for him to start slapping me around, or worse.

"Is everything ok, Winter?" Carsten asks with concern. I probably should've kept my mouth shut, but it's exhausting when you hide so many secrets.

"Yeah, my dad just drinks a lot and sometimes yells too much." I continue to lie though.

"Well, if you ever need my help you guys know where to find me." He looks concerned but I change the subject.

"Thank you so much again, Carsten. Seriously, you saved me tonight." I walk over and give him a hug, he wraps his warm, strong arms around me slowly, his muscles tightening around my waist as he places his large hands on my lower back. If I could stay here forever in this moment with his arms wrapped around me, I would. Something about him makes me feel safe, and it's nice to feel safe for once in your life instead of always being worried about what is going to happen next.

"Of course, Snowflake, I'm glad I was there to stop him." I step back from him before I get too comfortable and not want to leave his arms.

Emerald and I leave the bar and head to the diner to eat down the street. It was a fun night up until that drunk asshole went too far and tried to ruin it. Thankfully for Em she's an amazing friend and great at cheering me up. She's always been there for me my whole life, like a true best friend, like the sister I've always wished I had. We're both an only child and she's wanted a sister just as bad as I have so since day one, we bonded the way that sisters do. She's the one I go to for everything and same for her, we know everything about each other, all of each other's secrets, my issues with my family, well most of my issues about my family, some of those I keep to myself just because I know how pissed off she'd be because of them.

"So..." Emerald pauses. Looking at me with a big smile on her face, while wiggling her eyebrows. Like she knows something I don't know. I look back at her with a slight smirk, while raising one eyebrow in confusion, because I feel like I missed something like I have no clue what's going on.

"Soooo?" I ask, cause I'm not sure exactly what she's about to bring up. Now I feel even more confused, as I sit there and stare at her as she stares back at me still with this knowing smile. I'm about to start questioning her some more when she finally starts to speak.

"What did you think of that hunk of a man, Carsten?" Emerald gets a big smile on her face, wiggling her eyebrows even more. As she leans forward with a little excitement like she needs to be closer to me to hear my answer. Like if she sits back in her seat, it won't be as exciting for her. I'm surprised she hasn't jumped across the booth by now to get even closer, that's how excited she is to hear my answer.

I snort almost choking on my French fry while laughing. "Who says that? Hunk of a man, you nerd." I laugh at her; she always uses such weird phrases when she describes things and I love it. Especially when she says hunk of a man to describe someone she finds attractive. I laugh some more, shaking my head while taking another French fry, dipping it into my honey mustard and popping it into my mouth.

"Shut your face, you know I call men that all the time, you bitch, don't act like you've never heard me say it." She laughs tossing a fry at me as it lands on my plate. She tries to give me her best "I can't believe" you look but fails to because she can't stop laughing and now, I'm not sure if she's still laughing at what she said or laughing at the fact that she landed her French fry on my plate. Maybe it's both, I'm not sure she might be losing it at this point.

"My fry now, bitch." I pick it up, biting it as her jaw drops in shock like I was seriously about to give it back to her. She should be lucky I was able to eat it and it didn't fall to the floor. "Anyways, I know that's something you always say, I'm fucking with you, you know this. I always make fun of you for saying 'hunk of a man.' It's funny to me."

"Yeah, yeah. Now enough stalling I know you're just trying to change the subject and I'm not about to let that happen."

"Whatever, he was hot. I was thankful he was there to stop that drunk asshole, plus he seemed like he'd be fun to hang out with. So why don't you ever hang out with him?" I ask, raising my eyebrow hoping there wasn't more to the situation like they hooked up or something.

"You heard the man, he's always busy. Plus, like I mentioned to you before, he's usually working. Him and his brother work a lot, or they work out a lot, you can tell by that crazy fucking muscular body of his. But the only other time I see him at his house is outside working on this car he seems to be restoring."

"Oh, so he seems like a handyman, that's good to know, especially if you ever have car problems." I pause, afraid to ask the question, but I need to get it over with. "So, you guys have never hooked up or anything?" I look away after asking, embarrassed that I even cared.

"Girl, you know if I hooked up with his hot ass you would've been the first one I told. But no, he's hot, but he's just not my type." She takes the last bite of her burger as I'm finishing up my food.

"Not your type? Is there something wrong with him that I don't know about?" Hoping that's not the case, I patiently wait for her answer, as if she's stalling.

"No, there's nothing wrong with him, he seems like a great person, I just don't know him well enough to give an actual answer, so that's what I was trying to think, if I've seen anything crazy over the last few years of living next to him."

"Does he go to the same college as we do?" I ask since I don't think I've ever seen him there. Obviously, there's a ton of people who go there, but I feel like I see a lot of the same people all the time.

"No, if I remember correctly, I think he dropped out. He's also a year or two older than we are, I think. But he helps his mom at the bar, remember he said he's part owner and he also works at some of his uncles tattoo shops."

"Oh yeah, ok I remember you telling me that now." I glance at my phone to check the time to make sure it's not too late, so my dad doesn't flip and realize it's almost one thirty in the morning. "Shit, I gotta see if my dad's food is almost done, I gotta go or he is gonna freak the fuck out on me, Em." I sit there nervously biting my bottom lip.

"Don't worry, I'll go check with her real quick and see if Lisa can add any extra dessert for him to hopefully calm him down." She looks at me sympathetically as she gets up to head to the counter that our waitress is standing at.

I check my phone again, my anxiety spiking and my nerves going crazy. Em knows some of the shit my dad does but not to the extent. She'd kick my ass If she knew how far he took it sometimes.

She comes back with a big bag full of three food containers, all his favorite foods and a container of the rest of his favorite dessert. "You're the best Emerald, thanks for grabbing all that."

"No problem, babe. Now let's get your ass home before your dad kicks your ass." She chuckles softly. "I don't know why you won't just live with me, Winter. Seriously, I'm tired of worrying about you."

"I already told you, Emmy. I can't afford to, and I can't just leave my dad to take care of himself, he'd drink himself to death."

"I know, I know but the offer is still there."

I stand and follow her out the door of the diner, my stomach in knots knowing what is about to happen once I step into my house. I hate going through this all the time I just wish I had the balls to say fuck it and leave him for once to take care of himself.

5

CARSTEN

After I get home from closing the bar I'm bored. Chase went to some party that he had invited me to but after the night I had, I wasn't really in the mood. I lied to Brynn about being busy because I didn't feel like dealing with her but now, I'm wide awake and I'm fucking horny. It's three in the morning, so it's not like I can go out and find anyone different this late anyway, and I'm not going to some stupid frat party where every girl is going to be stupid drunk and slurring their words. I'd rather fuck a girl who isn't about to vomit on me. Fuck it. I'm sure she's just getting in from partying herself. I decide to send her a text to see if she's awake.

Me
you up?

Brynn
yep. wishing you were here baby

Me
stop with the baby bullshit

Brynn
sorry :(I can't help it

Me
wanna fuck?

I don't care that I'm being blunt, she knows that's all I'm wanting from her, so if she's going to continue to fall for me that's on her. You can only give a girl so many warnings before you break things off. The only reason I'm texting her is because I can't go out to find anyone else to fuck, and don't really feel like working for it with any of the other girls I've kept in my phone for just in case moments. I'm too tired for all that, at least with Brynn I can fuck her and leave, or if she comes here I can kick her out after. Then I can come home and get some much-needed sleep, or just wait for her to leave and go to bed. It's been a busy week with mom gone and taking on more of the responsibilities of the bar. On top of Tattooing at Crazy's I'm exhausted. So yeah, I'm going to be lazy about this too. A man has needs too and sometimes he has to be a dick about them to get what he needs and wants.

Brynn
My place? I drank 2 much

Me
sure. be there in 10

I get to her house, and she answers her door in nothing but panties. Her pink nipples are hard and usually that would turn me on, but her tits are too big for my liking. I'm a boob guy, but hers are fake, and that's not something I'm into.

She practically throws herself on me as soon as I shut the door, kissing me, pushing her tongue into my mouth. She's being very sloppy and it's a big turn off, so I push her away some.

"What are you doing? Why are you practically eating my face off?" I ask, sort of grossed out from how wet my mouth is from hers. It's not even too wet in a good way either.

"Sorry, I'm just so excited to see you. I missed you so much and I'm horny," she says as she's frantically undoing the zipper on my jeans.

She drops to her knees pulling my cock out. Usually I'm fully hard, ready to go, but today I'm only half hard and having a hard time focusing to get there. He usually does it for me, gets me hard no problem, but right now I'm focused on Winter, and I don't want to get hard for Brynn. Not feeling this one bit, I push her away. I've already spent ten minutes trying to get hard.

"What's wrong Carsten? Am I sucking your cock wrong?" she pouts. "I can do it differently if I need to," she asks, looking up at me.

"No, Brynn, I'm just not in the mood for it honestly." She stands up quickly, with an offended look on her face.

"Umm what? You come over here telling me you're in the mood, then I suck your dick, you can't get fully hard... Now you're going to tell me you're not in the mood?" She crosses her arms over her chest and lets out a breath.

"Nope, sorry, guess I wasn't. I'm probably just gonna head home." I put my dick back in my boxers and zip up my pants.

"Baby, wait, what about me? I'm horny." She bites her bottom lip and gives me a half smile. I can tell if I don't make a move to get out of here quickly, she's probably going to pounce again like a wild fucking animal and I'm not feeling that tonight. Especially that crazy side of Brynn.

"Not in the mood for that either, Brynn. I just want to go home, sorry for wasting your time," I say, heading towards her door. I honestly don't care that I wasted her time. I'm pissed I wasted my own time coming here, I probably would've been better off with my hand and the dirty thoughts of Winter that keep popping up in my mind.

"Wait, wait please. Let me try it again, or let's just go straight to sex. You can't just leave me hanging." She pouts again, I've never met a woman who pouted so much like a child. But Brynn is used to getting her way, she has the type of parents who are rich and give her everything. They even bought her this house she's currently living it. So, when she's told no, it can get pretty ugly.

"Brynn, I think it's time we call it quits. I can't keep doing this. Every time we're together to hook up you act like we're a couple, then every time I try to leave you get upset and pout–"

She cut me off. "No, you can't end this. I told you I'll work on it. Please don't do this to me Carsten, please." She gives a frustrated sigh grabbing her shirt off the floor and putting it back on.

"Brynn, it's over. I'm serious. No more hookups, no more texting. We're done. So, either leave me alone or I'll block you," I say as I walk out her door, shutting it behind me.

But it's like déjà vu, she comes running after me and cuts me off stepping in front of my car, blocking me from getting inside.

"Please." She starts to cry again. "What can I do to make you want to be with me, to love me?" Tears stream down her face as she stands there crossing her arms over her hard nipples that you can clearly see through her white t shirt that she must've been wearing before she decided it was a good idea to open her door topless.

"Brynn, please. I don't want to be a dick to you. I don't do relationships, I already told you, and you were fine with it." I take a deep breath, annoyed. "So, I'm sorry. I don't love you and I won't love you either." Then I pick her up and move her out of my way. I don't bother saying anything else and she doesn't either. I'm so sick of her shit, and her thinking that if she cries, I'll just give in and stay with her. I'm so sick of repeating myself to her on a daily basis, it's like she thinks I'll forget what I said from one day to the next and that's not how I work. That's not how it's going to start working with me either. So, I decide to stop wasting my breath on someone who isn't worth my time especially if she's not going to listen. Yes, I sound like a dick now. But I'm over it and I don't fucking care.

I get into my car and shut the door. I was hoping she wasn't going to stop me this time and I'm glad she didn't because that would have made this even more awkward than it already was. I put my key in the ignition and start my car, putting it in reverse. I back out of her driveway to head home.

6

WINTER

"You can just drop me off right here, Emerald." I hate the sick feeling I get when I don't know how my dad's going to be when I come home. Pulling off to the side of the road on my rundown side street she puts her car in park.

"What? I'm still about ten houses from yours, Winter. I'm not going to drop you off at almost two in the morning this far, even if it's only ten houses or so." She gives me a stern look; you'd think she was my mother and not my best friend that I've known since third grade.

"Well, I'll let you follow me like a stalker, how's that?" Laughing, I give her shoulder a slight nudge, hoping to bring a smile to her face.

"You know how my dad can be Em, I don't know if he's been waiting up for me or if he's passed out after drinking almost a case of beer for the day." My mouth curls up a little in disappointment. Sometimes I start to feel bad for myself and how shitty my life has been, but then I remember that sadly there are people out there who still have it worse than I do. So, I try to suck it up the best I can and try to keep moving forward no matter how much it fucking sucks.

"Winter..." She furrows her brows. I know she hates my living situation just as much, if not more, than I do, but there's not much I can do at the moment. "Why don't you just take me up on the offer and live with me in my townhouse? You know I'll pick up what you can't afford in rent, and before your stubborn ass says no, think about it, we've always talked about being roomies as kids and through high school, now we finally have a chance, and you refuse to do it." Emerald has never been stuck up or felt like she was better than everyone even growing up with money and great parents. She wasn't like the other stuck-up assholes in this town who have mommy and daddy paying for everything and still complain. She has always had jobs and paid for things herself, that's why her parent's gifted her the payment on her townhouse because they knew she wouldn't accept it any other way, and even then, she still fought them about it. So, her offering to pay for my half of rent until I can help pay is a completely normal thing for her to offer. Which makes me thankful to have such an amazing friend like her, because she would actually pay for it with her own money.

"I can barely afford the rent Emerald. I refuse to let you pay for my half. I mean you're paying the whole thing now. I'm not about to move in and still let you pay for almost all of it."

God, I wish I could just say fuck it and move in with her. I feel like we've had this conversation about twelve times tonight and it keeps ending the same way. I wish it could end differently but I just can't see myself moving in right now, not when I'm paying the small percentage of my college tuition that didn't get covered by financial aid. On top of taking care of myself and my dad.

"Besides, I have to stay and help take care of my dad, you know I can't just leave him as much as I wish I could." He's been a drunk my whole life and it's only gotten worse since mom passed when I was twelve. She was killed in a head-on collision when a semi-truck driver smashed into her car after he fell asleep on the road.

"But c'mon, you saw two of my neighbors. They are so fucking hot, Snow! How can you turn that down?" She starts wiggling her eyebrows again. I start to laugh at how ridiculous she looks since she can only wiggle them a little. It's something she's been doing a lot to try to get the hang of it, because it makes her mad that she can't wiggle her eyebrows like a normal person, so now every chance she gets she takes the opportunity to do it. That's another thing I love about her, when she's determined to do something, she won't give up on it. She won't stop until she gets the hang of it.

"Like tattoos, beards, mysterious looking hot men. So. Fucking. Hot." She sighs, giving a dreamy look. "Did I mention how hot they are? I mean you met Carsten; you saw his brother Chase, they have two more roommates that are just as hot, they too are mysterious bearded tattooed men." I can't control my laughter; she could sell anyone with that sales pitch. "It's like they're a part of a cult or something with how hot they are."

"How about I think about it, ok? I really gotta get to my house though before you mention your "bearded mystery tattooed neighbors" anymore, cause if he's up, he's going to be pissed. Plus, I have to work tomorrow. They want me to come to the bar during the day to help set up for two bachelorette parties going on, we're going to be slammed. I just don't feel like fighting with him tonight either, I'm too tired." It's never ending, this thing with my dad. No matter what I do I just can't win with him. He's never happy, I always do something wrong, it's always me. My fault and I hate it. I'd like to just flip out and go off on him for it. I'm so tired of being the blame for everything. I'm tired of being a punching bag that he verbally abuses while taking his anger out on me physically.

My dad is so exhausting no matter what you say to him. He doesn't care, he just gets angry and yells at me for stuff I didn't do.

"Fine, Snow, but if you need me to come get you, please don't hesitate to call. I'm serious, I'll be here in a heartbeat." She places her hand over mine, giving it a gentle and loving squeeze.

"I won't, Em. I promise I'll call if I need you." I lean over, hugging her and giving her a kiss on the cheek. "Love you, girl." Getting out of her car, I shut her door and hear her window roll down.

"Love you, girly... now get that ass moving. I wanna watch your ass shake while you walk home." She giggles out, trying to hold back her laughter.

I start walking and strut my stuff a little more obnoxiously than I normally would to help lighten the mood from our depressing conversation, and before I step into the gates of hell, that's what I like to call my home, because nothing good happens once you shut those doors. Even my nightmares are better dreams than my reality these days.

I walk into our dimly lit home, it smells like beer and body odor, like my dad hasn't showered in days. He honestly probably hasn't, half the time he's too drunk to remember if he did so he just says fuck it and doesn't bother doing it because "why accidentally shower twice if you don't remember if you showered once" is what he likes to tell me when I ask him about his hygiene. He's passed out on the couch, his arm draped over the arm of the couch holding onto his beer for dear life. Pretty sad that even in his sleep that's his main concern and one thing he'd never worry about wasting. His head is against the back of the couch, looking up at the ceiling mumbling and snoring heavily. I'm thankful that he's snoring, hoping I won't wake him as I walk through the house after putting his food in the refrigerator.

Right as I open the refrigerator, I wish I would've just left his food on the counter to spoil, because the light from the refrigerator wakes him up–but not the fucking flashing of the TV screen, right? Of course not, because my luck has always been shit.

"What the fuck are you doing making all that noise? Can't you see I'm sleeping." He sits up taking a sip of his beer before burping obnoxiously loud and pulling his filthy white shirt down over his beer gut.

"Sorry, Dad. Emerald and I just went to get food and I brought you back some of your favorites," I say, scrunching my eyes hoping he's too drunk to look at the time. But of course, because I have shitty luck...

"Why the fuck are you just getting in now? It's after two in the morning, Winter." He stands up slowly, trying to balance himself while his body sways. "What the fuck did I tell you about staying out late, huh?"

Fuck, of course he's angry. Over something as stupid as me having a life. "Dad, it was just Emerald and I, it's not a big deal."

"No big deal." Throwing his head back, he gives an angry, loud, laugh, taking another sip of his beer, downing the rest of it he then crushes the can. I flinch as he does it, the noise sounding so loud, like it's being crushed over a loudspeaker. He throws it into the recycling bin missing and not even caring to pick it up.

"I don't need you embarrassing me anymore than you already have. You're nothing but a disgrace." He practically spits as he's talking with how bad he's slurring.

He comes up behind me where I stand with the refrigerator door still open from putting his food in there and I jump when his arm comes past me as he reaches in for another beer. I know what's coming no matter how prepared I am for it there's nothing I can do to stop it from happening.

"Dad, I'm not an embarrassment," I say, a little angrier than I should have. But I'm sick of always taking his shit. I'm sick of just standing there and never sticking up for myself because god forbid I fucking speak without being given permission to speak.

"If I say you're an embarrassment, then you're a fucking embarrassment, you fucking bitch." He stands angrily in front of me, breathing so heavily I can practically taste the alcohol coming from him and it smells like stale beer and bad breath. He probably hasn't brushed his teeth either.

"I'm not arguing, Dad. I just don't understand how Em and I eating dinner at the diner is an embarrassment at all." I look at him frustrated and annoyed that this is even turning into an argument to begin with. But he would argue about anything with me just to have a reason to yell or hit me, like I said before it doesn't matter what I do, he always finds something wrong.

"Don't play dumb, Winter. You know damn well what I'm talking about." His body sways more as he reaches his arm out, then his big hand comes across my face, back handing me so hard my vision blurs, my head snaps to the left and my whole-body jerks. He comes at me again and I try to block myself but that pisses him off. He starts shouting.

"What the fuck do you think you're doing you fucking whore?" Spit flies and hits my face this time, his words slurring worse. But I don't lift my hand to wipe the spit off, I stand there as the little droplets of spit drip down my cheek, I don't want him to think I'm reaching my hand up to defend myself, I don't want him to think I'm trying to hit him back or anything because that'll just make things worse. Last time I fought back I ended up with a broken wrist, that I had to lie to everyone about and a busted cheek. That was a great story to come up with and I was thankful everyone I told believed me.

Here we go, he already forgot that we were just having a conversation. "Dad, I just told you. I was out with Emerald at the diner, we ate dinner. That was it. We didn't do or go anywhere else."

I lie, he doesn't have to know I was at the bar. I didn't get trashed and had one drink and a shot. He doesn't need to know that because then he'll use it against me. I say it as calmly as I can trying to hold back my anger, pissed that he hit me and pissed that this is even an argument.

"You expect me to believe you weren't whoring yourself out again?" He looks at me with his lips curling back in disgust. His breathing intensifying as he yells. To think I thought I was going to get away without being caught tonight. I guess the jokes on me.

This time he punches me in the stomach knocking me to the ground. That one fucking hurt, I'll probably have more bruises to hide by the time he's done.

Almost being raped at a party is me whoring myself around, he never wanted to believe that the "only respectful guy in town" is what he liked to call Preston, the asshole jock who thought it was ok to pretty much rape me. All I wanted to do was find Emerald and go home, but he apparently followed me up there and had other plans. The only reason I drank too much that night was to numb the pain from my dad kicking my ass again.

"Daddy," I try to say sweetly, attempting to stop his rage, reminding him I'm his daughter and not a whore.

"I brought your favorite burger with a side of half fries and half onion rings home. I even asked Lisa the owner if I could have some of your favorite dessert, her chocolate chunk caramel covered brownies, she gave me the rest to take home for you."

I scoot back on the ground trying to get far away before I stand up so I can show him his food, maybe then he'll believe me. But he just keeps stepping closer.

"I tell you all the damn time, Winter, that if you go out you need to get your ass home at a decent time. I'm sick and tired of you thinking that you don't have to listen to me, you're a disrespectful bitch." He backhands me across the face, snapping my head to the right this time and I can tell he split open my cheek from the force of the hit. I can taste the blood in my mouth and feel the blood dripping down my lip onto my chin from where he just busted my lip open.

"Goddamn, Dad. If you would just listen to me." I'm fed up and I'm fucking angry. He swings at me again, punching me in the eye. This time I smack him across the face to get him to stop or snap out of it.

"I am NOT a fucking whore. I was almost raped. If Emerald wouldn't have found me, then Preston would have had no problem finishing what he started. Doesn't mean he didn't touch me against my will. Or do other things I didn't ask for in the process. But I didn't ask to be called a whore. I am not a whore. I don't sleep around. I'm your daughter, dammit. And Mom would be pissed if she heard you talking to me this way, or even hitting me." He punches me so hard in the face it knocks me to the ground.

"You will not bring up your fucking mother like that." Sitting on the ground I look up at him holding my face, crying. I don't care if he sees me cry anymore.

"I didn't do anything wrong. This is why I brought her up. You're just hitting me and hitting me because you're a drunk, Dad, and you need some serious help. Please, you need help." He kicks me in the ribs, knocking the wind out of me. I try to gasp for air, but it hurts to even attempt to breathe.

I've officially lost, if I keep going, I might end up in the hospital, or worse, dead. This is what happens all the time, why Emerald begs me to move in with her, she just doesn't know exactly how bad it is. But I'm afraid if I leave and he finds out I left for good, that he really will come after me and kill me. I decide to try and end the argument, see if he forgets we were fighting to begin with. Sometimes it works and sometimes it pisses him off more but I'm willing to take my chances tonight. I need to get out of here once he passes out.

"Hey, Dad, do you want your food you had delivered from the diner? I can warm it up for you?"

"What do you mean, what food?" He looks confused, body swaying even more as he takes another drink and finishes his next beer.

"Remember, you called Lisa and had her deliver food for you, so we didn't have to leave? She delivered it when you were taking a nap. I figured I can get you situated on the couch while I warm it up for you and I'll get you another beer."

"Oh thanks, I forgot I ordered it. I must've been pretty tired, it's been a long day, busy week," He stops, scratching his head. I'm almost positive my plan is working. If I can just get him to the couch, I'll put his food away as he passes out.

I'm struggling to breathe from how many times he hit me and knocked me to the ground, but I'm trying my best to keep wiping the blood and breathing as normal as I can, so he doesn't ask me what happened. I finally get him back to the couch with a beer next to him on the table, hoping he'll pass out instead of opening it. "I'll be right back with your food, Dad," I say sweetly. Trying to keep whatever peace that came back from that argument. This is usually how it works with him. He's usually so drunk to the point where he forgets what is happening in the middle of it happening, it just sometimes takes a little bit to get him to the point of forgetting. Usually by the time we get to the point of him forgetting it's already too late for me and I'm usually the one left covered in bruises and blood, while he just sits back down with his beer and falls asleep. Then I'm the one left suffering while he just gets to continue with his life like nothing happened.

"Thanks, Winter. I'm just gonna rest my eyes while you warm it up," he says, leaning his head back against the couch, the same position he was in when I came home.

I quickly set his food in the refrigerator with a note with his name on it so he knows it's his and dart up to my room. I Text my boss to let her know I won't be able to make it tomorrow, there's no way the swelling will go down or I'll be able to cover up the bruises with how dark they'll be. I'll just have to take a loss on the extra pay and bigger tips from the bachelorette parties. I tell her I'm sick, hoping it'll be more believable with it being after three in the morning and hoping she'll be able to find someone to cover my shift for me as well.

I head to my closet and find my bags so I can start packing. I can't leave tonight but I'll start packing everything up so that way I can get a plan together to figure out how I'll get all my stuff out of the house without my dad noticing. I also sent Emerald a text to let her know that the argument was bad tonight, I didn't go into details with how bad it was, that's not important right now. What's important is asking her if the offer is still available to move in. Even though she told me it was a million times, I still want to double check before assuming and telling her I'm taking her up on it.

After gathering all my packing supplies, I quietly open my door to make sure I still hear my dad snoring. When I hear he still is, I shut and lock my door, bringing my chair up under the door handle just in case. Then I step into my bathroom so I can take a shower, but before taking a shower I strip down and take my pictures that I keep in a private folder on my phone. Pictures that show proof of all the times my dad hit me. So, when I finally have it in me to call the police I'll have multiple pictures showing proof. Not sure If I'll ever get the balls to call the police on my father. I still don't think that even after everything he's put me through that I would have the guts to unless maybe he puts me in the hospital then I don't think I'd have a choice about that.

7

CARSTEN

It's been about a week since I ran into Emerald and Winter at the bar, and I haven't stopped thinking about Winter. That gorgeous fucking girl, her smile, her laugh, her body, everything about her just keeps playing in my head. Her sexy voice—what's wrong with me, I can't believe I'm even obsessing over a girl like this—I never obsess over girls. Her voice was something else, the way she spoke, her tone, it was such a seductive sound that instantly made my dick hard. Her ass, oh my god, it jiggled as she walked. It wasn't even huge, but it was just enough ass to be able to see it jiggle. I'm sure it would feel great gripping her ass cheeks and hips while she rode my dick. I let out a frustrated groan.

"Thinking about that girl again, Carsten?" My brother laughs at me. He's such a dick, he knows I don't get caught up on girls like this.

"Yeah man I'm over here struggling to lift these fucking weights because I just can't stop thinking about her, my minds not focused. She's getting me all worked up, it's making my fucking dick hard just thinking about her voice man. What's my deal? I can go and get pussy wherever and now I can't stop thinking about her, or her pussy and how amazing it probably feels."

He's just fucking laughing at me, and I don't even blame him. I'd laugh at myself too. I probably sound like a fucking pussy. Shaking his head he decides to fuck with me "Sounds like you're just weak. It's why you're struggling with those weights' bro, it also sounds like you got it bad for her. She must have a golden pussy under there to be getting you worked up like this."

"Fuck off, I lift more than you, Chase, so I don't wanna hear anything about being weak. I'm not sure what it is, I even tried hooking up with Brynn the other day, ya know since I've been just hooking up with her, and I couldn't get my dick hard. Even if it was to save my fucking life it wouldn't work." His jaw drops and an odd chuckle comes out of his mouth, which I don't blame him for. It is pretty funny, depressing, but funny.

"Man, I thought I'd never see the day that Mr. Man Whore has a problem with getting it up, all it took was one girl to come along and now she broke it."

He sets his weights down and comes in front of me. "Maybe you just need to get her out of your mind, either hook up with her to see if fucking her gets her out of your brain and see if your dick starts working after. Or tell your mind to stop being fucking dumb and forget you met her."

"You think I didn't try the whole forgetting I ever met her and that she even exists for that matter bullshit, cause I have and my mind is not falling for it."

"Well, go talk to Emerald about her to see if she's seeing some-one, for all you know she could be married." Laughing he walks over to another machine.

"You shut your mouth, man. What am I gonna do if she is? Make her cheat to shut my dick up? I don't think she is though; she didn't have a ring on her finger and neither of them mentioned boyfriends." I can't believe this is even a conversation I'm having, I mean I'm thankful I have my brother to have this conversation with, but like I of all people have never had any issues with performing or getting things ready to perform. So, what the hell do I do if this chick broke my fucking dick?

"Just because they didn't mention it doesn't mean they aren't in relationships or married bro. A lot of girls pretend they're single or act single when they go out." I set my weights down frustrated with myself. Working out is one of my favorite things to do, it's always helped with clearing my mind and just making me feel better overall. So, I'm a little annoyed that not even working out is helping me clear my head of this weird bullshit that's suddenly decided to throw itself in my direction. Causing me and my dick all sorts of confusion.

"No, they don't. Usually, girls are the first ones to come off as bitches and freak out 'cause you talked to them when they're in a relationship or even married." I don't even mean that in a bad way either, you'll have a few women who flirt and act single but it's rare.

"Yeah, that's true, I wasn't thinking about that. So why don't you wait for Emerald to get home and talk to her about Winter then?" He turns back towards what he was doing and starts working out again while listening to me bitch like the pussy I'm becoming over this situation. Carsten fucking Hatcher, caught up in his feelings like a little bitch, gossiping over the first girl who caught his attention for the first time ever. Obviously, women catch my attention, I sleep around like it's my job. But I've never been interested in anything more than just fucking. That is what my issue is, I don't want to just fuck her and walk away. I don't know what I want, besides to talk to her again, feel her out. Try to see if she's my type before I continue obsessing. Who am I kidding. Of course she's my type everything about her is. It's like she walked out of my dreams and right into Black Velvet like she was fucking made for me.

"Dude, I've been waiting to see her pull into her driveway all week, every time I've heard anything that sounds like a car, I check out the front window to see if she's home, it's almost like she disappeared or something." I sigh. I've never had to work for anything when it has come to women. Ever. So, the fact that I've even gone this far is strange to me and I've barely done anything other than obsess and not stop thinking about her. Fuck, those perfectly pouty lips. Thinking about how they'd feel wrapped around…. But before I can continue my perverted fucking thoughts Chase starts talking again.

"Damn." He stops for a second, and stares. "That desperate huh? I've never seen you act this way. I wish I would've had the chance to really get to see her and talk to her. I caught a glimpse before you took over, but I'd love to have a conversation with her to see what's got your dick all excited over this chick." He smiles for a second. "Maybe see if she'd be interested in me, maybe that's why she's showing you no interest. She saw me first." He throws his head back a little, cracking up, as my jaw drops. The look of shock on my face. I never thought I'd feel... Jealous? Is that what this feeling is? Fuck him. I will kick his ass if he even thinks for one second that my little fucking Snowflake has any interest in him. Fuck him. She doesn't, she didn't even see him. Did she? Fuckkk. I hope she didn't.

I set the weights down and stand up, grabbing my water and chug down about half of it. Then I finally decide I think it's time for me to call it quits for the day cause I'm not getting much of a workout in obsessing over a stranger. Plus, Chase and his bullshit just pissed me off.

"Fuck you man. I saw her first. She didn't even see you." I set my water down and wipe the sweat off my brows with the back of my hand.

"I'm joking, don't get your lace panties in a bunch. No one wants to see that crusty shit." He makes a grossed-out face as he says it. Almost like he's picturing it. Nasty fucker.

"Are you ready to go home man? I'm not getting much of a workout in and feel like I'm just wasting my day. I gotta get home and sketch this tattoo out for one of my customers coming in this week." Maybe drawing up this tattoo will keep my mind off her and actually give me a chance to clear my head about everything going on. "Plus, I might just kick your ass if you don't stop talking about my woman like that. She may not be mine yet, but she will be I can promise you that. So back the fuck off." I give a quick smile before going back to a serious look, so he knows I'm not fucking around.

"Calm down man, I was joking. I didn't even see her." He shakes his head, his shoulders moving up and down a little, like he's laughing. Fucker. I can't see what he's doing because his back is towards me. But I'll kick his ass if he keeps laughing.

"Yeah, that's fine, I got some shit I wanted to get done anyway. Not really in the mood to keep working out today." He grabs his water and sweat rag and we head to the locker room to shower before we head home.

When we finally get home, I decide to make myself a sandwich to take to my room with me so I can eat while sketching. I gotta get most of it done today so my customer can come look at it tomorrow to let me know what she thinks of it, and I've barely gotten any of it done. I'm the best at procrastinating and I hate the stress that comes along with it.

Three hours later I'm finally satisfied with the final copy of my drawing. I decide to head downstairs to see what Chase, Creedence, and Axton are doing or if they're even home.

"What's up Carsten, haven't seen you all day man," Creedence greets me as I walk down the stairs.

"Hey man, been busy drawing up a tattoo. I just finished it." Now that I finally stopped, I didn't realize how tired my eyes were or how sore I am from sitting for so long. One thing I like about being part owner of the bar, and working at Crazy's tattoo shop is the change up of things. One job I'm sitting all day, which isn't terrible, but your eyes get tired and your body hurts from sitting for so long. At the bar I stand during my whole shift killing my body that way too. Basically, my body is fucked with both jobs. But I like the people, the atmosphere. Everything really. I get to see a different side to people at both jobs, which is interesting that's for sure. But I love the switch up and change of pace. It makes work tolerable at both places. Working with family doesn't suck like you think it would either, at least not for me. Whether I'm working at Black Velvet or Crazy's I'm around someone I'm related to. Maybe working with family since I was a kid and helping out where I could is what has made working together tolerable, maybe it's what made our family close.

"That's cool, anything different from the ordinary you get to draw up?" Creedence has been helping at my uncle's tattoo shop for as long as I can remember. Uncle Kane is the one who helped teach Creed and I how to tattoo. Watching him as I grew up is where my love for tattooing came from. His work is amazing and hope to be as good as he is one day. Creedence, Chase and I used to hang out at my uncle's tattoo shop when mom would work, and we had no one else to watch us. We'd organize his tattoo books, or he'd have us clean up his lobby and he'd take us to dinner or pay us and let us get some ice cream. He was like a dad to us, especially me and Chase. Since we grew up without a father.

I laugh thinking about all the tattoos that are the same but sometimes just slightly different. "Not really, pretty much the same, a bunch of flowers but all different flowers, and a couple fairies to go on them. It's cool." I say standing at the counter across from where he's sitting.

"That's cool man, so Chase mentioned you got it bad for some girl huh?" Fuck, sometimes I think men are worse with the fucking gossip I swear.

"Of course he did." I sigh "Fucker can't keep his stupid mouth shut." My brother has always sucked at keeping his mouth shut. Growing up he always had to have the last word in between the two of us, no matter what the conversation was he found a way to get the last word in. Even at night when we were kids before mom moved us out of the one-bedroom apartment we were all living in, he'd lay there at night and never shut up. Poor mom always had to come in our room multiple times before we'd finally stop fucking around and go to bed. But she never complained, even when the only expression on her face was pure exhaustion, she'd still keep a smile on it and do what she had to do for us.

Creedence laughs at that one. "No, he definitely can't, but it's all good. I'm your best friend man, you know you can talk to me. I may not be a hoe like you but I'm the relationship type of guy so I may have good advice." He leans back in his chair, crossing his arms over his chest.

"Ha. Ha. Ha. You're just jealous you can't be like me. I'm too young to settle down with one girl man, I can sleep around and have some fun." I pause thinking maybe a relationship might be nice for once. But push the thought aside as soon as it starts surfacing. Fuck that. "But yeah, I met her at the bar for country night last week, she's friends with our neighbor, Emerald. Her name's Winter; she's fucking gorgeous dude. She's covered in tattoos, curvy—like nice and thick in the ass, but not too much ass, nice size tits, she has pink and purple hair, beautiful brown eyes, she was my type that's for sure. Oh, she's a smart ass too, so that was the icing on the cake." She was fucking gorgeous. A fucking Goddess. Everything about her caught my eye, I don't think I've ever paid attention to details on one person the way I did with Winter last night. I even paid attention to the color of her fucking nails, black. I even noticed the way one eyebrow goes up just a little higher than the other one when she makes certain facial expressions. What is wrong with me? I think that's a question I'm going to be asking myself a lot of the more time I spend with Winter.

"Damn, she sounds sexy." Ha. She better not sound fucking sexy to him, she's mine. "Why don't you just talk to Emerald about her?" He gives me a look like I'm an idiot for not thinking of that idea before.

"Because I'm never home when she's home man. That's why I've been spying out the window like a fucking creep all damn week hoping to catch her at home and it's like she just disappeared or something." I run my hand through my hair letting out a long breath that I felt like I'd been holding from the stress of all of this. This right here is why I don't care to be involved, get involved or have any type of anything with a woman other than just sex. It's too stressful and I just don't have the patience or the time for it.

"Well bro, I'm about to make your day, Emerald is home right now. How about we head over there together, and I can help you out some. Plus, I wanna see her, she's hot as fuck. I'd like to get to know her a little more." He wiggles his eyebrows at me like he's gonna get lucky. Creedence isn't the type of guy to sleep around, at least I don't think he is. He's my best friend, my brother. But that's one thing he's kind of always kept to himself about and always stayed private about is his sex life. Which doesn't bother me much, I have enough of a sex like to talk for the both of us.

"Too bad you don't just fuck different girls and need a relationship to have sex man." I say in a mocking tone repeating it how he's said it in the past before.

"Shut up, at least I'm not a man who sleeps around bro," he says, slapping me on the back as a joke.

We head out the door to Emerald's and end up running into her in the driveway.

"Hey, Carsten. What's up. Haven't seen you since country night," she says, stopping and setting a box down on the ground in front of her.

"Hey Em." I pause looking over at Creed to introduce them. "This is my friend, Creedence, or Creed."

"Hey." She blushes a little. "I'm Emerald, it's nice to finally meet you." She reaches her hand out to shake his hand but instead he grabs her hand and kisses it. Making me smirk, he's always a gentleman no matter who he's being introduced to. Which isn't a bad thing at all, he's always been great with women of all ages with his charm and polite manners.

"Nice to meet you. Sorry, I just didn't realize how beautiful you were in person, I couldn't just shake your hand." Now I'm feeling a little awkward. Like I'm intruding on a personal conversation I shouldn't be a part of.

She giggles. "It's ok, I don't mind." She looks down at her hand, blushing like a guy has never kissed her hand before.

"I was actually just coming to talk to you, were you leaving?" I feel bad interrupting their moment, but I've been waiting patiently since I saw Winter on Thursday to find her again, and this is the first time I've seen her since. I'm not wasting anymore time.

"No actually, I was just carrying some of these boxes of Winter's in, trying to help her out some while her body heals." The way she says it seems off. Like something isn't okay, she has a sad look in her eyes. The smile she's giving us isn't a full genuine smile. You can tell she's forcing it. Something is not okay, and I need to fucking find out right now what is going on.

"What do you mean, is she ok?" I ask, grabbing the box from the ground for her. "Where do you want me to take this?"

"Oh, you don't have to help, it's ok." She's trying to avoid the question. I could tell by the way she was fidgeting. Which makes me even more curious about what the fuck happened to her.

"Well actually, I was coming over here to talk to you about Winter, so it kinda works out if you let me help you. What happened to her, is she doing ok?" I can tell she's still avoiding the answer, which is annoying me and I'm trying not to let my asshole side come out because she doesn't deserve it, I'm just... I don't know how I'm feeling right now, but nothing better be wrong with Winter. She probably really won't answer me if there is, would she?

"Yeah, I'll help too. Are there more boxes for me to grab?" Creedence asks her, walking towards her car.

"Um yeah, sure, but really you don't have too." She looks over at me. "Why did you come here to talk to me about Winter?" She avoids answering me, yet again.

"Look, I'm not trying to pry or be a dick, but the look on your face tells me something happened and I'm not just gonna drop it, especially after what happened to her at my bar. I'd like to know if she's at least ok."

She stops for a minute sighing. You can tell she's unsure of what to say or whether or not to answer me. I really don't want to be a dick and force her to answer me, but she mentioned it and now I need to know if she's ok or if there's anything I can do to help the situation. I haven't gotten this girl out of my head, and I don't think anything is going to change that anytime soon, so now that I feel like I should be worried the thoughts are only going to become worse, especially if she doesn't tell me what's wrong.

"Well, I don't know if it's my place to tell you guys honestly, she might kick my ass if I do because she didn't even want me to know, but since she finally decided to move in with me. That's one of the main reasons she gave in and told me." She looks around, with an uncomfortable look on her face. You can tell she's really conflicted about what to do.

"Look, I don't really know your friend, I came here to talk to you to ask you if she's single because I haven't been able to stop thinking about her. I don't know her situation or what's going on, but I promise you if she's in danger I'd do anything to protect her, especially after last week. I'd kick someone's ass if they did anything to her."

Right as I finish saying that a black car pulls up on the street and parks in between the front of our houses. "I guess now you can ask her yourself what happened to her and if she's single." She's smiling at me, and I give her a confused look getting ready to ask her why. "That's her car right there but be careful with your reactions when you see her, you're definitely going to be shocked and angry, but give her a minute she might not want to tell you exactly what happened, it was hard for her to finally tell me the truth." She turns her head to the right looking down the driveway, she looks really sad and angry.

"Emerald what happ... holy shit," I say at a whisper, barely moving my mouth, so Winter doesn't hear me, or hopefully see that I'm talking. But thankfully the only one who hears me is Emerald.

"I told you now, please don't say anything."

Looking at a sad, crying Winter, her whole left side of her face is bruised, her left eye black and blue, her cheek is cut but scabbed showing me that she's been like this for a few days meaning it could've been worse before this. Her right side of her lip is bruised and also scabbed like it was busted open too. It's hard to keep my jaw from dropping. Whoever put their fucking hands-on Winter is going to fucking pay. The look of heartache and sadness on her face, breaks my fucking heart. Making me want to kill whoever the fuck did this to her. They better pray that she called the police and that whoever is responsible is fucking locked up, because if they're not. It's not going to look good for them at all.

"What the fuck man. What happened to her?" Creedence says in a whisper.

"Emerald, why didn't you just say something?" I look back at her so I'm not staring as Winter is grabbing bags from her back seat.

"Look, I tried to tell you, but didn't even know where to begin. Please just go help her maybe she'll say something." She whisper-yells and my heart starts getting this weird fucking tightening feeling, is this what a heart attack feels like? I'm sure it's the terrible anxiety that decided to creep up on me knowing I have to go and talk to this gorgeously bruised up woman and not lose my shit and freak out asking her questions about who did this to her or if she's okay. Or the fucking fact that I have to go and have an actual conversation with a girl, I don't usually do much of those. Once I make my move, I'm usually taking the girl home relatively quickly or going back to their place. I keep conversation short. But now I have to actually go talk to her and my nerves are trying to fuck with me.

I walk down the driveway to Winter's car. "Hey, gorgeous." I greet her the same way because even though she's all banged up, covered in bruises, no makeup, and crying, she's probably the most beautiful woman I've ever seen. My heart starts racing as I get closer to her and for some reason now, I feel even more nervous. What the fuck? Don't be a pussy Carsten, you act like you've never talked to girls before, just because you don't have much of a conversation with them doesn't mean you've never talked to one before. And now you're going to be a shy fucking pussy? Don't think so, man the fuck up dude.

"Hey Carsten, nice seeing you again. You don't have to be nice about it though, please. I know I look far from gorgeous right now." She sighs. She wasn't saying it in a snippy way, but a hurt and embarrassed way. Her cheeks start to heat up, a light shade of pink covering them as she starts to blush some.

I gently reach out grabbing her chin to stop her from looking down, so I can see her beautiful brown eyes. "I'm not just being nice, Snowflake. I don't know what happened, but even with these bruises and cuts on your face, you're absolutely breathtaking."

She smiles at me, tears forming in those beautiful eyes. "Thank you." She tucks her hair behind her ears and blushes again, bringing a smile to my face. She blushes so easily for me, my little snowflake. She's perfect in every way but those beautifully flushed cheeks of hers that turn red when she blushes drive me wild. Making me think of all sorts of dirty things that involve my cock in her pussy and her flushed skin against mine. I snap out of my thoughts removing my hand from her chin.

"What do you need help carrying?" I ask her. I wanted to ask if she was ok but didn't want to ask her right away, I know she feels insecure right now with how she's looking and I'm sure the last thing she wants to do is have that be the first conversation we have.

"Umm, honestly, any of this would be great. I'm not as strong as usual right now so lifting anything pretty much in general hurts my body." She's holding bags that look very light, so I'm assuming this is all she can carry that won't hurt her.

"I'll grab everything, you just tell me where I'm going. Are you ok to walk with me to show me or does that hurt too?" I don't wanna cause her any pain. If anything, I can carry her on my back if it'll make it easier for her to get back and forth. Plus having her body that close to mine in a non-sexual way would be amazing.

"It hurts, but I'll manage. I'll show you where that stuff goes." That's all she says, she doesn't elaborate on why she's in pain when she walks and I don't want to pry, not yet.

We carry stuff back and forth for a little while before she sits down on the ground on the driveway. "Sorry I just need a break, come join me."

"So, I don't want you to feel like you have to tell me, but I need to know if you're okay, Snowflake." I reach over rubbing my hand on her leg to let her know she can trust me.

"It's just a lot. I'll be ok, it's why I finally said fuck it and decided I'm moving in with Em. I lost my job because of calling off from all this shit. I need to just start fresh, and she said she can help until I'm ready to look for jobs again. I'm just a big mess, I'll be ok though." She gives me a half smile before taking a deep breath.

"Listen, Snowflake." I pause thinking of how to word this, so I don't come off like a dick. "I'm not gonna pretend I don't see you're covered in bruises. I know you don't really know me, but you can trust me. I'll do whatever I can to help you, I just need to know what happened.

8

WINTER

I LOOK OVER AT HIS HANDSOME FACE, HIS LIGHT-BROWN HAIR messy on top like he's been brushing through it with his fingers from stress. He has the prettiest hazel eyes I've ever seen. He has this hard look to him, but gentle at the same time, at least to me he's not scary. He seems like he likes to be in control but not a controlling asshole. He's got two full sleeves of tattoos that cover every inch of his arms and big strong hands, I'm probably drooling just looking at him at this point. I finally snap out of checking him out and try to decide if I want to trust him and tell him what happened.

The one thing I'm unsure about is if I tell him, what will he do? The other night at the bar he kicked that guy's ass for touching me, which I was completely fine with, but what will he do to my dad. Yes, my dad's a drunk asshole and would probably deserve to get his ass kicked, but I couldn't stoop to his level and have someone do that to him. Maybe if I make him promise not to react he won't? I finally snap out of checking him out and try to decide if I want to trust him and tell him what happened. I never wanted to tell Emerald what my dad had done to me, I told her some, but I never fully filled her in only because I knew she wouldn't let me put up with it. The only reason I put up with it for as long as I have is because who is going to take care of my dad if I'm not there? That's my main concern is his health and safety, how will he survive without me? I want to tell Carsten because I don't want to start off hiding things from him, especially since he caught my eye the other night. I haven't been able to stop thinking about him and whether or not he was into me. But I want to start things off being open and honest with him.

"Look, I trust you, especially after how you protected and stuck up for me the other night at your bar. I just feel like if I tell you, it might make you angry, and you might want to react the same way, and due to the situation, I can't have you react that way."

He chuckles, running his hands through his hair, it must be a habit of his. "Ok." He stops to think for a second before he continues what he says, "I tend to react before thinking sometimes. It's a bad habit, but I like to protect what's mine and the people I care for." I can't help the smile that creeps up as I replay the words that just came out of his mouth. His? Did he just call me his?

I look over at him again with a bit of confusion on my face, since we had just met that night. "You like to protect what's yours; I love that. I don't mean to laugh, I only laughed because does that mean you're claiming me so soon?" I say in a sarcastic way, so he doesn't think I'm obsessing when I barely know him. "Oh yeah, I'm definitely in the process of claiming you, it's just in the beginning stages but after a few weeks you won't have to ask that. You'll just know that you're mine and that I'll be protecting what's mine." He doesn't even give me a chance to say anything else before he continues, "Now, what happened, Snowflake? I can't promise I won't get mad, but I promise I won't beat anyone up." He reaches over and takes his hand and holds mine.

"Thank you," I say softly looking down. I'm unsure of where to even begin with something that's been happening to me since I was twelve years old, and he's only gotten worse over the years over things that aren't even a big deal. This has always been a tough subject to talk about, that's why I've always just kept to myself about it and never spoke of it. The less people who knew about it and the details the better. That way I could live my life pretending like things weren't as bad as they were. It made it easier for me to cope that way.

9

CARSTEN

She turns to face me—still letting me hold her hand but so she's facing me. I feel nervous for her, completely unsure of where this is headed.

"So, my dad's an alcoholic, he has been my whole life. He wasn't always this bad either. After my mom passed away when I was twelve, he began to drink more and would buy a bunch of beer—enough to last weeks at a time so he didn't have to sober up to leave. That turned into he had more alcohol available to drink, so he drank more, he thought of it as why not it was there, and he was depressed. The depression turned to anger and the anger mixed with alcohol turned into him becoming abusive. It wasn't bad at first, he'd hit me here and there and I'd kind of just put up with it because I was angry about losing my mom too. I felt like I understood."

She pauses for a minute, seeming to try to compose herself from the memories and hold back the tears. I know this can't be easy for her to open to me and tell me. And it really can't be easy for her to have to relive the memories, she was so young when it started.

"But then when he started drinking liquor, it didn't matter what kind, usually cheap stuff so he could buy more at once." He became angry over little things and would hit me more and harder. Like me going out with Emerald and "whoring myself around, embarrassing him.'"" She uses air quotes when she says that, and it makes me wonder why he even feels that way about her. "That's what he told me the night I came home after meeting you. He doesn't even know we went to the bar; I only told him we went and got food. But he assumed I was out sleeping around because I was home late."

She pauses taking a deep breath before speaking again. The sad look on her face breaking my fucking heart and it takes everything in me not to just scoop her up and protect her right here even if nothing is harming her. "He was pissed because of how late it was when I got home, he didn't even care why I was home late, so he slapped me a couple times knocking me down." The look of hurt and heartache on her face. This poor girl is sitting here telling me and reliving the memories of all the times her dad kicked her ass and there's nothing I can do to take these feeling or the pain of the memories away. "He punched me in the face a couple times, then when he knocked me down, he started kicking me in the ribs." She leans back lifting her shirt showing me this huge bruise on the left side of her ribs, the whole area is bruised, it looks terrible. I'm beyond pissed at this point, drunk or not what the fuck is his deal? Who could sit there and just hurt her like that? But I wait to talk so she can finish what she's saying.

"Then he just kept yelling at me and hitting me, I seriously thought if I didn't get him to stop, he was going to kill me. But like I said, this time was the worst, and in the middle of it he forgot what was going on and went on like he wasn't just beating the fuck out of me." Her eyes fill with fresh tears as the old one's stream down her cheeks and I can't take it anymore. I lean forward and gently place my left arm under the bend of her knees and my right on the small of her back before pulling her to me and placing her into my lap. I don't care if this is the second time I've been around her. She needs this, to be hugged and comforted after everything that happened to her, she needs to know someone cares.

"Snowflake, how do you not expect me to go and kick your dad's ass after that? I mean I won't but babe." *I hope she didn't catch that part.* "What the fuck. That was too much, any of it is too much. I'm seeing red over here and the urge to go kick his ass to protect you is strong." I pull her close to me. "You're not going back there; do you understand me? Yes, I'm gonna tell you what to do with this one because either you live with Emerald or I'll make you live with me, but you're not going back there at all. Ok?"

I'm trying to control my anger because I don't want her to think I'm taking it out on her or I'm mad at her but I just don't get how her asshole dad can think it's ok to hit her like that at all, drunk or not it's fucking bullshit, if I ever see him come near her like that and I'm around I will personally kick his ass, she won't have to worry about him touching her again. I gently cup her cheek not wanting to hurt her, making her look at me. "I'm so sorry you've had to go through this, now and in the past. But I can promise you if you hang around me it won't happen anymore. I will make sure he doesn't touch you ever again." I stare at her beautiful face gently rubbing my thumb over her scabs and bruises.

"I appreciate that and thank you. It's been rough going through it. I stay because he doesn't have anyone else to take care of him and he's too drunk to take care of himself. Plus, he doesn't work so I help pay for things and the bills. I don't know what he will do now without me helping him." She lets out a quick breath, like she forgot to breathe while she was talking.

"Snowflake, Snowflake... my precious Snowflake." I lean a little closer to her face; the urge to kiss her pouty lips is harder to resist each time I look at her. I might say fuck it and kiss her before this conversation is over, but I don't want to rush her so I might wait. "Fuck your dad, no offense, stop worrying about him. Maybe this is what he needs to help him sober up and change his life around."

"God, I wish. I've tried so many things to make him want to sober up, including bringing up my mom, and it just makes things worse than he gets angrier and tells me nothing will change him that he drinks because I'm a whore, because my situation apparently makes me a whore."

"Situation?" I wanted to ask about it before, but I wanted to see if she'd bring it up again. Hoping she's ready to tell me, but I won't push if she's not ready, she's shared enough secrets with someone she barely knows.

She looks at me like she's pissed at herself for bringing it up. "Not tonight, I'm too mentally exhausted to share anymore about my stressful life." She laughs a sad laugh. "It's ok, we have plenty of time to get to know each other. If that's something you'd like to do, get to know each other better?"

She looks back up at me. "Yeah, I'd like that." Smiling, she looks away and leans her head back against my chest. I still can't believe all the bruises her dad has put on her, she's so small, it makes me wonder what her dad looks like, how big of an asshole he is to put his hands on her like that.

"You seem pretty tired, how about I help you carry the rest of your stuff into Emerald's house tomorrow so you can go relax? I'll help whenever you're ready to do it. Also, if you have more stuff at your dads I can go and get it with you." I want to make sure I put that out there, so she doesn't think she has to face him alone if she decides she needs to go there. I don't want her going alone so I'm hoping she stops fighting me and lets me help her out.

"Really, you don't have to help me. I'd feel terrible, you've done enough. You've helped me carry stuff already and listen to my shitty life and why I look like fucking shit and one big bruise. But I'd like to hang out when I'm done if you'd like to?"

Staring at her beautifully bruised face I can't help but smile, my heart gets this aching feeling I've never experienced before. There's something about this girl, I can't put my finger on it, but I don't want to ruin anything with her. "Listen snowflake, I'm not taking no for an answer, yes we'll hang out while I help you carry shit and I'll hang out with you during and after, how does that sound?"

"Sounds great to me. Once you see me outside you can come hang out with me, I'm not giving you my phone number yet, I'm gonna make you work for it." She teases, standing up and smiling down at me.

"Ooh, a challenge. I love challenges. So, my little snowflake, challenge accepted. I promise by the end of tomorrow I'll have your phone number," I say looking up at her.

"We'll see, you handsome devil." Then she blows me a kiss and walks up the driveway, leaving me sitting there. Not getting another word in and she doesn't even look back at me.

I'll get her phone number tomorrow even if I have to steal her phone and text my own number. Winter seems like she's going to be a very fun friend, more than friends, fuck I'd love to keep her around for a while.

10

WINTER

I WOKE UP EARLIER THAN I NORMALLY WOULD, SIMPLY DUE to not being able to sleep from being in pain and just from the stress of the situation. My anxiety has been terrible since the fight my dad and I had, and nothing I do seems to be helping it. Plus, Carsten's been on my mind all night, thinking about my feelings for him. How do you develop such strong feelings for someone so quickly when you're basically strangers? Carsten doesn't feel like a stranger though, he feels like someone I've known for forever, he makes me feel comfortable. I trusted him with stuff about my family that I don't trust a lot of people with. I told him about my dad, the alcohol and the abuse. Emerald just found out how bad it was with my dad and I'm sure it hurt her that I kept it from her. But I did it for a reason. With Carsten I just felt comfortable enough to share that with him, I was trusting Carsten right away with that secret and that's scary for me. I couldn't even trust my best friend because I was terrified of what she would think of me for staying there and why I still helped him out with money and whatever else. But for some reason with Carsten, it just felt right to tell him, like he would understand somehow or listen without judgment. Carsten seems different, different from any of the other guys I've dated and I'm excited to see where this goes with him.

I wanted to unpack some stuff before heading outside and bringing more shit in from my car and from Emerald's dad's work van he let us borrow to bring my stuff to her house. I never realized how stressful packing and moving was, so I can't even imagine what unpacking is like, or how stressful it's going to be.

I decided to start with my bathroom. Emerald gave me her whole second floor, the other master bedroom with a walk-in closet and an ensuite bathroom that connects to the bedroom and then the spare room up here for whatever I want to use it for. I'm not sure what I'm going to put in there yet either. I don't think I've ever had this much room to store my stuff before. At home I just had an over cluttered bedroom and my dad, and I shared the bathroom. After unpacking all my toiletries, towels, and feminine products, I move to the closet and start unpacking whatever clothes I have in here. I know the rest of them are in my car but I'm trying to start with the less stressful items before I get to the items that I'll need help moving.

All day Carsten has been on my mind. I wonder what he thinks about everything I told him. Is he still mad? Is he going to treat me differently now? Not in a bad way, but in an *I feel sorry for you,* kind of way. I don't want him to feel sorry for me. That wasn't why I told him. It wasn't a poor me, give me attention, confession, it was he deserved the truth and something inside me told me to trust him. He was pissed the fuck off after I told him, not angry with me but the obvious, my dad. I thought for sure he was going to go after him, thankfully I think I talked him out of it. Even though I'm sure my dad would deserve it, yes that's a shitty thing to say, but I don't want that for him. Because I don't want that for myself.

11

CARSTEN

It was a hot ass day, and I instantly regretted my decision to work on my car. I woke up earlier than normal to get a head start on my weekend list of stuff I need to do. I haven't worked on my car in forever so I made it a priority to spend as much time on it as I could until Winter needs my help. I'm a fucking idiot and thought I'd beat the heat being out here early, instead it decided to join me too. I've been working on this car for about six months. A friend of my uncles was selling it 'cause he didn't have time to work on it anymore, so I got it dirt cheap and I love working on old cars.

I hear something from my driveway, so I lower the hood halfway to check it out but don't see anything or hear anything more. I raise the hood back up and get back to work so I can get a move on. I'm not really into doing my car as much as I want to be because of how fucking hot it is, but I'm forcing myself to get a move on. I go to grab another tool and hear something again; it sounds as if someone is talking or sounds angry. Maybe a neighbor is fighting with one of their boyfriends. I put the tools down and go to check it out. Looking at the house opposite Emerald's, and now Winter's too, I stop and look and don't hear or see anything. Maybe I missed it, and they went back inside, or they were on the phone. Just as I'm about to walk back to my garage I hear it again and decide to look over to see if Winter is outside looking for me.

"Damn it, mother fucker, of course, gonna end up killing myself at this rate," I hear Winter say from her roof, what the hell is she doing up there, she's gonna get hurt especially if her body is still sore and bruised.

12

WINTER

THE AIR WAS HUMID AND STICKY AS I SAT OUTSIDE ON MY rooftop. I didn't care though I needed to get some type of fresh air after being cooped up in my room all morning unpacking my shit. I still haven't gone down to get the rest of my stuff yet, but I think after this break I'll go and see if Carsten is busy. My body is still sore from all the bruises, and I think more from falling each time I was hit now than from actually being hit. "This sucks," I mumble to myself as I rip up a leaf from the tree branch next to me. The view in this neighborhood is so pretty compared to how my dad's neighborhood was. There's so many beautiful trees and flowers, mine was run down, and nobody took care of it anymore. Houses were practically falling apart, the lawns were either overgrown or the grass was dying, it was pretty sad coming home to it every day.

Dark clouds start to cover up the sun and it looks like it's about to rain out of nowhere. I go to check my phone to look at the weather to see if the rain will ruin my plans to unpack my car when I realize I forgot it inside. "Oh well, guess I need to get a move on then. Shits not going to unpack itself." I start to stand up to climb back into my window but my foot slips under me and I smack my knee down onto the roof and catch myself from falling further. "Holy shit," I shout to myself, "nice job, Winter. Kill yourself when no one's here to even take you to the hospital." I stand up again and hear a deep laugh coming from below.

"Umm, I'd hate to bother you up there while you're talking to yourself on your roof, but uhh you good, Snowflake?"

Just great, my cheeks flush with embarrassment as I look down and see Carsten standing there, in a greasy wife beater and cargo shorts. He starts laughing as I stand there not sure how to answer him without him being upset that I almost just died. I mean it's not a far fall once I get down to the garage level but from here—yeah, I'd probably be dead.

"Oh sure, just find humor in watching me almost fall to my death off my roof," I say sarcastically, trying not to laugh myself.

"Well first, in my defense, I didn't realize that's what was happening. All I heard was you mumbling to yourself, you sounded angry."

I cut him off before he finishes that sentence. "Well yeah, because I almost died," I say dramatically, placing my hand on my chest. I look like shit. I have my hair up in messy bun pigtails and I'm wearing my cropped tie-dye shirt that comes to a stop right below my boobs, with no bra and black pajama shorts. My stomach is completely showing, and I realize how cold it is up here now that the temperature is suddenly dropping, and the wind is picking up.

"Well, if it makes you feel any better, I would have come to your rescue and caught you before you fell to your death. You know I'd do anything to protect you gorgeous." He gives me his sexy half smirk.

"Man, I don't know if I could trust you catching me that quickly." I smirk a little because there was no way around insulting him. Even though that was the last thing I wanted to do, it was a lose-lose no matter what.

He crosses his tattooed arms while shaking his head with a smile. "Are you underestimating my strength, miss?" he says playfully.

"Oh no, sir... I would never underestimate the strength of a man I've only hung out with two times and barely know." Laughing again I can't help but to hope this could go somewhere with the two of us.

"Mmm." He practically growls. "Call me sir again and I'm gonna have to come up there and throw you over my shoulder, maybe spank you some. Cause I'm not gonna lie that turned me on." He gives me the sexiest wink and smile ever. That growl was definitely a turn on, I think he just made my panties wet.

"So sorry sir, it won't happen again." I smirk as he growls again.

"Dammit, Snowflake. I'm warning you!" He shakes his finger at me. "You're lucky you're up there and I'm down here young lady." He laughs readjusting the crotch of his pants, it's hard to not notice his hard length as he shifts everything around.

"Ok, ok, I'll stop. I was actually about to come down there and see if you were busy." He's covered in what looks like grease from his car and his hands are filthy, for some reason it's turning me on even more how sexy he looks covered in sweat and grease.

"Yep, I was just working on my car until you were ready, you said you'd come find me, so I thought I'd make it easier for you to find me. Plus, I think it's about to storm. We can try to get as much in as possible before the rain if you'd like. I just need to clean up my tools real quick and I can meet you down here?"

"Yeah, that sounds perfect. I just gotta head back in and I'll be right down. Take your time, I can come to you in a minute," I say slowly backing up, so I don't fall this time while rubbing my hands over my arms because its fucking cold now. "Also, gonna grab a hoodie, it's fucking freezing now." He looks at me like I'm crazy.

"Hell no, that heat was terrible. It feels amazing now. I think I'll finally stop sweating some." He brushes his dirty hand across his sweaty forehead, leaving a little grease behind. Making his sexy face look even sexier. Who knew that was possible.

"Well, I thought the sweat looked good on you." I turn around to head back in. "I'll be right over there."

"Hey, Snowflake?" I love the way he says my name, well the nickname he gave me. It makes my stomach flutter.

"Yes, Carsten?" I sit down in front of my window.

"Your knee is bleeding; you might want to check it out before you head over." I look down because I didn't even notice I was bleeding. I never even felt a scrape at all.

"Oh shit, well thanks I didn't even notice." He smiles walking away and waving. I can't help but stare at his muscular, tattooed body as he walks away. The visible dirt and grease from his car stain his tattooed hands and arms, not fully covering his skin but scattered randomly, making him look even more delicious. It makes me want his dirty hands all over me, touching me in all the places that make my toes curl while I scream his name. Fuck, what is wrong with me?

"No problem, gorgeous. See you in a minute." How does he? How... how does he make the word gorgeous sound so fucking sexy? I swear he could make anything sound sexy, I'm sure of it.

I go to open my window since the wind blew it shut and realize it's locked. "Fuck, fuck, fucking shit." I put my hands over my face. "As if this couldn't get any worse, my fucking window is locked and my damn phones inside." I stand up slowly to walk down my roof again to see if Carsten is still outside. I climb down to the roof of the garage because if I absolutely need to, I can possibly jump from the roof.

"Hey, Carsten?" I yell hoping he hears me, or he didn't go inside. "Fuck... Carsten, are you still over there?" I yell even louder this time hoping I don't have to jump down. I'm sure I can but I'll probably hurt myself even more if I do.

"Winter? Everything ok?" he asks, walking out of his garage towards my yard again. He doesn't have a shirt on this time and damn I didn't think he could be any more attractive—but I was wrong, he is so fucking sexy, I could stare at him all day.

"Well, funny story..." I sigh. "Sometime between us talking before and me walking back to my window, the wind blew my window shut, the latch caught on the inside, and I'm locked out. Emerald's working until two in the morning and my phones inside." I rush out all of that in one breath and begin to shiver because it's really fucking cold and the winds blowing like crazy. As if my luck couldn't get any worse today, it starts to down pour. "And now I'm wet and freezing, and I'm stuck up on my fucking roof." I stomp my foot, pouting. "And I have to pee." I start laughing while Carsten is cracking up, standing with one hand in his pocket and a wrench in his other hand.

"Can you please help me down, with like a ladder or something, so I don't freeze to death, 'cause I'm a freeze baby. Or so I don't embarrass myself and pee my pants." He's still laughing and I'm standing here hoping the freaking wind doesn't knock me over. Yes, it's funny and I'm being somewhat dramatic, but I do feel the wind could knock me down with how bad it is. "Or you know, just laugh, it's cool, I'm just gonna jump down then." I stare down at him hoping he finally says something.

"I can help you down, Snowflake, I don't need a ladder."

I cut him off before he can say anything else. "What do you mean? How will you help me down then?" I stand there confused, not really sure what he has planned.

"I'll catch you, sit on the roof and slowly scoot towards the edge. It's not that far of a drop but when you push off, I'll catch you," he says with confidence, like it's no big deal at all. Not like my body isn't about to come flying down at him and if by chance he doesn't catch me I die. How horrible would he feel then? Maybe I should ask him if he's confident enough that he won't let me die. But then I don't want to make him nervous and overthink it while he's in the process of catching me then fuck something up and we both end up hurt. I'll just keep my mouth shut with that part.

Laughing, I look at him like he's crazy. "You're being serious? I'll hurt you falling on you like that"

"Winter, I'm telling you to do this." He pauses for a second, laughing nervously before he continues, "I mean not like I'm bossing you around or anything. I meant if I didn't think I could catch you I wouldn't offer, and I know you won't hurt me."

He throws his wrench in the grass in his yard and starts walking towards the garage more. I can tell he's very strong, I have no doubts he could lift me with no problems at all, I'm just afraid with the way I jump off, if I don't do it right, I might hurt him. "Besides…" He looks up at me, the corner of his mouth slowly curving up with that sexy smirk of his. "I wouldn't have this gorgeous neighbor to flirt with and take out on dates if I let something happen to you." He winks this time while slowly licking his bottom lip. I can't help the blush that creeps up on my face or the giggle that escapes my mouth.

"I don't know how you think I'm attractive looking like this." I feel like I look disgusting. I'm dressed like a bum and covered in bruises.

"Oh, Snowflake, you are so gorgeous. No matter what you look like, I don't think anything could change that." I can't believe I'm blushing again.

"Thank you, Carsten. I think you're pretty good looking yourself." He smiles.

"Why thank you, miss." He steps forward a little more, holds his arms up, then backs up a little and moves to the right a little and stops. "Ok, so I want you to scoot to the edge where your legs dangle off of the roof and when I lift my arms I want you to push yourself off then I'll catch you."

I sigh. "I'm scared though, but you sound so confident so that kinda helps me feel a little better."

He shakes his head and puts his hands over his face. "Winter, I promise I won't let you get hurt; you can do this."

"Ok, I trust you then, I guess," I say sarcastically with a smirk. I take a deep breath and start scooting down the roof a little more.

"A little further…" he instructs, waving his hands towards himself to show me to keep going. "Ok, now stop and slowly put your feet over the edge and just tell me when you're ready—although I'm not rushing you, but the wind sure is picking up and the rain is getting heavier again and I've seen quite a bit of lightning behind you, plus im kinda cold I didn't get to put my shirt back on."

"Tell me about it, I'm freezing my ass off too. I think my fucking boobs are gonna fall off from my lack of clothing." I put my hands over my boobs. "I also feel like the whole lightning thing was an important detail you should've told me sooner."

He looks back up at me growling again. "Damn, Winter, you're killin me and my dick here. First of all, please don't lose your boobs, I happen to be a boob guy and yours look like they'll be my favorite boobs ever. Second, I apologize, I'm not trying to be a perv, but keep it up with that dirty talk and you're gonna bring it out of me." He's laughing now while adjusting his dick again. "Anyway, I just didn't want you to freak out and fall off the roof from feeling rushed."

"Thank you, sir. I don't think you're a perv, I appreciate your honesty." I smile. "I'm actually quite a perv when I'm not stuck up on a roof or if I'm comfortable around you." I laugh again, now feeling a little more relaxed. "I think I'm ready now."

"Ok I'm ready for you... Do you want me to count down?"

"Yeah, I can see you're ready." Fucking blushing again, god I can't believe I blush so much around him, what am I a teenager talking to her first crush?

"Ha ha, ohh we're being playful now, I can show you how ready I am once you get down here." He winks, making my thighs tighten and my pussy throb. I don't think I've ever been this turned on in my life just from someone talking like this.

"Shit, well then, I guess you better count down. From three though, five will take too long and I'll chicken out or I'll hurt myself from overthinking it all."

"Alright then, get ready, three, two, one. Now push off," he says, holding his arms up.

"Shit, shit, shit," I squeak while pushing myself off. I closed my eyes on the way down and didn't realize my shirt slipped up as my body slid down against his shirtless chest. I could feel the warmth of his body against my skin making my nipples painfully hard. I think I let out a slight moan.

"Y—you can open your eyes now," he says, almost at a whisper. He's breathing heavier and his grip on my hips gets a little tighter. "Goddamn, babe." He growls, making my pussy throb yet again. I'm so turned on, it's ridiculous. I slowly open my eyes to his sexy ass smile and the look of hunger on his face. "Your tits babe, fuck." He gives a painful groan.

"Mmhmm," is all I can manage to say at the moment.

"Your body is so warm," I whisper, pulling myself closer to him. Looking up I notice he's staring at me.

"I—I've never wanted to kiss someone as bad as I want to kiss you right now." It's one of the sexiest things I think I've ever heard a man say to me.

"Please do." Is all I can get out without panting because I'm so fucking turned on.

He grabs my hips and readjusts the way he's holding me. I wrap my legs around him tighter, feeling his hard length against me, and he starts walking towards the garage behind me, he pins me up against it and I give a slight moan. The wind picks up sending chills down my body, I'm not sure if they're from being cold or from him. I can smell his musk cologne mixed with a hint of gasoline and I've never smelled something so sexy in my life. As he lowers his mouth towards mine, I can feel the warmth from how close he is.

His mouth crashes against mine. His tongue darting out gently, swiping my lips asking me to open my mouth. He sends chills down my body, I meet his tongue with mine, and he groans, swallowing my moan with his. He slowly lets me down but still keeps me pinned against the garage door. He moves away from my mouth, tilting my head to the side, gripping under my chin with his hand and starts kissing and sucking on my jaw, working his way down my neck. Moaning, I reach my hand down gripping his dick on top of his shorts, and slowly rubbing it up and down.

"God, fuckkk," he moans, still sucking on my neck. He starts working his way towards my collar bone when he pulls away panting, the rains coming down hard now, were both soaked. I don't even care that we're outside for anyone to see us. "Damn, I don't think I ever want to stop kissing you." He chuckles. "But we should probably get inside, it's getting pretty bad, and we should get out of these wet clothes," he says, still breathing heavy.

"I see you're not wasting any time trying to get my clothes off." I laugh.

"No, I didn't mean it that way. I just mean because I'm fucking cold, and if I'm cold I know you're cold." He's smiling, his beard almost covering up that sexy dimple of his on his left cheek. The way his lips curve up makes me want to run my tongue across them, it's so fucking sexy. This man is probably the sexiest man I think I've ever seen, and I thought I've seen sexy men before. But none of them compare to this Godly fucking man standing in front of me, Carsten fucking Hatcher. The things I hope to do to this man, make my panties wet, and my pussy throb. Clenching my thighs together I focus on the important thing right now. Making it into Carsten's arms safely.

"Shit, I don't have a key to get in or clothes to wear," I say, hugging myself.

He smiles. "Perfect. Either you can wear nothing, and we just warm up in my bed." He winks, "or you can borrow some of mine and I'll dry yours."

"Ohhh," I say playfully. "So many fun options to choose from, which one shall I choose?" I playfully tap my chin.

"Well while you think, let's go." He throws me over his shoulder and smacks my ass.

"Excuse me, I didn't agree to this." I playfully smack his back like my panties aren't soaking wet from how turned on I am right now. I've never moved this quickly with a guy before. Usually, I go on a couple dates and at least talk to them more, like way more than I have Carsten. But something just feels different with him, he doesn't seem like any of the douche bags I've dated or even talked to in the past.

"Yeah, yeah, Snowflake. Don't act like you don't like this, and if you keep smacking me, I'm gonna have to spank that ass of yours as a punishment, miss." As if I wasn't turned on enough. If I mentioned my panties were soaking wet... Well yeah, now they're dripping. I'll probably cum soon from just his talking alone.

13

CARSTEN

I CARRY HER SEXY ASS INTO MY HOUSE, SINCE SHE'S LOCKED out of hers, I walk in through the kitchen and see Creedence standing there making a sandwich. "Oh, uhh—hey, man." He looks confused while laughing. He goes behind me and leans down to look at Winter's face. "Hey there, Winter. How's it hanging?" He slaps his knee like he's a comedian, but I can't help laughing at how fucking cheesy that was.

"Hey, Creedence. Can you tell your friend here to put me down please?" she says, slapping my back again.

"Sorry, Winter, I can't do that..." she cuts him off before he can continue what he was going to say.

"What the fuck–" she gives a playful sigh. "You guys aren't fair." She pretends to pout and attempts to cross her arms, but it doesn't work too well since she's upside down over my shoulder.

"Hey, I'm not about to come between my best friend and his dick, ok?" He lets out a slight chuckle as he takes a bite of his sandwich. "You two have fun now." He starts walking down the hall towards his bedroom. Thankfully my room is upstairs, so he won't hear much, if things do happen between us.

"Alright babe, I'm about to carry you up the stairs, hang on," he says, turning in the direction of the stairs. I scrunch my eyes closed, scared of being carried up the stairs over his shoulder, afraid I'll hurt him.

"Carsten, I'm about to pee all over you. I have to pee so bad and you're putting so much pressure on my bladder." She practically squeals I'm assuming from the way I turned while holding her. Or maybe from the excitement of me carrying her. I'm not sure.

"Damn, when I thought you were into kinky shit, I didn't realize you were into giving golden showers, guess I'm willing to try anything once though." I smack her ass again. Making her shriek and giggle, sounds like she's excited from me smacking it if you ask me, my kinda girl.

"What? Hell no, I'm not into that stuff. I'm just saying if you take me up the stairs over your shoulder, chances are the bouncing is going to make me pee, plus all the blood is rushing to my fucking head man." From my angle it looks like she puts her hands over her head, while trying to pick her head up.

"Watch your mouth young lady." Smack—I whack her ass harder this time. Smiling to myself but also getting myself going, making my cock hard.

"Hey, stop smacking me dude, you must be really trying to get me to pee on you." She squirms a little in my arms and it makes me kind of wish she was squirming on my lap, on my cock. Even with our clothes on just to feel her juicy ass or warm pussy against my cock—mmm, fuck does she get me going.

"Maybe I am." I wasn't joking when I said I was willing to try anything once, but not sure if I'm willing to be peed on just yet. "I'll tell you what, the bathroom is up the stairs, once you get up the stairs you go down the small hall, and turn right, then the bathroom is the first door on the left, I'll give you a head start, if you can get there before I get you, I'll let you pee right away, but if I get to you before you get there I'm gonna throw you over my shoulder and tickle you..."

I look back at her as she stops for a second, a look of concern on her face. "First, I HATE being tickled, I kick and kick, so if I get your balls, you can't say I didn't warn you. Second, you're gonna hurt my ribs more, they're still sore from before but if you throw me over your shoulder again, I'm gonna have to kick your ass. I may be little compared to you but that doesn't mean I can't fight you." She puts her little fists up like she's about to fight me, and it's the cutest thing ever. Her tiny frame looking like she's ready to fight makes me want to pull her towards me and let her fight me, that way I can have my way with her. Maybe make her my dirty little Snowflake.

I can't help but laugh at how adorable she sounds but I gently set her down feeling like an ass because I forgot her ribs were still slightly bruised from her asshole dad. "Sorry snowflake, I'm not gonna lie, I was so excited to throw you over my shoulder and get your ass near my face that I forgot about your ribs." Leaning down I look at them and see they're slightly red from the pressure of her body against mine. So, I leave gentle kisses and slightly sucking on her skin. God, she tastes so good, like strawberries or cotton candy, maybe both, but I could kiss on her body all day long.

"Carsten," she slightly moans my name, which makes my hard cock even harder than it was. I didn't realize my dick could get this hard and it fucking hurts. I might have to go rub one out at this rate because I'm afraid I'll cum the minute I slide inside her pussy. "Carsten, oh god," she groans again. I start traveling up her ribs right under her left breast licking and slightly sucking on her under boob, licking my way up to her nipple. Her body is shaking; she's still wet from the rain, the water dripping from her clothes down her body, goosebumps spread across her skin.

"Hold on, hold on..."

I stop making sure she's not upset about what I'm doing. "Is everything okay?"

She smiles at me with a seductive look in her eyes. "I don't want to stop you but, please I really have to pee." She laughs.

"Shit I'm so sorry I just got caught up, I can't seem to control myself around you." I slowly stand up staring into her eyes while she looks down at me, smirking at her. She's not gonna be happy with what I'm about to tell her. "I'll give you a head start, Snowflake."

She scrunches her face in confusion. "What do you mean?"

My smirk turns into a full smile. "To get to the bathroom before I get to you." I wink. "Ready... set..."

She panics for a second. "Wait, wait, wait... I can't be tickled. I really have to pee. If you by chance catch me, I'll let you tickle me after." I step towards her, the right side of my mouth curling up into a smirk. Fuck, I can't wait to devour her.

I pause for a minute thinking of a new game plan. "I change my mind, Winter. If I catch you, I wanna continue doing to you what I was just doing." I whisper into her ear before pulling away. She nibbles on her bottom lip, and you can see she's turned on.

"But what if I want you to catch me now?" She smirks a little as she says it, but she says it so quietly you'd question if she was talking or if you're just hearing things. She's shy suddenly, like her confidence that she was feeling just disappeared and I'm not sure why, or if I'm the cause of it. That smirk of hers is doing things to me that I can't explain. But her confidence was a big turn on, making my cock twitch in response to it. My mind is instantly thinking dirty thoughts, about my cock pumping in and out of her pussy. Fuck I need to get my mind out of the gutter.

I look down at her, she's a lot shorter than I am so I lean back down to whisper into her ear. "Set... go!" I stand up smiling. Her eyes widen as she turns and darts for the stairs, I let her get up them before I start after her taking them two at a time. Even if she gets to the bathroom before I get to her, I'm still going to continue what I was doing, because fuck it, I can't get enough of this girl and I'm not going to stop myself. She's so addicting and I barely even know her.

I let her get to the bathroom because once I start again, I'm not stopping unless she asks me too. I get to the bathroom door the same time she opens it. "Better?" I ask as she steps out, shutting the light off.

"Much better, can I use a towel though? My clothes are dripping on me and I'm freezing." Her teeth are chattering as she hugs herself rubbing her hands up and down her arms.

"I can take care of that babe." I reach my arms down gripping the bottom of her ass by her thighs and slowly lift her into my arms, her legs wrapping around my waist, and her arms wrapping around my neck, I could get used to this. I lean in and gently kiss her, her lips parting instantly inviting my tongue into her mouth, and she whimpers. I walk slowly into the bathroom not pulling away, gripping her ass to lift her higher as I set her down onto the bathroom counter. Opening the cabinet in the bathroom without pulling away I grab a towel and wrap it around her. Kissing my way down to her jaw I start moving the towel down her arms to dry her off some, I stop and look up at her as I grip the bottom of her shirt. "Is it ok if I take this off?" I don't want to be a dick and just assume I'm about to get some, so I want to double check and not push her too far.

"Can we uhh..." She pauses, biting her lip like she's nervous. "Can we... go to your room?" She gives a slight smile, yeah, she's definitely nervous. She doesn't seem like the type to just randomly hook up with guys either, so that's another reason why I don't want to push her too far.

"Of course, that's fine, I can get you something dry too." I let her know, so she doesn't think she has to sit in wet clothes until Emerald comes home from work.

She smiles. "Thank you, this is fine too, I just think your bed will be a little warmer." She smirks, giving me the sexiest wink ever and holy shit if my dick gets any harder it's probably going to break. I put my hands under her ass and lift her up again, she wraps her legs around me tightly, puts her arms around my neck and starts kissing me. I could kiss her all day and never get bored of feeling her lips against mine. Everything about her is perfect.

14
WINTER

He sets me down slowly when we get to his room, breaking the kiss, which makes me pout. "Don't worry snowflake, I'm not done kissing those perfect lips of yours." He continues drying my arms off, then moves the towel to my hair, gently squeezing the excess water out. After drying my hair, he kneels down in front of me and starts drying my stomach off, kissing me as he's drying me off. He gets to my shirt again and stops looking up at me.

"Go ahead," I say breathlessly. I feel like he's done nothing but tease me. Who knew having someone dry you off could turn you on. He slowly lifts my shirt up pulling it over my head and lets out a sexy growl.

"God damn baby, your tits are amazing. You're so fucking sexy. This right here…" he grips my love handles. "This is my favorite, it's so fucking sexy and my favorite thing to grip onto." He gives me a devilish grin, slowly moving his hands to my boobs.

"Mmm, fuck." He readjusts his dick again with his right hand before bringing it back to my tit. "They're the perfect size, just enough for them to fit in my hands. And Fuck." He bites his lip and groans a little. "They're fucking perfect, babe." He looks up at me, I'm blushing. I've never had someone say so much about my body before or even be so turned on about it. I don't know what to do or even say about it, so I giggle and tuck my hair behind my ears. "What's wrong, Snowflake?" He asks, gently tugging on my nipple with his thumb and pointer finger.

I let out a moan, I'm breathing heavily, I don't even think I could speak if I wanted to. "N... noth... nothing," I say between moans. "Stand up please." I need to kiss him. He stands and I pull him towards me crushing my mouth to his and putting my hands in his hair, I start pulling it gently at first, then more aggressively as my needs grow stronger.

"Snowflake." He groans. "I fucking need to be inside you baby, please." He's panting and pushing my shorts down while I start unbuckling his belt. I'm left standing in my pink lace thong, while he's still standing in his boxer briefs. Water still slowly dripping down my ice-cold body making it hard to stop myself from shivering like crazy. He picks me up again and I wrap my legs around him feeling his hard cock against my wet panties.

"Mmm.... Shit," I moan into his mouth.

"You feel that baby, how fucking hard you make me?" he growls out, his husky voice deep, his voice sounds so fucking sexy.

"Mhmm." Apparently, I don't remember how to talk at the moment because all I can get out are mumbled words that don't make sense, but he doesn't seem to care too much.

He walks me over and lays me down on his bed. Hovering over me he stops and is staring at me with fire in his eyes, making me nervous. "Is everything okay?" Hoping I didn't do something that makes him want to stop.

"I just can't get over how fucking gorgeous you are, Snowflake. Your whole body is perfect. And these panties of yours..." He rubs his fingers over the outside of them, making a moan escape from my mouth. "They are fucking soaked... because of me. God, I can't wait to taste you." He licks his lips a little. "I bet you're going to taste delicious." He growls at me, lowering his mouth to mine with need. Then he starts kissing his way down my neck, kissing and sucking along the way, the moans coming out of my mouth are something I can't control, I probably sound crazy. My body has never felt this alive before.

He starts biting my neck, gently at first but gets a little more aggressive as he slowly works his way down to my collar bone. "My god babe, please let me taste you, tell me to lick your pussy." I pause. I've never really had someone this excited to want to taste me, and I sure as hell have never been with a man who's wanted me to tell him to do something to me. It's kind of exciting, but I don't know how to say it or what to say. He stops kissing my body for a second and looks up at me. "You okay, Snowflake?"

I blush a little because I'm embarrassed. "Yeah, I just...it's just that, well I've never had someone who told me to tell them to do that, or actually someone ever really go down on me." He cuts me off before I can continue what I was saying.

"What do you mean? How could someone be around you and not want to kiss and taste your pussy all the time? I haven't even tasted it yet but I'm practically drooling just thinking about it."

"I don't know. I've had guys go down on me, but it didn't really feel good, they made it seem like a chore or something, and they didn't do it for long." I look away from embarrassment. "They've also never been the type to have me tell them what to do." I blush again. I never thought it was possible to be this embarrassed and blush this much around one person. But I've also never had someone this attractive be this into me before.

"Well then, how about I start off like this." He slowly pulls my panties down, taking them off completely and throws them on the floor. Then he lays his body slightly next to me, to where he's leaning on his left arm for support to hold him up and starts kissing me again. He bites my bottom lip and sucks it into his mouth making me moan. He stops again and I pout because I want him so bad. "Now, now, gorgeous, no reason to be sad." He chuckles a little. "I'm about to make you forget about any man that's ever touched you." He slowly puts his hand on my breast and starts circling my nipple with his fingertip, making it even harder than it already was, then he leans down and puts my nipple in his mouth sucking on it at first, he pulls away and glances up at me while his tongue darts out and slowly licks my nipple, he lets out a groan the same time I moan. I've never liked watching someone touch me, but for some reason it's so sexy watching his tongue lick my nipple like that.

He goes back to sucking on my nipple while his right hand starts slowly moving down my body, past my belly button and he stops right above my throbbing pussy. Right as I think he's about to pull away he moves his hand down and gently swipes his finger through my slit. "Fuck." He moans. "Look how wet you are for me, Snowflake." He pulls his hand up and shows me his finger, it looks like he just ran it through water. That's how wet it is. Then he takes it and licks it. "Mmm, fucking shit." He lets out a frustrated growl the same time I groan from how sexy that was.

"Carsten, please." He sucks on his finger now and then swipes it back down my pussy, pushing his finger inside me, but not all the way, just enough to tease me, then he brings it back up.

"Taste yourself, Snowflake. Fuck, you taste so fucking good." I look at him because I've never done this before. I've had boyfriends and sex; they've just always been boring. "Stick your tongue out, Winter. I want you to taste what I'm about to feast on." I moan. God that was so sexy. I slowly stick out my tongue, still unsure, and he puts his finger on my tongue. I suck it into my mouth, closing my lips around it, and swirling my tongue to clean everything off it. "God damn, baby girl, your mouth is going to feel so good on my cock." This time he takes a finger and slides it fully inside me, sliding it in and out of me, slowly at first, then he picks up the pace a little, sliding it in and out before he adds another finger.

"Fuck, Carsten... please." Just as I think my body can't handle anymore pleasure, he places his thumb on my clit, gently circling it while pumping his fingers in and out of my pussy. "Oh God, Carsten."

"Yes, Winter?" He lets out the sexiest chuckle with a slight groan. "Tell me to lick your pussy baby, I wanna feel you cum all over my face." Holy shit. I've never had someone tell me to do that, I don't even know what to say. "Tell me, Winter. Tell me to lick your pussy. I won't do it until you tell me to, and please do it soon, I need to taste you."

"Oh my god, Carsten. I think..." I stop for a second not sure if I'm about to orgasm or not, it's embarrassing. "I think I'm gonna cum?" It comes out as a questioned moan. Then he pulls his fingers out. I blush instantly. I've never cum before, all the guys I've been with in the past have never had me this turned on, or even taken their time to try and get me there. And I've only cum once with a vibrator but stopped using it in fear of it ruining the real thing for me. So, I just stayed away, plus it took a lot to get me in the mood. It felt like I was broken after what had happened to me.

"Winter?" He asks, breathing heavily. He has the sexiest smirk on his face as he looks at me. The look in his eyes is pure hunger, like he's an animal about to pounce on his prey. I've never felt so desired before, this wanted, this sexy. It's a feeling I don't want to stop feeling from him.

"Ye... yes, Carsten?" I ask panting. My body's wound up so tight I feel like if I blink too hard it's going to explode. "Has a man ever made you cum before?"

I look away feeling so stupid. Here I am, twenty-two-years-old and a man has never given me an orgasm before. I cover my face with my hands and shake my head no. God, I'm so embarrassed.

CARSTEN

I'M IN SHOCK, I CAN'T BELIEVE I HAVE THIS GORGEOUS fucking woman laying naked in my bed and she's never had a man make her cum. I'm angry for her because—how? How has no one even tried begging her to let them make her cum, but I'm also excited that I get to be the first one to watch her beautiful face and body come alive the minute she has an orgasm.

"It's okay, Winter. You don't have to be embarrassed." I try to comfort her because I can only imagine how she feels.

"I just... I feel stupid," she says quietly, still looking away from me.

"Well don't. I can't wait to make you cum, Snowflake." I wink, then lean in and kiss her again. If i'm gonna get her off, I'm gonna make sure it's while I'm licking her pussy, I don't want her to ever forget her first orgasm from me.

I make my way back down her neck kissing and biting, making sure she's worked up and enjoying everything I do. I go back down to her nipples sucking and licking the left one in my mouth while pinching her right one with my pointer finger and thumb. Moving from her nipples I slowly kiss my way down her stomach until I reach the top of her pussy, licking around it but not where she needs it, making sure to tease her. "Oh god, Carsten, please don't stop." The way she says my name in her moans is so sexy. I spread her legs placing her thighs on my shoulders, while softly biting the insides of them. I start kissing my way down, it's like torture hearing her moan, I want so badly to stop and fuck her but I can't. I want to please her in more ways than one and show her what it's like to have amazing sex.

Finally, my face is right in front of her pussy and I am more than ready to taste her with my tongue, I slowly start licking her slit and she lets out the sexiest moan ever, it sounds like pleasure and torture mixed into one. "Oh. My. God," is all she says after.

"Mmm...Oh my god is right baby girl, you taste fucking incredible." I make my way up till I finally reach her clit, finding the spot that I know will get her off in the best way. I place my tongue on it and start swirling it around with just enough pressure to tease and just enough movement to get her body where it needs to be.

"Fuc, Carsten. Ple... please. Don't stop."

I stop long enough to tell her, "Don't worry, Snowflake, I'm not stopping until you cum all over my face, and even after that you'll probably have to pry me off of you with how delicious you taste." Her whole body shakes, so I know she's getting close. I put my lips around her clit and start sucking. She instantly starts thrusting her hips into my face, so I push two fingers inside her, she's already soaked so I didn't have to work one in at a time. Pumping them in and out of her I keep sucking and swirling my tongue around her clit.

"Shit... I'm about to cum, please don't stop," she says breathlessly. I enter a third finger and push them all in and curl them up and she loses it. Her tight pussy clamps down, while pulsing on my fingers. I feel her wetness all over my mouth and I am so fucking hard, I need to fuck her. Her body goes limp, and I lick up her pussy one more time before getting up to remove my boxers.

She turns her head to look at me. "You okay?" I ask while smirking at her.

"Never been better." She blushes. "That... damn." She lets out a breath like she forgot she was breathing. "That felt so good, I've never experienced anything like that." She smiles at me.

"Good, I can't wait to do it again." I put my fingers in my mouth one by one slowly licking the rest of her off of me. She tastes just like a drug that I just can't get enough of. I push my boxers down and slowly climb back on the bed, my dick fully hard and ready to feel her. She looks down and her eyes go wide "What's wrong, Snowflake?" I ask, not sure if I did something.

"Nothing, I just...wow." Her face turns red. I smile knowing exactly why she's saying wow to—my hard length. Then she pauses. "I'm on the pill, so it's ok if we don't use protection, if that's ok with you."

I pause and smile. "That's fine with me, I'd rather feel you without a condom." I lean down and start kissing her again, her lips are addicting, I could kiss her all day long. I spread her legs and move myself closer, putting the head of my dick at her entrance and slowly pushing inside her. "Fuckkk..." I groan, her pussy is so tight I might cum before I'm all the way in.

"Oh...god" She opens her eyes and right as I look down at her, she wraps her legs tightly around my waist and pushes my cock all the way in.

"Fuck, Snowflake, your pussy is so tight. I'm gonna cum if you move me again."

She moans. "I want you to fuck my pussy, Carsten."

I groan, stopping for a second so I can calm myself down. "Are you trying to kill me, talking like that?"

"No, your cock just feels so good, I don't want you to stop." She pants, her chest rising and falling quickly, I watch her nipples harden even more, it makes me want to put my warm mouth around them as I lick and suck, listening to her quiet whimpers and throaty moans. As my cock slowly pushes into her little, by little. Fucking torturing me in the process, because it takes everything in me not to fuck her nice and hard, but I wanna take my time with this sweet little pussy of hers and make sure she feels and remembers every inch of me filling this tight pussy of her with my cock, and my cum.

I shut my eyes painfully because the way she's talking alone is enough to get me off. You'd think I haven't had sex in forever. No, it's been two days and I'm about to cum like I just lost my virginity. "It's ok if you cum, Carsten," she says shyly.

"Hell no, it's not. I wanna feel your pussy throbbing all over my cock, Snowflake. I wanna feel how wet you are as my cock slides in and out of you, baby girl." I don't even wait for her to respond this time and start fucking her pussy, slowly at first, then I pick up the pace. I reach down and start massaging her clit hoping to get her there before I cum. I pump into her deep and quick.

"Fuck, Carsten. Please... please don't stop. I'm getting so close." She's panting as her body starts trembling. I pick up her hips so I can get deeper and start pumping into her harder, rougher, and she's moaning—cursing my name, and right as I think I won't be able to take it anymore, her pussy clamps down on to my cock, pulsing and squeezing my dick so tight, I groan.

"Fuck babe, I'm about to cum." I pump into her a few more times and I'm done, my cock pulsing inside her. I'm going as deep as I can, emptying inside her. She feels so good, I'm not ready for this to end yet, but I keep pumping until I'm finally done. I let go of her hips and fall on top of her laying my head on her chest. I don't even care about pulling out, I just lay there and she wraps her legs around me, snuggling her face into my head. "God, that felt so good." She let out a satisfied sigh. "You have no idea, Snowflake. That was amazing."

16

WINTER

Carsten gets up out of the bed and puts his boxers on, I'm not really sure what he's doing but I don't ask since I feel like it's not my business. He walks into the bathroom turns the water on for a few minutes and then comes back out holding something in his hand.

"Here, let me clean you up Winter," he tells me, making my cheeks turn what I'm sure is a bright shade of red, from embarrassment.

"No need to be embarrassed baby girl, I'm just trying to take care of what's mine. I don't want you to be uncomfortable or anything." Why the hell is he so sweet? Is everything about that sexy ass man perfect? Because I'm convinced it is.

He slowly spreads my legs, his touch making me shiver. Then gently places a warm washcloth against my sensitive pussy, holding it there for a minute before gently cleaning me up with the rag, wiping away the rest of his mess he left inside me. He doesn't talk as he does it, just wipes softly, slowly. Like he's afraid to hurt me. Which is so sweet that he cares. When he's done, he leans down and places a kiss against my pussy. Making my already sensitive bud throb from the contact. He gets up. Walks back to the bathroom I'm assuming to dispose of the washcloth and then comes back out and goes over to his walk-in closet. He comes out holding something in his hands and I raise a brow in confusion at what he's doing.

"Here, try these on." He throws me a shirt and a pair of basketball shorts. "They'll obviously be big, but I wanna make sure they at least stay up on you if you roll them a couple times until your stuff is dry." He smiles at me. The smile on his face is so sexy, the way his lip curls up in the corner. It makes my heart race and my stomach flutter. This man does things to me that I don't even know how to explain. I've never experienced anything like this before and what I mean by that is someone as attractive as Carsten being into someone like me. Not that my past boyfriends were ugly or anything they were definitely attractive, they just weren't Carsten's level of sexy.

"It's fine, I'll make it work. I appreciate it." Slowly getting up I stand and put the clothes on, they're huge. The shirt comes down almost to my knees and the shorts I had to roll up a ridiculous amount just to get them to stay, and even then, they'll still slide down some. "I can go wait at my house if you have stuff you need to do, it's not a big deal. It stopped raining so I can wait till Emerald comes home," I say awkwardly because I'm not sure if he still wants me here. I look down and tuck a few loose strands of hair behind my ear while waiting for him to respond.

He walks towards me, lifting my chin with his hand so I'm looking up at his handsome face. "Baby girl," he starts, his smile growing as he looks down at me. "You think I'm gonna send you out there until she gets home in the middle of the night? You're crazy." He chuckles a little. "I would never let you go sit outside alone until she came home. Besides, I have nothing important to do and if I did I could do it with you around." He kisses me on the lips slowly both times before he swipes his tongue across them, I open to let him in, swirling my tongue against his before sucking it into my mouth. God, I can't get enough of him. What is wrong with me—I barely know the guy and I'm becoming obsessed. He pulls away with a groan. "Why'd you do that? Now look at what you did." He looks down at his now hard cock that you can clearly see from his shorts.

He's definitely bigger and thicker than average, so I'm sure you could see it even when it's not hard. The thought makes my thighs tighten together a little in response to thinking of how big he felt inside me, how full he made me feel. I swallow slowly at the thought, trying to stop myself from possibly moaning out loud from the thought alone.

"Aww you poor thing, I'm so very sorry," I say sarcastically. His jaw drops, and the corner of his lip curls up again, showing off his signature smirk. It's almost like he's surprised I would say something like that.

"Listen here, Snowflake. Keep teasing me and I'm gonna bend you over and shove my cock in that tight, pretty pussy of yours." Pretty pussy? Did he just refer to my pussy as pretty? Fuck, he sure knows what he's doing with his words. I can't help but let out a moan with that. So much for holding back a moan before I couldn't even control myself with this one even if I tried. He licks his lips slowly, giving me a devilish grin. He could probably get away with anything with just that smile alone.

"Sir!" I put my hand on my chest as my jaw drops dramatically. "I would never tease you." Laughing I lean in to kiss him again, then pull away.

"Good girl," he says in a deep, cracked like tone. Boy is he dreamy. I don't think there's anything about this man that isn't attractive, or hot. "That's what I like to hear, baby girl." His deep voice sends chills through me. I could listen to him talk all day just for the sound of his voice alone. It's hard to believe how comfortable I am with him, like he's never been a stranger, just someone I was waiting to meet again after a long time of searching for that one person. Is he that person? Clearly, it's too soon to tell, I'm just caught up in my hormones driving me crazy from the things he's doing to my body and the way his voice stirs up the butterflies that have decided to take over my stomach since I met him.

"I was gonna say, let's head outside while the weather is some-what nice. We can sit on my porch swing, before it gets dark." He walks over to me, grabbing my hands in his and captures my mouth with a soft kiss. A soft moan escapes his lips and I want to know what it tastes like, to feel his breath against mine as our lips collide and tongues go to war with each other as they fight for dominance. I snap out of it, pulling myself from those dirty thoughts before we're back in his bed and finally give him a response.

"I'd love to. Especially if the rain stopped finally. I need to warm up some because I'm still fucking freezing." I shiver, the cold chill piercing through my body painfully, it's going to take me a while to warm up. I'm always cold and I hate it.

"How about when we come back in, we can come back up here and I'll warm you up some more?" He stops talking for a second and let's go of one of my hands before squeezing the other. "And I mean I can actually warm you up, we don't have to do anything else, just so you know." He gives a slight smile, making my stomach flutter some more. I don't think the butterflies have stopped yet. They've just made a permanent home right in the pit of my stomach, and every time I see Carsten, they come to life.

"I'm ready whenever you are." I'm not sure if he's waiting on me so I let him know just in case. He interlocks his fingers with mine now, holding my hand differently than he just was and we start walking out of his room towards the stairs. As we get to the end of the hallway, right as we reach the stairs one of his roommates starts running up them.

"Hey, dick face." He gives Carsten a big Cheesy grin as he says it. "Damn, who is this fine girl you got here, Carst?" He wiggles his eyebrows while looking at me and it's so hard not to laugh. He looks me up and down for a second like he's trying to decide his next move.

"Get lost, cock breath." He pushes his hand in his face, rubbing it all over him, you can tell they're close, I just don't know who he is. My smile widens as he continues to rub his hand in his face before the guy finally backs up and moves out of his reach. His eyebrows scrunched together when he looks back up.

"Wow, harsh...Just tryin' to see if she's taken." He smirks at me.

"Did you finally get rid of that skanky blonde you were banging. What was her name? Brenda, Brittany, Brynn? Yeah, yeah, it was Brynn." He's pretty much talking to himself. But as he says it my stomach drops, and I instantly feel sick to my stomach. Was he just cheating on someone with me? Would his friends have said something to him or to me if he was? Would Creedence have given me a heads up when he saw me the other day in Emerald's driveway? All these questions are swarming my brain, and my mouth is just afraid to move and ask.

"Shut up, asshole. Chase, this is our new neighbor, Emerald's friend, Winter. Winter, this is my asshole brother, Chase." He slaps Chase on the shoulder some, you know one of those moves that guys do for some reason.

"Damn girl, Winter is a fine name." He makes kissy faces at me as he looks over at Carsten, trying to block his moves as he messes with him and pretends to fight him. He's obviously just trying to piss Carsten off, making me laugh in the process. Now that he said he's his brother I can see the resemblance. I can't help the smile that forms on my face as I watch them fuck around, I'm an only child and had always wondered what it would be like to have a brother or sister growing up. Just watching Carsten and Chase makes me see how fun it could have been, making me miss something I've never experienced before.

"Man shut up and leave her alone. We're headed outside if you wanna go meet us on the porch when you're done." He lets his brother know as he grabs my hand again and walks down the stairs with me. I think it's cute that he likes to hold my hand this much already. I didn't think he'd be the touchy type of guy. But I love it. None of my boyfriends in the past held my hand, or even really acted like we were together. They never kissed me in public or held my hand. So, I'm not used to this much attention from someone I'm not even dating... yet? I'm not complaining though, I'd love to have all of Carsten's attention.

"Alright man, I'll probably be out in about twenty-minutes."

Chase pats Carsten on the back as he says it, walking in the opposite direction of where Carsten's room is, down another small hallway.

I can't help the sick feeling I feel as we're walking down the stairs as the thoughts of him possibly having a girlfriend sinks back in. I was caught up in watching him and his brother that the thought slipped my mind for a second. Shit I was even caught up in the possibility of us being something more than friends. I'm an ass, I'm glad it came back to me though. I usually keep quiet when I'm uncomfortable and not sure how to deal with the situation, but this isn't something I can avoid. If he's talking to someone, and it's nothing serious yet, then I'll just leave and walk to Emerald's work. It might take me an hour or so, but I refuse to stay here. And if he just cheated on his girlfriend and made me the "other woman" I will freak the fuck out. Before my mind continues to wander and drive me crazy, I stop in my tracks the second we get to the front porch and look over at him, my stomach twisting in knots and those butterflies that were swarming earlier have suddenly died and turned into nausea and anxiety.

"So uhh... Brenda, Brittany, Brynn huh?" I sound a little more nervous saying that than I wanted to, and maybe a little bitchier than I wanted to sound, but for some reason right now, I just don't care. I'm a little hurt and hoping my mind is just making shit up. I throw in an awkward laugh making the situation worse for myself. I'm such an idiot. I quickly blink back the tears that threaten to fill my eyes and hope he doesn't notice that they officially have a glossy look to them. I close my eyes for a second and let out the breath that I keep holding, because apparently holding your breath gives the answers that I'm searching for and blink a couple more times before opening them again.

"I'm sorry about that, my brother is an asshole, has no brain to mouth filter. But no, she's no one important. There's nothing to worry about." He steps towards me cupping my bruised cheek and gently starts rubbing the bruise and my cut with his thumb. His brows scrunch together. "Snowflake?" It comes out as a question as he softly kisses the bruise on my cheek, and I let him. Because I'm an idiot. I blink again, trying to hide the tears that keep trying to form. He then kisses my cut and works his way down to my mouth. Before I can think about stopping him, he kisses me a couple times before he starts talking again. Why do I keep letting him kiss me when I don't have any answers yet. "Brynn isn't someone I was serious about. I know that sounds bad, but we just hooked up a few times and it's already over." I look down trying not to look bothered, unsure if I should believe him or not. Plus, with all the rumors I've heard about "Man whore Carsten Hatcher" has me worried. Would he waste his time making it seem like there's a possibility for more here when there's really not? He sounds serious, like the kind of guy who wouldn't waste his time telling a lie like that. But then again, I've dealt with plenty of lying assholes in the past. But he just doesn't give me a vibe like he's lying. I just hope I'm not reading him wrong. "I know you've probably heard about the kind of guy I am, and I can explain." He almost looks ashamed as he says the words.

"It's fine, you don't have to explain yourself to me. I was just making sure she wasn't your girlfriend. I'm not that type of person." I sigh, trying to contain my emotions so he still doesn't see I'm sad.

"I'm not that kind of person either. I would never do that to you, or to anyone in general. I'll be honest with you, I'm not usually the type of guy who has girlfriends. I might hook up with them once or twice, then I move on with no strings attached." He shakes his head as he says it. Almost like he's finally realizing how much he's fucked up, or maybe him actually having to explain his life to someone other than his friends makes him embarrassed.

I feel so stupid, is this all that was? Is this what he's telling me right now to let me know that we won't be more than just a hookup or two. "Carsten, please you don't have to expla…" But he cuts me off before I can finish the word.

"Please just listen. Once in a while I might find something in common with a girl and stay around a little longer, but it never gets any more serious than that. Brynn had known from the beginning what she was getting herself into and that it wasn't going to be anything serious." He pauses, tucking his free hand into his pocket while gently swinging our interlocked hands. "She kept pushing and pushing when I wasn't ready for anything, so I cut ties completely the night I saved you at my bar. She's the one I was with when you came outside. But after everything that happened and me helping you, I cut things off with her because I can't see myself being serious with her." He takes a deep breath, and slowly lets it out. Like he was holding it to rush out what he was saying. "I know the fact that I sleep around makes me seem disgusting or something. I've just never found someone worth settling down for, which sounds worse than what I had said previously, but I'm just trying to get my truths out on the table. I don't want you to think I'm hiding anything or not being honest with you. About anything, ever.

"Carsten, you don't have to explain, please. I know this isn't anything. It's ok, you didn't hurt me." I look down because I feel like an idiot as my eyes swell up with the tears that I can't hold back anymore. I can't believe I'm about to cry.

"That's the thing, I would never do anything to hurt you, or in general to anyone like that. Every girl I've been with has known from the beginning that there were no strings attached. But I didn't tell you that." He pauses looking into my eyes, a serious look on his face.

"I understand." I sniffle still blinking away tears. He steps in closer to me and puts his fingers under my chin, bringing my head up to look at him. Right as I do the tears fall. I feel like such an idiot.

I don't sleep around; it took me a long time to actually be comfortable having sex whether I was dating the person, or it was just a hookup. I don't care that Carsten sleeps around. I just don't know if I can only hook up with him and nothing more. Is that what he'd want?

After almost being raped by Preston I started therapy because I couldn't stop the flashbacks that would take over every time I tried to have sex. It was another reason I couldn't orgasm during sex too or when I'd try getting myself off. Besides the men just not caring, I couldn't stop my mind from going back there. So now when I have sex, I have to actually have a lot of trust in the guy and for some reason things felt different with Carsten, I barely knew him, but I felt like he was never a stranger at all. But now I feel like an idiot, and for some reason all of that makes me feel very emotional. I've always been an emotional person; I've always been one to stop and let my body feel what I'm feeling in that moment. But right now, I'm confused. My body doesn't know how to react to any of this. My mind doesn't know how to feel, will I be able to trust him if he does want to be with just me? He really hasn't given me any reason to think otherwise. Maybe I just need to relax, take a couple deep breaths and trust him. He said he slept around and didn't do relationships. Doesn't mean he's telling me that this isn't going to be anything more. Or that he just wants sex.

17

CARSTEN

The tears continue to fall down her face, falling onto my hand that's holding her chin up and her black T-shirt that I gave her to wear. I feel like a fucking asshole. Part of me wants to punch myself for not giving her a heads up about Brynn and part of me wants to go find my brother and punch the shit out of him for his stupid... fucking... big-ass mouth. I feel like such an asshole. I've dealt with crying girls before; trust me I've had my fair share of crying blubbering messes in front of me that I've either had to dodge from trying to hit me or pry off me because they couldn't handle the fact that I didn't want anything more than sex. But Winter, she's different. She's crying because she's hurt, she's not throwing herself on me. Yelling at me for my past or anything in general. I actually feel bad about how she's feeling right now. Which is new for me. I never care how I make women feel, espccially when it comes to sex. They know from the beginning what it is and they're the ones who choose to promise that they'll be okay with it and lie and freak out in the end. Winter so far hasn't done any of that except cry from the hurt she's feeling because I'm an asshole.

"Please, Winter, don't cry. You're breaking my fucking heart baby. I wasn't trying to hurt you. I was actually trying to do the exact opposite." I remove my hand from hers. She has such a sad look on her face. Her eyes look up at mine and she sniffles. "What do you mean?"

I pause thinking of how to say what I've been wanting to tell her without sounding obsessed. Because I think for the first time in my life—I might be actually obsessed with this beautiful girl right in front of me and I have no idea what to do with this information. Or how I'm supposed to be around her. Do I want her to be my girlfriend? Do I want someone to call mine for once instead of constantly bouncing from girl to girl. Is this what I need?

"I like you, which is funny since I barely know you. But I haven't been able to stop thinking about you since the night I met you. You've been on my mind nonstop, making my stupid dick painfully hard." She snorts at that one. Making me smile because I was hoping she would find that funny. "And I've done nothing but try to find a way to talk to you again, I've literally watched daily for Emerald to be home so I could go talk to her about you. I don't know what this is yet, but I like it, I like you." I go to sit down on the swing and pull her with me, pulling her onto my lap. She turns her head to look at me, puts her hands around my neck and kisses me, slowly but with need. The tears still fall down her cheeks as she kisses me until I pull away, to make sure she's okay.

"Talk to me, Snowflake. I know I've upset you, but I want you to be honest with me like I just was with you, please." I'll beg if I have to, not that she knows this. But I need to know what I did that upset her, so if that means I have to get down on my knees then you bet your sweet ass that's what I'm fucking doing. I'll get on my knees and beg my little fucking Snowflake so I can fix whatever my dumbass did wrong. And I won't stop begging until she forgives me. I'm determined to make something of this with her and I refuse to give up.

"Honestly–" She lays her head against my shoulder as I start swinging the swing with my feet. "You scared me, I thought you were going to tell me that this was just a hook up and nothing more, which would've been fine, I just...I don't usually just hook up." She pauses again like there's more. But I don't want to push her to tell me if she's not comfortable. "I'm just glad I wasn't wrong about you." She sits up wiping the tears from her face. "I'm so sorry, I can't believe I'm crying. I feel so stupid." She covers her mouth, shaking her head in embarrassment.

I pull her towards me, holding her closer. "Don't be sorry and don't be embarrassed, my little Snowflake," I whisper to her, while she lays her head down onto my chest. My heart is racing in my chest, I'm sure she can hear it or feel it against her ear. I'm not used to this much physical contact with someone. I mean I touch girls, fuck girls, hang out with girls, stuff like that. Sure, girls sit on my lap. But I don't cuddle, I don't let girls snuggle against me or on my lap like that. Usually when a girl is on my lap, I'm drunk on some couch at a frat party, or drunk on my own couch trying to find my next fuck and there's usually a girl on my lap grinding her pussy against me because she's looking for the same thing I am. A hook up. So, this is new to me.

We sit there in silence while I continue to swing us, glancing at each other here and there. I feel like a child in school looking at a girl I have a crush on, every time I look at her, I get this strange feeling in my stomach that I don't know how to explain and I can't help but just smile at her. This beautiful girl on my lap, how can someone so perfect and so smart be into someone like me. I'm an asshole. The man who hates relationships. The guy who uses women for their bodies. The town man whore, I usually sleep with a girl once before getting rid of her, unless your pussy is fucking addicting. I'll sleep with you maybe five times before tossing her aside for the next girl to offer me her pussy. Yet something told her to trust me that if she slept with me, it would be more than once, and most definitely more than five times. Because her pussy might be the tightest pussy, I've ever put my cock in. Yep, typical guy thinking with my dick. Honestly, I'd be an idiot to let her go. Thinking with or without my dick, I'd be stupid to let her get away from me. I don't want anyone else having the chance to be hers, near her, inside her. Nothing. She is mine and I refuse to let anyone else get her now that I've had a taste of my little snowflake.

What the fuck is my problem? I told you I was an asshole. This girl is perfect, she's too fucking good for me, and I want her, for me and only me. She won't ever let another man touch her for as long as I live, because she's fucking mine. No. One. Else's.

My brother finally comes out and of course breaks the silence.

"Damn guys, did someone die? Why so quiet and sad looking." He chuckles, crossing his arms and leaning against the railing. Waiting for one of us to give him an answer.

"Nah man, just enjoying each other's company is all," I tell him, making myself sound fucking old because what twenty-something-year-old just enjoys being home in the company of someone they care about? Especially when they aren't even dating, this is technically our first time hanging out together besides meeting at Black Velvet. I mean at least I never thought I'd see myself being this into someone this quickly and not wanting to do anything but be around her.

"Ohh." He scrunches his eyebrows. "Fucking weirdos. Y'all are like an old married couple and you're not even dating." He shakes his head, trying to stop himself from smirking as he does it. I know exactly why he's shaking his head, because he can't actually believe I'm into someone like this. I still can't believe I'm into someone that I actually want to make my girlfriend. Who ever thought the day would come when Carsten Fucking Hatcher wanted to settle down. At least I think that's what this is, because I can already tell you right now. I won't let her get away. She's a hit of fucking heroine straight to my blood stream and I refuse to give up this addiction. Ever.

"What's wrong with being comfortable in silence with someone else? Are you jealous?" Winter asks jokingly, with a sexy smirk on her face. Well shit, if I think it's sexy than I know damn well Chase thinks it's sexy, and he better fucking not even try and make a move on my woman. I'll kill his ass and he knows this. It wouldn't be the first time we've fought over women before either. Not that we've gotten into bad fights or anything. Just stupid banter and brotherly fights with a few punches, that's how we fought over women. It was another way to give mom a heart attack growing up. I started sleeping around when I was fourteen. Not even sure why honestly. I only had one girlfriend growing up, Natalie. That was the only time I was ever in a relationship, and she was the one who ruined them for me. After her family moved away. I loved her, you know, young love. But she was my first love and it fucking hurt when she moved away. That was the last relationship I had. It took me some time to get over her, used a lot of girls in that time too, probably hurt a lot of them too. But that's when I started sleeping around more and not caring about what I was doing or who I was hurting in the process.

"Yep. Totally jealous of your old people relationship—not relationship—y'all got goin on there." He stops laughing and tries to give a serious look but sucks at it. You can tell he's just fucking with us. "What are you guys doing after this? Wanna order some pizza and watch a movie or something, I don't wanna go out tonight." Chase asks looking back and forth at the both of us.

"That's fine with me, Winter here can't go home till Emerald's home. She's locked out and her phones in her room too, so she's with us for a while. So, I'm down if she's down."

"Yeah, that sounds fine with me as long as you guys are ok with me hanging out. If not, I can go sit on my porch till Emerald comes home." Winter looks back and forth at the both of us.

"Don't be stupid." My dick of a brother says to her. Her jaw drops. "Kidding babe, or should I say, Snowflake." He winks at her. He's such an ass, but I love that he's comfortable bickering with her already. Like she's always been around or something.

"Don't you take my nickname for her. And no, Winter, you're not gonna go sit on your porch until like three in the morning, you're crazy. You can stay here. I already told you that Baby girl, I promise you're not a bother or anything." I say in a little harsher tone than I meant to, but I want her to know I'm being serious.

"Thank you, guys, I appreciate it." She looks back and forth between Chase and me. She must not have caught my accidental harsh tone because she didn't say anything about it. Or maybe it just didn't bother her, and she realized she was being ridiculous wanting to go sit alone on her front porch in the dark.

"Don't thank Chase, he's a dick." I grab a twig off the tree next to me, the branches come through the porch some because of how close the tree is to it. Then I throw it at him.

"Hey, what did I do?" He asks, trying to sound innocent. He's such a dick sometimes, but not in a mean way. I don't think he has a mean bone in his body until you fuck with what's his. That's one reason we've gotten along so well growing up and even now as adults. We're a lot alike. We've always had each other's backs. Especially being close in age, I think it made us closer growing up. Because we always had each other, no matter what the situation was. It always made mom proud with how much we stuck up for each other. He's my best friend, aside from Creedence who is basically like another brother to both Chase and I. He was my friend first but instantly became Chase's best friend too when he met him. Then it was the three of us growing up until high school when Axton came along.

"I was fucking with you, but you don't get credit, she's my girl not yours." I tug her into me like a child stealing back their toy that someone took. Like he's trying to pull her away from me and glare at him. Making sure he's aware how serious I am about the fact that Winter is mine, and she's not up for grabs.

"Calm down over there, you're going to break her if you squeeze her any tighter." Chase pauses, shit, I think to myself, because now I know what's coming next. "Speaking of breaking, you ok Winter? I couldn't help but notice the bruises?" he asks in a way you can tell he's not trying to be a dick.

"Yeah." She sighs and glances at me. "I moved in with Emerald because I have an abusive alcoholic father. The night I went home after meeting your brother at your bar he beat the shit out of me and this…" she waves her hand up and down at herself. "Is the result of it." She lifts her shirt enough to show her healing bruises.

"Fuck man, I'm so sorry you had to go through that." He shakes his head with an angry look on his face. The anger obviously not meant for her, but he and I are very much the same when it comes to abuse, especially from someone who can barely fight for themselves.

"Thank you, I'm just trying to move forward and deal with him as little as possible now that I no longer live there." She says shifting on my lap some, her ass rubs against my half-excited cock making it twitch a little, hopefully she doesn't feel it. Right now is the worst time for my cock to be paying attention to anything sexual. But what can I say? It's in my nature, I wouldn't be Carsten if I didn't have a random boner over a girl at the worst time.

"What do you mean as little as possible?" I pause looking at her worried face. "You're not going back around him, are you?" I ask, my voice laced with concern. She better not be going back around him. Not anytime soon at least.

"I haven't yet but I have to sometime this week to make sure he's ok." She says looking away from me, you can tell she's nervous just thinking about going near him again.

"Winter, I know it's not my place, but you shouldn't go around him, especially not alone." Now it's my turn to have a worried look on my face. I'll kick his ass if he tries to put his hands on her again, I don't care if he's her dad. Don't put your hands on my Snowflake and everything will be fine. It's that simple.

"It'll probably be best if I go alone, he'll freak out either way, but it would be better if no one else saw him that way," she says looking back and forth at the both of us.

"Hell no, you are not going alone if that's what he did to you, I'm with my brother on that one," Chase says to her, shaking his head. He crosses his arms with a somewhat angry look on his face. I like that he seems to care just about as much as I do about her safety.

"Fine, you can come with me if you'd like, and I'll go in alone, but you can stay in my car in case I need you. That's my only offer, or

I'll go alone." She looks over at me, then over at Chase before looking back down at her shaking hands.

"Deal, just let me know when, that way if I'm working, I let either Chase or one of my uncles know so they can cover me at the bar or tattoo shop." I place my hand on top of her shaking ones and bring it down onto her thigh and squeeze it, hopefully reassuring her that she's not alone. I hate that she has been dealing with this alone for as long as she has. To think that she didn't even confide in Emerald during all the abuse is crazy to me. But I get it, especially when no one has her back, it's probably hard for her to trust who she does tell. That's probably why it took so long to finally get it out in the open. I don't think she would have if the fight that her and her father just had didn't escalate the way it did.

"That's so awesome you do tattoos." She changes the subject, I get it though, I'm sure it's an uncomfortable topic for her to talk about in front of people and I don't want to push her if she's not ready to move further on the topic.

"Yeah, I love it, it's something I enjoy doing a lot. You should let me tattoo you sometime." I'd love to give her a new piece or add onto something she already has. I think it's so sexy that she has as many tattoos as she does. Something about a girl with tattoos the way she has them scattered all over her is so fucking sexy.

"Definitely, let me find a job and get caught up on things and I'll let you know when I'm ready, I already have a couple ideas I've been wanting to get." She smiles down at her visible tattoos. Her smile is so beautiful, the way her perfectly pink lips curl up higher on one side than the other. Makes me want to kiss her even more.

I look over at my brother the same time he looks at me, we've been looking for extra help for a while and can't seem to find anyone reliable, or willing to work late hours. He nods to me giving me the okay, so I figure when she's ready I'll bring it up to her, I don't want to throw too much at her right now while she's trying to get better and unpack. I don't want her to stress over anything unimportant like a job, when her healing, her healthy and her safety is the most important thing now.

"Awesome, I'd love to draw something up for you," I say leaning down a little to kiss her. She's still shorter than me sitting on my lap. She leans in and opens her mouth for me, instantly making my dick hard, and she giggles because I'm sure she feels it on her ass.

"Get a room you two." Chase smiles while taking the twig I threw at him and throwing it back at me. "Let's go order some pizza and pick a movie out now before I get hangry, no one likes a hangry Chase." He snorts, grabbing his cell phone from his pocket, I'm assuming to look at the pizza places. I don't know why he looks around when we order from the same place every time.

"No one likes Chase even when he's not hangry." My voice drips with sarcasm as I shrug my shoulders like I didn't just offend him. "Just fuckin with you man before you go and get butt hurt."

"Oh, I know you are, you can't resist my Chase charms." He crosses his arms, bringing the one hand up to rub his chin with his fingers while wiggling his eyebrows.

"Wow, that was really lame. Chase charms?" Winter shrieks with laughter, snorting in the process. "Sorry, I can't help it. I'm not trying to be mean, that was just perfect." She holds her stomach as her laughing settles down. Probably hurts to laugh a certain way from the bruises.

"Right? Feel bad for me. This is what I've been dealing with my whole life. It's pretty rough," I say, holding my hand to my chest being dramatic like I'm wounded or something.

"Fuck you guys, I'm a fucking riot, everybody loves me." Chase says with a cheesy grin on his face. You can clearly tell he's not this conceited and just joking around, he's such an idiot. One thing he's good at is making everyone laugh. He always has been, he was the troublemaker growing up in school, the class clown. Who always worried more about making everyone laugh than he would his schoolwork or paying attention in class. It drove mom crazy all the call she'd get from his teachers, but she took it like a champ and powered through parenthood as a single mom of two boys like the bad ass she is.

"Keep telling yourself that man." I watch him walk to the front door, holding it open for us. Winter slides off my lap, exciting my cock even more, before she fully stands up. As soon as she does, I adjust my stupid dick and follow them inside.

"What kind of pizza do you like, Winter?" Chase asks her, opening his phone again, scrolling through the Menu of the same place we always get. I laugh to myself, we're both stuck in our old ways. I didn't even have to look at his phone to know.

"Umm, well first I'll pay whoever back for what I eat, and uhh either pepperoni or just cheese. Either is fine." He stares at her for a second. This is great, I'm happy to see he likes her and that they're comfortable fucking with each other.

"No wonder you're so skinny." He looks her up and down, he's not checking her out just looking. "You don't eat anything on your pizza. Let me guess, you eat half a slice then you're full too?" He winks to show he's fucking around. Those are the types of women we're used to. It's rare to hang out with a girl that actually eats and isn't afraid of what it'll do to her body. I love a woman who has an appetite, to me it's sexy.

"First, I am not skinny, I have plenty of chunk on my body. Second, I eat more than half a piece, just depends on how hungry I am, and I haven't eaten yet today so I'll probably eat a decent amount, you dick." She sticks her middle finger up at him.

"Babe, babe," I say pulling her towards me, placing my hands on her hips. She's not your average twig, she's thick and curvy, but she's definitely not chunky, she's fucking sexy. "This, all this right here... mmm... mmm." I growl. "This is fucking sexy, I love your curves, I already told you this is all my favorite." I grip onto her, making my dick painfully hard. I've already learned I'm just going to have a constant boner around her, most of the time it's tolerable, except for times like this where she makes it rock hard. I lean up to whisper in her ear. "I'm about to need a round two here in a minute."

She blushes, Chase doesn't care, he's not even paying attention to know what I said. I want her to know how badly I want her. How much my body craves Her's. These delicious fucking curves, I'd love to bite and suck on. Then grip onto them while she's riding my cock, or while I'm fucking her from behind. My cock pulses from the thought alone. Fuck, I need to be inside that tight pussy, soon.

"Can you show me where your bathroom is please?" She asks and I'm hoping it's for a round two. "I forgot how to get there, sorry." She gives an apologetic smile.

"I'm gonna show her the bathroom, just order the pizza you know what I like." I tell Chase as I grab Winter's hand. "No need to be sorry my little Snowflake. Unless you've been a bad, bad girl. Then you don't need to apologize," I whisper into her ear while she shivers against my words.

"Ok, have fun with your quickie bro," Chase says, shaking his head while laughing, not even bothering to look up while talking as he scrolls through the menu, adding God knows what to the cart.

"Will do man, will do." I give Winter a devilish grin. Hoping she's in the mood for another round just as much as I am.

"Hey, I said I had to pee, no one said anything about a quickie." She blushes after she says that, and I love how easy it is to make her blush.

We head upstairs so I can show her the bathroom again, since she actually did forget and I patiently wait for her in my bedroom, hoping she'll get the hint and come find me.

18

WINTER

I COME OUT OF THE BATHROOM AND SEE THE HALLWAY IS empty. "Carsten?" I say quietly because the house is so quiet I'm not trying to yell. His room is close to the bathroom so I wonder if he's in there and just can't hear me. "Carsten, are you up here?" I start walking towards his room, trying to calm down my racing heart, making sure he's not up here before I head downstairs to find him. Walking to his doorway I stop for a second, his door is open so he must be in here since he shut it when we walked out. "Carsten where'd you..." And then a hand is over my mouth while the other one comes up over my eyes and I instantly freeze. The only thing that's moving is my shaking body and chest from trying to calm down before I have a panic attack.

FOUR YEARS AGO

I stumble into the bedroom looking for Emerald. I thought she said she was coming in here because she needed to lay down. Both of us are pretty drunk so I'm ready to head home, that's why I'm trying to find her before she passes out into a deep sleep.

"Em, you in here?" I'm met with silence, other than the base from the music downstairs. The room spins a little and my vision is begin-

ning to blur from all the shots and drinks we had. I usually don't drink like this when I go to parties, but my dad kicked my ass tonight and I needed something to help numb the pain. Physically and emotionally.

"Emerald... where are you?" Then suddenly something comes over my eyes, it feels like fabric or something, I'm not quite sure what it is. Then a hand flies over my mouth before my brain gets the chance to register what's happening and I don't get the chance to scream. All I hear is a muffled noise while I start trying to hit whoever put what I think is a blindfold over me. I end up smacking someone.

"Ugggh," is all I hear, it's a male voice but I can't tell who. My heart starts racing and my body starts shaking while I try to calm down my breathing. I feel like my heart's about to fly out of my chest. I have no idea what's going on but if Emerald is playing a prank on me then this isn't fucking funny.

I'm shoved up against a hard surface, a wall? A door maybe? I'm not quite sure all I know is it was so hard it practically knocked the wind out of me.

"Stop moving, you stupid bitch." Yep, it's a man's voice and it definitely doesn't sound like it's a prank. I start shaking my head, trying to tell him to stop but he doesn't care.

"If you just stay still, it'll make this easier for the both of us, now stop fucking moving." He says with an angry growl. His voice is so familiar, I know who he is, but I can't put my finger on it.

He lets go of me for a second to readjust the way he's holding me, and I try to run but he yanks me back by my hair and quickly put his hand back over my mouth, I try to scream but all you hear is my muffled voice behind his hand.

"I don't fucking think so you fucking bitch." Then I'm shoved down onto what feels like could be a bed. It loosens the blindfold and slides up where I can see a little bit with my eyes, and I start screaming. Holy fucking shit, I can't believe this is happening. He was pissed because I wouldn't sleep with him, he just took me out on a date last weekend and I refused to have sex because I'm a virgin and I knew he only wanted to date me to add another notch on his belt.

"Surprise." Is all he says as he completely removes the blindfold. He keeps his hand over my mouth, and I try biting it but he slaps me with his other hand. "Calm the fuck down." He reaches on the nightstand grabbing duct tape and ripping a piece off with one hand and his mouth. Then he grabs a longer piece and starts taping my hands together.

"It's ok, I'll keep your eyes open. I want to watch you cry as I fuck that tight pussy of yours, then when I'm done, I'm gonna fuck that tight little ass of yours. You deserve those tears after telling me no, no one tells me no. You should be lucky I was even into you." He finishes taping my hands and then leans down and starts kissing me over the tape, then down my neck until he rips my shirt open down the middle from my breasts down to my stomach, then he pulls my bra down.

"Mmm, Winter, I knew those tits would be amazing." He says, leaning down biting my nipple very hard. I scream into the duct tape, the tears pouring down my face faster than they fill my eyes. "All that's missing is me getting to hear you scream with those tears, but this will have to do." He starts to lick one nipple, I start kicking and screaming, the screaming does nothing cause all you hear still is muffled noises behind the tape. I'm trying to hit him with my taped together hands, but he grabs them and pins them above my head.

Then he continues licking and sucking my nipple before he moves onto biting and licking the next, he's moving quickly and being extra rough and I know he doesn't care. Snot is shooting out of my nose as I try to breathe, but I'm crying so hard I'm beginning to hyperventilate. He starts to undo my shorts and pulls them down. "Let's see if this pussy of yours is wet." He rubs his fingers over my underwear while the other one works my shorts further down.

"Such a shame, you're going to wish you were wet. Either way this will hurt and the more you cry the harder you're going to make my dick. You whore, you're my fucking whore. No one's gonna want you by the time I'm done with you." He snarls. "You'll come begging me for more by the time I'm done with you." The disgusting smile on his face

makes me wish I could punch him. It makes me so angry. Hot tears flood my vision as they pour down my cheeks more.

I'm whipping my body back and forth trying to get him off me, but being a football player he's a lot stronger than I am. He puts his knee on my right leg and pushes my leg open, leaving his knee there to stop me from moving. He licks his way from my jaw line down my neck. I feel the bile rise in my throat the more he touches me, making it so hard to swallow down. I don't have a choice, unless I want to choke on it, and it wouldn't matter to him. He'd still continue to violate me. "You might as well stop fighting. I know this is what you want." He's sucking on my neck now. "Whores like you love the fight, love to feel like you're innocent when really you're begging for it." He leans down licking the tears from my cheek and I start kicking my legs and hit him in the junk. "God damn you, stupid bitch, now you're definitely going to get it."

He rips my underwear off, screaming under the tape from the way it rips my skin before the fabric finally breaks. I'm pretty sure there will be blood from the way it ripped against me, and if not, it's going to leave a mark.

"God this is gonna feel so good. I can't wait to shove my cock in this tight Cunt." He pushes my legs further apart and shoves two fingers into me so hard I scream, and fresh tears start falling down my face faster this time. It feels like he ripped my skin, or his nails scratched me as he shoved his fingers into me. I wasn't wet at all and now he's just shoving his fingers in and out of me. "Come on you whore, get your fucking pussy wet for me. Don't act like you're not enjoying this as much as I am." I feel bile rise in my throat that I struggle to swallow down and start coughing, but it doesn't matter the tape is still there, even if I choke on my puke he'll still continue. He finally stops with his fingers inside me, when suddenly, I hear a female voice. Everything sounds so far away so it's hard to hear exactly what's going on.

"What the fuck is this, Preston…What the fuck are you doing to her?" She's screaming so loud she's probably going to lose her voice from it. "Get the fuck off of her."

"Dude, calm down. She told me to bring her up here, she wanted this."

"No, no, no, Winter did not want this. Oh my god, she's bleeding. What did you fucking do?" She finally gets him off of me and I see its Emerald. "Jason, get in here please, Jason, help me."

"What the fuck, dude? What the fuck is going on?" He punches Preston in the face so hard he gets knocked to the ground. Emerald is shaking and crying just as much as I am. She removes the duct tape from my mouth.

"Em, I came up here looking for you so we could leave. Then he came up behind me and blindfolded me at first but then it came off, then he put duct tape on my mouth and hands. I didn't ask for this." I start dry heaving. I'm shaking uncontrollably, my nerves are going crazy, I feel like I'm going to pass out and the alcohol doesn't help one bit. "Emerald, please get the duct tape off my hands."

"Dude, she asked for this. Jason, c'mon man. We're friends. You know I wouldn't do this without her wanting it. She's into the kinky shit, she asked me to tape her up." Jason punches him in the face.

"No girl asks to be tied down against their will and raped, you fucking asshole." He kicks him in the ribs and then in the face.

"He... he didn't rape me. He just–" I start crying even more, "shoved his fingers inside me."

"Oh, Snow." Emerald pulls me to her. "I'm so sorry. I'm so sorry it took me so long to find you." She hugs me tightly, rocking me back and forth in her arms. "Babe, we need to go to the hospital, he may not have used other parts, but he still forced himself onto you and in you, that's still rape, sweetie."

Nothing ended up happening with it. I decided not to tell anyone since I knew nothing would happen if I did. Due to his rich family, his social status and future football career, I would've just wasted my time.

19

CARSTEN

"SNOWFLAKE...SNOWFLAKE, WHAT HAPPENED?" I SAY IN A panic. After she came into my room, I put my hand over her mouth and my other hand over her eyes because I was trying to excite her. Instead, she started breathing really heavy and gasping for air, her whole body started shaking and she started crying.

"Winter, it's me, Carsten. I'm so sorry, baby. What did I do?" I grab her onto my lap.

"Don't touch me," she cries. "Please don't let him hurt me again, please." She hides her face into my chest as she tightly grips my shirt with both hands.

"Who, your dad?" I have no idea what's going on. I'm trying to get her to snap out of it but no matter what I say she just keeps telling me to not let him hurt her again. "Winter, it's me, Carsten. Please, its ok. I won't let anyone hurt you. Ever." I start pushing her hair out of her face and wiping her tears, rocking her back and forth trying to calm her down. Her breathing slows down some but she's still crying. I reach up onto my nightstand and grab the box of tissues I keep there and wipe her tears away again.

"It's ok, Snowflake. I'm so sorry, I don't know what I did but I'm so, so sorry, baby." I pull her closer, turning her where she's facing me and her legs are wrapped around my back, and she lays her head on my shoulder. "Babe, look at me." I gently lift her head and turn her face to look at me. "It's ok, it's me, you're safe, I won't let anyone touch you ever again."

"He... he tried to rape me." She cries, trying to look down but I stop her, lifting her chin with my hand. Mother fucker. I see red. I don't know who tried to rape her, or when, but I'm not ok with this. "Winter, who? You're dad?" She's sobbing on my lap, this fragile, beautiful fucking woman has been through enough with her dad. But this too? She... She was raped? Fucking hell.

I don't want to push her and freak her out again, but I need to know what is going on. "No." she whispers. "Preston... he... I was a virgin." She starts crying again, her body trembling, her breathing barely there.

"He covered my eyes with a blindfold, I was drunk, he covered my mouth with his hand then duct tape." She's sobbing and I'm beginning to understand.

"It's ok baby girl, it's ok. You don't have to continue. Please, I don't want to make you relive this. I'm so sorry I triggered this." God I'm a fucking idiot. Here I thought I was going to excite her but then I just triggered this.

"He...ripped my clothes." She takes a deep breath. "Ripped off my underwear and shoved his fingers inside me, he made me bleed from not being wet, he ripped me with his nails." I hug her because I don't know what to say. "He was about to do more but Emerald finally found me." She whispers between sniffling while wiping at her tears that keep falling down her now red cheeks.

"God baby. I'm so fucking sorry." I kiss her forehead not wanting to startle her by pulling her face up again. She looks up at me and kisses me.

"Thank you, for listening and understanding." Her breathing is almost back to normal now. I have no idea why she's thanking me, but I don't argue. I don't want to upset her. I'm more than happy to be here for her. To be the one she trusts to talk to about anything with.

"You're welcome, Snowflake. You can trust me, I would never, ever do anything to hurt you. As long as I'm around I'll protect you, I promise. I'll help you get through any of this the best I can."

I kiss her forehead before she lays her head back on my shoulder. I think she's falling asleep or was until Chase comes running up the stairs to my room.

"Hey guys, did you get lost?" He says, opening my door. "Oh sorry, didn't mean to interrupt, just wanted to let you guys know pizza just got here."

"Thanks man, we'll be down in a few." He signals to me by pointing at Winter with a thumbs up or a thumbs down, asking if she's ok, and I kinda just shrug my shoulders because I don't know if she's ok, or how long she's been going through all this alone. I don't want her to be alone with it anymore, that's too much bullshit for one person to carry and I want to help her with the weight of it all. I won't push, I'm going to let her know she can trust me to open up to. Even if nothing happens between the two of us, as far as more than sex. I still would like to be her friend; I won't be one of those guys who is butt hurt about being turned down or whatever. Yeah, it would fucking suck because she's mine and no one else can have her especially if I can't. So, fuck it, she's still going to be mine even if she tries to turn me down. I won't stop trying to convince her to be mine until I win her over and even then, I'll still spend my days trying to convince her not to leave me. But who am I kidding. Even if she does leave me. She'll be alone forever. So, she might as well be with me, Right? I probably sound crazy. But I don't care. I'd do anything to keep my little snowflake happy with me even if it is becoming a little obsessed and crazy over her.

20

WINTER

After I settled down, we finally headed downstairs for pizza. I expected Chase to say something, but he must've known it was a more serious moment and not a time to be a smart ass.

"So, I figured while I was waiting for the pizza to get here I'd pick a couple movies for you guys to pick from. Scary or funny?" He asks, holding the remote for the TV looking over at us.

"Doesn't matter to me, I'm down for whatever." Carsten says, looking over at me. "How about you pick since you're the guest, Snowflake."

"Man, I wish I had an awesome fucking nickname like that." Chase laughs but you can tell he's being completely serious. "You guys, I'm being serious, how does it feel to be called something as unique as Snowflake?" He asks.

"I love it honestly. I've only ever been called Winter or Snow, but no one's ever called me Snowflake, surprisingly." It's true, of all the nicknames I've had in my life I'm surprised no one has ever called me Snowflake before. Especially Emerald with all her crazy nicknames she's come up with for me over the years. No one has called me that. But I love it. Especially since Carsten gave it to me.

"Snow is cool too though. Let's just say I'm jealous." He chuckles a little, his mouth curling up more on one side than the other. He's definitely very attractive, both him and Carsten are super-hot. But to me Carsten's personality adds to his attraction and his bad boy appearance. Chase looks like a bad boy too, he's covered in tattoos, same as Carsten. But goddamn, just thinking about the bad boy vibe Carsten gives off makes my panties wet, makes my pussy throb. It's what all girls dream of the typical "bad boy" that all girls want. That's what Carsten Hatcher is. The bad boy of my dreams.

"Anyway, Chase, enough with your weird ass. Let's pick a movie," Carsten says to him while shaking his head.

"How about you pick, Chase, since you can't have a cool nickname like me, I'll let you pick." I laugh at him. Happy that they seemed to brighten my mood some and that it doesn't seem like I'm going to spend the rest of my evening in a funk.

"Let's go with something funny, but first let's drink or something, maybe take a shot? We don't have to get crazy but I'm in the mood for something, are you guys down to join me?" He asked setting his plate down before opening the pizza.

"I'm fine with either, doesn't matter to me. I could probably go with a shot before pizza and a drink after, I've had a shitty week and I've been stressed the fuck out." I sigh looking over at Carsten and Chase. I put my hands over my face shaking my head, dragging them down it while letting out a long slow breath.

"I'm down. Let's go out back to the patio, I just restocked the whiskey and vodka back there. We can do your favorite lemon drops, or just a plain old shot of whiskey to really take the stress away." Carsten smiles at me at that one. I'm sure he understands just what I need, especially after that breakdown in his room. Hell, I'll chug the whole fucking bottle, that's the type of mood I'm in.

"Hell yeah," Chase chimes in making sure all the pizza boxes are closed. "We can do both, whiskey and vodka. I'm sure it's a terrible thing to drink one after the other, but you only live once, right?" He grabs the pizza box, stacking it onto the other one.

"What are you doing with the pizza?" Carsten asks him, raising one eyebrow in confusion.

"Let's eat outside, if we're doing shots and we have pizza, might as well sit out here for a bit before we come in for the movie." He has a good point, I'd rather be outside enjoying this nice, warm weather while it lasts.

"Sounds like a plan." Carsten grabs plates and some red solo cups from the cabinet, and little plastic shot glasses that are placed right next to it.

"I forgot to replace the cups and shot glasses." He shrugs, placing them in his arm holding it against his chest while he tries to grab some napkins with what little free space in his hand he has left.

"Here, let me grab these for you." I take the plastic shot glasses and napkins and walk behind Chase as Carsten walks behind me. I let out a small yelp as I feel something come down and smack my ass.

"Hey!" I shriek. "I didn't take these things from you so you can slap my ass, sir," I say over my shoulder to Carsten.

"Oh, I'm so sorry, miss. I thought you grabbed it and said, "Hey make sure you smack my ass when I get in front of you." He has the sexiest smile on his face as he laughs. When doesn't he have a sexy smile on his face? I mean really, even him just blinking is sexy.

"No sir, you must have read the sign wrong." I shriek again as he pulls me back to him before I can step outside fully, my back to his chest and his hands come around my stomach as his face comes to my neck, sending chills down my body. I shiver as he kisses my neck. His warm breath blows across my skin as his lips come down again, placing gentle kisses while he slowly sucks my skin into his mouth. Just as I'm about to give into the pleasure he stops.

He groans in my ear. "Snowflake, Snowflake... I can't handle it when you call me sir, it sounds so sexy coming from your mouth babe." He grabs the stuff from my hands and sets it on the small table set up in his garage and does the same with the plates and solo cups in his hands. Then he comes back up behind me.

He lightly bites my neck and I turn my head to look up at him. "So sorry, Sir," I whisper as my mouth finds his and starts kissing him. He turns me around, picking me up by my ass and pushing me gently into the back door. Chase can probably see everything and part of me wants to stop him, but the other part of me says fuck it, he's turning me on, again. "God, Carsten, you can't keep doing this to me or I'm never going to want to leave your room." He laughs leaning in to kiss me again. I know we aren't in his room right now as we do this, but that's where we'd spend most of our time if that's what we were doing.

"That's totally fine with me, I'll have Chase bring up food every couple of hours." He places another soft kiss on my neck. Before nipping the skin and sucking it back into his mouth. God whatever he's doing to me I don't ever want it to stop. The way his mouth and tongue glides across my skin like they're one, making me moan. Spreading goosebumps across my body. His breath whispers across my skin as he moves from one spot to the next. Tickling me as my lips curve up into a big smile.

I stop and look up at him. "I wish, unfortunately I'm gonna have to leave come September, I'll be starting school." His face falls and he sets me down. He looks like he's seen a ghost as his face suddenly pales and a worried expression takes over.

"Wait, what do you mean, leave? You're going away to school? Fuck." He pushes his hand through his hair and starts pacing. I have no idea what's going on, why does he think I'm going away to school? Duh, because he just learned that you go to college, idiot.

"No, no, wait, just the college a couple blocks over, not anywhere else. Sorry, I should've been more specific."

He looks relieved. "Damn babe, 1 thought, this is just my luck, I meet a girl I could actually see myself being with and she's going away to college." He puts his hand over his face, embarrassed. Even if that were the case, I don't think I'd be able to leave. Not now, I don't think I'd want to pass up on the chance at what this could possibly be with Carsten. That may sound stupid or even childish to some people. But to me that's just the type of person I am, when I want something, I do what I can to get it and to keep it. Even if it's a new relationship I'd still work hard on it the same way I would a longer relationship because I'd want it to work.

"It's ok, if that were the case I wouldn't leave. Besides I'm only going for half the year, then I'm done."

"You really wouldn't leave if it meant staying here with me instead?" He asks, rubbing his hand on my cheek. A love laced look in his eyes.

"If it meant losing the chance to possibly have something with you, no, I'd transfer." I gulp hoping he doesn't see me do it, or even hear it. Especially with how quiet it is around us right now.

"Wow." He pauses, smiles, then relaxes his face. He gives a serious look, chuckles a little then smiles again. Is he speechless? I think I made him speechless. Or he just feels bad for my attempt at trying to see where things will go with this and doesn't know what to say without hurting my feelings.

"Well, unless you didn't want things to get any further, I mean." I say, hoping his *wow* wasn't a bad thing. I'd be so embarrassed if that's what he had meant by his wow. Traumatized really. What am I going to do if that's the case?

"Oh, I do want to see where this goes. I don't think I can ever get enough of you." He leans down and kisses me then pulls away. "I'm afraid I might be obsessed with you, I hope that doesn't scare you away," he whispers my ear, his tone so deep it sends a chill through my body. As if he doesn't give me the chills enough, he just keeps adding to it.

I pull away to look up at him. "No, not at all, I was afraid of the same thing." I smile, turning around to walk away. I can't get too serious too fast yet and I feel like I already am. I don't want to get hurt, so I walk into the house to hopefully save the conversation for another day.

We spend the rest of the night eating pizza, drinking a little and watching movies with Chase and his roommate Creedence, who came home after the first movie was over. I actually really enjoy being around them. I've never felt so comfortable being around a bunch of guys, especially with my past with Preston. I laugh to myself wondering what my dad would think if he knew I was hanging out alone in a room, scratch that—in a house with three grown men, obviously nothing is going on but to him nothing has to be happening to still be a whore.

Emerald finally came home at three-thirty in the morning, right as I started dozing off with my head on Carstens lap. She was confused as fuck as to why I wasn't home or responding to her texts. She ended up knocking on Carsten's door hoping I was here and that I didn't go home to my dad. We all head to the front porch as Em and I head outside to go home.

"Girl, don't you know my number by now?" She laughs at me over the fact that I got locked out. I should have her number memorized by now with how much I've had to call her for rides home from parties and other things I've needed her to rescue me from over the years.

"Actually, I know most of it but the last few numbers always fuck me up. I know them but never in the right order" Not even sure how it's possible to remember the numbers out of order, but at least I got some of the numbers right.

"Makes sense, well I'm glad you had somewhere you were able to go and someone to hang out with until I came home." She says, wiggling her eyebrows at the both of us. I feel my cheeks heat up, probably a bright shade of red. I must look guilty if you pay enough attention to my facial expression right now.

"Also, what happened to your clothes?" She raises an eyebrow, looking me up and down in confusion. As she smacks her gum in her mouth obnoxiously, trying to be annoying. Making me smirk in the process.

I forgot I didn't have my clothes on and start laughing again. "We got caught in the rain when I was stuck up on the roof and our clothes were soaked so he had to give me a shirt and some shorts to wear until my stuff is dried."

"That's not the only thing he gave her when her clothes were soaked." Creedence says, slapping his leg, being a smart-ass. That must be a new thing of his or something.

"Those were my thoughts exactly, at least what I was hoping would be what happened," Emerald says with a big smile on her face. She is such a weirdo. She is the type of friend to be excited and celebrate for you when you fuck someone. She'd probably buy you a cake or something if the sex story was exciting enough for her. But I love that about her, I love that she gets excited for things about her friends lives and isn't all about herself.

I start to blush, not wanting us to be the center of attention. "Ok guys, shut up. I just needed dry clothes that was it, nothing more."

"Nothing more? Damn, babe…Here I thought we had some great sex, guess I gotta work on my moves more." Carsten laughs, then pouts. Looking over at me with a sad look in his eyes.

"Oh my god, you too? Fine guys. Carsten and I did sleep together. Ok? Is that what you wanted to hear?" I say covering my face laughing. "And it was amazing, I have nothing to complain about with the sex or the dick. There, is that better?" Everyone claps and cheers all being smart-asses.

"See, Snowflake, that wasn't too bad, now was it?" Carsten wraps his arm around my waist pulling me closer to him.

"God, I just love the nickname Snowflake. I'm kinda jealous not gonna lie." Emerald sighs dramatically.

"Right, that's what I said earlier and got made fun of for it," Chase says, shaking his head like he's disappointed.

"Now, now, guys, no need to be upset, we can think of cool nicknames for you cry babies." Carsten says while patting Chase on the back like he's comforting him.

"Well, I'm beat guys. We were slammed at work, and I have another long day tomorrow. Should I leave a spare key with Carsten in case you get locked out again? Or you trying to repeat tonight tomorrow again and get "locked out" again." Emerald uses air quotes like she's hilarious or something.

"Ha. Ha. Ha. Very funny bitch." I shove her shoulder playfully.

"She doesn't have to pretend to get locked out, if she's not busy I'd like to take her out."

"Ohh, gonna be fancy before you take her to the bedroom this time huh?" Chase gives a loud obnoxious laugh slapping Carsten's arm as he laughs. Carsten just stands there shaking his head like he's ashamed of his brother. But obviously in a joking way. That's one thing I missed about not having any siblings growing up is the bickering over stupid things and the unwanted stress we'd cause our parents, that's assuming life would have been different for me if I did have a brother or sister. The thought making me sad. Mouring the life I never had the chance to have in this lifetime. A life with a sibling or the life with a mother. The life with my father was like watching someone you love slowly forget you every day because as the alcohol took over the worse his memory started to get. I mean he still knows who I am but his memories of life with me and my mother are long forgotten. Which is sad, I don't even know if he remembers life with my mother anymore.

"No, but I think she deserves to be treated good and I wanna take her out and have some fun together, just us two." Carsten looks over from me to Chase as he says it. Like he needs me to know he's changing for me. Which makes me feel special that he cares enough to want to change. I don't want him to change who he is, I like Carsten as he is for a reason. I just obviously don't want him sleeping around if we're together and I don't want other girls forcing themselves on him whenever we go out places because that will not be okay with me at all. I think I have the right to feel that way though especially if we are together.

"Guys... I'm umm right here ya know?" I say crossing my arms over my chest.

"Well, Snowflake." He pulls me into him, snuggling his face to my neck spreading goosebumps all over my body. "What do you say? Wanna go out tomorrow night with me? If you're free of course." He kisses my neck then up to my jawline.

"Get a room, you guys," Creedence says like he hasn't been

flirting with Emerald while everyone's talking. He thinks I didn't see them talking or the way they were looking at each other all googly eyed and everything.

"Shut up, Creed, don't hate," Carsten says back to him then goes back to lean down and kiss my neck again. "What do you say babe, go out with me tomorrow night?" He stops and looks over at me, cupping my face with both hands, titling my head up gently to look up at him. "Please, pretty please?" He pouts looking down at me.

"Of course, I'd love to, you didn't even have to ask that many times." I stand on my tippy toes to kiss him but that doesn't even help me get close enough to kiss him since he towers over me, so he has to lean down the rest of the way to kiss me back.

"Well good night, Snowflake." He leans to whisper in my ear, "I hope you dream about me." Then he kisses me one last time.

"Good night, handsome devil." I smile up at him, hoping he remembers me calling him that yesterday and he smiles.

We head back home and don't even talk other than saying good night, we're both exhausted since it's after four in the morning now and just head straight to bed. Not only do I not dream about Carsten, but I just can't sleep at all because I can't stop thinking about him and the whole day we had together. Or how excited I am to go out with him tomorrow. I've never been this excited before to go on a date and I've been out on plenty of dates, but none of them have even come close to matching the excitement I'm feeling right now over going out with a guy as attractive as he is.

21

CARSTEN

I wake up the next morning tired as fuck, I couldn't sleep at all last night due to the fact that I couldn't stop thinking about Winter. I have never been so into someone before. Into is an understatement, because I'm fucking obsessed over this gorgeous fucking girl. She has done nothing but consume my fucking thoughts since the minute I laid eyes on her. I can't wait to see her again, I've never been this excited to be around a female before, which makes me feel like a little bitch. Do other guys feel this way when they're this caught up in a woman or is it just me? I think it's due to the fact that I'm not used to being so obsesses with a girl that I can't stop thinking about her. About her touch, her softy pouty fucking lips against mine. Her creamy pale skin under mine, as I watched my cock slide in and out of her tight pussy. Fuck, now I have another boner. This chick is going to break my dick. Which reminds me that I don't even have her phone number because she never gave it to me. That in fact is the first time I've ever had a girl turn me down when I asked for their phone number, she actually told me no. Then had the nerve to tell me I needed to work for it. I've never had to work for anything when it has come to a girl before, usually they're all over me and throwing themselves at me, and prac-tically typing their phone numbers in my phone for them. Or handing them to me on ripped up pieces of napkins or pieces of paper, whatever is available at the time when they decide it's necessary to give me their number, even if I'm only interested in one thing. Anyways, back to what's important. My little Snowflake.

I'm not being cocky either, I like the challenge this time. Especially since the result is that gorgeous fucking girl who won't get the out of my fucking thoughts. No matter how hard I try to think of something else she pops right back into my mind. Fuck, why do I've got it so bad for her? Well, she will be mine, I wonder if I'm consuming her thoughts the same way she's taken over mine? I can't wait to see what the answer to that question is. I'll be able to tell the minute I see her if she's been consumed by thoughts of me all day. It's something I've picked up on over the years with women.

I'm looking forward to taking her out. I don't want to overdo it but I also want to do something nice for her, so she has a good time. "But first I gotta fucking go next door to talk to her about these plans." I mumble to myself, walking down the hall to the stairs.

"Talking to yourself again, Carsten?" Chase asks, coming up behind me. Always sneaking up on me like the fucking creep that he is. I swear he's always there and he never makes his presence known, it's always him creeping up, scaring me and shit.

"Fuck, a little warning next time would be nice." I shove him with my hand and start running down the stairs, so he won't shove me back, unless he plans on murdering me and burying me in the backyard, then he better not fucking shove me. I don't even give him the chance to respond before I continue, "No. Well, I fucking guess. Winter turned me down about giving me her phone number the other day, she told me I had to work for it."

He cuts me off. The look of shock on his unshaven face. The scruff taking over, which doesn't look terrible, actually makes him look more attractive and that ugly face needs some kind of help. I laugh to myself, but I don't think he notices since he doesn't react. "So, let me get this straight, the girl sleeps with you but doesn't give you her phone number? Damn You must be smooth with the ladies then." He rubs his hand over his chin like he's thinking. Maybe he's going to ask for advice on ways to get more pussy. He sure needs all the help he can get if you ask me. But what do I know I'm just a man whore, I obviously need more help with not sleeping around and more help with how to be a good boyfriend. You know, just in case Winter decides she wants more eventually.

"See I told you I was, but you never want to listen to me. Anyway, now that we're going out tonight, I have no idea how to discuss anything with her beforehand about tonight, so now I have to go over there and trick her into giving it to me, although the challenge would be fun to work for it." I wiggle my eyebrows, rubbing my hands together thinking of all the fun ways I can tease her or trick her into just giving me her number. I wonder if she'll still make me work for it or if after going without a way to talk to me if she'll just give it to me without making me work for it.

"Yeah, that does seem like it would be a good challenge." He pauses for a second. "You working tonight then, or are you dipping out early?" Fuck. Of course, I would forget that I have to work tonight, I was so caught up in making sure I was going to see Winter again I asked her out without thinking of my schedule. Fuck I'm an idiot.

"Shit." I mutter. "I might have her meet me there and work for a bit, so I don't leave you alone." I grab my phone off the counter and shove it into my pocket. "Honestly, I kinda forgot I have to be at work. I wasn't thinking when I asked her out." I put my hand through my hair, frustrated at my stupidity.

"You guys are more than welcome to come hang out up there." He walks over to the table and pulls out a chair. "But no, don't be stupid. Don't work while you're on a date with her bro, that would be a shitty thing to do." He shakes his head like he's even disappointed in my shitty life choices. What the fuck is my deal. This is why fucking around and not dating is just easier. Too many rules to follow, always checking in on each other, knowing everything that the other person is doing at all times. Am I ready for something like that? To be that committed to someone. I'd like to think I am, at least for my little Snowflake I think I can be.

"Yeah, I guess you're right. I just felt bad leaving you solo but guess what? Fuck you, bitch, I don't feel bad anymore." I stick my middle finger up at him and he gasps, placing his hand over his heart in pretend shock. He always fucks around with me the same way I fuck with him. We've always been close growing up, I don't even think we went through the phase where you hate each other as siblings. No, I think we were always just close. Yeah, we fought and drove our mom crazy with it. But it was always fun fighting and wrestling or just stupid arguments. My brother truly is my best friend, I don't care if that makes me a pussy for admitting that either.

"Wow, straight to my heart with that one man, thought you loved your little bro." He wipes at pretend tears being the dramatic fucker that he's always been good at being. Fucking dick.

"Ehh, I guess I do, that's why I was gonna hang for a bit. Maybe we'll just stay there then, that way if you do get slammed, I'll be there to help. I don't know, I'll see how she feels about it and what she wants to do." I'm talking to him and myself at the same time, thinking out loud, like I catch myself doing more than I'd like to admit. But who isn't fucking crazy in their own fucking way, huh?

"You are one confusing son of a bitch man." He's still giving me this crazy look, but I don't even care, let him think I'm crazy. If this is what being into someone does to you, being fucking obsessed with someone does to you, then call me fucking psycho because I'm just getting started with my Winter obsession and I have a feeling my obsessions only going to grow stronger.

"Yeah, yeah. Suck a dick. I'll be right back man." I mumble to him as I head towards the front door. I walk out the front door as Creedence and Axton are walking in.

"Hey man, you still live here?" I joke. "I feel like I haven't seen you in forever," I say to Axton. He's been staying over his girlfriends a lot so he's never home. I also work a lot for the most part, so we never really crossed paths to begin with.

"I know, it's been a minute." He pats me on the back. "Where are you headed?" We give each other our normal man handshake hug thing—you know that one handshake, hug that all men seem to be programmed to know how to do.

"Next door, Emerald's friend moved in last week and we're going out tonight," I tell him, looking over in the direction of Emerald's house, hoping Winter is actually there and I don't have to go chase her down somewhere, because I will fucking find her if I have to. That's how badly I want to see my little Snowflake and get her phone number.

"Ahh, already trying to hit that huh?" He cracks a smile, nodding his head like he's proud or something. He was a man whore too before he met his girlfriend. Whatever the fuck her name is. I'm not a fan of her so I don't care to know it. She's a bitch and he deserves way better than her. She must have a magical pussy or something because she's not going anywhere anytime soon, I think she's got him under her control. You know the old saying pussy whipped. Yeah, I think that's what he is due to her being a controlling bitch.

"He already did, but ready for the shocking part? He's actually really into this chick man, but she's super cool. She hung out over here last night. You'd probably like her too. She has a cool personality like we do man," Creedence tells him in an excited voice, which makes me laugh because he sounds excited, like he's talking about himself. That's how he is as a friend though, he puts his all into his friendships. Always excited when it's needed and always there no matter what. That's why he's more like a brother to both Chase and I instead of a friend.

"That's awesome, Carst. I hope this goes somewhere for you bro, it would be nice to see you with someone for once." He laughs but then slaps me on the shoulder letting me know he's fucking with me. Deep down I know all my friends, including my brother would like to see me in a relationship. Especially my mother, every time I talk to her she's always asking me if I'm dating anyone or if I think the girl I slept with is the one. I'm pretty open with my mom. She's not fond of the fact that her son sleeps around because of course as a mom she wants her little boy to have a girlfriend or get married and give her grandbabies. Maybe I'm finally ready for all of that myself and it just took meeting Winter for it to all click in or me. Better late than never, right?

"Thanks, dick." I shake my head. "I'll be back in a little bit. I'm going to talk to her about our date later." Hoping she'll still come even though it's going to the bar I partially own, instead of somewhere else, like out to dinner or something. God, I'm going to fuck this up because I don't know how to date, I don't know how to be a boyfriend, I don't know how to be the man she needs me to be, because I only know how to be the man that fucks women and leaves them. Will I be enough for my little Snowflake? I wonder if how much I need her to be mine will be enough for her. Enough to make her want me back the same way I want her to be mine.

"Alright man, see ya," Axton says, slapping my back again.

"See ya, brother," Creedence says, doing our stupid handshake we made in middle school, when we thought we were bad asses, and just stuck with it since then. Because why not? It's become so natural that sometimes I don't even realize we're doing the handshake until it's over with. "See ya, guys."

I finally get out the front door. I thought I was never going to get out of the house and I'm dying to see Winter. It's like I crave her. Her touch, her kiss. Her smell, everything about her, I need it all. Like I won't be able to get my next breath of air without her. I just need to touch her, feel her body against mine again, feel her in my arms, it doesn't even have to be fucking naked. I just need her. As I start walking next door, I see Winter sitting on her front stairs to her porch.

"Hey, gorgeous." I smile, the nerdiest fucking smile I've probably ever given a woman, because I've never been so happy to see a girl before. My smile grows bigger the closer I get, and my cheeks are sore already. That's how big it is, and I can't even stop it from forming, the smile just keeps naturally curling up on my face.

"Hey there, handsome devil." And she gives me her sexy smirk and wink with it that instantly makes my cock fucking hard for her. Here we go again, another day of my dick painfully straining against the inside of my jeans because it doesn't know how to act around a female anymore and just thinks it's normal to walk around with a painful, awkward hard on all day.

"How are you today?" I ask, not sure how else to start a conversation since I don't usually care to talk much to the girls I fuck.

"I'm pretty tired, struggling to wake up and stay awake. I was about to head inside and grab some coffee, do you want some?" She yawns after she says it and her body does this cute stretch with it that looks to me like she can't stop from happening. One of those stretches that completely take over your body. And it takes everything in me not to pick her up and just take her back to my bed and go back to sleep. I definitely need it after the lack of sleep from last night. But at the same time, I'm afraid to close my eyes and miss out on my time with her.

"Whatcha tired from baby girl?" My voice is scratchy and deep. Something that happens when I don't sleep well, it'll take a while for my voice to return to normal. I walk towards her leaning down and kissing her on her warm, wet lips. "Mmm, your lips Snowflake, are amazing." I lean back in, closing the space between the two of us again. I don't think I'll ever be close enough to her, no matter how close I am. It'll never be enough.

"Mhmm, so are yours, handsome." She practically moans against my mouth. "Do you want me to make up a reason why I couldn't sleep, or you want the honest truth?" She laughs as I sit down next to her.

"First I forgot to answer you, I'd love to drink some coffee with you, and I want the truth, don't you lie to me." I use a playful serious tone with her as I scoot closer, closing the leftover space between our bodies. I could get used this.

"I couldn't stop thinking about you, and then I couldn't stop thinking about today and going out with you, then I wanted to text you but then I'm an ass and forgot I never gave you my phone number. It took everything in me to not scream across the window to your room because I realize my room is across from yours." She laughs putting her hand over her face, probably embarrassed. It's fucking adorable in every way possible, and I'm just convinced that everything this girl does will always be adorable or cute in some way.

"Yes! So, I can peek at you through your window and get free shows of you changing any time I want?" I crack a smile at her, nudging her lightly with my shoulder before putting my arm around her and pull her closer to me "Baby girl, you should've come back over and given me your number. I wouldn't have cared about how late it was." I'm kind of bummed that she didn't come over to give it to me, but then I don't think I would have let her leave then if she did come back over. "I couldn't sleep for shit last night because I was thinking about you, and I was thinking about kissing your lips again." I look down at her pink pouty lips as I say it, she has the perfect pout to them. That's why I love biting on her lip so much, she's got just the right amount to nibble and suck on. Shit, I need to stop with these thoughts of mine.

"Yeah? You were? Because I was thinking about…" then she leans in to whisper into my ear, "your thick hard cock inside my wet pussy." And she smiles at me, this devilish smile that knows she made my painfully hard cock even harder. And I'm not going to sit here and take this kind of abuse from her anymore. Nope I'm putting my foot down, her pussy is going to be mine here shortly and I can't fucking wait.

"That's it miss, I'm afraid you're gonna have to come with me." I pick her up and throw her over my shoulder. "Forget the coffee, I'm about to take you to my room and spank your ass."

"Wait, Carsten. Let me at least grab my phone. It's on the table right when you open the door." She says in a panic, probably so she's not locked out without a phone again like she was yesterday.

"Winter—I don't even know your last name to call you by your full name since you're in trouble—but you need to stop leaving your phone in your house. Didn't you learn your lesson?" I use my pointer finger, pointing it at her, and attempting to use a serious tone with her but it's hard because she literally has control over everything, I do without her even doing anything and I don't want to be mean to her, even in a joking way.

"Vega," she says with a struggle.

"What?" Cause I barely heard what she had said. "My name. It's Winter Vega. And apparently not, cause I keep leaving it inside. Guess you will have to spank me then." She

I open her front door and grab her phone, then shut it and walk across her porch and jump down the stairs.

"Ow you dick, my ribs," she says in a painful voice. I close my eyes and scrunch up my face because I completely forgot about the pain she's in. How could I forget something so important like that?

"Oh fuck, I'm sorry, Snowflake. I'll make sure I give you extra kisses for hurting you babe," I tell her in a serious tone. I don't want her to think I don't really care about what I just did. I didn't mean to hurt her, and I need to keep reminding myself that she's still not one hundred percent yet.

"It's ok, I forgive you this time." She squeals out as she giggles. "And you better give me extra kisses, I missed your lips all night." It sounds like she's pouting, either that or the blood is rushing to her head from being upside down. I'm going to go with her pouting though because that sounded like something that would be said in a sad pouty way.

"Don't you worry, baby girl, don't you worry." My voice still a little raspy as I say it in a seductive tone.

22

WINTER

We walk up his front porch and I see a strange man sitting on the stairs that I've never seen before; I assume is his third roommate that I had never met. Or maybe it's just another friend who stayed the night.

"Hey Carst, brought company?" He smiles looking over at me as Carsten swings me back so I could see his face fully. "Hi, I'm Winter. I'd love to shake your hand but I'm afraid I can't from this angle." I snort, sounding all funny and stuffy from being upside down.

"Hey, Winter. Nice to meet you. I won't take offense, don't worry." The guy says, still not telling me his name. I'm not upset by it; I just feel rude not knowing what to call him.

"I'm heading upstairs man, make sure no one bothers us, we'll be busy talking about... our feelings and stuff." Carsten says with a big cheesy grin on his face, like a child waiting to open their gifts or something. I guess he does have something to be excited about though.

"Ahh yes, your feelings and stuff." He lets out a laugh as he shakes his head at Carsten. "Whatever you say man, whatever you say."

We walk into his house, and we're greeted by Chase and Creedence.

"Snowflake! What's up? Happy to see you back so soon." Chase says with a huge smile on his face. it makes me feel good that Carsten's brother likes me, actually that his roommates like me too, it makes things a lot easier.

"I already told you yesterday man, don't you call her Snowflake. That's my nickname for her and she's mine." Carsten practically growls at his brother and it's such a sexy sound it makes my thighs tighten together to control the constant throbbing he causes between my legs.

"Calm down man, I was just saying it to fuck with you. I like how you're claiming her and she's not even your girlfriend yet, bro." He calls him out. Hopefully that doesn't push him to ask me to be his girlfriend yet, cause although we already slept together, I'm not ready to rush into a relationship just yet. I'd like to see where this goes a little. Who am I kidding if he asked me to be his girlfriend I'd probably say yeah because I'm crazy like that.

"Alright fuckers, no one come knocking on my door, we will be busy having important conversations." Carsten says in a firm voice as he walks towards the stairs.

"Important conversations?" Creedence finally says something, with such a confused look on his face. The facial expressions this man give are the best, he never seems to know what is going on or is always confused by something Carsten says.

"Yep. You heard what I said, important conversations about our feelings and stuff." He lets out a chuckle using the same excuse as he used with that nameless guy from the front porch with them.

"Alright gorgeous, let's go." He smacks my ass and starts running up the stairs, my whole body shaking from it in the process. The pain I feel in my ribs making me wince with the movement. I feel so bad that he keeps forgetting so I don't want to bring it up again, I'll manage, I've done it all the other times I've had bruises from dad so there's nothing different about it now. I just don't want to make Carsten feel like an asshole, so I don't want to bring it up.

"Please, I don't want you to hurt yourself, don't run." And he has the nerve to laugh at me like what I just said was funny or something.

"Babe, I bench more than you weigh at the gym. Don't worry I won't hurt myself." He shuts and locks his door, double checking with the door handle to make sure it's locked. Then he walks over and tosses me onto his bed before climbing on top of me. "Now, miss, where were we?" He gives me a look I've never seen before. Something I can't put my finger on, but then he snaps out of whatever thoughts he was just lost in and smiles at me before he leans in and brushes his lips gently against mine. Just the softness of his lips alone is enough to get me in the mood. Why is he affecting me like this?

"I think we were at the part where I told you I thought about your nice, hard cock in my tight, wet pussy." I slide my tongue into his mouth before biting his bottom lip.

He lets out a sexy growl before biting my lip back and then he flips me over on my stomach and starts pulling my shorts down. "Is... is this, ok?" He asks, sounding concerned like he doesn't want to trigger anything or make me panic. It's sweet that he cares how he's making me feel as he touches me and before he does things.

"Yes, thank you." And I leave it at that because I don't want to ruin the moment. I'm too turned on and want to see where this goes. Hopefully it goes where I want it too.

He takes off my shorts and panties and grips my ass with his hands, jiggling it for a minute before smacking my right cheek hard, but not enough to hurt, and I let out a moan, then he rubs it with his hand and smacks it again a little harder this time and rubs the sting with his hand before he leans down and bites my ass.

"Mmm. Fuck" I am so turned on right now, I can feel the wetness from my pussy making my thighs wet. I don't think I have ever been this wet, or even this turned on before.

"You like that, Snowflake?" He groans and smacks my ass cheek again this time loud and hard. "You're a bad, bad girl my little Snowflake." He lets out a deep chuckle before his hand comes down again. It stings and burns, but nothing about it hurts. My pussy throbs in response. God, I need more, I need to feel his hands on me.

"You're a bad girl that needs to be spanked." Holy. Shit. Did he just say that? He then leans down and kisses right where he spanked me. Shit is he turning me on even more. I have never had someone do these things to me before and it's driving my body absolutely wild. Making me crave his next touch like an addict. Is this what it feels like to need another hit? To crave something so much that you feel like you'll die without it? That's how my body feels right now. He makes me want things I never knew I needed until I felt his hands on me. Then it was like my body started piecing things together making me crave more of it.

"Mmm, Carsten, please." I don't even sound like myself. My voice is raspy as I pant between breaths.

"Fuck." That was sexy. "Tell me baby girl, are you enjoying this?" And he swipes his finger across my pussy, and it's so wet he moans. "Goddamn, Snowflake." He flips me over and shoves his finger into his mouth and licks my wetness off him. "God, you taste like fucking candy." He sticks his finger into me pumping it in and out of me.

"Oh god." I can't seem to say anything else, it's like I forget how to speak every time he touches me. He makes my body melt into this big puddle of mush with every touch. I need his body on mine, to feel him against me, inside me. His sweaty skin against mine. His mouth on mine or roaming my body. My thoughts are getting me even more worked up than I already was.

He pulls his finger out and sticks it back into his mouth and starts licking it clean, again. "Mmm, I could taste you all day." His voice gravel as he speaks. He stares at me like he can't get enough of me, like he would eat me alive if I let him. He sounds like he's about to lose control, the ache in his tone as he talks, like no matter how much he gets it'll never be enough. Like he can't hold back anymore, like he's an animal watching his prey trying to time it perfectly on when to attack. And I can't wait.

"Carsten, please." My body needs to be touched; it needs to feel him inside me. My body craves him like it's never craved anything before. I'm filled with this want or need; I can't even begin to explain what I'm feeling. I'm not even sure. I've never felt these feelings before. All I know is that I like it and I don't want to feel anything else besides what I'm feeling right now.

"Please what, baby girl... is this what you want?" He licks right up my pussy and stops right on my clit. He starts swirling his tongue around it, finding the spot again that gets me so close to an orgasm and teases me. Slowly licking and sucking my clit like he's starving, but instead of scarfing down his meal, he's taking his time to enjoy every. Single. Bite. Every. Lick. Every. Taste. My core clenches tight as pleasure starts building deep inside me. He's torturing me with pleasure, teasing me and I love everything about it. I never want this feeling of pleasure to end.

"Fuck, Carsten. Please, I need—"

"Need what, baby? Huh?" He places his lips back around my swollen clit and begins sucking on it again before he sticks his two fingers inside me and starts pumping in and out of me, then he adds another finger and I lose it. My pussy clamps down on his fingers and starts pulsing, my body trembles as my orgasm soars through me, waves of pleasure pulsing through me until my body goes limp, needing a second to catch my breath because of how intense it was. He doesn't give me that chance before he's flipping me back over on my stomach and pulling my ass back towards him and pushes right into me without warning, stretching my pussy in the most delicious way. Our moans mingling together as he slowly slides himself in and out of me in a torturously slow way, feeling every inch of his length as it glides against my wet walls.

"Fuck." He groans, pumping in and out of me with his rock-hard cock. I look back at him as he throws his head back, his Adam's apple bobbing up and down in his throat, and god is it sexy, yes it's one of those weird things I find attractive on a guy but I just can't help it.

He grips my hips to thrust a little harder. "God, baby girl, your fucking pussy feels so amazing." He leans down over my back, gripping my hair in his hand and pulling my head to turn back at him again. His mouth crashes down on mine, his kiss becoming wild with a need I feel through my entire body. He lets go of my hair as he stops kissing me and leans back up.

"Do you like the way my hard cock feels in your pussy, Snowflake?" He asks with a growl. "Tell me baby, tell me how much your pussy likes my cock.

"I... oh, god, Carsten. Your cock feels so, so good." He stops for a second and I let out a whimper. "Tsk, tsk, tsk, I told you to tell me how much your pussy likes my cock, baby girl. Tell me before I spank you again." My pussy clenches around his cock at his words, making me grow wetter with each thrust.

"Shit, Carsten." I moan. "My pussy loves your cock." I breathe out between pants. "Don't stop." I say a little louder as the pleasure takes over and my body is getting turned on from his words. "Please don't fucking stop."

"Fuck, that was sexy. I wanna feel you cum all over my cock, Snowflake. I wanna feel you pulse all over it while I fuck that tight pussy." He smacks my ass so hard, my body explodes and my orgasm shoots through me, my whole body shaking as he grabs my hip and slams into me. "Shit, Snowflake, I'm about to cum." He says as he grips my hips hard enough to leave bruises, but I don't mind at least these are bruises from pleasure. His body starts tightening up as he pumps in and out of me before he slams into me one last time. Then he collapses next to me pulling me close to him.

"Shit, that was amazing." He leans in and kisses me.

"Mhmm. Amazing." I manage to get out as my heavy eyes start to flutter shut, the next thing I remember is him covering up our naked bodies and snuggling close to me.

23

CARSTEN

I WAKE UP IN A PANIC, FORGETTING WHERE I WAS, HOPING I'm not late to help my brother open the bar. I went to Winter's at nine in the morning, so it was still pretty early when we fell asleep. I try to roll over forgetting she was on my arm and have trouble moving it because it fell asleep. When I finally move it out from under her head I roll over and see it's one in the afternoon. We aren't opening the bar until four today so I have a little more time to spend with her so we can discuss our plans for the night.

I roll back over to Winter, who's slowly opening her eyes. "Hello, gorgeous." I lean in and kiss her slowly.

"Hello, handsome devil." She smiles, I love hearing her call me that. "Did you have a nice nap?" She asks me, and if I'm being honest, I haven't slept this good in a long ass time.

"Yes, I did. I haven't slept in that deep of a sleep in a long time." I stretch a little, staring at her beautiful face.

She laughs. "Same here, I actually forgot where I was when I woke up for a second."

"Yeah, I panicked hoping I didn't sleep past helping my brother open the bar."

"Oh, you have to work?" she says, sounding disappointed.

"I just have to help him set up and open the bar and then I'm free to do whatever you want, Snowflake." I smile a little hoping she isn't mad or upset with me.

"If you need to work it's not a big deal, I can come hang out at the bar with Emerald and our friend Chastity." She smiles and it sounds like she's being serious. She doesn't sound angry. Unless she's holding back the hurt and trying to put on a happy face for me. Fuck, did I just mess things up?

"No, we are just short on bartenders and it's just me and Chase right now so the only issue is I might have to hang around for a little bit to make sure he doesn't get slammed. I'm such an asshole, I didn't even think about what day it was when I asked you to go out with me." I pause to push her hair behind her ear. "I just wanted to take you out so bad that I said fuck my job." I laugh because it's true, I wanted to forget about everything but her in that moment. Nothing else mattered, apparently not even my job.

"It's ok, we can hang out there. I enjoy being around you, and your brother is hilarious. So, whatever you need to do I'm down for, as long as I get to hang out with you, I'm happy." She shy's away, her cheeks growing a slight shade of pink from her words.

"Sounds perfect," I say as I lean in to kiss her again. I get on top of her and slowly kiss her, taking my time, exploring her mouth with mine. I lift her right knee, bringing it up to make more room for my body. "I wanna be inside you, Snowflake."

"I wanna feel you inside me..." But I don't even let her finish what she was saying before I gently slide inside her, taking my time with her body, not being rough at all, just enjoying the feel of her pussy sliding against my cock as I thrust inside her. I don't even know if this is what it's like to make love, because I've only ever had rough sex. But the way it feels is amazing. If this was the only way I got to have sex with her every time we slept together, I wouldn't even be upset.

"God, you feel so good, Carsten." She lets out a tortured moan, the sounds of pleasure radiating through her moans.

"You feel so good, Snowflake. I don't want to stop feeling you this way." It's true, having her pussy around my cock is my personal form of heaven. If she decided she didn't want to sleep together anymore after today I don't know what I'd do or how I'd react. But I'd put up a fight, I don't think any other pussy will ever feel as good as the way hers feels on my cock. It's like she was made for me, her pretty pussy fits perfectly on my cock like a glove. It's tight like one too.

"Me neither. Your cock, oh god..." She lets out a moan, she's getting close to cuming I can tell by the way her body is reacting. "Your cock feels so good."

"Goddamn." I let out a groan. I reach down and around the front of her and start massaging her clit and that's all her body needs to send her over the edge. Her body trembles and I lean down and kiss her, slowly kissing her and swirling my tongue around hers while sucking on her bottom lip. I thrust into her a couple more times before I finally explode, releasing all of my cum inside her.

We lay there for a little longer, snuggling and talking before she has to go home and get ready.

"Give me your phone."

"Did I finally earn your number?"

"Well, no. But I get lonely and like talking to you, so I'm giving in." She laughs typing her number into my phone.

"Wow, I can't believe you just said that. Here I thought I swooned you with all my charm and earned your phone number." I pretend to pout, making her jaw drop.

"Aww, babe." She laughs, kissing my pouty lip. "I was just kidding; you did a good job earning my number. Now I'll text you when I'm ready, ok?"

"Yes, make sure you do. We'll be leaving here around four to get the bar ready."

"Alright, handsome devil." She winks, kisses me, and walks out the front door to her house. Leaving me there with my heart pounding in my chest, and this weird fluttering feeling in my stomach.

24

WINTER

We're sitting in Carsten's car, his brother and Creedence in the back seat. We decided they could just ride with us, and the guy who's name I still don't know would be taking them home since he's coming up with his girlfriend. He made sure to invite Emerald and she invited Chastity and her friend Saylor that I have only met a handful of times. That way we can all hang out together at the bar and if it ends up getting busy, I have people to hang out with and am not alone waiting on Carsten. I'm not even upset that this is our date, so far, his friends all seem awesome and I think my friends will get along with them, so it should be a great night.

"I actually wanted to ask you something, Snowflake," Carsten says while placing his hand on my thigh. He stares straight ahead at the road while talking, gently rubbing his thumb up and down my leg, while his hand creeps a little closer to my center. The smirk on his face grows when I tighten my thighs.

"What's up?" I ask because I'm curious what it's about. The smile on his face is enough to make me wet alone. I like to call it panty dropping, because the minute I laid eyes on him, I imagined what it would be like fucking him, and now that I know what it's like to fuck him, I don't think I could fuck anyone else.

"Well, Chase and I need help at Black Velvet and my mom doesn't really bartend anymore like she used to, and we actually wanted to know if you would like to come work with us. When you are fully healed and ready of course." He says to me, glancing over here and there, I think to gauge my reaction. I could stare at this handsome man all day. His beard hugging his jaw just right, just enough to pull and run my fingers through. His gorgeous eyes, the way they linger on my body in all his favorite places. Fuck, he's addicting.

"I was actually gonna start applying for jobs within the next two weeks, I wanted my bruises to be fully gone or at least almost gone completely so they were easier to cover up just in case I was called in for an interview." I look down as I talk, still embarrassed and ashamed of how I look, nothing about me feels pretty. I feel like I'm looking at a stranger, who's broken, when I look at myself in the mirror. Yet the way Carsten looks at me he makes me feel beautiful, like I'm the only girl in the room and I love it.

"See, it'll be perfect, Carsten," Chase says from the back seat. "I think Mom is back at work tonight so maybe she can meet Winter and get a feel for her." I pause and turn in my seat, glancing back and forth at them both. My heart falling into my ass, we might have actually lost it on the road at this point. He wants me to meet his mom? Tonight? Well fuck, I guess if I'm going to be working with them, I have to meet her sooner or later.

"You guys want me to meet your mom?" My nerves showed more than I thought they would. I suck at hiding things, especially when it comes to how I'm feeling. Usually with my resting bitch face and my inability to control my facial expressions, that is my first giveaway right there, my face tells on me, therefore I can't hide anything for shit.

"Only if you're ready to babe, but it could be as someone looking for a job and not as you being mine, if you'd rather it be that way." Carsten lightly squeezes my thigh a couple times. Something about his big strong hands is just so sexy, the way it makes my thigh look so small in his firm grip as his thumb goes back to rubbing my leg.

"Oh, I'm not nervous." Of course I'm nervous, is he crazy? But I pretend I'm not, more for him than for me. "I just was more concerned about her questioning my bruising is all, I know it's faded but it's still very much there." I bite my bottom lip out of a nervous habit.

"Well, I'll pull her to the side and tell her not to question it so you don't have to, Carsten." Chase tells him, smacking his hand against his shoulder.

When we pull into Black velvet, we pull around back where the employee's park and see a woman getting out of her car. She stops after shutting her door and waves to us as she's opening her back door to grab a bag. She stands there waiting for us.

"Does she work here?" I ask out of curiosity. She's absolutely gorgeous. Her sandy-brown hair hangs just past her shoulders, she has half of it up and half of it down. The color of her hair shows off the different colors in her hazel eyes, the same color as Carsten's.

"Yes, that's our mom. She just got back from an extended vacation with her friends." Chase leans forward as he says it, looking through the front window like he's excited his mom is home or something. Maybe he is and they have a really close relationship. That would be nice to see for once instead of dealing with my family drama all the time.

"Oh wow, she looks so young." I swear she doesn't look old enough to be a parent.

"She had me when she was eighteen," Carsten says, and I feel like an idiot because I don't even know how old he is, and I've slept with him multiple times.

"I'm an idiot, how old are you guys?" I place my hand over my face embarrassed. I can't believe I slept with a man I know so little about. I don't even know his fucking age. *Nice going idiot*, I think to myself. Yes, I just thought that thought, but I'm not the kind of girl who sleeps with someone knowing so little, so that's why it freaks me out some.

"I'm twenty-three," Carsten says trying to hold back one of his panty-dropping smiles that I love so much. I'm convinced all of his smiles are considered panty dropping.

"I'm twenty-one, I'm not old like you guys."

"Yeah, yeah, fucker. So old." Creedence laughs. "I'm twenty-three as well."

"Ok, I knew we were close in age, I just never thought to ask really, I'm twenty-two," I say, feeling a little better now. I'm definitely going to take the time to ask Carsten some questions tonight to get to know him more.

We all step out of the car and their mom rushes over to hug them all, including Creedence.

"My boys, I've missed you so much! Thank you for keeping up on the bar while I was gone." She has the biggest, prettiest smile on her face. It's a kind, loving smile. It makes my heart happy that they have such a loving mom. But sad, because it makes me miss my mom.

"No problem, Mom, we enjoyed it." Carsten says to her as she hugs him again. You can tell she loves her boys, I mean duh, they're her children. But you can tell they share a close bond.

"Who is this gorgeous young lady just standing here with you guys?" She comes over towards me, her pretty smile still spread out on her face. She looks even younger up close, making it even crazier to think she's a mother of two adult boys and doesn't look older from the stress I'm sure they've caused her over the years.

I smile at her and step forward. "Hi, I'm Winter." I smile again, feeling a little insecure about my bruises but hoping she doesn't really notice them.

"Wow, what a gorgeous name to go with a gorgeous girl." She grabs my hand and gently squeezes it. Her hands are a little cold, but soft and her touch gentle. It's a mother's touch, that sweet loving touch that only a mother knows how to give.

"Winter, this is my mom, Ms. Hatcher," Carsten says, moving his hand from me to his mom and then back again.

"Carsten, really? Ms. Hatcher?" She rolls her eyes, and it takes everything in me not to laugh, because I can tell I'm already going to love this woman. "I may be old but c'mon." She winks at me. I see where they get their good looks from, their mom is absolutely gorgeous. I could say that every time I look at her and not in a weird way, she could be a model. Carsten has her smile and her beautiful hazel eyes, where Chase has her cheek bones and smile.

"Please do not call me Ms. Hatcher, call me Presley." She waves her hand at me.

"I love your name, it's beautiful." I say because I haven't heard the name before.

"Thank you, sweetheart. Now Carsten, does this mean you finally have a girlfriend?" Her smile grows even bigger than it was, making her hazel eyes sparkle.

"No, Mom, she's just my friend." He rolls his eyes in a joking way, gently shoving her arm.

"Carsten!" I smack his arm lightly. "Don't roll your eyes at your mom." My jaw drops with a look of shock on my face, although you can tell that I'm messing with him. I love that we joke around already, like we've been joking around forever. Like this isn't something new.

"See, I like this girl, Carsten. Sounds like she's keeping you in your place." She chuckles and sticks her tongue out at him. "Alright let's go get this bar ready to open up." She's walking towards the door holding her keys to unlock the door. "Are you coming to work with us, Winter? Did they hire you while I was on vacation and actually listen to me about needing the extra help?" Her voice is laced with excitement, and it makes me feel a little better about them asking me to come work with them, without asking her first.

"Actually, I will be looking for a new job soon." I'm not sure how to word my situation "Um, I just moved in with my friend Emerald, who actually lives next door to your boys, after a family issue, so I'm not exactly ready to start yet, if that's ok." For some reason that comes out quiet and shy, almost like I was afraid to give my answer and be yelled at or something. That's something I started from my dad, when he would yell at me, I'd get quiet and shy, not sure how to act around him. Afraid that if I said the wrong thing, or spoke too loud, I'd get yelled at, or worse, hit.

Carsten cuts in, I think he senses my discomfort. "Of course it's ok, we're not going to force you to work until you're ready, the position is yours. If mom is ok with it, we will hold it until you're ready for it, Snowflake. Don't worry, there's no pressure." He puts his arm around my shoulder kissing me on the cheek as we walk into the bar.

"Carsten, that was so sweet," Presley says to him, with her hand over her chest. "I wasn't rushing, I was just curious, is all. If you have experience, awesome. If you don't, awesome, we will train you. We're just happy to have the extra help is all, and like Carsten said, the position is yours when you're ready."

"Thank you so much. I was a bartender at my last job but when I called off due to personal issues they fired me. I wasn't physically able to come in and they just didn't care."

"Oh my god, dear, I'm so sorry to hear that happened. Well, I hope everything is ok now, we are more than happy to have you a part of our work family."

"Thank you, I truly appreciate that."

"You're welcome, sweetheart." She squeezes my arm gently before walking away to go turn all the lights on. Carsten, Chase, and Creedence start putting all the chairs down, so I decide to help instead of just standing there.

"Snowflake, Snowflake," Carsten says, walking up to me slowly. Then he leans down and whispers in my ear, "You better sit that sexy ass of yours down or else I promise to spank you later."

He kisses my jawline before making his way to my mouth and kissing me. I open to let his tongue in, and he groans into my mouth, it's such a sexy sound and instantly makes me wet. "You're not here to work, baby girl. Sit down and I'll get you a drink if you'd like one."

I pause, still thinking back to what my dad would say, and remember I don't have to worry about that anymore.

"You know what? I think I will have one, for once I don't have to worry about what my dad will say when I come home. Maybe I'll get drunk for once, who knows." He laughs. "Don't worry, Snowflake, you're safe with me, no matter what you decide to do, I'll protect you, love."

I pause and look up at him as his face turns bright red from embarrassment and he instantly changes the subject. "Cherry vodka and Sprite, right?" he asks, and it makes me smile.

"You remembered?" I know it's an easy drink, but I'm still kind of shocked that he cared enough to remember what my favorite drink was, especially with all the drama that had happened that night.

"When a girl comes in here who instantly takes my breath away from how gorgeous she is, then you think about her non-stop for the next week until you see her again, it's kinda hard not to forget the little details like that." My heart stops for a second, did he really mean all of?

"You're amazing, Carsten." He has been nothing but amazing since meeting him and I'm thankful that I'm lucky enough to get this side of him.

"You're quite amazing yourself, Snowflake." He comes around the bar handing me my drink. He turns the stool and stands between my legs, his muscular arms come around my waist, pulling me closer to him as he puts his fingers under my chin lifting my head up and leans down to kiss me.

"Are you sure she's not your girlfriend, Carsten." I jump away when I hear his mom ask the question, embarrassed that she saw us kissing.

"Not yet Mom, but I'm thinking soon. I'm not stupid enough to let her get away." He looks over at her. "Sorry, I'll get back to work." He gives her an apologetic look.

"No, take the night off. Seriously, I'll cover for you. You two just hang out and enjoy yourselves." She tells him as she picks stuff up and wipes off the counter to the bar.

"How about I tell you what I told Chase—if you need the extra help, I'm here," he says.

"Sounds perfect. God, you guys are adorable together." She smiles, leaning over the bar, her hands under her chin holding her head up. "How long have you guys known each other?"

"Umm... I think about two or three weeks, but it feels like a lifetime," Carsten says, smiling over at me with this look in his eyes that I can't quite figure out what it is.

She doesn't speak, she just smiles at us for a few minutes and walks away. I wonder if it's possible to love someone you just met, you know like in movies—love at first sight, I've never experienced it before, so maybe it's just the newness of getting to know each other that I'm confusing with love. Or maybe I'm just scared, scared of being hurt again. So, I'm denying that that's what this could be.

25

CARSTEN

"Give me about five more minutes to help them babe and I'll be done for a while, unless it gets slammed, and they end up needing me," I tell her, carrying boxes behind the counter to unload this weekend.

"That's fine, handsome, take your time. No need to rush, we have the whole night to hang out," she says to me with a relaxed smile on her face. She's already done with her first drink, and you can tell it's helped melt away some stress and loosen her up enough to have some fun tonight. In fact, I feel like it's the first time since I met her where she is truly relaxed and isn't hiding a smile over a scared face. I haven't known her for long but even the first night I met her it was like she kept looking over her shoulder, scared, waiting for something to happen. I'm hoping that is finally over now that she is no longer living with her dad.

I'm excited to be out with a girl I like. Sure, I've been out with girls before, and this isn't anything fancy. But I'm excited to get to know her, to be around her, to eventually have something more than just sex for once. I don't know what it is about her, but she makes my fucking heart skip beats, I'm falling for this gorgeous girl, with this awesome personality, and for once I'm completely ok with that.

I walk up behind her about ten minutes later, it took a little longer than I had expected but we're done, and the bar is finally open. I slowly wrap my arms around her waist. "Oh my god, Carsten, you scared me." I lean down to kiss her cheek and then lay my head on her shoulder.

"Sorry, Snowflake. I just couldn't wait to get over here and kiss you." I place soft, slow kisses across her jaw, making her shiver with each kiss, a sexy smirk growing across her face. She closes her eyes as I start to kiss right below her ear, I can feel a soft moan vibrate against my lips, sending a jolt of excitement to my already half hard cock.

She turns around wrapping her arms around my waist, placing her chin on my chest looking up at me. "I couldn't wait for you to come over here so I could kiss you too." She grabs my shirt and pulls me down into her for a kiss. I kiss her gently at first, then with a little more need, a slight moan sliding out of her mouth, which causes me to groan.

"God, Snowflake," I growl. "I just don't know what it is, I can't get enough of you." She kisses me again, this time pulling in my bottom lip and sucking on it before biting it softly.

"Wanna take a shot together?" She asks, which I'm not sure I should, since I have to drive, and I might have to work. She continues talking, not waiting for a response. "To celebrate... Hmmm." She taps her finger on her chin. "Us meeting each other." She smiles a cute smile; I think she's slightly buzzed. Maybe I'll have a shot and a beer, we won't be leaving until later and I won't even catch a buzz from either of those.

"What kind of shot do you want to do my little Snowflake?" I lean in kissing her again. Man like I said before I think I could kiss her all day and never get sick of her perfectly pouty lips.

"Chasseeee." She drags out his name almost like she's singing.

"Yes, Winter." He laughs, shaking his head at her.

"Can your brother and I get a blowjob shot please?" And there it is, my half hard dick is fully aware of what is going on now and pushing against the fabric of my jeans.

"Well, you do know how this shot is done right?" He asks, laughing at me because he knows damn well, I'm not going to do it. "You have to keep your hands behind your back and take the shot with only your mouth holding the shot." He smiles again. Fucking asshole. He acts like he would happily do this shot. I mean I have no issues doing it if I weren't in fucking public. But nah, I'd rather watch Winter wrap her pink, plump lips around that glass and pretend it was my fucking cock between those sweet, sweet lips of hers as her tongue is licking up the rest of the glass, I'd like to pretend it was her sucking the rest of the cum out of my cock. That is why I don't want to take my chances with turning my head. My mind is too dirty and I'm too much of a guy to ignore these dirty thoughts and these dirty images of my little Snowflake that are in my mind.

"Oh yes, I'm fully aware of how it's done, that's why I want to do it, to see Carsten's blow job skills." Now he's cracking up.

"Ha. Ha. Ha fuckers, very funny. You go ahead and show me your blow job skills, Snowflake, but I'm good on that." Even though there aren't a ton of people in here yet, I'm still not trying to do that for people to see, even if it's just for fun. Chase goes to make the shots for us while Winter just smiles at me.

"The girls should be here soon, Emerald just texted me saying she was just waiting for Chastity and Saylor to get to her house and then they're leaving."

"Good, that way if you want to do blow job shots with anyone else you can do them with your friends." I laugh at her, smiling, and she pouts.

"Hey, no fair, I wanna do shots with you too." She pushes her bottom lip out more as she exaggerates her pout.

"I'll do maybe one more shot after this, but I gotta drive us home and I need to get the both of us there safely."

"Okay, we can always get an uber if you don't feel comfortable driving, I'll pay for it."

"First of all, no you wouldn't. And second, I'll be ok, don't you worry. Just relax, let loose, and have some fun babe, you deserve it.

Be a normal twenty-two-year-old for once." I kiss her right as Chase sets the shots down.

"Get a room you two, every time I look at you guys, you're kissing." He's joking, but part of me thinks he's serious, only because I know he's been looking for a girl.

"Shut up, you're just jealous," I say fucking with him, hoping I don't rub him the wrong way.

"Part of me is, but the other half knows I'll meet the girl of my dreams soon." He gives a half smile while tapping his fingers on the counter then walks away to go help other customers. Making me feel bad for my brother.

"Alright babe, show me whatcha..." And before I can finish what I'm saying she puts her hands behind her back, opens her mouth around the shot glass, then tips her head and takes the shot. Then sticks her tongue out and swirls it around the inside of the glass, cleaning out the rest of the shot. Holy. Shit. All I could think of was her on her knees, hands behind her back, and my hard dick sliding in and out of her warm, wet mouth.

Then she takes her finger and swipes some of the whip cream from my shot and sucks if off her finger, slowly and seductively with a look in her eyes that tells me she's ready to fuck me. My dicks probably going to break at this point. If it gets any harder, I'm gonna have to go take care of things myself. But then she stands up, pulls me down, again, by my shirt to kiss her, and then whispers in my ear "I need to suck your cock now, I see how hard you are and I wanna fix that for you, baby." She pulls away, biting her bottom lip. You can tell she's feeling shy, like she never spoke like this to anyone before. My eyes go wide and my mouth falls open slightly. This woman is going to kill me if she keeps it up with this dirty little mouth of hers. I kinda like this side of Winter. It's fucking sexy.

"Umm–" I choke out because I wasn't expecting that at all.

She pulls me down to her again so she can talk in my ear. "Please, Carsten, I need to taste your cock. I wanna feel your soft, silky cock against my tongue baby." She pauses and then smiles before going back to my ear, meanwhile my fucking cock is about to snap in half from how hard she has me. "I wanna feel you cum in my throat." I don't say anything, because I'm afraid whatever I say might come out mumbled, I feel like I don't know how to speak right now. Like I've never spoken to a girl or heard a girl say naughty things to me. I think she made me speechless.

The next thing I know I'm pulling her behind the bar, walking through the back room down the hall. I'm checking around as I go to make sure my mom isn't anywhere near, and I walk into my office. We each have our own office so I don't have to worry about anyone knocking. I shut and lock the door but keep the light off, pull the window blinds down on the door and the windows to my office and turn on my desk lamp. I turn around and pull her towards me and lean down to kiss her, she kisses me with hunger, moaning into my mouth. My god I am so fucking horny, I can't wait to feel my dick in her mouth. "Shit." Is all I can manage to get out. She pushes me down into my desk chair and starts quickly undoing my belt. I stare at her beautiful face as she watches me, she's breathing heavy, and that's all you hear in this room is our heavy breathing, both of us panting like we've already had sex. We don't take our eyes off each other, I feel like I'm glued to her, or afraid that if I blink she'll disappear.

26

WINTER

I UNDO HIS BELT AND UNBUCKLE HIS PANTS, THEN UNDO HIS zipper as he takes off his shirt. I can't take my eyes off of him. The look in his eyes is so sexy, it's turning me on and making my pussy wet. I push his boxers down and his hard cock stands at full attention, practically making me drool with how delicious it looks. He lifts his ass up and pushes his jeans and boxers down some. I get down on my knees right in front of his dick. "Fucking shit, Snowflake." He groans in a whisper. I look up at him and his eyes are heavy as they flutter from how turned on he is from me. I did this to him, I am the reason his cocks this rock fucking hard and something about that makes me feel so sexy and in control, making me feel desired and needed. Something I've never experienced before.

I lick my lips then grab his cock in my hand, I start moving my hand up and down his shaft, and he lets out a moan. It is so. Fucking. Sexy. The sound of a man moaning from the pleasure that you're responsible for. God, I just love it. I stick my tongue out and slowly swirl it around the head of his cock, then wrap my lips around it and suck, while swirling my tongue. "Fuckkkk, Snowflake." He growls and grabs the back of my head as I take his cock to the back of my throat. I start pumping him in and out of my mouth and sucking at the same time, his moans turning me on making my panties grow even more wet than they were when I started. "Goddddamn, baby girl, your mouth..." He throws his head back for a moment before looking back down at me. "Mmmm." His voice deep and raspy as I shove him back into my throat and make the movements with my mouth like I'm swallowing.

He's panting, his chest rising and falling quickly, his tattoos defining his muscles every time he breathes in, making me drool even more than I already am with his large cock filling up my mouth. I look up into his lust filled eyes and he's biting his bottom lip, dammit he's so sexy. I grip his cock with my hand again, my fingers barely closing around his thickness, and pump up and down while sucking his head, his hips move on their own, I don't even think he realizes he's doing it. He grips my hair a little tighter and moves his hand with my head, not forcing me to go faster, just going with what I'm doing. His body starts to move a little quicker. "Shit, Winter, I'm so close. Get ready to taste my cum, baby girl." And it makes me moan, because fuck was that hot. Although I think Carsten could make anything sound hot. But that right there was so. Fucking. Sexy.

"Mmm." The vibration of my moan sending him over the edge, his body stiffens a little as his warmness fills my throat, I keep sucking as it's coming out making sure to get all of it, groaning in the process from how turned on I am. I suck one last time and then open my mouth, swirling my tongue around his shaft to clean the rest of his cum off before I pull him out of my mouth and look up at him. His head is thrown back, eyes closed and he's panting.

"Fuck." He says in between breaths. Making the corner of my mouth curl up in a smile. I can't believe I just made him feel that good. I bring my hand up to wipe my mouth a little to hide the smirk some more.

"That. Felt. Fucking. Amazing, Snowflake." His voice is raspy and he's still out of breath. He finally looks down at me, smiling and pulls me to stand. "God, that was amazing." I bite my lip, I don't know what to say or how to respond. It suddenly makes me feel shy, yet even more excited that he loved it.

He pulls me into him to kiss him, then slowly pulls away. "I want your shorts and panties off. Now, Snowflake. I want you to sit on my hard cock and ride me." He groans, making his cock even harder from what he had just said. He starts unbuckling and undoing my zipper. I step out of my shorts as he pulls them down, then he pulls me onto him and into a kiss. Straddling his lap he swipes his fingers across my pussy. "Mmm." He moans. "So fucking wet, Snowflake. So. Fucking. Wet." Then he licks his fingers and starts sucking my wetness off of them. " I had a feeling your pussy was going to be soaked baby girl, especially with the way you were moaning while sucking my cock." He practically groans when he says the last part that's how much talking about me sucking his cock affects him now apparently. Not that I'm complaining.

"I can't wait to feel your pussy swallowing my cock, baby girl." He places his hands on my hips as he says it. Then I sink down onto his cock, throwing my head back in a moan as I grip his shoulders.

"Fuck, Carsten." Instant chills cover me from head to toe, as my body comes back up.

"Goddamn, you feel so fuuuccking good, Winter." He groans out gripping my love handles as I start moving up and down grinding into him, rotating my hips as I come down.

"Fuck, I love these. They are so fucking sexy." He pants, his thrusts matching mine, coming up right as I go down.

"Thank you, I hate them." I'm not sure why I said that right now during sex but it was the first thing that came to mind. "We'll save that for another day." I add in between breaths.

I decide to change the subject and start kissing him; he pushes me away in shock, his eyebrows scrunched, he's panting trying to find his words. "Goddamn, Winter. Don't say that about yourself, I already told you that's one of my favorite things about you." He crushes his mouth to mine, and I ride his cock faster. He slides his tongue into my mouth; we're both swallowing each other's moans, meeting each other halfway when I come down his body thrusts up deep inside me.

"I'm so close, Carsten." I moan out and he reaches down and starts massaging my clit with his thumb. My body starts to shake and his body starts to grow tight. His thrusts meet mine, rougher with each thrust, we both cum at the same time. He's gripping my hips, I'm gripping onto his shoulders, my nails digging into him while I grind into him finishing out our orgasms.

Both of us panting, covered in sweat, trying to catch our breath. I've never had sex feel this good before, or feel this comfortable letting loose in front of someone before, and I love it, I love that I can be this comfortable around him and be myself for once.

27

CARSTEN

I'M GOING TO CALL MYSELF A RETIRED MAN WHORE BECAUSE after the sex we just had, I don't think sex will ever be the same with anyone else. I've been around and I've never had sex this good. I've always felt like I had to go over the top to make sure I was impressing and pleasing the girl I was sleeping with, and with Winter I don't have to try, it just comes natural.

We both clean ourselves up and put our clothes back on. We both take a shot of my secret stash of whiskey I have hidden in my office before heading out. If I need to, Mom can give us a ride home or we can sleep on my air mattress I have tucked away for emergency drunken nights.

Winter finishes buckling her shorts and lets out a breath that seemed like she was holding in.

"What's wrong, Snowflake?" I ask, concerned. Hoping I didn't hurt her or do anything to trigger anything.

"Nothing, babe." Babe, I've been called babe before but coming from her stirs up something inside me that I just can't explain. "That just felt so good, now I'm sleepy." She laughs. "But I'm sure everyone is here and wondering where the hell we are." She puts her hand over her mouth almost as in 'oops I forgot where we were' kind of thing and we both start laughing.

"Oh well, they can keep wondering. They're at a bar, I'm sure they've found plenty of things to entertain themselves." I grab her hand as we walk out of my office and I shut the door behind me. "Let's go out to the patio for a bit before it gets crowded." I let go of her hand real quick and slap that juicy ass of hers making her let out a shriek and a giggle while she tries to squirm away from me. But I grip her hand again interlocking our fingers together. Her tiny hand getting lost in my large one.

"Ya, let's go see if everyone's here and if not we can just wait for them on the patio, they'll see us walking in." She looks over and up at me as she walks next to me, a smile on her gorgeous face and something about this just feels so normal, like we've been walking this walk together in life for quite some time and nothing about us is new. Fuck, what is going on with me? I can tell myself what's going on with me, I'm fucking obsessed. I want to eat, sleep, breathe, and live all things, Winter. There's nothing wrong with that right? Ha. I'm sure if I was talking to a therapist, they'd probably tell me I was crazy for wanting that much of one person, but even all of that that I just named. It still isn't enough of her.

We walk out from the back room and all our friends are right there at the bar, Chase is shaking his head. "That was some long quickie you guys had there." He laughs shaking his head in a joking way but still knowing exactly what we did.

"Hey man, I was wondering when you'd be joining us." Axton says, standing behind his girlfriend, his arms wrapped around her waist.

"Um excuse me, Winter?" Emerald says with her wiggling her eyebrows, or at least attempting to wiggle them. "And where were you young lady, huh?" Winter blushes and it's fucking adorable. That's another thing that'll probably never leave my list of things I love about her. Fuck, I'm not IN love with her. I... I don't think? Nah, it's too soon to love her right? It's just things I really like about her, so it means I love these things about her. What is my deal these days?

"She was helping me with something in my office, something I had to get done before the night was over." I say laughing, having a hard time making up a lie when everyone knows we just had amazing sex. Well they know we had sex but they don't know exactly how amazing it was.

"Ohh yeah, "needed help" with your dick, huh?" Creedence makes air quotes as he says that, like the dick he is.

"Shut the fuck up man, you're just jealous. Now let's stop talking about me and Snowflake's sex life and let's go get some drinks, they're on me." We all start heading outside as someone else starts talking.

"Oh. My. God. That is so fucking cute," a blonde girl says to Winter. "Is that what he calls you? You're so lucky to have such a cute nickname."

"Right, we all say the same thing." Everyone else kinda mumbles off.

"Yes, I love it." Winter blushes as she looks down since every-one's staring at her. "By the way, Chastity this is umm–" She pauses like she doesn't know how to introduce me. "Carsten, Carsten this is one of my best friends, Chastity."

"Nice to meet you, Chastity," Carsten says to her as he extends his hands out to hers, what a gentleman, making my stomach flutter from the act alone.

"Nice to meet you too, I've heard so much about you from both these girls here." She pulls her hand away as she moves her thumb back and forth between Emerald and Winter.

"Guys this is Saylor," Chastity introduces her friend to us after giving her our names.

"Nice to meet everyone. Who is that muscular Greek God over there again?" She says looking at Chase, who's jaw drops as he blushes. "Sorry, I tend to blurt things out when I'm drunk." She hiccupped, putting her hand over her mouth like even she was surprised the words came out. Her cheeks flush a little like suddenly her confidence disappeared, or maybe it's from the alcohol and I didn't notice I'm not sure. All I know is whatever she said made Chase forget how to speak.

"It... it's fine." He stutters before picking up his jaw. "I'm uhh, Chase." He walks over to her to shake her hand. With the cheesiest fucking grin on his face. Well I think Mr. Chase just might have met his dream girl. I'll have to remember to ask him how things went.

"So, what made you give her the nickname, Snowflake? Besides the obvious, her name being Winter." Chastity asks me with a smile on her face. Like a little kid staring into a candy store or her favorite toy store. That's the kind of excitement Chastity has on her face while she waits for an answer about something as simple as a nickname. Although to me it's more than just a nickname, it actually has meaning to me.

I look over at her and smirk. I can't get over her beauty. I look at her and feel like my heart stops or time stands still. Then I glance at them. "It's simple really." I step a little closer to her, pushing her hair behind her ear.

"No two snowflakes are exactly alike, she's so unique in so many different ways." I stand in front of her caging her in with my arms. "Winter is my favorite season, and so far, she's becoming my favorite person." I brush the hair away from her other ear, grazing her cheek, watching her shiver. She gulps hard, I don't hear it but I see it. "To me the snow is so beautiful and when it snows, every time I see it, it's like it's the first time. Every time I see my Snowflake, it's like the first time I've ever laid eyes on her, every. Single. Time," I end with a whisper, leaning in to kiss her.

"Holy shit," Creedence says. "I think I just fell in love with you, bro." His deep voice just above a whisper.

"Yeah, me too," everyone kind of mumbles to themselves.

"If you don't tell this girl you love her soon, then love doesn't exist anymore," Chastity says to me with a big smile on her face. Which it's all true, that's exactly how I feel about her.

28
WINTER

Holy shit. I feel like I can't breathe, or even swallow. My mouth is too dry to even try to swallow anyway. He leans in and kisses me as my stomach begins to flutter more. I can't believe he just said all of that to me, in front of my friends, in front of his friends.

Right as he pulls away from me, I see a girl walking up behind him, tapping his shoulder, she looks familiar, but I can't remember why.

"Carsten, what the fuck. I've been texting you for two weeks now, why are you ignoring me?" she says, crossing her arms after stomping her foot like a child.

"Brynn, hey." He says, sounding completely uninterested, annoyed if anything. Like she's the last person he wants to talk to.

"Well, this is awkward." Chase says, turning away a little almost like he's peeking over his shoulder like he's afraid to see what happens but doesn't want to miss it.

"How about we head back in for some drinks?" Creedence says, breaking the awkward silence, anything but talking to Brynn. Yep, I'd rather just walk away like we didn't see her, but she wouldn't allow that, she's too immature, too much of a child. She would follow Carsten like the psycho bitch she is. I know she just saw him kissing me. I don't know if she heard anything he said, I'm hoping she did though. But even then, I don't think she'd get the hint.

"Well, Carsten?" She comes up to him and wraps her arms around his neck trying to kiss him, but he pushes her off him. "Don't put your fucking hands on me. You can't just walk up to someone who wants nothing to do with you and act like everything is normal." He says in an angry tone.

"So, I'm gonna need you to stop, Brynn. I told you a couple fucking weeks ago that I wasn't interested anymore." Mmm, something about him being angry like this is sexy. Do I feel bad for her? Nope. Will I feel bad if he embarrasses her because she can't take a fucking hint and just leave him alone? Also, nope. Does that make me childish? Not sure, but do I care? Not. At. All.

"Well, what the fuck. I didn't think you were being serious, I thought what we had was different, baby. C'mon, Carsten. We can go back to my house and... well you know." She winks at him grabbing his hand trying to put his finger in her mouth.

"Brynn. If you could just leave me alone that would be fucking great." Then he grabs my hand and looks away from her like he wasn't just talking to her. Like he doesn't even see her. She scoffs, rolling her eyes. Clearly offended. But does he care? Nope, and that's one more thing I love about him, I don't mean it like I'm in love with him... yet. I think I could fall in love with him, Hell. Maybe I am in love with him. Now is not the time for this Winter, I think to myself trying to get myself back to what is currently going on.

I kind of wish he would've introduced me to her, but I felt like he didn't even acknowledge that I was here. Maybe he just didn't want to deal with her childish drama.

"Sorry about that babe, I didn't know she'd be here."

"It's ok, you can't control how she's going to act when she sees you."

We start walking towards the bar when the song 'One Man Band' by Old Dominion starts playing.

"Oh my god." I shriek.

"What's wrong, Snowflake?" He asks concerned.

"I love this song." As I get out the sentence, he grabs my hand pulling me to the dance floor.

"This is one of my favorite songs." He says to me. "Dance with me."

He grabs my right hand with his, putting his left hand on the small of my back. He pulls me close to him and I close my eyes, laying my head on his chest as he sings the song to me quietly in my ear. After the song is over, he leans down and kisses me softly, slowly moving his tongue into my mouth.

"Hey, Carsten, sorry to interrupt. Mom said she needs you quickly." Chase comes up from behind him and tells him.

"I'll be right back, gorgeous." He kisses me one last time and pulls away.

"You know he's not really into you right?" I turn and see Brynn standing behind me with another girl, both standing with their arms crossed. Almost like a scene from a movie, it's quite comical honestly. It's hard not to laugh at them.

"Why do you say that?" I ask nervously, hoping she doesn't know something I don't, thinking she's just saying it to be a bitch.

"He does this to every girl he sleeps with. Makes you think he really likes you, makes you fall for him." She snarls and looks away as she talks almost like she'll catch a disease if she's caught looking at me any longer.

I cut her off, not wanting to hear anything else she has to say. "That's not true. Now if you'd just leave me alone, I have nothing to do with him breaking things off with you."

"You're not even that pretty either, I don't know what he sees in you. You're nasty." She says, laughing while roughly shouldering me on her way by. By the time she's fully out of sight I have tears in my eyes as Carsten walks back over.

He looks down at me with worry in his eyes. "Snowflake?" My tears fall and he wipes them as quickly as they drop with his big, calloused thumb.

"What's wrong, baby girl? Did something happen when I walked away?"

"No." I pause for a second not wanting to start unnecessary drama. "It's ok, I'm fine." He follows my eyes and sees me staring at Brynn. She's standing across the room pointing in my direction, laughing. From where she stands you can't see that Carsten is standing next to me, so it just looks like I'm standing here alone, crying.

"What the fuck happened, babe? What did Brynn do?" he asks, wrapping his arms around my waist. "Please talk to me."

I sigh. "It was nothing, Carsten. Don't worry about it. I actually think I'm gonna be headed home soon." I'm over the bullshit of Brynn. I don't know why she has to be such a nasty bitch to me because Carsten doesn't want her. It's not my fault she's an ugly person inside and out.

"Winter, you need to tell me what she did or said, please?"

"She told me you're not really into me. That you're messing with me to make me think you like me, to make me fall for you. That you do this to all the girls you talk to. She told me that I wasn't pretty." I can't believe I'm crying right now in the middle of the fucking bar. "She told me I'm nasty and she doesn't know what you see in me."

"What the fuck, that stupid bitch. I'm so sorry, babe. None of that is true. Seriously, she's just pissed because I broke things off with her and now, I'm seeing you."

"Carsten, it's ok. You don't have to explain it to me." He grabs my hand and starts pulling me towards Brynn and her friends.

"What the fuck did you say to my girlfriend." My eyes widen and I look over at him, the same time her eyes widen and her jaw drops.

"Your girlfriend?" she says in shock like she's pissed. "Since when do you date?"

"Since I met her and started falling in love with her. That is when I started dating Winter, Brynn." He says her name in an angry tone.

"I didn't say anything to her, I just walked past her, that was it."

She rolls her eyes. "I can't believe this." She waves her hands up and down.

"This what, Brynn?"

"The fact that you're dating her." She looks at him with disgust.

"What the fuck is that supposed to mean?" He balls his fists up in anger at his sides. And I'm sure she's fucking lucky that she's a girl right now because I'm sure if she wasn't Carsten would be kicking her ass.

"It means—that how could you be attracted to something like that, after having someone as attractive as I am." She looks over at me and smirks.

He walks up to her, getting in her face. "Don't talk about her like that. Now I want to know what you said to her when you stopped and talked to her."

So, I speak up because I'm tired of Brynn's bullshit. "Just forget it, Carsten. She's not worth it, let's just go back outside with our friends."

He looks from me to her. "Brynn, you will never be anything or anyone better than this gorgeous girl right here." He pulls me to him, wrapping his arm around my waist. "That's why I'm with her and why she's my girlfriend, not you." Then he grabs my hand and has me follow him back outside. As we're walking away, I glance back behind my shoulder, smiling when I see how pissed off Brynn is.

29

CARSTEN

WE'RE BACK OUTSIDE ON THE PATIO, AS IT'S GETTING crowded inside, we decided to come back out for more fresh air when Chase reminds me of the fire we planned tomorrow night that I completely forgot about. Honestly, I'm not really in the mood for it, I'd rather hang out with Winter, but it's too late to tell everyone that we're canceling it so I'll just go with it.

"What's everyone talking about?" I ask as we join the conversation after coming back outside from going off on Brynn.

"The party tomorrow night, remember, bonfire, backyard party." Chase looks over at me as he says it.

"Fuck, I forgot about that. We invited a lot of people too," Axton says to us as he looks over at his girlfriend who looks very unhappy.

"Yep, it's our end of summer party we do every year." I sigh dreading it. It's fun but sometimes too many people show up and it becomes annoying.

"It shouldn't even be an end of summer party at this point, fall came early this year with how shitty our weather is, it'll be snowing by Halloween." Creedence shakes his head with a disappointed look on his face.

"Right, the weather sucks this time of year." I look over at Winter and her friends "You guys are invited too, just so you know, it starts around nine at night, but come whenever."

"Awesome, we'll be there." Emerald responds for her and her friends, without even asking them if they want to go, but none of them speak up and tell her no so I guess we just invited four more people. Not that I care, as long as Winter is there, that's all I care about. I wouldn't even be mad just hanging out inside with here and avoiding the party, that's how much I'd rather be around her and how much I'm not in the mood for partying.

"Is that cool with you?" I look down at Winter, talking quietly so no one can hear me just in case she's uncomfortable going, I don't want her to feel forced.

"Yeah, that sounds perfect. I'd be happy to come, especially since you'll be there. I love spending time with my *boyfriend*." She gives me a look like what the hell. But it's not a bad look, a confused one especially since I called her my girlfriend without properly asking her to be my girlfriend. Oh well, she doesn't seem to upset by it. Maybe that'll give me the push I need to ask her to officially be my girlfriend. But I don't think I want to wait anymore, what's the point of waiting we both know that we're interested in each other, why stop it from progressing.

"Ha. Ha," I say, thinking she's messing with me. "So, you aren't mad I called you my girlfriend to Brynn? Without officially asking you first?" I say to her, because I want to make sure it didn't upset her at all. Not that I truly care, not in a dick head way either, she's going to be mine either way is what I mean. Whether it's now or in a week. She's not going anywhere; I won't let her. Not anymore, it's too late. I'm already invested and no one else can have my little Snowflake.

"No, I wasn't upset at all." She leans her head against my arm, hugging it with both of her small arms hugging around my arm. I love how small she is next to me.

"So then, does that mean you're my girlfriend now?" I ask,

double-checking because I've never done this or cared about doing this before.

"If you wanna be my boyfriend, then I'd love to be your girl-friend." She looks down blushing. A little giggle escaping her lips.

"Damn, I have a girlfriend and she's coming to my party as my girl," I say as she laughs at me. I never thought I'd see the day where I finally had a girlfriend. Or be excited to actually have a girl to call mine.

"You're funny, I love how cute you are right now because I want to be your girlfriend." I lean down putting my fingers under her chin and softly kiss her lips.

"How about we get out of here and go to my place to watch a movie?" I ask, not really in the mood to be here anymore when I'd rather be spending time with her.

"Sounds perfect to me, I'm getting cold so I'm gonna change at my place first then I'll head over to you." She shivers a little as the wind blows around us. It's still pretty warm for this time of year. But the temperature has been dropping a lot at night so it's starting to get pretty cold.

"You won't need any clothes in my bed, I promise to make sure to keep you warm." I lean down whispering in her ear. Fuck, I can't wait to get home now and have her in my bed with me.

"I'll take you up on that offer if you pinky promise to keep me warm." She giggles, sticking her pinky out and just like that, I feel like a little kid again reaching my pinky around hers.

30

WINTER

THE NEXT DAY I SPEND MOST OF MY TIME UNPACKING THE rest of my boxes so I can finally be done, I'm sick of unpacking. Plus, I need to find the rest of my clothes so I can pick out a cute outfit for the party tonight. I know it'll be somewhat chilly, so I have the perfect idea in mind.

I decide to head downstairs to make some lunch and see what Emerald is up to since I haven't seen her yet today. It's nice living with her, she's one friend I don't think I'd ever get sick of being around.

"Hey, babe." She greets as I walk down the stairs, a big smile on her face. She has a natural beauty to her; she doesn't have to worry about covering her face in a bunch of makeup. She's one of those girls that could get away with leaving the house with nothing on her face, or even a little mascara and still look just as beautiful.

"Hey, lover." I say laughing to her. We've always had little nicknames or talked to each other like we're into each other. It started when we were old enough to go places alone. When we'd go to the mall, or dinner, pretty much anywhere if we didn't want a guy hitting on us, we'd act like we were a couple. It was our thing to protect each other from creepy men.

"What are you up to? Are you hungry, I was just about to make some grilled cheese sandwiches, do you want one?" She asks me knowing I love grilled cheese. It was one of the easy things we loved to make as kids. Something we both could make without fucking up, and another thing our parents trusted us cooking. At least her parents did. We stayed at her house more than mine, especially after Mom passed.

"Oh! I haven't had grilled cheese in so long, I'd love one." I say excited like a little kid excited for candy. My stomach growling from the smell of her already cooking them.

"What are you wearing to the party tonight?" I ask her curious to see how she'll dress. I haven't been to a party in so long I'm not even sure I know how to dress for one anymore.

"Probably some jean shorts and a crop top with a zip up hoodie in case I get cold. Cute but comfortable, I don't need to impress anyone, I'm not looking for a man." she says waving her hand like it's no big deal. "What about you?" She bites a piece of cheese that she's holding in her one hand while holding the spatula in the other hand.

"I'm gonna wear a crop top, with black fishnets, ripped jean shorts, my hot pink converse, and a hoodie in case I get cold." I say laughing because we are so much alike and somehow always pick similar outfits without even planning it. But then when we do go places everyone assumes that our somewhat matching outfits were planned.

"Oh my god, we need to stop doing this." She laughs. "But like, not stop doing it at the same time. I can't believe we always end up dressing alike without even planning it." Even through high school our friends thought we planned our outfits together because we'd always end up matching somehow. I guess that's another thing we have in common. We're so much a like that we even dress similar.

"I swear you sneak into my closet when I'm picking out my clothes so you can pick something similar." She snorts, flipping the grilled cheese over in the pan. A pleased look on her face when she sees the bread is toasted perfectly.

"If I had time, I probably would just say fuck it and let's plan matching clothes, but since I don't have time, our minds just do it for us." She pauses. "You would think that we shopped together all the time and purposely bought matching clothes." It's true, we do go shopping together, but we end up buying more things that match when we're not together than when we are together, it's pretty funny.

"I love you, Emerald, thank you for being my best friend." I hug her and steal the grilled cheese off the plate that she had just sat down next to her, it was probably mine anyways since she always makes her food last, but I run away just in case she decides to chase me and smack my ass with the spatula she's cooking with.

"Girl, you're lucky that was for you anyways, bitch, and I love you too. I'm glad I have you as my bestie." She sets the spatula on the counter and turns around placing her hands in the air like a truce.

After we finish eating lunch I go back upstairs to lay down for a little bit before showering. I decide to check my phone when I see I have a text from Carsten.

Carsten
miss you snowflake

Me
miss you too handsome devil

Carsten
What r u up to babe?

Me
laying down, I need to shower but I'm lazy lol

Carsten
Can I join u for the shower? We'll save water
that way.

Me
u perv, no.

Carsten
lol y not, I'll behave?

Me
do u ever behave though?

Carsten
ur right, I don't lol

Me
see I know u so well

Carsten
fine can I join, I won't behave

Me
lol no but I'll make up for it tonight?

Carsten
sounds perfect , what time u headed over? U can
come early

Me
I'm sorry I can't but I'll probably be there around
9:30

Carsten
damn, I'll miss you until you're here

Me
I'll miss you too handsome

I decide I need to get up before I fall asleep and head to the shower so I can make myself look hot for him. I want to do my makeup for the first time since I've moved in. I haven't bcen able to from my swollen eye and now that the swelling is gone, I can look like a normal person for once.

Me
headed to the shower now, I'll think about you ;)

Carsten
please do

I set my outfit out on the bed and look at the time before heading to the bathroom so I can see how much time I have to get ready. I can be there at nine, but I don't want to be early. I want to make him miss me so I'm showing up a half hour late, along with Emerald. I want him to be excited to see me, not that he wouldn't be if I showed up early. But I just want him to miss me and feel what it's like to be missed by someone who cares about you.

After my shower I stand in my towel and do my makeup, while waiting for my hair to air dry some more before I blow dry it. I decided to go for a smokey eye with cat-eye eyeliner, and I take my time doing it so I can make sure it looks sexy. I blow dry my hair and decide to wear it down. That way I have the option to put it up later if I need to. After putting my clothes on I check the time and it's nine-fifteen. Perfect, almost ready to go when Em knocks on my door.

"Knock, knock, bitch." Emerald barges through my door, thankfully I'm dressed. Not that she hasn't accidentally seen my boobs or other body parts over there years of our crazy friendship.

"Come in, hoe," I say standing in the mirror checking out my outfit, adjusting my fishnets around my waist.

"Holy shit, girl, you look fucking hot!" She whistles after saying it. I look at her through my full-length mirror in time to see her eyebrows wiggling up and down as she whistles.

"Thanks, that's kind of the look I was going for tonight. You look fucking hot too, bitch." I say putting my hands on my hips looking her up and down. Yep, we practically have matching outfits.

"Thanks, boo." She says, blowing me a kiss. "Now are you ready for your boyfriend to see your fine ass?" She slaps my ass as she says it, making me yelp. "And drool over how fucking good you look."

"Excuse you, that's my ass bitch! Yeah, I'm ready, let me just grab my phone and we can head next door." I walk over to my nightstand removing my phone from the charger, not really sure why I even care to have it since everyone I talk to is going to be with me.

"Oh yeah, I need to go grab mine too. I'll meet you in the

kitchen." She says rushing out my door. She hates being late to anything even if it's parties, she's usually early like a weirdo.

Walking through the gate to Carsten's backyard the first two people I see are Chase and Creedence.

"Hey, Snow. Damn you're looking hot tonight." Chase walks towards me and greets me with a hug. It's funny that he practically hits on me, but I think at this point he does it to fuck with Carsten. Not that it bothers me, I know he's just joking when he does it. It's funny, especially watching Carsten's reactions every time he does it.

"Hey yourself, and thank you, how's it going?" I ask him, hugging him back. It's always a quick pat on the back but never awkward. It's like he's family, it feels like I've known Carsten, Chase, and all their friends for a long time. I never had to go through the awkward part of meeting friends, because they never felt like strangers.

"It's going, Carsten wouldn't shut up about you at all today." I try not to laugh because it makes me feel giddy that he hasn't stopped talking, but I bite the side of my lip instead, trying to hold back this nerdy smile that's trying to escape. "Winter this, Snowflake that, like a teenager talking about his first crush." He tries to pretend like he's annoyed by it but you can clearly see he's happy for his brother.

"What? Shut up, no he wasn't." I say in denial, because I think he's fucking with me. Part of me prays he's not, because I've never had someone so into me before and I'm not going to lie, I kinda like it.

"Hey, Winter." Creedence hugs me and I hug him back.

"Hey there, is he lying to me about Carsten talking about me all day? I feel like he's fucking with me." Creedence will tell me the truth. I know he doesn't want me to be excited for nothing if it's not true. But something tells me Chase isn't fucking with me, and it makes my stomach flutter in ways I've never experienced before.

"No, he's not fucking with you for once. The guy was talking about you non-stop. I've never seen him talk about a girl so much in my life, but it's nice to see him happy." He pats me on the back, the smile on his face is a real smile for his friend, like he's finally happy that his friend has someone. He and Carsten are close like Emerald and me. They've known each other for forever. Practically family at this point.

"Where is he anyway? I'm surprised to see he isn't attached to you guys like normal." They're usually together. So, to see him somewhere else that Creedence, or even Chase isn't is very odd.

"Don't make fun of our bromance," Creedence says dramatically, the look on his face like he's truly offended while he's trying to hold in a laugh and keep the smile off his face.

"So sorry, I only make fun of you guys in a joking way, it's cute. I am one hundred percent for your bromance." I pat his shoulder in reassurance.

"I know, everyone loves our bromance." He chuckles a little. "Anyways, he's further back in the yard talking to some guys we haven't seen in a while. I think he's on the picnic table sitting." He points his thumb in the direction he's talking about, his hand balled in a fist as he does.

"Thanks guys, I'll see you later." I wave to them as I start walking towards the direction of the picnic table, my heart racing from excitement, my stomach flutters the closer I get to him, and it takes everything in me not to pick up my pace and run to him.

"See you." They both say and wave as they go back to what they were doing before I walked up to them. Some kind of yard game, I'm not exactly sure.

I start walking further into the back yard, I lost Emerald the minute I got here, she said hi to Creedence and Chase and then stayed by Creedence when I left. I think they have a thing for each other. I always end up losing her to talking to him. Not that I'm complaining, I think it would be great if they ended up together. As I walk a little further, I end up running into their other roommate, who I still don't know his name and I'm assuming his girlfriend and stop to talk to them.

"Hey guys, how's it going?" I ask, a smile on my face. I'm going to ask his freaking name this time because I can't keep referring to him as the nameless roommate.

"Hey Winter, we're doing good, how are you?" He asks me, wrapping his arm around the girl's waist and pulling her to sit on his lap in the chair that he's sitting in.

"I've been doing pretty good. This is a huge party, you weren't lying when you said you guys invited a lot of people, this is awesome." I look around, thankful it's inside and out, because if the party was just inside, I'd probably leave from how many people are here. "By the way, this is rude, but I never caught your name. Carsten never introduced us, and I just keep calling you the nameless roommate." I laugh a little, feeling awkward especially with his girlfriend here, I don't want her to think I'm interested in him.

"Well shit, I'm sorry." He holds his hand out to shake mine as he says "I'm Axton, and this is Daisy, my girlfriend." He continues to shake my hand as Daisy just gives me "the eye" like I better back off her man. Don't worry sweetie, he's not my type. My type is sitting on a picnic table waiting for me. And I can't wait to see him.

"Well, it's nice to officially meet you." I chuckle, dropping his hand and not even bothering to say anything to his girlfriend who, no offense, seems like a total bitch. She didn't even say anything when he introduced her. *That's just fine sweetie, I didn't want to know your name anyways,* I think to myself. Feeling proud for the internal argument we just had where I had the balls to be a bitch to her.

"I can't believe how many people actually showed up, we were expecting people to forget." He pauses for a second wrapping his arms around Daisy's waist and pulling her closer. "Carsten's back there by the fire sitting on the picnic table." He points the same way Creedence did, fist balled, and thumb pointed in the direction he's apparently sitting.

"Thanks, I'll see you guys later." I walk off a little quicker this time, ready to get away from bitchy Daisy. He seems too nice for her.

I finally make my way over to Carsten and he looks super sexy in his dark ripped jeans with his white T-shirt that's hugging his muscular, tattooed arms and chest just right. His light-brown hair—messy like he's been running his finger through it—and his beard is perfectly in place. I'm practically drooling just looking at my boyfriend. Boyfriend, looking at him and thinking he's all mine, makes my pussy wet and my heart flutter. God I'm so fucked up.

"Hey, Snowflake, get your ass over here gorgeous." He's buzzed I think, which is fine, I've just never seen him drink more than one or two beers. He pulls me to him and instantly buries his face into my neck, sending a chill through my body as he breathes me in. "Mmm, baaaby girllll," he drags out a little, I think from the alcohol. It's sexy, that's one thing I know for certain. "You look and smell so fuuucking. Delicious. Seriously that outfit is fucking sexy." He pulls away wrapping his hands back around my waist but under my unzipped, oversized zip-up hoodie that I have on.

"Hey there, handsome devil." I move my head to give him a kiss. Then move my head back a little, to appreciate how good he looks a little more. "Carsten, you look fucking hot." I giggle, feeling a little confident from his compliments, not holding back this time. I hug him tight and breathe him in, he always smells like musk and mint, it's something I could smell all day and never get sick of.

He pulls me back to him and starts kissing me again, swiping his tongue across my lips for me to open. I stick my tongue into his mouth, swirling mine around his before sucking on his bottom lip, then gently biting it as I pull away, making him growl. It's something I know that drives him crazy and I love to do it to him. "Goddamn, always torturing me and making my dick hard." He starts squeezing my ass and stops before slowly going down lower, sliding his fingers up my shorts over my tights. "Mmm, baby girl, your soft fucking skin, I could rub this all day. Even through these holy things." His voice deep and rough.

I giggle a little, he always makes me feel so giddy, I don't know why. "These holy things are fishnets," I whisper back, not even sure why we're whispering in a loud crowd of people and music, but something about our closeness and us whispering together makes the moment seem a little more intimate. "And I'm sorry babe, you know I'll take care of it later." I wink at him biting my lower lip. He always turns me on so much, making my thighs tighten and my panties wet. I can't wait to feel him inside me later. Just the thought of the way he feels inside me sends a chill through my body.

"I'm thirsty. I'm gonna go find Emerald really quick and make a drink. I'll be right back. Do you want anything?" I ask him but he pulls up a red solo cup and shows me he's already got a drink in it.

"I'm good, Snowflake, I have mine right here. But hurry back, I'm already missing you and those pouty lips of yours."

"I will, don't worry." I smile walking backwards as I talk. I place my hands in my butt pockets, it's a habit, something I've been doing for as long as I can remember. It's hard to turn away from him. I feel like if I blink, he'll disappear. Plus, if I turn away, I won't get to stare at his handsome face. But the quicker I get there the faster I'll be back next to him. So, I blow him a kiss, he catches it and places it to his heart and I turn. Keeping my cheesy grin hidden to myself as I do.

I spot Emerald and start walking in her direction, once I get to her, we lock our arms together and we head inside making our Cherry vodka and Sprite mixed drinks before heading back out towards the fire. Creedence said he'd wait for us back there.

As I'm walking towards the picnic table, I see a guy sitting where Carsten was with a blonde girl between his legs. She has her arms over his shoulders, and it looks like she's whispering in his ear, but he doesn't seem too interested. I'm looking around for Carsten since he obviously got up in the time it took me to find Emerald and for us to make our drinks. But as I glance back at the picnic table the guy who is with the blonde pulls away from her long enough to laugh and go back to her ear to talk some more and I instantly feel sick. I drop my drink and Emerald stops walking right in her tracks to look back at me.

"Shit, do we gotta go back now since you dropped your drink? Not even drunk yet and spilling things, Snow." She laughs until she sees my face. My hands are shaking, and I feel like I'm going to puke. I swallow the vomit that's trying to creep up my throat and take a step back.

"I...I can't believe what I'm seeing," I say as Emerald looks from me to the picnic table and her jaw drops.

"Is that ... Carsten with Brynn?" she says in an angry, disgusted voice.

"That's exactly what it looks like to me, what the fuck?" Tears instantly fill my eyes and suddenly I don't want to be here anymore. I don't even want to wait for a lie from him as to why he was hugging Brynn and whispering in her ear.

"I'm leaving." I go to turn and see Carsten look my way, his face falls and he jumps up after pushing Brynn off him. She falls backwards on the ground looking up at him in shock.

"What the fuck was that for?" You hear her shriek out. But I turn and start running for the gate. Not caring that there are tons of people standing around staring, wondering why the crazy girl with pink and purple hair is running like she's about to be fucking murdered, looking around like should they run too.

I don't even stop as I hear Carsten yell my name. I don't want to hear his lies or excuses. I keep running as I hear Axton ask me if I'm ok, and same when Chase tries to stop me. I'm so fucking stupid to think that he was different from any other man I've been with. I thought maybe we had something. But apparently when he told Brynn he was falling in love with me it was all just a lie to make her jealous. All it took was me walking away to get a drink for him to let her throw herself at him. The fact that he was letting her hug him, and he was whispering in her ear, I'm so stupid. I thought things were going to be different, but no, it seems that nothing about him changed. I was just another stupid girl who fell for the wrong guy.

I don't stop, I keep running all the way to my house and up the front porch. I open the front door slamming it shut as I see Carsten running up the stairs behind me. I slam the front door shut and slide down to the floor to sit down. I stop wiping away my tears, smudging my makeup all over my face, I slowly lay down onto my side in a fetal position, hug myself tight with my arms and just cry. I let out the pain, the emotions and everything I am feeling right now. Everything—I don't want to feel anymore. I don't want to feel anything that has to do with feeling things for Carsten. I don't want to remember what it was like to possibly love him. Because how fucking stupid am I? I thought a girl like me could change him, that he would want to be different for me. But I guess I just wasn't enough and that just sucks, it breaks my fucking heart to feel this pain.

31

CARSTEN

I'M WAITING FOR WINTER AND EMERALD TO COME BACK with their drinks when I see a familiar face walking towards me. I'm pretty buzzed and not in the mood for her bullshit. I just want to have a good time with my girlfriend, but she ruins that instantly.

"Hey there Carsten, are you finally done ignoring me?" she says, wrapping her arms around my neck, resting them on my shoulders in the process.

"What do you want Brynn? I already told you to leave me alone when I told you off the other day." I make sure to keep my voice monotone, uninterested. Hoping she'll get the hint and just leave. But she's Brynn, it could be staring her in the face, and I don't think she'd understand.

"C'mon Carsten, you know we have chemistry and that you can't keep running from me." She's leaning into my ear now whispering, and I try shoving her away, but she doesn't budge.

"Brynn, no man is going to want a desperate whore like you." My friends laugh around me as I say it next to her ear where it looks like I'm about to whisper but I don't. Although who am I to talk, I'm a whore myself. It honestly doesn't bother me that Brynn sleeps around. If a girl wants to sleep around and not have a boyfriend, good for her. If a girl doesn't want to sleep around and have a long-term relationship, good for her. I just don't like the person she is now; I didn't realize how much of a nasty bitch she is.

"I thought you got the hint the other day when I told you I was with Winter, that she is my fucking girlfriend. Oh yeah, and that I am falling in love with her." I say loud and clear into her ear so she can't even tell me I didn't tell her that. She backs away long enough to reposition herself, but right as she backs away, I catch a glimpse of Winter standing there, her drink falling to the ground. "Fucking shit man," I say pushing Brynn off me as she falls to the ground. "Goddamn Brynn, why did you fucking do that you bitch." I usually don't like to call women names unless they really fucking piss me off and goddamn this fucking woman pissed me the fuck off. I'm livid, I can feel my body heat up as my blood pressure rises. I tighten my fists into a ball as my heart feels like it's about to explode right out of my fucking chest. I can't lose this girl; I cannot fucking lose her. She is everything to me, my world, the fucking air in my lungs, the blood in my fucking veins, the reason I am living. Because without her, I am nothing. Without her I can't breathe, without her my heart simply cannot beat. I think, fuck dude, I think I just fucked up the most important thing in my life. Fuck everything else right now. I need her.

"What? Someone had to show her that you have feelings for me, and I knew it wasn't going to be you unless it was me showing her with you right in her face." She pauses, smiling. "It's about time you realize you're in love with me and stop denying it," she says in this disgusting attempt at a seductive voice, the look on her face is an attempt at being sexy but it's the furthest thing from sexy. Her face makes me angry and what she just said even angrier.

"Brynn, I don't fucking love you, get it through your fucking head. I will never love you." I'm so fucking irritated and frustrated. I need to fucking hit something, punch a wall, hit someone in the face. Something. But I can't, I need to go after Winter.

"Winter wait, wait up Snowflake, let me explain," I yell after her trying to get her to stop but she just keeps running. I chase her all the way to her front door where she slams the door in my face and I turn around to an angry Emerald crossing her arms over her chest, with the scariest—yes, I said scary, she's scary when she's angry. She has this pissed off look on her face and right now I feel like I should hide or something before she comes swinging. Fuck she's scary.

"What the fuck was that Carsten?" she yells at me, coming at me, arms raised like she's going to hit me. She yells in this loud, scary tone, like that tone your mother gets with you when you know you fucked up.

"It's not what it looked like, I swear to God, you can even ask my friends. I leaned in so she heard me tell her loud and clear that I was falling in love with Winter. I swear Emerald. I would never do anything to hurt her." I say sighing, running my hands through my hair in frustration trying not to flip the fuck out, because I'm afraid if I do then it'll make me look fucking crazy. I mean I am crazy I'm absolutely losing it right now not being able to talk to her and explain myself or be near her and just fucking touch her. That's all I want, and I just fucked it up.

"You... you said what?" She says, her jaw hanging open, eyes wide in shock. She doesn't look so scary now that she's calmed down some. Her small frame backing away from me a little.

"I told her that I thought she got the hint the other day when I told her, with Winter standing next to me, that I was falling in love with her. It's true, the minute I laid eyes on her I knew something was different. I've never seen anyone like her before, she's the most gorgeous person I've ever seen." I zone out saying this to her, thinking about the pain Winter must be feeling right now, alone in her house with me standing right outside her door while her heart is being torn right out of her body, and she's taking my heart right along with hers. Just ripping it right out of my fucking chest. I won't stop until I get her back. I need to get her back. She's mine and I refuse to let anyone else think they have a chance with what's mine.

"Why didn't you tell her that?" she asks, still in shock, trying not to smile about what I had just said.

"I was running after her to tell her, but she slammed the door in my face, she wouldn't stop to listen and now I've fucking fucked up." I'm so fucking stupid, if I were home right now, which it's a good thing I'm not, I probably would've punched multiple holes in the walls by now. I can't believe Brynn and her fucking bullshit; she just can't be happy until she fucks things up.

"Maybe just give her a day or two to cool down and then try talking to her again." Emerald has a sympathetic look on her face. You can tell she feels bad for being angry at me, and she feels bad for what just happened, but she also knows she can't do anything to help fix it, this is just between the two of us—Carsten and Winter.

"That's the thing, I don't want to give her time, I need her to understand what was going on and what I was doing. I would never cheat on her." Just the thought of cheating on Winter makes me sick to my stomach, makes my anxiety rise like crazy.

"Winter is usually the type of person who needs time to think or cool down before talking to someone when she's angry, it sucks, but you need to give her a couple of days. I'm sorry," she says, giving me a sad look, which quickly turns to an angry look when Brynn comes running up to us.

"Carsten, I've been trying to catch up to you." I don't even give her the chance to finish speaking before cutting her off. She doesn't deserve the chance to speak, not after what she did tonight. It was fucking bullshit.

"Brynn, for the love of God, leave me the fuck...." But this time she cuts me off in a panic, a worried look painted across her face.

"I'm pregnant, Carsten. I've been trying to tell you, but you keep blowing me off." she says, looking down, her hands fidgeting.

"What the fuck did you just say?" I say angrily charging up to her. If she were a guy, I wouldn't waste any time beating the shit out of her. But since she's obviously not a guy, I need to approach this situation differently and try my best not to put my hands on her because that's how angry I am.

"You're what?" Emerald says, her jaw dropping, that scary angry look appearing on her face again. Making me slowly take a step back before she either comes at me or comes at Brynn or fuck it maybe both of us. How the fuck is she pregnant? We used protection every time we fucked, and she said she was on birth control? Did one of the condoms break and we didn't know? Did she put holes in her condoms to try and trap me?

Then suddenly the front door opens, and Winter just stands there, a shocked look on her face. "You…you got her pregnant?" She cries, her body shaking as her hands come up to her mouth, her sobs breaking my fucking heart. It takes everything in me not to run up to her and pick her tiny body up in my arms and wrap her legs around me. Feeling her warm body against mine. Fuck I need to hold my her so fucking badly, it makes my heart ache.

"Carsten, please baby, I've been trying to tell you." Brynn shouts at me, tears streaming down her cheeks, and I roll my eyes. I can't help it, just hearing her name makes me roll my eyes.

"Stop fucking calling me *baby*. I am not your *baby*. I don't want to be with you," I say pulling my hair because I am fucking pissed. "I thought you were on birth control? We used a fucking condom." I trusted her when she told me, that and I've even seen her take it before.

"I … I …" She pauses, stuttering. "I was, until you told me you didn't love me." She takes a deep breath. "Then I stopped taking it, because I figured if I was having your baby, you'd love your baby so then you'd have to love me." She gives a slight smile like that makes everything better.

"What the fuck is your problem, Brynn?" I'm so pissed, if she was a dude I'd hit her. "So, you purposely got pregnant?" I shout throwing my hands down at my sides, my hands instantly ball into fists still wanting anything, just something to fucking punch.

"Yes, Carsten, I love you." She starts crying again. You can tell she's being over dramatic, forcing herself to cry harder. And it just pisses me the fuck off even more. Not sure why she feels the need to even be dramatic about this horrible fucking situation she got us into. Not that a baby would be horrible. I would obviously love and care for the baby and be a good dad. But still, I can't believe she purposely tried to trap me. Well jokes on her. Hell yeah, I'll take care of my baby, but not with her.

"God dude, you're fucking psycho. I will NEVER love you, even if you are carrying my baby." I yell, I don't even care if I bring attention to us in any way, let them see how fucking crazy she is.

"I can't believe you got her pregnant." Winter is still breaking my fucking heart, as she sobs from the doorway. I can't believe I hurt her, well Brynn hurt her too. But she thinks I'm responsible for her pain. I mean I am responsible for some of it. But Brynn is the reason this all fucking happened. Fuckkk I am sooo fucking stupid dude.

I turn to her, afraid if I walk to her, she'll shut the door again. "Winter please, I had no idea, I promise you, you have to believe me." I push my hands through my hair again. My head is pounding, not sure if it's from the shot of whiskey or the couple beers I had. Or this whole nightmare. I wanted to have fun with Winter tonight and actually be able to party with her since I wasn't at work. I wanted to unwind a little before she got here so I could enjoy my time with her and not be so fucking nervous, because for some reason she makes me nervous as fuck around her.

"Winter, let's just go inside." Emerald starts walking up to her, but she stops her from pushing her in.

"Did you really even care about me?" Winter says, shaking her head. "I just—a baby, Carsten? I could move past that and be ok with you being a dad, but I feel like I was just a joke to you. Just another person to fuck. God, I'm so stupid." Shattering my fucking heart even more than it was already shattered, the pieces are everywhere. I don't think I'll be able to fix my heart after watching her cry like this. Fuck she's ruined me, I will never be able to look at another girl the same way I look at her because there is no other Winter and I don't want anyone but her.

She rubs her hands down her beautiful face, smudging her already smeared makeup. "All I was to you was a game, when this whole time Brynn was the only one you were serious about." Then she walks inside with Emerald behind her. She doesn't stop and look back, or just look back in general. Once Emerald shuts the door, that's the last of my Snowflake that I see that night. My mood ruined; I'm fucking heartbroken. I can't even imagine how she feels. Fuck I feel sick. Like whatever little alcohol I consumed is going to come up. I hear the lock turn and I know I won't hear anything else from her tonight.

"I have nothing else to say to you Brynn, get the fuck away from me, go home. I don't want to see you anymore, the only time I want to hear from you is if it's about the baby. But go the fuck home." I walk away, not waiting for her to respond. Fuck her and her response. I walk up my front stairs and in my front door, locking it. I'm done with this party, I'm no longer in the mood to be around anyone. So, I head upstairs to my room locking my door behind me. I take off my shoes since I didn't do it downstairs. Then I walk over to my dresser grabbing a wife beater and a pair of gray sweatpants changing into them. Fuck this night. After changing I go over and lay down in my bed, resting my hands behind my head replaying the night, but only the good things that happened. Like my face in the crook of Winter's neck, her sweet strawberry or cotton candy—I have yet to figure it out, scent. I take a deep breath and I swear I can feel my heart stopping in my chest, the beating slowing down. My chest is tightening along with it. Shit is this what heartache feels like?

32

WINTER

The next week without Carsten is terrible, I miss him so much, I feel like It's been the longest week of my life. The day after his party Emerald had told me what had really happened between him and Brynn before she came over and told him she was pregnant, I'm still having a hard time with that. A hard time believing what he's saying is true and a hard time forgiving him. I don't really care that they had a past together, because obviously people date. But now that she is carrying his baby, I don't know what to think or what will happen between them. Or if anything could ever happen between us again.

Pushing my thoughts aside for now, I decided today I'm going to look for a job. I know that Carsten said I can work at the bar but right now I don't have it in me to go work there when I'm not ready to face him yet. As I'm getting dressed my phone rings and I look down to see it's my dad. "Fucking great, another thing to ruin my mood." I mumble to myself.

"Hello." I answer, trying to sound happy to hear from him. But it's kinda hard to sound happy to talk to someone who abused you half your life. Or the fact that this is the first time I've talked to him in weeks.

"Hey Winter, it's Dad." His voice doesn't sound like it normally does. I instantly start to worry that something is wrong.

"I know, Dad." Not sure why he always does that when I have both his name and number saved in my phone.

"Well, I wasn't sure if you blocked my number, I wouldn't blame you if you did." My eyes widened at that, confused because he doesn't sound drunk for once.

"No, Dad." I pause thinking of what to say next. "I should have. Last time was too far but I didn't block you, I couldn't do that to you." My eyes burn, with tears that are threatening to escape. I try to blink them away but it's no use if they fall faster than I can blink. I won't make it obvious; I don't want him to know I'm crying because of him.

"Well, I appreciate it, I was calling because I need your help." He stops talking and takes in a deep breath. I wait for him to continue but he doesn't.

"What do you need, Dad? Because I don't have any extra money right now." I'm assuming that's what he's calling for because that's usually the only reason he takes time to call.

"No, I don't really need money. Well, I might, but not right now, and not for what you think." Now I'm even more confused than I was before, but I wait for him to talk. I don't want to ask any questions or say anything that might make him angry.

"What do you mean?" I sigh, getting annoyed. "Can you just tell me what's wrong please?" I don't want to make him mad, but I guess I can just hang up if he starts being a dick, I don't have the patience for him to keep dragging this out.

"I've cut back on drinking, after what you said to me, about Mom and what I did to you, I've cut back." His voice sounds a little shaky, like he's afraid to say what's really on his mind. Or his nerves are getting the best of him and he's not sure how I'm going to react to this news.

"Well, that's good." Cool so he's still drinking, not sure why he called to tell me that.

"I'm going to go to rehab. I talked to my doctor, and he said to cut back first and then think about what I want to do, and I think rehab will be best for me." I think my jaw nearly hits the floor. I don't speak, I'm in shock. More tears form in my eyes and fall quickly. I have no idea what to say, or how to feel. Is this really happening?

"You... you are?" I hesitate because I don't want to say the wrong thing and make him change his mind or piss him off and start a fight with him.

"Yes, that's what I need help with." He says kind of quietly, like he's ashamed. I don't want to bring that up either, talking to him is like talking to a bomb, not knowing when it's going to go off. When he'll explode. He's unpredictable and I hate it.

"Are you being serious? You're gonna go Dad?" I'm afraid that this is going to be the thing that makes him snap. It's always been hard for me to talk to him and have a conversation because it's like walking on eggshells around him.

"Yes, Winter, I don't want to lose you. I lost your mom; I've lost our relationship. I don't want to lose you permanently, you're all I've got left." He chokes out, and I lose it. Here comes the water works. Or I should say more tears, I've been crying this whole time. I'm sobbing uncontrollably now, almost having a hard time even breathing. I've been waiting to hear these words my whole life, because I didn't just lose my mom the day she passed, I lost my dad too. He was already halfway gone before she passed but I lost him fully the day she died. He wasn't my dad; he was an angry monster who hurt me and took his anger out on me.

"Are you okay, Winter?" He asks, almost like he's afraid of how I'm going to react.

"Y...ye." I hiccup, trying to catch my breath. "Yes, Dad. I'm just– God, I'm so happy. I feel like I've been waiting for you to say those words for forever." I cry even harder now, trying to talk but having a hard time controlling my emotions. Barely able to get the words out between sobs. "What do you need help with? I'll do what I can to help you." I'm still afraid I might say the wrong thing and trigger the monster inside of him. So, I choose my words wisely, like all my conversations with him, like I said, you never know when he's going to explode.

"Well, I don't know how to say this, but my insurance won't cover the full cost of my rehab." He stops talking for a second, I hear him taking a deep breath like this is the hardest part of the conversation. "I can't afford to pay the house and the rehab payments, and I was wondering if you could help me pay for some of it, not all of it, we can work something out if you can agree to help me." He sounds ashamed, or embarrassed.

I cut him off before he finishes. "Yes, Dad, I'll do whatever I can to help you. I just need you to promise me that you're going to take this seriously." I pause, not sure how to say the rest of it because I don't want to make him angry.

"I know sweetheart, I promise I will take this seriously." He sounds serious. He's never once talked about getting sober. I was always afraid to bring it up so I just didn't. So that's the one thing that makes me feel like he's being serious, that he's never mentioned rehab before. Fingers crossed he's not gonna chicken out and change his mind.

"Dad, it's just that, I can't just throw away money I don't have for you to go through rehab and go back to drinking right after you get out." I stop waiting for a response. My eyes scrunched closed tightly like I'm hiding from him and his response even though he can't see me through the phone.

"I know Winter, this isn't going to be a short-term thing. I'll be staying for six months, or I can choose to stay longer if I feel like I need to, but this is an extensive program that has a good outcome. The percentage of people who stay sober after is very high." He sounds happy, positive. Like he's proud of himself and it makes me smile. Dad hasn't sounded this hopeful in a long time, about anything. I wonder if he's smiling and proud of himself for making this choice.

I'm afraid to be too excited though, because he can change his mind in an instant but I wanna be happy for him. "That's great Dad. This is so great! Really, I'm proud of you." I tell him, because I truly am, I just hope he sticks with it and doesn't back out. "When does the program start?" I ask hoping it's soon, so he doesn't have time to change his mind. Plus, the sooner he gets in there the better so he can start getting sober.

"Well, that's why I called you today, do you have time to take me tomorrow morning? They have a room available, and I don't want to wait too long in fear of changing my mind." I feel like he's reading my mind or can hear my thoughts. Am I thinking out loud and talking? I'm so glad he feels the same way about being afraid to change his mind, so maybe he really is being serious about all of this.

"Yeah, Dad, I'm available all day tomorrow, I can take you whenever, what time?" I ask in hope that it's early that way he doesn't have the day to think about whether or not he really wants to go.

"I have to be there at nine in the morning, you can come in with me so we can discuss the payment plans and everything else." He pauses, "Winter?" He sounds nervous again. Which I'm sure he is, this is going to be a huge life changing decision he's making. He has every right to be and sound nervous.

"Yeah, Dad?" I ask fighting back the tears again so I can finish this conversation without being a blubbering mess. My eyes are already swollen from crying so much over Carsten. I don't think I'll have normal eyes for a while. No amount of makeup can hide the swelling or redness. It's terrible.

"I really appreciate you helping me and supporting me, not just financially either," he says in a serious voice, or at least what a serious voice sounds like to me. I've never heard him talk in a serious voice if he wasn't slurring his words he was yelling or passed out. I never had a normal father daughter relationship with him.

"You're welcome, Dad. I'm proud of you, very proud of you for doing this." It's true, I am proud of him, and scared at the same time. Scared he's just going to go right back to drinking once he gets out.

"Thank you, sweetheart. Well, I have to go now, I have a lot to do before I go tomorrow." He sounds panicked now, anxious maybe. Like the reality of it all just hit him with how serious this is.

"Ok, Dad, and don't worry I'll check on things at the house while you're gone too." I reassure him, so he knows I'm being serious about helping him out.

"Thanks, Winter, I love you, sweetheart." Here come the tears, I don't remember the last time he told me he loves me. In fact, it's been so long all he has told me for so long is how disappointed he is in me and how much he hates me.

"I love you too, Dad. See you in the morning. I'll text you when I'm on my way." These damn tears won't stop. I'm so tired of crying.

"Ok sweetheart, bye." He hangs up and I sit there and sob, happy tears, scared tears and for once I feel like a weight has been lifted off me, something I didn't realize I was carrying around for so long. I wish I could celebrate this information with Carsten. Or that he could go with me. It sucks that we aren't together anymore. I mean yes, I can not wait to tell Emerald obviously she's going to be so excited. But there's something different about telling someone you're in love with, funny there's that word again, something that's important to you especially this new information about my dad. I know he would know how important this was to me.

Now that I am going to be helping him out financially, I finally figured out my school stress. I'm going to have to take a year off, just in case he stays in rehab longer, so I can worry about helping him and not trying to figure out how to juggle both. I grab my phone, purse and keys and head out the door.

33

CARSTEN

THIS HAS PROBABLY BEEN THE WORST WEEK OF MY LIFE. Between Brynn trying to trap me by purposely getting pregnant and then ruining things with Winter. I've been in a shitty fucking mood from it all.

I never thought I'd miss a girl this much; in fact I've never cared about a girl enough to the point of missing her. I know that sounds bad, but I never kept them around long enough to develop any kind of feelings for them. I decide I'm done laying around today, my mom gave me a couple days off at the bar due to me "moping around too much" is what she had told me.

"We can't have you here zoning out in between customers. You've been moping around too much. Which I understand honey, I've been there. But go home, you look exhausted. Get some rest and focus on you for a few days." She's the best mom anyone could ask for. She basically kicked me out of my own bar. I didn't have the heart to tell her about Brynn being pregnant yet. I need to figure things out with her first before I tell my mom, just in case something happens to the baby.

I've been laying around, playing video games, and attempting to eat. But who knew that when you're heartbroken you have a hard time eating, and I've been attempting to sleep too. Another thing that doesn't fucking work when you're heartbroken. Love fucking sucks. Yeah love, I really think I'm in love with this girl. I've never felt this way about anyone before, I'd do anything for her. Hell, I'd probably kill someone for her if it meant I could keep her safe. That's how much I care about her.

I decide I'm going to go outside and work on my car. I've been neglecting that beauty for too long now and I miss it. Working on cars has always been something I've enjoyed doing, it's always helped relieve a lot of stress for me and right now I'm fucking stressed, dude.

I change into a wife beater and some of my work shorts and head downstairs to open the garage. As the garage door is opening my heart sinks, I see Winter walking to her car, and she looks so fucking beautiful. She's wearing a T-shirt and ripped skinny jeans, and her hair in messy pigtail buns, but she just looks gorgeous. I think about going to talk to her for a minute but then I remember what Emerald told me, basically to give her time so I don't push her away or something like that. So, I decide to just stand there like the fucking creep I've apparently become, in my garage and watch her through the door so she can't see me. After watching her leave I decide to start gathering all my tools that I'll need for the parts on my car that I'm working on at the moment.

Absolutely nothing is fucking going right, I keep dropping my fucking tools, not putting the parts in right, I've tried fixing the same damn thing for about an hour now, but no luck, I'm too distracted. All I keep thinking about is Winter and I can't take my mind off her no matter what I do. Thinking about my little Snowflake has been my main hobby these days. Her touch, her soft, pink pouty lips against mine. The way she smells, the way her fucking pussy tastes as she's cuming all over my face. Fuuuckk, I miss her. Sick of working on my car I decide to sit in the trunk of my truck and drink a beer.

Right as I sit down Creedence comes home and decides to join me. "Hey man, getting a decent amount done on your car?" He asks, grabbing a beer from the refrigerator in the garage and joining me on the bed of my truck.

"Fuck no, no matter what I do, I put the part in wrong, I keep dropping shit, hurt myself a few times. It's fucking stupid." I sigh, taking a sip of my beer, staring straight. It's taking everything in me not to stare next door at Winter's to see if she's out there or up on her roof. It makes me laugh to myself thinking of that day I had to save her from being stuck up there. Fuck, then the memories of her wet body pressed against mine outside flash and I have to bite the inside of my fucking cheek to not moan out loud. Shit I miss the way her tight pussy feels sliding up and down on my hard cock. Fuck I miss laying with her after we fuck, the feel of her small body lying on top of mine or next to me. I miss her so fucking much.

"This shit with Winter is really getting to you huh?" He glances over at me before taking another sip of his beer. He has a concerned look on his face.

"Dude, it's eating me alive. I can't eat, can't sleep. Hell, I can't even stop thinking about her for more than five minutes. I feel sick to my stomach all day. Who knew a fucking break up could kill you this way." I sigh again, I feel worse than how I described it, but I didn't want to sound like a little bitch. My fucking heart aches all goddamn day long.

"Sounds like you really love her, huh?" he asks, trying not to laugh at my misery.

"I mean, I've never been in love before. But I'd say yeah, I fucking love this girl. I'd do anything for her, man." I would, nobody knows how far I'd really go to protect what's mine, and she is just that, mine. She's always been, she just hasn't realized it yet.

"Then you need to give her some space for now, but in the meantime come up with a plan." He takes another sip of his beer and then crosses his arms. Then looks over at me.

"Plan? What do you mean?" I ask, taking another sip of my beer before setting it down next to me. I look back over at him, raising an eyebrow since he didn't answer me yet.

"A plan on winning her back man, something to show her how much you really care about her." He smiles at me, a look on his face like he's been in my shoes before and knows exactly how I'm feeling.

"I could kill someone, does that work? Cause when I say I'd do anything for her I mean it, I'd kill someone for her if I had to." I sound ridiculous, of course I wouldn't kill an innocent person, I'd make sure they were a bad person that deserved it. The things I'd do for her are things I never thought I'd see myself doing, ever.

He laughs. "I don't think it has to be that drastic. But I think if you just tell her how you truly feel along with maybe something romantic, it could help you. Like I said though give it a couple weeks before you come running at her with this." He gives me a serious look. "You don't want to scare her off with being too obsessed, Carsten." He shakes his head, like he can't believe he's having this conversation with me of all people. The man he'd lecture all the time about how I need to find a girl to get serious with and stop being a man whore. Well, I hope he's happy now. Because not only am I a retired man whore. But I'm fucking heartbroken. I'm slowly dying every day without her. Fuck, I just wanna feel her little body in my arms. Not even for fucking sex, just her. Fully clothed. I miss the feel of her body next to mine.

"A couple weeks? Fuck man, I won't have to kill anyone. I'll fucking die before it hits a couple weeks. How do you do this?" I ask because I'm curious, if this is what it feels like to be in love and get your heart broken when you know that person might be it for you.

"Do what?" He asks, throwing his beer in the recycling bin and grabbing another one for the both of us, even though I still have half a beer left. Ehh fuck it. I chug the rest of my first beer down and toss it into the recycling bin. Sounds like it cracked or shattered after hitting the other bottles. Fuck, my bad.

"Date, do relationships, go through breakups. This heartbreak shit fucking sucks. I'm constantly questioning if I'm having a heart attack because my chest has been hurting, here, it's just anxiety. It's terrible." I let out a half sigh, half laugh. I don't know anymore. All of the sounds I make these days sound sad and depressing.

He starts laughing too. "It's worth it man, to fall in love and be in a relationship, it's worth it even if the result is heartache," he pauses for a minute, "my goal with each relationship has always been to find my soulmate, and each time one of my relationships ends it just motivates me to get back out there and find her." He smiles at me. "But with your case, you found her, just don't lose her." He pats me on the back. He and I have been through some shit growing up together, but he's never seen me experience any kind of heartache because I never let it get that way. Not sure why but I never thought the idea of dating someone to see if it works out, or if you'll be heartbroken, sounded fun so I just stuck to fucking them once, or maybe a few more times. But no relationships I'm twenty-three and this is my first ever relationship and I fucked up big fucking time.

"Thanks man, I appreciate the advice instead of making fun of me." I look over, as I open up my new beer that Creed just brought me.

He opens his other beer at the same time, chugging half of it on the first sip. "Of course, man, I'd never make fun of you for being in love. Maybe once you get her back, I'll make fun of you some. But until then I'd be a dick if I did." He throws his head back and laughs. Such a great fucking friend. Asshole. He's lucky that he truly is a good friend, or I'd kick his ass for that.

"Thanks dick." I elbow him in the side making his laugh turn into a funny sound. Which makes him elbow me back a little harder than I did, but on purpose.

I pause, not sure if I want to mention Brynn but it's eating me alive. I didn't tell anyone, not even Chase, and I need someone to talk to about it.

"There's something else too though, man." I say, waiting for him to respond since I'm stalling.

"What's that?" He looks over at me taking a normal sip of his beer this time.

"It's Brynn." He rolls his eyes and I close my eyes, shaking my head. "She told me she's pregnant." I peek through one eye to look at him and try to get a feel for how he's going to respond. Hopefully he won't yell at me like Emerald did.

His eyes widened in shock. "Well fuck man, what are you gonna do?" He asks with a serious look on his face. That's one thing I love about this guy, he never judges the dumb shit I do, and this right here, Brynn, is some dumb shit I shouldn't have done.

"I don't know, I told her not to talk to me anymore unless it's something to do with the baby. She told me right in front of Winter, so now she's pissed and heartbroken. I don't think she'd care about the baby; I think she just cares about it being with Brynn." I rush out in one breath. Not sure why I do, I'm nervous my whole life spiraled out of control out of nowhere and I have no idea how to handle any of this.

"Well yeah, Brynn is fucking psycho, you should've dropped her a long time ago man. I thought you said she was on the pill?" The look on his face is hard to read. "Did you use a condom?" He's obviously confused, or maybe he's pissed at Brynn. Fuck maybe he's pissed at me for being a fucking idiot.

"Yeah, that's the thing, she purposely got pregnant to make me love her." I sigh, just the thought pissing me off, but I try not to get caught in that right now. I need to stay calm for my own mental health.

"Are you fucking kidding me? That's fucked up man. I wish I had advice to give you." He's shaking his head. I don't blame him. I'm shaking my head too. This whole situation is just so fucked up.

"It's fine man. I kinda just told you to get it off my chest, no one else knows so don't repeat it until I figure more shit out." I give him a serious look, because I'll be pissed if he does. Word travels fast where we live. Everyone and their fucking mother love to gossip in this town. I mean who doesn't love to gossip? I know chicks fucking love to gossip and Brynn needs to keep her fucking mouth shut too.

"I got you man, your secrets safe, just update me when you find out more." He says before drinking the rest of this beer and giving me a fist bump, his way of telling me he's heading in which I might too. I can't sit out here and not just stare next door like a fucking creep in hopes I get to see my little Snowflake. On the off chance I don't see her, I'd just look like a creep to the neighbors.

"Will do man, thanks." I take another sip of my beer, not even in the mood to drink, just drinking to help numb the pain that I don't want to feel anymore but I have to because I'm a huge fucking fuck up.

After talking with Creed, I end up feeling a little better or maybe it's the whiskey I switched to after finding it hidden in the freezer. I hide it from our guests when we have parties. It's my fucking whiskey I don't want anyone drinking it. I get back to working on my car. I spend about another hour getting things done before calling it quits for the day. Mainly because my thoughts start to go back to Winter, and I get that ache in my chest that has me questioning if I'm dying or if it's heartache. Either way, this fucking sucks. So, I head inside so I can brainstorm some ideas on how to get my little Snowflake back.

34

WINTER

AFTER LEAVING THE SCHOOL AND TALKING TO ADMISSIONS and my counselor about taking the year off due to personal reasons, I head towards the diner down the street that we usually go to put in an application, hoping that Lisa is there so I can talk to her to see if I'm wasting my time or if they're hiring.

Pulling into a parking spot I shut my car off and sit there for a minute. I take a couple deep breaths to calm my nerves before opening my car door and heading inside. Right as I walk in, I see Carsten sitting at a booth with Creedence, Chase, and Axton. They all stop talking and watch me for a second. "Fucking awkward," I mumble under my breath looking down.

I walk over to the counter right as Lisa walks out from the back room carrying plates.

"Oh my god, Winter, it's been so long honey!" she says, smiling at me.

"Hi Lisa," I say waving my hand.

"God, you look just like your mama, dear, so beautiful." She pauses for a second and lets out a breath.

"Thank you, that makes me so happy to hear. I sure do miss her," I say, giving a half smirk. Trying not to let the mention of my mom phase me. I can't cry here, not right now in public, especially with

Carsten so close and not being near me, I'd lose it and wouldn't be able to stop. The heartache of my mom is still heavy, some days it's a little lighter and some days my heart is so heavy I'm surprised I can keep my body standing upright. Most days it's just a normal heaviness that I'm used to weighing me down, waiting for something to help fix that empty feeling.

"Well, let me set these plates at the table and then I'll take a quick break and we'll talk." She's carrying four plates in two hands and it's very impressive to see her carry them like that, but I feel bad just watching her carry them without offering to help.

"Here let me help you," I tell her, with a big smile on her face. I don't want to just stand here and feel awkward especially with Carsten and his friends so close. I don't know if they're watching me still and I don't want to look.

She cuts me off before I can finish what I was going to say. "Oh no honey, it's ok it's not a far walk at all," she says, getting ready to walk away with a kind smile on her face.

"Lisa, please, I insist." I take two plates and we head straight to Carsten's table. Great. I definitely wasn't thinking about the fact that these could've been their plates when I took them from her.

"Here you boys go, Creedence this is yours, Chase honey this one's yours." She looks over at me. "Carsten's is the burger," she tells me, pointing to Carsten. "That would leave the chicken sandwich for Axton." She points to him. "Boys, this is Winter." She smiles looking from me to them, they all say hi and I say hi back not having the heart to tell her that I already know them. "Do you guys need anything else?" she asks them with her hands on her hips waiting for their response.

"No thank you, Lisa, we appreciate you," Carsten says as the other guys follow behind him thanking her as well.

"Hey uhh, Winter?" I look over and Carsten is talking to me. Fuck. Why does he have to do this here, right now?

"Yes?" That's all I managed to get out because my heart is in my throat, and I feel like I'm going to puke. It's been over a week since we spoke, and I miss him. We weren't even together long but it felt like we were together forever. He never felt like a stranger and that was my favorite thing about him.

He stands up and reaches out his hand to me. "My names Carsten, it's nice to meet you." He says, shaking my hand with a shy smile.

I shake his back while his friends stare up at us in confusion. "It's umm... nice to meet you, Carsten." I say, shaking his hand back, trying to keep calm and not make things weird.

"I love your name, it's unique and beautiful." He pauses for a second. "Just like you," he says and sits back down.

"Th... thank you," I stutter out, because I'm not sure what else to say, my heart is racing too fast to think, my stomach a ball of nerves, making me feel nauseous for some reason.

"That was so sweet Carsten," Lisa says, wiping her hands on her apron. "Now you guys enjoy your food." She starts walking away and I follow her. Really fucking confused.

"What the hell was that about?" I hear Chase ask him as I walk behind Lisa, so I slow down to hear his response.

"Just trying to break the ice, hopefully start fresh," he says, taking a bite of his burger. I follow Lisa and sit down in a booth with a cup of coffee, catching up for a few minutes before I finally work up the courage to ask her.

"Are you guys by chance looking for help?" I give a half smirk waiting for an answer, feeling nervous for some reason even though I've known her my whole life.

"Actually, we have a waitress leaving in a week. Then I was going to put a sign up. Why do you know someone looking for a job?" She looks at me, tilting her head to the right a little, smiling. She is always smiling, always looking happy.

"Me actually. I umm, was let go from my last job, personal reasons with Dad." She gives me a knowing look. Lisa has been in my family since I was a baby so she knows what kind of person he can be and what he turned into.

She gives me a sad look. "Honey, I'd love to have you work here if you'd like a job." She reaches across the table and squeezes my hand.

"Really?" I say getting excited. "I would love more than anything to work here if you'd have me." I scrunch up my eyes a little. Biting my bottom lip. It's a nervous habit, something I've done for as long as I can remember. Every time I get nervous or I'm uncomfortable, I've drawn blood before, in uncomfortable situations, from biting too hard. It's a bad habit that's for sure.

We discuss the hours I'd be willing to work and the pay. Then I fill her in on everything going on with my dad and how I'll be helping him pay for rehab and his house while he's gone. After two cups of coffee and a long break she finally has to get back to work, so I head out the door not even looking in Carsten's direction, hoping he won't see me leave.

As I'm unlocking my car door and opening it, I hear footsteps behind me and jump. "Holy shit, you scared me." I hold my hand to my chest holding my heart that now feels like it wants to explode in my chest.

"Sorry, I wasn't trying to scare you, I just wasn't sure how to approach you." Carsten says with a half smirk.

"It's fine, maybe just next time try yelling my name or something," I say with a slight laugh.

"So, I figured while I caught you here, I'd just ask, can we talk?" he says, licking his perfect lips. I miss kissing him so much, I miss him. It's taking everything in me not to pull him down for a kiss.

"Carsten, I just-" I stop looking for the words to say without sounding like a bitch. Even though after what he did maybe he deserves my bitchy attitude. "I don't think I'm ready to talk yet, it's still too fresh." It's true, like I said I'm not gonna come off nice if we talk right now. It's too fresh and I'm just simply not ready and that's okay. He hurt me, it's his fault I feel this way, he can wait until I'm ready to talk. I don't care if it hurts him.

"That's fine, I just wish you'd let me explain things. Well at least the things I know I can explain for now."

"Carsten please, when I'm ready I will come to you, but until then I'm just... I just need time. Please. Please I need you to just leave me alone."

"Ok, well you know where to find me, Snowflake. Just know that... I miss you." He turns and walks away back into the diner to go sit with his friends, a sad look on his face that breaks my heart. I can't just give in. My fucking heart hurts and I'm not ready to listen yet. Even if what I saw isn't what I thought it was, it still hurts to see.

I get into my car to head home, it's been a long week and a long day, I'm mentally and physically exhausted. I think I'm gonna head home and just go to bed early.

35
CARSTEN

I GRAB MY LEATHER JACKET SINCE IT'S FUCKING COLD AND starting to snow some and I head to the bar for the first time in over a week. It's been about two weeks since Winter and I have spoken and this sucks. She's been on my mind non-stop. The need to touch her, kiss her, and just have her body against mine. God I fucking miss my little Snowflake. Goddammit, I just wish things would go back to fucking normal and it's driving me absolutely crazy knowing I can't do anything to fix it right now. So, I'm hoping the bar will keep my mind off things.

Tonight is hip hop night at the bar, so it tends to be very busy. There's usually a large crowd and a lot of dancing, so that means a lot of alcohol and a lot of food. We've been slammed for the last two hours and I'm ready for a break.

"Hey Chase, you cool if I take a break?" I ask yelling over the music to him.

"Sure, go ahead, take your time bro." He yells back to me. I don't know how he's not tired from this. It's not like I'm fucking old either, but he always seems to just push through it without needing a break. He says if he stops it makes him tired, I get it but right now I just need some kind of break.

"Thanks man." I grab a beer from the refrigerator, grab my coat, and walk outside to take a break and get some fresh air. I'm fucking tired and all I keep thinking about is Winter. I miss her so fucking much it hurts. I know I just said that but those have been my only thoughts. I can barely eat, or sleep, so I just walk around like a fucking zombie all the time from exhaustion. But what else can I do? I don't think I'll be able to sleep again until I have her back, and I will get her back. It's been too long without touching my little Snowflake and my fucking heart hurts. It kills me to see her and not be able to touch her, kiss her, smell her. Shit even just look at her. I feel like I can't stare at her like I used to without looking like a creep. Or coming off as a stalker, fuck it I'll stalk her. I need to know everything she's doing and if she's happy without me. She better not be fucking happy without me. That'll only break me more and I'm too exhausted, mentally and emotionally to keep breaking like this.

The air is so cold on my fucking face, but it sort of feels good after being cooped up in that hot ass bar. The snow is finally starting to stick to the ground, so I walk further into the parking lot and stare up at the sky, breathing in the cold air. I can see my breath as I breathe out, making me wonder how I'm even still alive when I feel so empty and my heart fucking hurts so goddamn bad.

I walk back towards the bar and open my beer, leaning against the building to take some kind of relief off my body. I don't want to sit because that'll just make everything worse, so I stand drinking my beer in silence, watching the snowfall around me. I hear talking on the side of the building, giggling, then someone gets loud and that someone sounds like Brynn. Fucking great. I had no idea she was here unless she hasn't been inside yet. I quietly walk over and listen very carefully so I can hear her.

"So, then I panicked and had to tell him I was pregnant." One of her friends gasps and then giggles. What the fuck? What the fuck does she mean, had to tell me she was pregnant?

"You're what? You're pregnant Brynn?" Whoever is with her, I'm assuming Colette and Daisy, no not Axton's Daisy either, this Daisy is the bitchy snotty one. Axton's girl, ehh she can be a bitch but she's nice.

"Oh my God, what are you gonna do?" one of them asks her? I only met her friends a couple times so I can't really tell them apart by their annoying voices, I just know their names.

"No, you idiot I'm on the pill, I told him that to make him love me, so that way he can't leave me. He's mine now, Winter will never forgive him. She'll never want him back now." She laughs about it and holy fucking shit am I fucking pissed. Son of a bitch, I can't fucking believe her. She was lying that whole fucking time? I step out so she can see me.

"What the fuck is your goddamn problem, Brynn? You fucking lied to me about being pregnant?" I walk out further so they can see me more. They stand there with their teeth chattering, in short skirts and barely there coats, huddled together, smoking.

She gasps dropping her drink, glass shattering everywhere, I guess she was inside, and I just didn't see her. I don't care thought, I'm fucking pissed. I can't believe Chase didn't say anything to me about him seeing her. "Carsten... wh... wha... what?? No, I'm pregnant. I promise, I just didn't want them to be ashamed of me." She looks away lying again, to her friends and then back to me with a pissed off, yet shocked look on her face.

"You psycho fucking bitch." I say stepping towards her, breathing heavily, you can see it in the air from the cold. I don't even care that I just called her a bitch either, like I said before I don't really like to talk to women like that, but she deserves it. "I can't believe you would lie about something like that, I was about to tell my mom and everything, dude. What the fuck is your problem!" I am seeing fucking red. If she was a guy she'd be on the goddamn ground by now with my hand around her throat and my fist hitting her fucking face. She's lucky. She's also lucky I'm not an asshole who just says fuck it and kicks her ass anyway, girl or not.

"Carsten, I'm sorry ok." She breathes out, puffs of smoke from her cigarette and the air hitting me in the face. God she is so nasty I don't even know what I saw in her. "I just... I just want you to love me like I love you. I'm so sorry baby." She pauses, looking at me. A sad look on her face as tears build in her eyes. Fucking pathetic. She pretends to be pregnant and then she's upset now that I'm pissed.

"Brynn, enough," I yell. I don't even care that I'm yelling either she can go ahead and fuck the fuck off. "I don't love you and stop fucking calling me baby. I never want to see you again." I ball my fists at my sides. "Listen to me and listen to me good, Brynn. I will never love you, not now, not ever. I don't want to see you near my house, near Winter, or in my bar ever again. Do you fucking understand me?" I don't even care if I'm being dramatic with any of this, I want her out of my fucking life at this point.

"Carsten, but please. I'm so sorry." She chokes out. "Please I just want a chance to be with you, why don't you understand that." Tears are pouring down her face and I don't even feel bad. Usually, I hate to see a girl cry but for some reason with Brynn, it just pisses me off even more.

"I don't want to understand it. God, you're fucking psycho. I love Winter. I fucking love her and you might have ruined that for me because you're a crazy bitch." I throw my hands out in front of me, trying so hard not to pull at my hair in frustration because if I do, I'm afraid I'll rip it out. "Get the hell out of here before I call the police, seriously. I can't believe you lied to me, lied to Winter. You disgust me." I say, shaking my head at her. Her friends stand there with their mouths open in shock like they can't believe I just said that to her.

"C'mon Brynn, let's just leave this bar and get away from this asshole." Colette says, grabbing her hand and I can't help but laugh at her, like a psycho, crazy laugh.

"What, are you serious right now? I'm the asshole?'" I take a deep breath because I'm about to lose my shit. "She lies and fakes a pregnancy and I'm the asshole. You guys are losing it right along with her." I have no idea how to even feel right now. I'm shocked. Pissed.

These girls are fucking idiots if they think I'm the bad guy, and I don't even care if I sound like an asshole.

They roll their eyes at me and cross their arms. "Right, we're losing it, let's go ladies." Daisy says, grabbing their hands, her whole-body trembling from the cold. I guess that's what happens when you barely wear any clothes outside.

I stand there in shock. I can't believe what just happened, brushing my hands over my face and letting out a deep breath. I turn to go back inside when my brother comes out. "You ok man?" He asks with a concerned look on his face. "Fuck it's cold." The dumbass says to me as he stands here in a T-shirt and jeans, no jacket.

"You have no idea," I say with a laugh. "It is cold, but I love the snow."

"You're crazy man." He shakes his head. "Well, I'm all ears, fill me in." He opens the beer he grabbed and takes a long sip. We don't usually drink while working but it's been a busy night for the both of us. So why the fuck not, everyone else is drinking, why can't we?

"The night of the party, Brynn came and sabotaged mine and Winter's relationship. Then she told me she was pregnant." The expression on his face goes from a normal one to a completely shocked look, kinda like his jaw is gonna hit the floor or something.

"She what? Dude what are you gonna do? You can't be stuck with that psycho bitch for life." He practically shouts as he throws his hands up into the air.

"Those were my thoughts exactly, until I walked out here to get some fresh air." I stop taking a sip of my beer. "Then I heard some girls on the side of the building, one who sounded like Brynn, so I stood close to listen and here she was lying the whole time."

"What do you mean?" He looks confused. He's not the brightest when it comes to stuff like this.

"She lied to me about being pregnant to try and trick me into loving her because she loves me and is upset that I don't love her." I pause, taking another sip of my beer." She wanted to break us up because she thought if she was pregnant, I'd get back with her and just forget Winter like I didn't love her."

"Bro, I knew it man." He pauses, giving me this big cheesy smile.

"Knew what?" Now I'm the idiot who's confused. I have no idea what his smile could be for.

"That you loved her man." He says, nudging my shoulder, still wearing that cheesy smile.

"You did?" I stare over at him, curious what he's going to say next. I'm sure it was written all over my face with how obsessed I am with her, I'm sure one look at my face around her and you could tell she was it, that I loved her. I'm sure everyone around me knew before I realized what it was. She's always been and always will be mine. That's one thing I know.

"Yeah, I could just tell, the way you are around her, you can see it on your face, that you're in love with her." He laughs a little, shaking his head. "Never thought I'd see the day, but I'm happy for you man." He pats me on the back, smiling at me. A truly happy look on his face, that's one thing about Chase he's always been supportive of me, no matter what my crazy ass decides to do, and even through these years of being a man whore, he's always had my back.

"Well damn, I'm glad other people can see it. That's probably what pissed Brynn off the most. She could tell I was in love with Winter and not her and she panicked." I shake my head, annoyed still by what she did, not sure how I'm going to get Winter back now. But Brynn's plan to fuck everything up isn't going to work. I won't let it; I can't lose my little snowflake. She won't make me fucking lose her. Just the thought of being without her makes my fucking chest hurt, it makes my heart feel tight and heavy.

"Yeah man I'm glad you found it out before doing anything crazy, I can't believe she went that psycho on you and told you she was pregnant." He shakes his head, taking a sip of his beer.

"Right, then her friends had the nerve to say I was the problem. They're all fucked up." I chuckle. "But we won't have to worry about that anymore. I told her I don't want to see her around here ever again, so hopefully she listens." We both head back inside the bar before it gets too crazy again with customers.

"So, when are you gonna tell her?" Chase asks me, grabbing a beer for one of the customers.

"Not sure yet, Emerald told me to give her some time and after I tried talking to her at the diner the other day, she still needed time." I sigh filling up two vodka and cranberries for the two girls checking Chase and I out. "I don't want to push her away more, ya know?" I sigh again. I'm frustrated, I miss her so fucking much. I need to touch her. I need to fucking be in her air, I need to fucking be inside her again. My cock craves her pussy, and my fucking hand isn't doing the job, it's not even close to as warm or wet as she is. Nothing will ever compare to my little Snowflake. I just fucking miss her.

"Ya man, chicks are hard sometimes," he says walking away to go give someone else their drinks.

We finish up the rest of the night slammed, no time for anymore breaks, but that's ok it keeps my mind busy, my only thoughts of Winter, besides the fact that I miss her, are how I'm going to get her back, and how I'm going to tell her that Brynn was lying since she wants space.

After closing the bar for the night I head home to shower and go to sleep. Exhausted from how busy we were and how stressed I've been. I'm hoping that I can get some sleep for the night.

36
WINTER

ANOTHER WEEK GOES BY WITHOUT TALKING TO OR SEEING Carsten and I fucking miss him. It's taken everything in me not to just say fuck it and go talk to him. But I know I need space and at this point I feel like if he wanted to talk to me he probably would have tried to again. I wonder if he decided to get back with Brynn since she's carrying his baby, or if they have even discussed anything about it. Every time I want to talk to him I remember he's having a baby with her and it makes me sick to think about. I still can't believe that she purposely got pregnant. What a fucking psycho, what kind of person is that desperate for someone's love, that they would go that far. They would purposely get pregnant, I can't believe her. Brynn is pregnant with Carsten's baby, what the fuck is going to happen now?

Trying to push my thoughts aside, I head to the bathroom to shower before work. I finally started my job at Lisa's Diner the other day and so far I love it. The customers are friendly, my coworkers are great.Well, most of my coworkers are great, Stacey has been an issue since starting here.She acts like she owns the place, or is in control of everything, and she's always in everyone's business. The money isn't bad so I guess that makes up for Stacey being a bitch.

After my shower I start drying and styling my hair, deciding to wear it in a messy bun so it's out of my face. I put on a black T-shirt and black leggings with my hot pink converse. We don't have a dress code as long as the clothing is appropriate, we just need to wear the aprons provided. I grab my winter coat, since it's fucking cold and head downstairs to leave for work when I run into Emerald. She stands at the counter with what looks like bread, cheese and some butter. Mmm I wonder if she is making grilled cheese. Those are my absolute favorite and I haven't had any in forever, if she's making them I'm going to convince her to make me some too. Although I know she won't have a problem making them for me, I still don't want to assume.

"Hey bitch," I say walking past her. We've always had

"Hey bitch yourself." She laughs, attempting to slap my ass but misses because she has horrible aim.

"I'm about to head to work. Do you want me to bring you home anything from the diner?" I ask because we both love the food from there. That's one plus about working there, I get to eat there every day.

"Mmm, decisions, decisions. Can I text you if I want something, or do you want to know before you leave?" she asks me with her arms crossed and hand on her chin like she's thinking.

"Yeah, whenever. I'm working from five-thirty until midnight so as long as you let me know by at least ten-thirty so I have time to put the order in in case we're busy that's fine," I say grabbing my keys and walking towards the door.

"Awesome! Thanks, Snow, I'll let you know as soon as I make up my mind babe," she says. "Have a great night at work." She waves bye to me as she's walking down the hall towards her room.

I get into my car and shiver as I put the key in the ignition, thinking that I should've warmed it up before getting in and I start driving towards the diner. I could probably walk if I wanted to, that's how close we live to it but because I work so late I don't like walking that late at night, plus i'm not trying to walk when it's freezing cold and snowing.

I pull into the parking lot and park in a parking spot, getting out and locking my door. I rush quickly through the parking lot to the door, the wind blowing down my neck through my jacket, sending chills through my body. I stomp my feet to get the snow off on the rug and start slowly walking towards the back room to put my stuff in my locker and put on my apron on as my co-workers walks up to me. "Hey winter, you have a request in your section. Just so you know, they just got here so take your time," she says in the doorway.

"Thanks, Stacey. Do you know who it is?" I ask, confused since I haven't been here long enough to have regulars yet.

"I don't know his name. I've seen him in here before. He's super tall, like a freaking giant, or I'm just really short." She giggles. "He's got light brown hair, beard, covered in tattoos. He's fucking hot that's all I know." She laughs, walking out and my stomach drops, my heart starts racing. I wonder if it's Carsten.

I walk into the bathroom real quick and check my makeup and outfit in the mirror to make sure everything looks okay before heading out to the floor. I walk out and am immediately slammed with five tables of people. I started walking over to the first table that requested me. I look up and butterflies swarm my stomach as I see Carsten's hazel eyes staring up at me. His sexy panty dropping smile plastered across his face. I think I just fell in love with him. God he is so fucking sexy.

He smiles. "Hello my little Snowflake." His voice a deep, sexy cracked tone.

"He... hey, Carsten." I swallow nervously. " What can I get for you?" I bite my bottom lip, not sure if I can form another proper sentence.

He stares at me, a serious look forming on his face. "I miss you, Winter. You can't stand here and tell me you don't miss me," he whispers hoarsely. I'm not sure what to say. I miss him but I'm not ready for him to know that yet.

"Carsten, I ... I'm–" I pause for a minute but Carsten talks before I can continue.

"Don't say anything. You belong to me Winter, and you know this. We belong together and you feel it too." He takes a deep breath and I look around making sure no one's watching. I don't want to get in trouble. "Please baby girl, I'm losing my mind without you. I can't eat, can't sleep. You're on my mind every second of the day." God, my fucking heart. I think this is probably one of the sweetest things a guy has ever done. But I'm just... I just can't jump back, not yet. Too much has happened and I need time to think even though he's breaking my heart. I fucking miss him. I still haven't said anything and I feel like an ass.

"Carsten, I'm sorry. Please I... I can't talk about this right now," I whisper-yell looking around, noticing Stacey is staring over here.

"Shit, I'm sorry." He pauses for a minute. "I just want a milk-shake for now please." He winks. Giving me fucking whiplash changing the subject so fucking quickly like that. Now I'm confused.But thankful I don't have to respond to what he was saying.

"Okay, what kind would you like?" I ask fidgeting my hands, I don't know why I'm so nervous. I feel like I've never even talked to the guy.

"I'll take a peanut butter chocolate milkshake please, with Reese's cups on top." He slides the menu back to me.

"Ok, I don't know how you can drink a milkshake when it's so cold." I shiver a little because I'm freezing, like always. I write down what he wants so I can go to my other tables really quickly. " Are you sure you don't want anything else with that?"

"You know what, maybe some french fries too please." He winks again slowly and it's so sexy, then he smiles like he knows what he's doing to me. I can't help but smile back, like we don't have issues going on or something. "I drink milkshakes year round. Plus I love the snow. Winter is my favorite season, remember?" he smiles again, this time it's almost like a nervous smile and I wonder what he's thinking.

"I don't think I could forget a crazy thing like that." I laugh "Ok, I just need to go to my other tables really quickly to take their drink orders then I'll put your order in," I tell him slowly, starting to walk away from him.

"Sounds great, take your time gorgeous." He picks up his phone as I walk to the rest of my tables.

Walking to put the orders in at the kitchen I'm stopped by Lisa. Fuck, I hope she's not mad for how long I took at Carsten's table.

"I see Carsten requested you." She smiles at me, a gentle smile.

"Yeah, I was surprised when Stacey said I had a customer request in my section." I look over at her and Stacey walks up

"Damn, Winter, the way he looks at you, it's like he's in love with you girl. What's your secret?" she asks, biting her lip and checking Carsten out, with a look on her face that tells me she wants him.

"Um, I don't have a secret." I laugh "Plus, he's definitely not looking at me like that. He's just looking at me the way he would anyone else." I lie, I don't really want to go into details about what is going on with our relationship because I'm honestly not too fond of Stacey and she doesn't seem like the type to listen and give advice.

"Well if he's single give him my number," she says giving me a piece of notepad paper with her cell on it. Lisa stands there rolling her eyes as she walks away.

"Give me that paper please." I look over at her confused.

"What do you mean?" I asked her.

"Her phone number, don't you dare give that to him, you know damn well he requested you for a reason, Winter. Now don't you let her fuck it up." I laugh because I wasn't expecting her to say that. I love this woman, she's the best. She pats me on the back and walks to the break room.

I walk over and pick up Carsten's milkshake and my other tables drinks and walk over giving him his milkshake last. I do it on purpose in case he wants to talk to me

"Sorry it took so long, your fries will be up next."

"It's ok, take your time with me, worry about your other customers, Snowflake." He pauses for a second then adds, "You look beautiful today by the way." He says it in such a sexy voice it sends butterflies straight to my stomach.

"Oh I umm." I look down at my outfit in my plain shirt and leggings. I did my makeup so I didn't look like a bum but I didn't think I looked good. "Thank you, I appreciate that."

"You're welcome, gorgeous." He wink at me right as Stacey walks by and her jaw drops as he says it. I love that he winks at me, it's like it's his signature move or something. Whatever it is, it does funny things to my insides. I've never seen him wink at anyone else either, so I'm beginning to think he does it just to me.

"I'll be right back with your french fries, babe." I pause. "I mean Carsten. Sorry, I didn't mean to say that. Habit I guess." I quickly walk away as he laughs, the half smirk on his face that curls up and forms right to his dimple, it's so sexy. It's hard not to look back and stare, but then I'd lose track of time and forget about my other customers because I'd be too busy wrapped up in staring at Carsten the rest of my shift.

Walking back to grab the food for my tables I quickly grab them and deliver them then head back for Carsten's french fries.

"Holy shit, he is flirting with you, he called you beautiful and gorgeous. What the hell, I'm jealous," she says, crossing her arms with a pout. It almost looks like she stomps her foot too, such a child.

"I'm sorry," I say looking down at his fries in my hands. "I umm... have to go give him his food." I walk away feeling awkward, like I stole her man who was never even interested in her to begin with.

"Oh yeah, go ahead, slip him my number too, since you don't seem interested." She rolls her eyes at me as she says it. I can't believe her. I guess we aren't going to have a friendship after that, since she seems like a bitch. I knew I felt a weird vibe from her, I just couldn't put my finger on what it was. She's just a bitch, there's nothing to figure out now.

It's eight o'clock by the time I get to take a break, I have a half hour to do whatever so I grab some fries and head outside. Even though it's cold, I need the fresh air and to get out of this place. Carsten is still here, at his table, when he walks over to Lisa as I walk outside. Not sure why he's talking to her but that's none of my business since he isn't my boyfriend anymore.

I go to sit on one of the benches outside the diner, that surprisingly isn't covered in snow, but it's fucking cold through my leggings. I pop a hot fry in my mouth, loving the heat since it's freezing. I probably look like a crazy person sitting out here freezing just to eat in peace. I look up as Carsten starts walking out of the diner.

"Shit," I mumble to myself looking down like I don't see him.

"Can I sit here with you?" he asks, pointing at the space next to me.

I assumed he was leaving so I'm caught off guard. "Uhh, yeah sure, that's fine," I say, my body shaking from how cold I am.

He sits down and scoots closer to me. "I'll help warm you up, since you're shaking." Then he pauses. "I miss you so much, Winter," he says right away. In a desperate voice, like he's dying without me, and it hurts my heart so much, my stomach twists in knots at the thought of not being with him anymore, God what am I doing?

"Carsten, please." But he cuts me off.

"Brynn lied." He stops talking for a second which leaves me confused, right as I'm about to ask what he was talking about he continues. "She's not pregnant."

"She... She's not?" I ask him, now confused. There's no way this is true.

"No, she did it because she's upset." He stops again and I'm getting aggravated, I just want to know what he's talking about.

"Why is she upset Carsten?" I ask, not sure if I want to hear the answer.

"Because, I don't love her," he says looking over at me. My heart stops for a second when he says that for some reason and I'm not sure why it affected me so much.

"So she pretended to be pregnant because you don't love her?" I ask even more confused, I feel like I'm missing information or something.

"She made the whole thing up. She's jealous because I don't usually do relationships. She wanted to be with me and when she found out you were my girlfriend she was pissed." He pauses looking over at me as if he's trying to read my facial expressions or wait for a reaction. "So she lied and I needed to tell you so you knew." He looks over at me again, a sad look on his face. Why does he do these things to my heart?

I put another fry in my mouth before responding to him. "Wow, I can't believe she lied to you about that. I don't even know what else to say." I shake my head looking at him. "What a psycho bitch." I laugh in disbelief, I can't fucking believe her.

"Right, I was furious when I found out. I kicked her out of the bar and told her she's not welcome there anymore." He looks down at the ground. "I know I hurt you, and I'm sorry. I didn't mean for any of that to happen, Snowflake." He takes a deep breath, puffs of breath float through the cold air as he lets out a breath before he pauses. So I take that as my turn to talk.

"I appreciate you telling me the truth about her not being pregnant, I still can't believe she lied about that." I don't know what else to say because I'm not ready to just jump back to how things were before.

"I understand if you're not ready to pick back up where we left off at." He looks over at me and grabs my hand. "I'll give you whatever time you need, just know I'm here for you no matter what. I'm not going anywhere, Snowflake. I'll wait for you until whenever you're ready. Just come to me when you are." Then he kisses my hand and gets up and walks away leaving my heart racing, my palms sweating and my stomach swarming with butterflies.

I sit there sort of in shock, watching as he walks to his car. He'll wait for me. I've never had anyone care enough to give me time to decide when I'm ready for something and it's nice to not feel the stress of the pressure for once.

I finish up the rest of my break and then head inside to finish the rest of my shift. I walk up to the table and see something written on a napkin at the table Carsten was sitting at. I walk over and pick it up to see that it says, "I'm sorry Snowflake." I grab it and smile, putting it in my pocket so I can save it.

As I walk away from the table Stacey walks up behind me. "So is he leaving you love notes?" She crosses her arm with a snotty look on her face, almost like she's jealous.

"No, he's not." That's all I say. She doesn't need to know more, whatever happens between Carsten and I is our business not hers. I'd never trust to tell her anything.

"Hmm, it sure looked like it to me. But anyway, did you give him my number like I asked?" So I lie to her that way she doesn't question what I did with it.

"I placed it on the table for him, I'm not sure what he did with it though, he might've taken it," I say with a fake smile. I'm not sure what crawled up her ass with her snotty attitude towards me. But I can play her game too,I can play dirty if I have to.

The rest of the night was slammed, I finished my shift later than I was scheduled to due to my last table taking longer, which is fine because I'd rather be busy than slow. Plus it gave me time to put Emerald's food order in.

I'm finally done for the night so I clock out and put my apron in my locker, taking my note from Carsten with me and setting it in my purse. I head to the counter and grab Emerald's food and head out the door. I'm exhausted and ready for bed by the time I get home so I give Em her food and head upstairs to shower.

37

CARSTEN

I CAME UP WITH A PLAN. I ASKED LISA FOR WINTER'S schedule that way whenever I'm not working, I can show up there and eat. Like I said, I'm obsessed. If I can't have my little Snowflake yet, then I'll find a way to be around her. I'll take her breaks with her. I've known Lisa my whole life, which is funny because Winter has too, so I'm surprised I never met her before.

I gave Lisa a brief rundown on why I'm doing what I'm doing, and she loved the idea so I hope my plan will work. I don't care if it sounds obsessive or if I look like a stalker, I am obsessed and I'll fucking stalk my little Snowflake if it comes down to it. I miss her and I'll do what it takes because I want her back. I need her back, I need what's mine and that's her, my Snowflake.

I walk into the diner the next morning right after I watch Winter walk in, I don't want to come in at the same time and I don't want her to see me, so I make sure to walk in after she's already in. I walk up to the counter to wait to be seated when Stacey walks up. "Hey there handsome." She smiles at me then licks her lips.

I take off my coat, trying not to roll my eyes at her. "Hey, I'd like to be seated in Winter's section please." I don't even acknowledge the whole handsome thing, in fact I'm not even looking at her, I'm looking around making sure Winter doesn't walk out while I'm waiting to be seated.

"Why not my section? I don't know what you see in her anyway." She rolls her eyes at me, and her lips curl up in disgust. It's not a good look on her.

"I don't want your section, I'm here for Winter. She was my girl-friend, now I'm trying to prove to her that I'm sorry and that I love her. So, I'm trying to get her back. It shouldn't matter to you what I see in her, she's gorgeous to me and I love everything about her." I let out an annoyed breath. "Now if you don't mind, I'll just seat myself in her section, since you apparently don't know how to do your job anyway." I say as her jaw drops. I don't bother saying anything else, I just walk away and seat myself in my usual booth and wait for Winter.

As she walks out, I hear Stacey say in a bitchy tone. "Carsten is here for you in your section." Then she rolls her eyes, yet again.

"Thank you." She's trying not to smile as she walks over to my table.

"Hey gorgeous." I greet her like I always do. It's hard not to call her gorgeous when she's absolutely breathtaking.

"Hey, what can I get you?" She pauses. "I'd ask if you wanted your usual milkshake but it's breakfast time. You're here awfully early." She smiles.

"I'll take some coffee." I look right up into her eyes. "I try to usually show up when my favorite waitress is working. I'm not a fan of the other one." That makes her blush and laugh. It makes me feel like I'm making some kind of progress.

"That's all you're here for is coffee?" she asks with one eyebrow raised. Usually, I order more in the morning.

"And the view too, I love watching you." She blushes and shakes her head laughing.

"That's not creepy at all." She places her hand over her mouth trying to cover her smile.

"Says the girl who told me she wanted to be at home in her

pajamas watching crime documentaries because she loved them, the first night I met her." I wink at her.

"You remember that?" She says as she bites her bottom lip.

"Oh, Snowflake." I smiled at her. "I remember everything you tell me," I say, placing my hands together and resting them on the table.

"Wow, I … I don't even know what to say to that, that's so sweet." she says, looking away blinking quickly. Shit, I think I might've made her cry. "I uhh, I'll be right back with your coffee," she says as she rushes off to the back room. I jump up to follow her. I don't work here but Lisa doesn't care if I go back there.

"Winter, are you okay?" I ask grabbing her arm lightly to stop her.

"Carsten, what are you doing back here?" she asks, looking over my shoulder waiting for someone to come back here and say something.

38

WINTER

It's been a month since everything happened between Carsten and I and I think I'm finally ready. Ready to talk to him regularly instead of just at the diner and on my breaks, ready to kiss him, and just ready to be an us again. I miss him.

I go into work for the third day in a row and walk to the back room to check in and get my apron on. As I'm tying my apron Lisa walks in behind me.

"Hi, Winter. I'm not rushing you, but I'm just letting you know you have a customer that requested you waiting in your section," she says, smiling at me with a different look on her face than normal.

"Oh ok, well I'm almost ready, do you know who it is?" I ask because I'm impatient and don't want to wait a few more minutes to find out.

"Um..." she pauses like she's not sure how I'll react. "It's Carsten, again." She covers her smile with her hand and giggles while walking out of the back room.

I can't believe him. I just worked from five-thirty this morning until noon, and he was here for breakfast. I came back at five-thirty this evening for the dinner rush and here he is, again, in my section requesting me.

"Hey there, handsome," I say to him as I walk up to the table and his eyes light up at what I said.

"Hey, gorgeous." He has a huge smile on his face, which makes me smile even more. It's contagious, and so, so sexy.

"What can I get you this evening?" I pause, then look at him again. "Wait, you better be ordering an actual meal, I feel like you only order little things, and you don't eat enough." I look at him concerned.

"Sometimes I eat before I come here." He laughs a little, and suddenly I'm confused.

"Wait then why are you here if you eat before you come?" I raise my eyebrow at him, trying not to laugh at how crazy it sounds.

"Well, I don't eat a lot, but I eat something. Plus, I told you, I'm here for you. I'm not really worried about eating." He says to me, shrugging his shoulders. Like what he just said was no big deal, like it's normal to spend all your free time at the diner, your once girl-friend that you're trying to win back works at. It makes my stomach flutter with butterflies, knowing that he comes here just for me.

"Will you be here when I take my break?" I ask, hoping he says yeah.

"Aren't I always?" He asks, handing me the menu. "I'll have a bacon cheeseburger, no onion or tomato, and some fries with ranch please." He smiles, placing his hands on the table, drumming his pointer fingers lightly.

"Good boy, I'm proud of you. I'll go put your order in for you and I'll be right back with your drink.'" I start walking away then stop... he didn't tell me what he wanted to drink, so I turned around. "You never told me what you wanted to drink," I say, slapping my hand over my face feeling like an idiot because that's usually the first thing I take care of.

He just laughs. "I'll have a Coke, please." I think I might be in love with this man. Everything about him drives me crazy, he is so fucking attractive, it makes me wet just looking at him, thinking that he could be mine again, soon.

"Yes, sir, coming right up." He glares at me because I know when I say "Yes, sir" it turns him on.

I walk over to put his order in and fill his drink when Stacey walks up to Lisa and starts complaining. "How come she is allowed to spend most of her free time at work talking to Carsten, when she has other customers to tend to?" she asks, crossing her arms across her chest with a pissed off look on her face. Seems to be her signature move, she's worse than a toddler throwing a tantrum at this point with how often she stomps her foot, crosses her arms, and pouts.

"Stacey, she spends a decent amount of time on all her customers, she doesn't just favor Carsten, and he doesn't demand all her time. He already talked to me about why he is here and I told him it was ok." She tells her in an annoyed voice. Apparently, Stacey just likes to piss everyone off.

"The only time I give him all of my attention is on my break, and that's my time so it shouldn't matter to you what I do with my free time," I say, rolling my eyes back at her like she does everyone else and I walk away to give Carsten his drink. After setting his drink down I make my rounds checking on my tables before heading back behind the counter waiting for food to be ready when Lisa walks up next to me.

"He's been here every time you work, sitting in your section, is there something going on with you two I don't know about?" she asks and I wonder how much he had told her when he said he filled her in on the situation.

I sigh looking over at Lisa not exactly sure what to say. "It's complicated." That's the best thing I can come up with.

"Complicated?" she asks with a don't bullshit me look.

"We were a couple and a girl he was seeing kind of got in the way and ruined things on purpose. It kinda hurt me and pushed me away. There's more but that's his business not mine. But the way everything happened it just made it hard for me to let things go so quickly. I told him I needed time, so he gave me some space until recently." I smile, looking over at Carsten as he sits on his phone in his booth. He's wearing a black shirt that hugs his muscular arms perfectly, it makes me want to go over there and hug his arm and rest my head on his shoulder. His dark washed ripped jeans hug his legs just right. Then he wears converse—I always see him in converse, which I love because they're my favorite shoes. I always wear converse too. I just stand there and smile until Lisa snaps me out of it.

"You love him, don't you?" she asks me, tilting her head to the side, with a smirk on her face. I feel like this should be a conversation that I should be having with my mom, I wish I had her to go to with boy problems and advice on what to do with this whole situation.

"Wait, what?" I ask, pretending I didn't hear her because I need a second to process what she just asked me. I think I do love him. But I've never been in love before to know for sure if this is actual love.

"Carsten, you love him, don't you?" She raises her eyebrows at me with a knowing look on her face.

"I'm not sure honestly, I think I do." I pause looking over at her. "I've never been in love before, so I'm not sure." I give a shy smile because for some reason talking about my feelings with her makes me shy, I'm not used to talking about my feelings with anyone really, besides Emerald and Chastity. But I haven't had an adult to talk to about this kind of stuff with, well ever. I was too young when my mom passed to have these problems. I never actually got a chance to have a conversation with her about love and boys.

"Trust me you'll know. When you experience butterflies that never go away and an overwhelming feeling that you can't describe, that's when you know you've found love." And with that, like always, she just walks away.

"Winter, food's up." But I guess that was perfect timing for the conversation to be over anyway. I grab four plates and hand them off to my table of three before giving Carsten his food.

"Here you go, bacon cheeseburger, extra onions, extra tomatoes."

And he just stares at me, I can't help but laugh at the look of disgust on his face because I know he hates both.

"I'm just kidding babe. If you look down at your burger you can clearly see that neither of those things are on your burger." I pat his shoulder and walk away to tend to the new couple that just sat at the booth next to Carsten's.

The next hour and a half is non-stop which I love, it makes my shift go by a lot quicker before my break. I grab my salad and head to the booth that Carsten is sitting at and sit down across from him.

"Hey, gorgeous," he greets me, rubbing his leg against mine from under the table.

"Hello, handsome." I smile and take a bite of my food because I'm starving and didn't eat before my shift like I normally do.

"I like it." Is all he says as he sits there. I look at him confused. "What do you mean? Like what?" I raise my eyebrow at him.

"That you're calling me handsome again, I like it." He stops taking a drink of his Coke. "It makes me feel like we're making progress." He shrugs his shoulders, smiling, and the smile is enough to make me want to climb on his lap and kiss it off his face. It is so fucking sexy.

"I think that's because we are making progress." I smile and go to take another bite of my salad but pause. "What are you doing tomorrow?" I ask hoping he's free.

"Nothing actually, I worked at my uncle's tattoo shop today during your shift so I won't have to tomorrow. I was hoping since you were off that if I was off too, you'd want to hangout, but it looks like you beat me to asking the question. If that's what you were going to ask, that is." He gives a nervous laugh as he rubs my leg with his. I miss the feel of his body touching mine, and I don't mean it in a sexual way. I just miss his touch.

"Well, I'd like to hang out and talk if you're ok with that," I ask nervously, biting my bottom lip.

"If I say yeah, will you please stop making my dick hard by biting your bottom lip," he whispers. "It's been a while and you're turning me on." He gives another sexy smile while saying that. This man drives me and my body absolutely crazy.

"Carsten! Shhh." I put my finger over my mouth when I say that. "You can't talk like that here. And you better be saying yes because you want to, not because you want to fuck me." I barely whisper the word, I pretty much mouth it so no one around me can hear me say it.

"I promise you; I am saying yes because I miss you Snowflake, not for any other reason." He gives me a reassuring look and I know he's being serious, I never actually thought it was for sex only. I knew he was wanting to see me, I just wanted to make sure he knew I wasn't jumping right back into bed with him, at least I'm hoping I can control myself to keep from jumping back into bed right away.

"Ok, I believe you," I say, looking down at my salad. "Do you want a bite of my salad?" I ask him, holding the fork out and scooting my plate over to him.

"What kind of salad is it?" He asks, looking at my lips and not my salad, with a look like he wants to kiss me, but I'll make him wait for it a little longer.

"Just a chicken salad with cheese, croutons, and ranch dressing." I smile, and look away quickly, his intense look on his face making me feel nervous suddenly.

"Can I use your fork?" He looks at my mouth again while licking his own lips, waiting for my answer.

"Of course that's why I'm holding it out to you." I set it on the plate and scoot it towards him more.

"I'll take anything from you as long as it had your mouth on it first," he says, winking at me and stabbing the fork into a piece of chicken with some lettuce and cheese.

I blush and look up at him pulling my cup towards me. "Then I guess you'd want a sip of my drink then too, huh?" I put my tongue on the straw and lick up it before closing my mouth over it slowly and then taking a sip.

"Umm... ye... yes, please." He clears his throat and adjusts his pants. I push the cup towards him smiling.

"Here you go, sir." I might as well keep teasing him. It's fun watching him get all worked up, and I love seeing the effect I have on him, while he moves around adjusting his hard cock in his pants.

He glares at me again. "That wasn't nice, Winter. You're lucky we're not alone." He says in a rough whisper, before taking a sip of my drink, the same thing he's drinking. I just had my mouth on it first.

"Well since you don't want to be alone with me then I guess you won't follow me outside for some fresh air." I know it's still winter, but it just gets so stuffy in here, it's nice to get some fresh air during my breaks." I get up from the booth and grab my coat that I had set down and walk towards the door. I look over at him and nod my head towards the door, telling him to follow me and he practically jumps out of his seat and runs after me.

Once outside, I zip my coat as I walk to the side of the building so I'm not right in front of the diner and he follows behind me. The second he gets close to me he keeps walking towards me until my back bumps into the brick wall of the building, the snow that was stuck to the brick wall sprinkles down around us, and he puts one arm up next to me and the other under my chin lifting my head to look at him. I can hear his breathing pick up as he stares at me. I'm sure he can hear my heart racing too. It's beating so fast and loud that it feels like everyone inside the diner can hear it through the brick wall. He moves his head in slowly until his mouth is inches from mine and I slightly stick my tongue out to wet my suddenly dry lips.

Right when I think he's about to change his mind he leans in and gently brushes his warm lips against my cold ones, and then he slowly starts to deepen the kiss. He swipes his tongue against my lips and right as I'm about to open up, his phone rings making us jump.

"Shit, I'm sorry Snowflake." He reaches for his phone in his pocket and pulls it out. "I'm sorry it's my mom I have to get this." He swipes his phone to answer it.

"It's ok, take your time," I say as he walks to the front of the building.

I grab my phone to check the time, my break is almost over anyway so I don't have much time. After he gets off the phone, he walks back over to me. "Hey, I'm sorry. I have to go; my mom needs my help with fixing something at the bar. But are we still on for hanging out tomorrow?" he asks, putting his phone in his pocket.

"Yes, if you don't have any plans I'd like to hang out and talk." I put my phone back in the pocket of my apron so I can focus on what he's saying.

"Of course, I'll text you in the morning," he says, putting his phone back in his pocket.

"I'll see you around, Snowflake." He winks at me. I love his winks, something about the way he looks when he winks is so sexy and drives me crazy.

"I'll see you around, sir." I wink back, smiling as I walk away to head back inside to finish my shift.

39

CARSTEN

The next morning, I wake up in a great mood, I get to see Winter. I get to talk to her. I get to hold her. I'll get to kiss my little Snowflake, I'll get to breathe again, I'll be breathing in Winter. My fucking world will be whole again, all because I get to see her. I head downstairs to grab something to eat and run into my brother on the way down.

"Hey, dick face." He says to me while standing at the counter eating cereal.

"Hey, ass breath." I say, patting him on the back, then I stop and think. "I'd rather be a dick face than an ass breath." I laugh. We're fucking weird but I love our relationship. We've always been close; I mean we have our moments like normal siblings but other than that we've always had a great relationship.

He stops mid bite and looks over at me. "Yea, same honestly." Shaking his head he tosses a piece of soggy cereal at me but misses and it lands right next to me on the floor. Shitty aim.

"What are you up to today?" I ask, pouring myself a bowl of cereal at the counter next to him where he's standing instead of sitting for some reason.

"Not much really, Mom gave me the night off, said her friends are gonna come in and work with her so we can both enjoy a night off."

He takes a bite of cereal, talking with his mouth full, "What about you?" It comes out to where I just manage to understand it.

Chase and I used to play this game when we were younger. We'd stuff our mouths with food and say a sentence to see if we could understand what the other was saying, so after a while we got pretty good at understanding each other with our mouths full. My mom used to hate when we did it, but she couldn't help herself and she'd crack up right along with us. That's one thing about her, she always knew how to give in and have fun with us, even when we were driving her crazy.

"That's awesome, what do you have planned for tonight?" I am curious since I barely get to talk to him outside of work.

"Remember that girl, Saylor, who came to the bar the night we all hung out?" He smirks at me and takes a sip of his coffee. "She's friends with Winter's friend Chastity. I think she came with her." He says, giving more details.

"Yeah, what about her?" I ask, confused as to what she has to do with this conversation.

"Well, we hit it off that night and we've seen each other twice since then, so we're hanging out again tonight." He says, wiggling his eyebrows. "If you know what I mean."

I can't help but laugh at how cheesy he is sometimes. "Nice, she seemed pretty cool. You'll have to let me know how it goes with her. And I don't mean the bedroom details."

"Well, I'll tell you right now, she's great in bed." He gives me this big cheesy grin, but you can tell he's actually happy.

"Shut the hell up man, before I start filling you in on my sex life." Now it's my turn to throw a piece of soggy cereal at him, but it somehow lands on his face and sticks to him.

"Damn man, that was fucking awesome. I can't believe that just happened, what are the chances of that ever happening again." He says with a shocked look on his face.

"Hell, if I know, I wasn't even trying to do that. That was pretty funny though." I throw another piece and it lands on the countertop.

"What are you doing tonight, got any plans?" he asks, taking another bite of his cereal.

"Yep, Winter finally asked me to hang out so we can talk, so I'm hoping everything goes well with that," I say, drinking the milk from my bowl before walking it to the kitchen sink.

"Hell yeah! I hope it all goes well for you guys too. She's perfect for you dude." He shakes his head at me like I'm the idiot who fucked things up and not Brynn. Speaking of Brynn, I'm glad she finally got the hint and gave up. I load my bowl into the dishwasher and take Chase's from him and do the same then I turn back around to face him.

"I think I'm going to tell Winter that I'm in love with her tonight." I pause waiting for his reaction, hoping he doesn't make fun of me for it. Well actually, fuck it if he makes fun of me, I don't care, it won't change how I feel about her.

"Holy shit, really?" His jaw practically hits the floor from how shocked he is. He's fighting back the big cheesy grin that's trying to fight its way out. Making me smile even bigger because fuck man, I'm in love with the most unique Snowflake there is and I'm so fucking happy.

"Yeah man, after losing her I don't want to lose her again." I get angry thinking about the way it even happened to begin with. It wasn't even necessary, if Brynn could've just gotten the hint in the first place. Winter and I would have been very happy still. At least I think we would have been. Who knows maybe I was just destined to mess this relationship up. It was doomed before it even started. Because I'm a fuck up.

"Well man good luck with everything, I gotta get going though I have a busy day ahead of me." He pats me on the back as he walks out the front door and locks it behind him.

I head upstairs and text Winter, hoping we still have plans for the day.

Me
hey gorgeous

Winter
hey there handsome

Me
what you up to

Winter
about to shower, what about you?

Me
about to shower too

Me
we could save water and just shower together 😏

Winter
Ha. Ha. wishful thinking

Me
a man can try can't he?

Winter
yeah that was pretty clever, i'll give you that

Me
thanks babe

Me
we still hanging out today?"

Winter
definitely, are you fine with it?

Me
been counting down the minutes. I miss you.

Winter
miss you too, Carsten

Me
well go think about me while you're showering

Winter
only if you think about me 😊

Me
i probably do too much

Winter
good. Same

40
WINTER

I ASKED CARSTEN IF WE COULD TALK YESTERDAY WHEN I WAS at work, so we made plans to hangout and talk today. I think I'm finally ready to talk things over. No, I need to be ready to talk things over, it's been too long, and I miss him. I'm just hoping everything works out like I want it to because I'm finally ready to tell him how I feel. I'm done being a chicken and backing out. I just hope maybe he beats me to it and says it before I have too.

I grab my coat and gloves, it's colder today than yesterday and it sucks. I leave my bedroom and walk down the hall and down the stairs, through the living room stopping to put my boots on and then walk out the front door. After shutting my front door, I turn around and see Carsten standing there on the sidewalk, you can see his breath in the air, his hands are in his pockets, and he looks so handsome.

"Hey, gorgeous," He winks at me. I love the way he looks when he winks, something about the smirk on his face and the way he winks is so sexy.

"Hey there." Suddenly I feel shy. I had this whole plan for what I was going to say and do and suddenly I feel like this is the first time I've met him, like he didn't just spend the past few weeks at the diner every chance he got sitting in silence when I wasn't ready to talk or slowly starting conversations when I was ready. Or like he didn't just kiss me on break yesterday. I'm sure if I wasn't at work more would have happened, and I probably would've let it happen.

I tuck my hair behind my ear and take a deep breath, trying to calm my nerves, which is hard when I'm already shaking from being cold. Now I'm on the verge of shaking from my nerves. But I tell myself it's ok, it's just Carsten, the man you love. Love. Yep, I realized during our time away that I hated living without him, and I missed everything about him. I'm ready to stop being stupid.

"I'm sorry," I start with because I'm not sure what else to say. "I've been an idiot and I'm sorry." I rushed out again, because I felt the need to get it out quickly for some reason because I felt terrible.

"You're sorry?" He looks at me confused, like he didn't understand what I was saying. "Snowflake, you have nothing to be sorry about. I'm the one who should be sorry, and I am, I'm so sorry baby girl." He takes a step closer, and I don't waste any more time.

I run across my front porch and down the front stairs, snow getting all over my pants from the stairs. I run right into his arms. He picks me up, gripping my hips to lift me and places his hands on my ass to hold me. I can feel his cold hands through the fabric of my leggings. My heart is racing as butterflies form in my stomach. I've never experienced these feelings as intensely as I do with him, and it scares me. Who knew loving someone could feel so terrifying.

"God, I've missed you Snowflake, and I've missed feeling you in my arms." He looks at me as I wrap my arms a little tighter around his neck.

"I've missed you so much, Carsten and I'm so sorry it's taken me so long to realize I was being stupid."

"Shut up, you're not stupid." He says, staring down at my lips. "I understand why you needed space and there's nothing to be sorry about." He smirks a little, staring at my lips again. "Winter, I wanna kiss you more than I need air baby girl." He leans down and softly presses his lips to mine. Before pulling away his heavy breathing matching mine. Then our mouths crash together, sloppily teeth clashing as our tongues dance in a war together. He lets out a groan. "God I've missed your lips, Snowflake," he says before leaning back in to kiss me again. He slowly sets me down bringing both his warm hands up to cup my ice-cold face before pulling away. "I love you, Winter." He looks at me, giving me his sexy panty dropping smile. "God, I'm so fucking in love with you."

Tears fill my eyes, not because I'm sad but because I've been waiting my whole life for a man to tell me that he's in love with me and actually mean it. "I love you, Carsten, so, so much." I grip his shirt at the collar, pulling him towards me to kiss him.

"And I'm obsessed with you, baby girl." He looks down at me. "When I tell you that I love you I feel like it's an understatement, because beyond obsessed is definitely what I am, which to me feels equal or stronger than love. I can't find a way to put into words how obsessed I am with everything about you. If I'm not with you breathing in your air, I'm just not ok, I feel lost, I feel empty. Like something is missing and I just can't explain how much you consume all my thoughts." He looks at me waiting for me to say something, but I'm struggling to get words out because I can't control my tears.

"I feel the same way, I never thought I'd be so obsessed with someone, and feel so incomplete when you're not around." I say between sniffles, I can't believe he loves me.

"Well, you don't have to worry about feeling incomplete ever again." He stops, wiping the warm tears off my cheeks again.

"It's funny because during the winter it's so cold that it's hard to breathe, sometimes it hurts to breathe. But for some reason I can't breathe without you, I can't breathe without winter. Because breathing you in has been the easiest thing I've ever done in my life." He leans down and kisses me, not even giving me a chance to respond.

Which is fine. I don't think I can say much since I can't control my crying. But I push away and manage to choke out, "God, I love you Carsten. I never want to be without you ever again."

"I'm never going anywhere again, Snowflake." He places his cold fingers under my chin, lifting it to look up at him as his head comes down and gently presses his lips to mine, swiping his tongue out as I open my mouth to allow him inside as he swirls his tongue against mine before pulling away. He whispers to me in a husky voice, "I need you, Snowflake."

I smile up at him and ask, "My place or yours?" He picks me up and throws me over his shoulder, this seems to be his favorite way to carry me. He slaps my ass as he starts walking towards his house. "Excuse me sir, my ass is too cold for that." I smack his back playfully. "Well, I'll be warming it up once we get inside, while I spank you for calling me sir." He growls out.

"Wait, why are you spanking me?" I ask giggling.

"Because you like to tease me too much with calling me sir, and I love watching your ass jiggle when I slap it." He smacks it again. "I love watching it turn red too."

"Hey, that's not fair." Before I can finish what I'm saying, he turns his head and bites the side of my ass. "Umm excuse me, now you're biting me too?"

"Yes, I am just warming you up for when we get inside, my little Snowflake." He shuts his front door and starts walking into his house, pauses and pulls off my boots, setting them on the ground, then removes his own boots before heading towards his room.

"Going to have important conversations again?" Creedence yells out as we start walking up the stairs. I laugh since that was Carsten's excuse he used the last time he carried me up the stairs.

"Yep, gonna be in there for quite some time, they're very important today." Carsten yells back to him as I laugh.

When we get upstairs to Carsten's room, he shuts the door with his foot before turning around and locking it. He turns around in the other direction and slowly sets me down.

Not wasting any time he starts taking my coat off, followed by my shirt, leaving me in my black lace bra and leggings. His hands come up and cup my face and then his lips are on mine, he kisses me with need and with passion. Like he's making up for all the kisses we missed out on from our time apart.

I stand on my tiptoes and wrap my arms around his neck and lean into him. I press my body against his, feeling his hard cock against my lower stomach. I pull one arm away and move my hand down to his jeans, quickly undoing the button before unzipping them. I waste no time pushing his boxers and jeans down to his ankles, making him groan as my hand grazes his dick. Then I slowly get down to my knees, scratching my fingernails down his bare thighs. I look up as he's taking off his T-shirt and he stares down, his eyes devouring me. As he grips the base of his cock in his hand and starts pumping his hand up and down. I swipe my tongue out and slowly lick the tip before wrapping my lips around the head and sucking.

"Holy fuuucckkk." He growls, his breathing starting to pick up. I push his hand off his cock and grip it the best I can myself, my fingertips barely touching. I slowly stick my tongue out to lick my lips before opening my mouth and taking him as far back as I can to the back of my throat. Swallowing his cock before sliding back up to the tip. He lets out the sexiest moan. "Ohhh goddd, Winter." It makes my thighs tighten and my panties wet. I tighten my hand around his shaft and start quickly pumping it up and down, taking him back in my mouth, swirling and sucking him in. I can feel his body start to tense and I know he's getting close, but he stops me.

"I'm not ready to cum yet, Snowflake." He pulls me up from the floor, then pushes me down onto his bed. He climbs on the bed and slowly crawls over me until his lips are right above mine. "I love you, gorgeous." His mouth crashes into mine. He kisses me deeply, devouring my lips. Then he pulls away and starts kissing my jawline, trailing kisses and nibbling down my neck. My breathing picks up, I'm panting and moaning his name. I start pushing my hips up into him trying to get him to give in.

"Carsten, I can't wait any longer... I need to feel you inside me, please," I say breathlessly.

"Not yet, Snowflake." He starts nibbling his way down my collarbone, then licking his way down to my nipples, licking and biting the sensitive skin.

"Oh god, Carsten, please." He picks me up and places me onto the bed, laying me flat on my back before climbing over me. His muscular body caging me in making me feel so safe under him.

"Please what, Snowflake? Tell me what you want, baby girl." He groans as he works his way down my stomach stopping right above my throbbing pussy, he throws my legs over his broad shoulders and holds my hips in place with his hands.

"Mmm, I can't wait to taste you." He slowly licks his way up my slit, stopping right before he licks my clit. Then licks his way back down, then he starts fucking my pussy with his tongue before licking his way back up to my clit finding the spot that drives me crazy, taking turns swirling his tongue around my clit and sucking on it. Pushing me over the edge. He moves one of his hands from my hips shoving two fingers inside me and I come undone, my legs shaking, my pussy throbbing and squeezing his fingers, he groans into my pussy while I cum all over his face.

My body finally settles down, going limp and he gets up from between my legs, kneeling in front of me. His hard cock ready to be inside me. He pauses for a second before licking his fingers clean one by one. "Fuck, you taste so good," he says in a husky voice. "Mmm, my god." He growls.

I wrap my legs around him and pull him towards me wrapping my arm around the back of his neck, pulling him in for a kiss. I lick his cum covered lips, licking what's left of me off him. "Please Carsten, I need you to fuck me," I say panting, still wanting more even though I just got off.

"Don't you worry Snowflake, I'm not done with you yet." He flips me over on my stomach pulling my ass up into the air. He grabs his dick rubbing it up and down at my entrance and slowly pushes himself inside me. "Ffffuckk." He hisses in a breath.

"Oh god." I moan into his sheets while gripping them with my fingers. "God, you feel so good, Carsten."

"You feel fucking fantastic, Snowflake." He starts pounding into me, quickly moving in as deep as he can go, my body thrusting back to meet his movements. My body starts shaking as my orgasm starts to build. "I'm getting so close, Carsten." He reaches around putting his fingers on my clit, gently massaging it.

"I don't know how much longer I can hold back," he says in a groan.

"Don't, I... I'm coming," I moan out as I cum all over his cock.

"Shit, Winter." He thrusts back into me while cuming inside my pussy.

His body gently collapses onto mine before he rolls off me onto the bed next to me. I stay on my stomach, too tired to move, and turn my face to look over at him. "I love you," I say in almost a whisper, too tired to fully speak.

"I love you, Snowflake," he says as he pulls me closer to him, while he scoots in towards me. I turn over, my back to his chest, snuggling in close. He pulls the blankets up over us and wraps his arm around my stomach and I lace my fingers through his. Too tired to stay awake, I close my eyes and start to fall asleep.

41

CARSTEN

I LAY THERE NEXT TO HER, EXHAUSTED, BUT HAVING A HARD time falling asleep. It's not nighttime, but I could use a nap, especially with Winter. I miss being with her, lying next to her and sleeping next to her. I miss everything about her. God, is this what happens to men when they fall in love? They turn into sappy pussies.

Not that I mind, I'd do anything for Winter, I'd do anything to protect her. I'm sure if my friends saw how much of a sap, I am around her they'd probably make fun of me. Creedence might not since he's the relationship type. Either way I don't care.

I decide since I can't fall asleep, I'm going to put this energy into making her dinner. I had just bought some steaks yesterday in hopes I could get her to come over for dinner. She doesn't know there will be dinner yet, but I'm sure she'll be starving when she wakes up. I gather the seasoning I need for the steaks and some baked potatoes to cook with them. I turn the oven on for the baked potatoes, wash them off and prep them, wrapping them in foil to help them cook. After setting the potatoes in the oven I head over to the steak to season them so they can sit for a few minutes before I grill them. As I'm washing my hands I turn around when I hear a noise behind me. Since I'm the only one down here it makes me jump.

"Sorry, I didn't mean to scare you," Winter says, covering her laugh with her hand.

"Holy shit. I didn't realize you were up," I say, placing my hand to my chest. Feeling my racing heart. "I'm sorry for leaving you. I couldn't sleep and I was getting hungry," I say, leaning down to kiss her.

"It's okay, I'm sorry I fell asleep on you." She smiles looking down.

"You don't have to be sorry." I stop her from looking down by cupping her face and leaning down to kiss her again. I love the way her lips feel against mine, soft, and warm. I start deepening the kiss while gripping the back of her hair, I swipe my tongue against her mouth before I start moving to her jaw, then I pull her head back to give me access to her neck. She sucks in a breath, letting out a moan. I bite the sensitive skin of her neck, forcing her to whimper. Then she pulls away, reaching down, gripping the bottom of my shirt and pulling it up over my head. She places her hands on my shoulders and leans in leaving a trail of kisses down the middle of my chest, scratching me with her nails on the way down. Stopping right before my jeans, she slowly licks her way back up. My dick is painfully hard again and she looks up at me and smiles, like she knows how much she's driving me crazy.

Then she grips my cock in her hand over my jeans and starts rubbing it up and down. But then I stop her and lift her up onto the counter and go straight to her mouth to kiss her. Right as I'm about to lift her shirt up I hear the front door unlock and my brother walks in.

"Well shit..." He laughs. "I umm. Should I leave?" he asks smiling, shaking his head.

"No dick face, we are in the middle of cooking dinner," I say, helping Winter off the counter.

"Ahh okay, I wasn't aware making out on the counter... shirtless was making dinner." He throws his head back laughing and I toss my shirt at him.

"Shut up dick. We were in the process of cooking steaks and Winter distracted me." I pick my shirt up off the floor and put it back on.

"Woah, woah, don't you blame me." She crosses her arms laughing. "You started it, sir."

I raise my eyebrow at her. "Excuse me? What was that?" The corner of my mouth curls up as I try not to laugh, she knows calling me sir gets me going.

Her eyes go wide, and she starts to back away, putting her hands out trying to stop me, and I slowly start walking towards her. "Umm, I said you started it." She leaves out the sir part like she thinks I didn't catch it.

"I started it, what?" I back her into the wall caging her in with my arms.

"You guys need to get a room; I feel like this is about to get intense," Chase says, grabbing some food from the cabinet.

"Nahh man, you need to just go. Now." I lean down to start kissing her again. I hear Chase leave the room laughing and wait for him to run up the stairs.

I take my hand and lift the shirt of mine that she's wearing and to my surprise she's not wearing any underwear. I let out a low growl as my finger swipes her wet pussy. "Fuck, Snowflake," I hiss out. "I was gonna take you upstairs." I whisper by her ear, and she moans. "But I don't think I can wait that long." I bite her neck and start sucking on it, hoping to leave a mark. She lets out a soft whimper when I bite down hard on her sensitive skin. "Goddamn, baby girl." I groan and quickly start undoing my pants and zipper, I don't even bother to pull them down as I pull out my dick. I quickly pick her up by her hips, she wraps her legs around me as I wrap one arm around her, grab my dick and thrust it inside her. She lets out a soft moan, trying to stay quiet so my brother doesn't hear her. I readjust the way I'm holding her and grip her by her ass cheeks lifting her body up and slamming it down on my cock as my body thrusts up deep inside her.

"Oh god, Carsten." She moans. Her head rolling to the side as she closes her eyes from pleasure.

"Yeah, baby girl?" I ask, because I wanna hear her tell me how my cock feels in her pussy.

"Oh, fuck." She's panting, her body shaking, and I know she's already getting close.

"Tell me Snowflake, tell me how my cock makes your pussy feel," I growl into her ear.

"Oh god, so good Carsten, so fucking good," she cries out. "Your cock feels so good in my pussy."

"Fucckkk, Snowflake. You're gonna make me cum," I groan.

"Please Carsten. I need it, I'm so close." I start thrusting into her faster, wrapping one arm around her and taking the other between her legs and start massaging her clit with my thumb, that sends her over the edge.

"That's it Snowflake, cum all over my cock, baby girl," I tell her as I'm about to cum. "Oh shit." I thrust into her one last time, filling her with my cum.

"Oh my god." She pants in my arms. "Fuck that was... amazing," she says breathlessly.

"Goddamn babe, I love your pussy," I say, pulling out of her and slowly setting her down. I look down at her, "I love you, Snowflake." And kiss her one more time.

"I love you, Carsten." She smiles while readjusting her T-shirt making sure it's pulled down around her completely. I zip my pants up and turn around as the front door opens again, perfect timing.

"Hey, man," I say to Creedence as he walks through the front door.

"Hey, something smells good, what is that?" he asks, lifting his head and smelling the air.

"I made steak and baked potatoes. Help yourself, I made plenty for everyone," I say as I hand Winter her plate.

"Thank you, this looks delicious."

"Well eat up, you're gonna need your energy for later." I wink at her.

"Alright you two, keep this PG please," Creed says, shaking his head with a smile on his face.

"Yeah right, they just fucked in the kitchen right before you walked in," Chase says, walking into the kitchen.

"Damn bro, can't even keep your nose out of my business." I laugh.

"Kinda hard to when I can hear you guys upstairs in my room from the kitchen."

"Ya, ya... you're just jealous," I say jokingly.

"No way, I just got mine right before Saylor left for work, that's where I came from."

"See, then don't be a bitch and complain."

"All right you two, do we need to separate you?" Winter asks laughing at our bickering.

"How's everything going with Saylor?" Winter asks, taking a bite of her potato.

"It's going really well. I like her a lot... like a lot. It's weird," he says, smiling while answering.

"Wait, why is that weird?" Creedence asks with a confused look on his face.

"Not sure yet. I'll let you know when I figure out why it's weird," he says taking a bite of his steak.

"Are you in love with her?" Winter asks him with a smile on her face.

"Honestly, I couldn't tell you. I don't think I've ever been in love before." He shrugs his shoulders like it's no big deal.

"Typical man's answer." She rolls her eyes laughing. "You men suck at this stuff." She places her hand on her forehead and starts rubbing it, like he's stressing her out.

"Are you okay, Snowflake?" I ask her since she's still rubbing her forehead.

"Oh yes, I just have a headache, but I'm ok." She stops rubbing her forehead long enough to look over at me with a smile.

"I can get you something for it, do you want Tylenol?" I ask because I'm not about to watch her sit there in pain.

"If you have some, that'd be great," she says as I get up and go to the medicine cabinet. I grab the bottle and take it back to her.

"How was your food?" I ask looking down at her almost empty plate.

"I haven't eaten yet today, so it was delicious. I get to cook for you next time."

I frown. "That's probably where your headache came from, from not eating."

"Hey, we're heading out to a party tonight if you guys want to come?" Chase says. "Creed, you're obviously invited too, I think Axton and his girl are going to be there too."

I look over to Winter, who smiles at me. "Yes, I'd love to go if you want to?"

"I'm down, I just wasn't sure how you were feeling about it since your head hurt," I say, grabbing the Tylenol bottle and putting it back in the cabinet.

"Oh, I'll be fine once the Tylenol kicks in."

"What time are you heading to the party?" I ask cause I'm not trying to show up without friends.

"Probably around ten or so, I don't want to be too early, but I'm not trying to stay out too late cause I have to work in the morning," Creed says, emptying his plate in the garbage.

"What about you, Chase? What time are you going to this party?"

"I'll probably head there around ten-thirty."

"Well, I'm gonna head home then so I can go and get ready. Gotta make sure I look good for my boyfriend," Winter says, walking over to me. She leans down and kisses me. "I'll be back around nine-thirty."

"Love you, Snowflake." I kiss her back.

"Love you, handsome devil." She pulls away, then winks at me, and starts walking towards my front door.

42

WINTER

We head into the party, looking for Creedence and Chase. They left the house before we did so we have no idea where they are. "I'm gonna go check the backyard, do you want to come with me?" Carsten yells over the music to me before letting go of my hand.

"I actually wanted to go find Emerald so how about you check the back for the guys, and I'll check inside for her. If I find the guys, I'll come find you with them." I yell back, looking around to see if I find Emerald before he leaves me.

"Alright, gorgeous." He leans his head down to kiss me as I stand on my tiptoes to reach him. "Did I tell you how fucking sexy you look?" He practically growls into my ear, sending goosebumps through my body from how sexy he sounds saying it.

"Thank you, sir." I say winking and he pulls my body into his, in the middle of the room. There are so many people around us, yet it feels like it's just the two of us.

He presses my body to his and leans down into my ear. "Do I need to throw you over my shoulder right here for everyone to see and spank that sexy ass of yours, Snowflake?" he says in a husky voice and nibbles on my earlobe, sending chills down my body, making me shiver. "Because I will." He nibbles my ear again.

"No, sir," I say, teasing him, knowing he won't do anything that'll make me uncomfortable. But it's still fun to get him worked up. As he leans down to talk to me, I turn my head to the left to hear him better and my heart stops. I tense up, balling my fists and I freeze. I swear I stop breathing, but I don't hear anything. Everything in the room blurs, except for him, Preston. I haven't seen him since high school. At least I think it's him, but then I'm snapped out of it when Carsten gently shakes me to get my attention.

"Winter, are you okay?" he asks, turning my head to look up at him. "You look like you've seen a ghost." He looks down at me with a concerned look on his face. I look back over to my left and relief washes over me because he's not there and I realize I was just seeing things. I feel like I always panic at parties, especially with what happened that night with Preston. But I've managed to work through the panic pretty well and remind myself it's just in my head for the most part.

I snap back out of it again and turn back to Carsten. "Yeah, sorry. I thought... I thought I saw something, but I was just imagining it. I'm okay," I tell him, just because I'm not trying to cause him to panic for no reason.

"Alright, I'll be quick. I'll meet you at the back sliding door over there." He points back to where I was just staring. I'm not really paying attention to what he's saying because I'm trying to make sure my mind was just messing with me, and that Preston isn't actually here. "So that way you know where to find me, come over there in ten minutes, even if you don't find Emerald. Then we'll look together. I don't want to lose you in this crowd. Is that okay?" he asks he rubbing his hand over mine.

"Sounds good to me. I'm not trying to get lost in this crowd either." I laugh, trying to calm my nerves.

I head off in the opposite direction of where I was just looking to get my mind off of Preston so I can go back to enjoying my night with Carsten. I check through all the rooms of the house including the bathroom line and in the bathrooms looking for Emerald and I'm wondering if either she's not here yet or if maybe she's with Chase and Creed. I decide to check one last time in the kitchen to make sure she's not in there getting herself a drink before I go meet Carsten where he told me to meet him.

As I'm walking back, I make sure I double check everywhere to make sure I didn't overlook her. My guess is she probably found them outside before we got here, unless they came together. I start walking through the hallway that connects the kitchen to the dining room to find the back door but I think I took the wrong way, this house is a little confusing the way it's set up, so I turn around and walk back down the hall and through the kitchen to the other hall-way, this is the one that leads to the back sliding door. I check my phone and it's been six minutes, so Carsten will be there soon.

I start rushing through the crowd, the amount of people in this house has doubled since we first got here. I'm close to the door so I still try to calm my anxiety, maybe once I get outside, I'll feel better. I get over by the door the same time Carsten walks through, with Chase, Creed, and Emerald behind them. "Hey, baby girl." He hugs me and nuzzles his face into my neck. One of my favorite things that he does, I love the feel of him being that close to me. "I missed you." he whispers, and I love how he expresses himself. He wasn't away from me long, yet he missed me.

I lean into him standing on my tiptoes. "I missed you." I whisper back and he tightens his arms around me more, his hug calming my anxiety.

I look over and see Creedence and Emerald holding hands and my eyes look up at hers. I smile and she winks at me. I don't call them out on it, I just keep it to myself because I don't want to make things awkward. But I would love for something to happen between the two of them. It would be so fun if my best friend dated his best friend.

"Who wants to get a drink?" Chase asks.

"Yesss! Let's go." Emerald shouts, throwing her hands in the air.

She loves to party. She doesn't overdo it, but she loves having a good time.

We head over to the table, and all do a round of shots first. I definitely needed one to help calm my nerves some after I thought I saw Preston. Then we grab our drinks and head back outside to go by the fire. All the sudden a smack to my ass makes me shriek.

"Hey what was that for?" I ask, rubbing my butt since it left a sting.

"Your ass looks delicious in that skirt, too bad you're wearing those fishnets, I can't just lift your skirt up... you just had to make things difficult for me huh?" Carsten laughs smiling down at me.

"Exactly. Because I knew if I came to you in just a skirt and nothing else, we'd never leave your house and we'd miss the party." I smack his arm playfully. It's true, there's no way we would have even made it to the party if I was just wearing a skirt, so I had to make it a little difficult with my fishnet tights. Too bad he didn't think about how easy they'd be to rip. But I'll keep that secret to myself for now and let him know when we get home.

The boys go over to the other side of the patio to play beer pong while Emerald and I stay by the fire under the patio to get warm, since the air is chilly. The snow melted some over the last few days and there's very little left on the ground. Winter hasn't even started yet, but it always snows early here, I'm dreading when it finally does start though.

"Hey, I'm gonna head inside and use the bathroom, I'll be right back." I tell Emerald. I knew I should've gone before I came out here, but the cold made it worse.

"Ok babe, do you want me to come with you?" she asks with a worried look on her face.

"No, I'll be back. You know where to find me if I go missing though." I wink at her walking away. My nerves have calmed down a lot with the shot and drink I had so I'm not as freaked out as I was before when I thought I saw Preston.

I walk upstairs to find the bathroom, surprisingly it's empty which is a huge difference from the lines that were there earlier when I was looking for Emerald. I walk into the bathroom locking the door and look at myself in the mirror, my makeup smudged under my eyes a little. "Ew, I look like shit," I mumble to myself. "Gotta fix that when I'm done." I sit down and use the bathroom. Then wash my hands, grabbing some toilet paper to wipe under my eyes since I can't seem to find anything else and I'm not trying to go through stuff that isn't mine. I unlock the bathroom door, open the door and shut off the light and walk out.

Looking down as I'm walking out and am caught off guard when I run into a hard surface, almost knocking me on my feet, I step back grabbing the wall to help me balance and look up. *Holy shit* I think to myself as my heart starts racing again. I think I'm going to throw up. I look up to a smiling Preston standing in front of me. He gives me the biggest grin telling me he's happy I ran into him.

"Winter, baby, I'm so glad I ran into you," he yells, his words slurring a little.

"I thought that was you before... but then I thought to myself, there's no way I'd get lucky twice with her at a party." Fucking great, he's drunk. So, I don't even respond. I'm not trying to give him a reason to think it's ok if he touches me. All I have to do is get around him and run down the stairs to get away from him, then once I'm downstairs I can run out the back door to Carsten, it's not too far from the stairs.

"Leave m alone Preston." I try to push past him but it's no use, he is so much stronger and taller than me.

"Aww, what's wrong baby. Not drunk enough to play yet?" He gives a disgusting chuckle, making my stomach turn at the thought of what he can do to me now.

"I'm here with my boyfriend, he'll come looking for me and kick your ass." I try to calm my shaking voice as I say it, trying to show him I'm not scared. Even though right now I'm terrified.

"Oh Winter. You really think that your boyfriend is going to help you? I'll be done before he even notices you're missing." His lips curl up. "I'll make sure I ruin that pussy for him. He'll never want to touch you again once I make you a dirty whore for cheating on him." He laughs again before lifting his glass to his mouth and chugging it down before throwing it to the side. It lands somewhere on the ground next to us along with all the other garbage that's scattered around from the party. Then gives me an evil grin.

"You have no idea what he's capable of. He'll fucking kill you." I spit in his face. Literally spit right into his eye.

"You fucking bitch." He places his hand over his eye wiping it quickly and I use him being distracted as my chance to hopefully get away from him.

I quickly step to the side trying to get away from him so he doesn't block me anymore, but he steps with me. I take a deep breath and step the other way making it past him, but he grabs my arm last minute and spins me around pinning me to a wall.

"You thought you were gonna get away this time without letting me fuck you huh?" he slurs and then laughs. I can't hear it over the noise of the music, but I could see it in the way his head and chest moved. I don't respond this time. Fuck him, he doesn't deserve anymore of my energy. Plus, I'm not trying to give him any reason to think that I wanted it then or that I want it now. I try pushing away, but he slams me back into the wall even harder with his body, gripping my wrists with one hand. He has them held together like they would be if he tied them, but with one large hand wrapped around them. I can't move at all because of how close he is to me. I attempt to shove into him, but my body barely moves from how close he is to me while he pins me. I try pushing again but he just laughs.

"Tsk.Tsk. Why are you trying to get away, don't act like you don't want my cock to fuck you, Winter. You've always been obsessed with me, don't you remember? How much you liked me before we went on that date." He practically spits out. His body seething with anger.

"But then you turned me down, you made it seem like you fucking wanted me. Teased me, practically begged me to fuck you with all those looks and the ways you would act around me. Then you go and turn me down. No, fuck you. I will get what's mine." He gives me a creepy smirk.

"Get the fuck off of me Pres..." His mouth comes down on mine slamming my head back into the hard wall, while shoving his tongue into my mouth. I head butt him, but he doesn't budge, I didn't do it hard enough. No one around us is even bothering to look, the way he's standing he has my hands blocked by his body and it looks like we're just making out, right along with all the other people who are going to hook up tonight, so no one even pays attention. Plus, it's too loud to hear me yell even if I tried. He takes his tongue out of my mouth kissing me again and with his free hand starts grabbing my boobs. I turn my head away, but he moves his hand from my boob and holds my head in place kissing me aggressively and biting my bottom lip so hard I can taste the blood, then he starts licking my jaw.

"Get off of me." I yell and try kneeing him in the balls, but he shifts right in time, and I miss.

"Nice try bitch, I told you, you're not leaving here without giving me what you owe me." His tone is angry as he stands there breathing like he just got done running. He's out of breath from how worked up he is. Fucking pig. I can feel his fucking dick pressing into me each time he moves and it's making it so hard not to vomit. Please let them find me.

"What, I owe you?" I shout. "I don't owe you shit." I spit in his face again.

"You fucking whore." He wipes the spit off with his free hand, then he grabs me and opens a door next to us shoving me inside onto the ground. He falls on top of me knocking the wind out of me. I start coughing from the impact and try kicking him but the way he's on me I can't move my legs. I'm struggling to breathe from his weight and the fall. I try to shove him again but I'm not strong enough, he doesn't even budge. He pushes my hands above my head, still wrapping his hand around both my wrists, then uses his other hand to start lifting my skirt up and I'm thankful for my tights so it'll make it harder for him.

"Get off of me, Preston, please," I yell, crying hysterically now. I was calm up until this point because I didn't want him to see I was afraid. Now I'm terrified. I'm stuck in this room with him, and no one knows I'm not in the bathroom, they might not even be concerned because they might think there's a long line.

"You think begging me is going to make me stop?" His laugh is evil this time, like something you'd hear in a movie. Sending chills through my body making me realize this might actually be it. Preston might get what he wants now after all these years.

"All you're doing is making my dick harder. Don't you know the more you fight the harder I'll get," he whispers next to my ear. Bile starts rising in my throat at the thoughts of what's to come next and I start choking on it. I cough in his face spit splattering along with it, but I could care less. The bastard deserves it.

"You stupid bitch, stop fucking fighting Winter. You want this." He smiles as he reaches his hand back down between my legs.

I start thrashing my body back and forth trying to break my arms free from his hold but it's not helping, he's too strong. I need to figure something out. Quickly.

"You're not leaving here until I get what you owe me, you fucking tease. Don't act like you don't want this, Winter. Now just stop fighting me." He leans down to kiss me again while trying to get my skirt up. "The faster you give in and stop fighting, the sooner I'll get to destroy your cunt and ruin you for every other man. No one wants a fucking whore, Winter." His slurring is worse the more he speaks making it harder to understand him. How much did he drink? I start kicking my legs hoping to hurt him and end up getting him in the balls this time, he rolls off me grabbing his junk. "Goddamn it, you fucking bitch," he yells, rolling onto his stomach.

I manage to get up and run for the door but he's too quick, He grabs me by the ankle and pulls as hard as he can. Making me fall to the ground on my stomach with a hard thud. Knocking the wind out of me yet again. I gasp trying to get some air into my lungs but it's not working. Fuck it, I need to get out of here. I start using my arms to pull my body away from him, but it's no use he just keeps pulling me back to him.

"Get back here you fucking whore. Give me what you owe me." I manage to kick his hand off my ankle.

"Fuckkkk," he shouts shaking his hand in the air. "You fucking bitch."

I don't have time to waste. I pull my body up to a standing position and start running towards the door again. But I'm not fast enough. He pulls me back and shoves me into the wall again pinning me close with his leg between mine and his shoulder into my chest pushing me into the wall, hard. He grabs the waist of my tights, pulling the fabric away from my body, ripping it and pulling my skin along with it. But it doesn't break.

"God dammit," he screams and reaches into his pocket. Please someone help me. Is all I can think of right now. Please someone help me.

I look down and see he's holding a pocketknife in his hand and an evil smile on his face.

"Stop. Please stop," I shout, spit flying out of my mouth. Salty tears fill my mouth as I shout at him. I need to find a way to stop this.

"I keep telling you baby, if you stop fucking fighting it'll hurt. But it will go a lot easier if you just stop. Fucking. Fighting. Me." He growls placing the tip of the knife to my throat. "Now, where were we." His laugh is fucking crazy, it's scary. Like something from a horror movie. It sounds like something nightmares are made of. Vomit tries to force its way up my throat just thinking about what he might do next. Is he going to kill me?

He slowly takes the tip of the knife and pushes it into my skin, and I stop moving. Scrunch my eyes closed and hold my breath, afraid moving will cause the knife to cut me if he isn't already with it. He's pushing it into me so hard I wouldn't be surprised if it was. It's taking everything in me to not to freak out. I try to slow my breathing as he takes the knife and starts trailing it down my neck, slowly down my body. I'm afraid to open my eyes. I'm afraid to look down and see that I might be covered in blood. I stop fighting. I don't want him to get any more ideas or end up killing me. He slowly drags the knife between my breasts, tracing the outline of what you can see from my bra before he finally moves the knife away.

What is he going to do? I tighten my eyes even more. I don't know if I want to look at this point. He places the knife on my stomach and slowly traces his way down until he gets to the top of my belly button.

"See how much fun this is now that you're not fighting me," he says before bringing his lips down to mine while he swirls the knife around my belly button.

"Please," I whisper. "I won't tell anyone." Why do people say that. Obviously, that's the first thing I'd do if I get the fuck out of here.

"Winter. Winter. Now, now." He laughs and I open my eyes a little and look at him. He takes the knife placing it in one of the holes of my fishnets and cuts up all the way to the waistband slicing it in half. Then takes the same hand and rips them down my body the rest of the way. Leaving them at my feet, before pushing my skirt up with one hand.

"Now where were we?" He places the knife to my hip right where my lace thong sits.

"Please, stop," I scream out. "Please." I push myself forward trying to move his body but all that does is make the knife push further into my skin. Not caring if it cuts me anymore. I need to get away from him.

"Baby, Baby. Calm down," he whispers. "I'm almost ready," he says undoing his belt and pants with his free hand still holding the knife.

I feel like we've been in this room for hours when it's probably been about five minutes, why haven't they come looking for me yet? Is this really happening, is he going to kill me after he rapes me? Is he that crazy? My whole body is shaking. I feel like I might pass out, but my adrenaline is keeping me going.

"Preston, think of what you're about to do please. Stop." I cry. I need to do something; this can't be happening. I try moving my arms that are above my head but it's no use, the grip he has on my hands is tight enough that my arms are numb, and my hands are tingling, I'm sure I'll have bruises.

"I've been thinking about this moment for four years Winter, you think you're going to stop me now?" He takes his knife and pushes my panties to the side with it, holding the fabric over with the tip. "Fuck, look at that pussy of yours, only thing that's missing is how wet you're supposed to fucking be from how excited you are Winter." He drops the knife by my feet and relief washes over me. Did he do that on purpose?

"Let's work on getting this pussy wet for me Winter, should I taste you? I've always wondered what you tasted like. But you never gave me the satisfaction of knowing, did you?" His fingers trail to the band on my panties

"Maybe I'll just fuck you we don't have much time, do we?" He gives another crazy laugh.

"Preston please stop." His mouth crashes down onto mine and I bite his tongue, hard. I taste blood, and he pulls away from me.

"You fucking bitch." He wipes his mouth. "You made me bleed." He looks at me in shock like he can't believe what I just did. Then he smiles, his once white teeth now stained red as the blood fills his mouth. "That's alright we don't have to work on making you wet, do we?" He laughs as blood and spit drip from his mouth. He tightens his grip on my hands above my head making me wince from the pain. He moves his fingers back to the waistband of my panties. I gotta get him off me. I start thrashing my body attempting to kick my legs, but I can't with the way he has me pinned to the wall. Headbutt him. It suddenly comes to me, I've never headbutt anyone before but I'm willing to do anything at this point. Right when I'm about to smack my head into his, his whole body is jerked back away from me.

43

CARSTEN

CHASE AND I ARE IN THE MIDDLE OF A GAME OF BEER PONG when I notice that Winter isn't by Emerald anymore. Emerald and Creedence are talking to each other, that's what made me realize she was gone. "Hey, where did Winter go?" I ask in sort of a panic because I didn't notice that she walked away and I'm not sure how long she's been gone for.

"She said she had to go to the bathroom. She didn't want me to go with her though, she said she'd be fine." She says then goes back to talking to Creed. I don't want to seem like a controlling boyfriend, so I wait until we're done with the game before I go to find Winter since she isn't back yet.

"Hey guys, I'm gonna go wait with Winter and I'm gonna get a drink. Anyone else want another drink?" I ask, trying to calm my panic. Hoping she's just stuck in a long line and that nothing is wrong.

I head inside and run up the stairs to the bathroom but it's empty. The door is open, and the light is off. I try to calm myself down. Maybe she's getting a drink now that she's done in the bathroom. I start walking back down the hall to head back downstairs when I hear a yell coming from the room across from the bathroom. Panic sets in. I rush back up the hall to the first door, I see and open it the rooms empty. The next room I try is locked, I bang on the door, and no one opens so I bust it open.

"Hey what the fuck." I barge in and get a full view of some guys ass.

"Shit, sorry." I slam the door shut and turn to see one last door I rush over to the door and bust it open fuck checking the locks. I see Winter against the wall with a man in front of her. I walk up behind them and pull him off her. Pissed, I can't believe what I'm seeing. Winter's tights are at her feet and he's holding her hands above her head, skirt scrunched up at the waist.

"What the fuck is going on here," I shout, really fucking angry. Then I notice someone I used to be best friends with. What the fuck? And why the fuck is Winter crying?

"Preston?" He looks over at me, confused.

"Yoo, Carsten, long time no fucking see man," he says, going to slap my shoulder but my anger takes over and I shove him.

"Why the fuck were you just kissing my girlfriend," I yell, balling my fists up at my sides. Trying to control my anger, because if someone calls the cops—I can't get arrested for fighting, again.

Preston puts his hands up, backing away a little. "Woah man, ask your girl, she came on to me. I was standing there waiting for the bathroom and she started flirting with me. I didn't know she was yours or I wouldn't have touched her." He pauses looking over at a sobbing Winter as she tries to push her skirt down. But I don't run to her, not yet. I need to figure out what the fuck is going on.

"Winter?" Is all I say. I'm not accusing her but I'm giving her the chance to explain. She doesn't speak, she looks like she's in shock. I know something is off, her face is ghost white and she's shaking. I stand there, staring back and forth between the two of them until it hits me. Preston... he's the one who tried to rape Winter. Now I'm fucking pissed and seeing Red.

I lunge at him and punch him right in the face. If I get arrested tonight, it'll be worth it for Winter.

"What the fuck man, why are you hitting me?" he says, grabbing his nose.

"Don't you fucking play games with me, Preston. Once upon a time I would've believed you. But I'm not fucking stupid anymore." I can't believe I used to be best friends with this fuck. He was the one who did this to Winter all those years ago?

"Man, I don't know what you're talking about. Like I said, she came onto me." I look over at Winter she's so pale. I'm afraid she's gonna pass out.

"Winter, go find Emerald, please." She just stands there.

I punch him in the face again. "Who the fuck do you think you are, you tried to fucking rape her." I punch him again, now he's leaning over holding his mouth and nose in his hand. "I remember you telling me this story years ago, but you made it seem like she was willingly giving herself to you and she chickened out. You didn't tell me you fucking raped her, you piece of fucking shit." I knee him in the face knocking him to the ground.

"Carsten, man, stop. Let me explain." He's got tears running down his face.

"Explain what? That you fucking raped her? She's fucking traumatized from that already and now you fucking try to do it again? To my fucking girl." I kick him in the side multiple times.

"Carsten, please stop." I hear Winter crying behind me. "He's not worth it. Please." She falls to the ground hugging herself. Crying. I rush over to her and grab her off the ground and put her onto my lap.

"Do you want me to call the cops, Snowflake?" I ask, holding her close to me. "I will."

"No, please. I don't want the police involved. Just take me home. Please." She's shaking in my arms, hysterically crying and on the verge of hyperventilating when Emerald, Chase, and Creedence come walking in.

"What the fuck?" both Creed and Chase say at the same time, as Emerald is rushing over to Winter.

"Oh my god, Winter. Please tell me he didn't." She starts crying. "Winter, I'm so sorry. Are you okay?" But she doesn't talk, she just cries.

"I got to her just in time," I tell her as I lift Winter in my arms while I stand.

"We'll take care of him for you Carsten, just get her home." Creed says.

"I'm gonna stay back with them." Emerald pauses and looks at Winter crying in my arms. "She needs you right now, you're gonna be the best person to comfort her."

"Thanks, I'm gonna do my best to comfort her the best I can. Let me know what happens. I'll see you guys back at home." I stop in the doorway looking back at my brother and Creed and nod my head. They know what to do with Preston and that will stay between the three of us, I'll tell Winter eventually. I start carrying her out the room and down the hallway. I get to the stairs and walk down. People are staring as I carry her through the party, not bothering to move. "Get the fuck out of my way, there's nothing to see here," I yell at them as I struggle to get through everyone. Winter is snuggled up into me holding her fishnet tights in her shaking hands that she refused to take off until we get home. She said it's the only thing keeping her together letting her know he didn't get to her this time, making her feel less exposed even though they aren't on her all the way.

Once I get to the door someone opens it for me. I look over to thank them and it's Brynn. "Here, let me get the doors for you. I'll help you with the car too," she says, following me out of the house.

"Umm, thanks. I appreciate that," I say, giving her a slight smile. Not really sure what made her help me but right now my main focus is getting Winter back to my house to make sure she's okay. We walk outside towards the street where my car is parked as Brynn starts talking.

"Is she okay?" is all she asks.

"She will be, I can't explain right now, it's not my place. But seriously, I appreciate you helping," I say to her, not wanting to be a dick, but really it isn't my business to tell, especially to Brynn.

"No problem, glad I saw you coming down the stairs." She opens my door as I set Winter down in the passenger seat. Then I lean in and grab the seat belt and buckle her in.

"Well, I gotta get her home." I say to Brynn, walking around to the driver's side. "Thanks again."

"You're welcome," she says and starts to walk away.

I get into the driver's side and look over at Winter, she's curled up on my front seat, her knees to her chest, head down crying. It's breaking my heart to see her like this, but I don't really know what to say that isn't going to be the wrong thing.

"Winter?" I say in a slight whisper. "I'm gonna take you to my house okay, Snowflake?" She slowly shakes her head and finally manages to look up at me a little.

"I'm sorry, Carsten." She sniffles.

"You're sorry?" I ask, because she doesn't need to be sorry and right as I'm about to tell her that she starts talking again.

"For having so many issues, and for being broken." She lets out a sob, her body shaking. I undo her seat belt and pull her onto my lap. I gently cup her face and turn it to where she's looking up at me.

"Listen, Snowflake," I say calmly. "You do not need to be sorry. You did nothing wrong." I go to continue but she cuts me off.

"He kissed me, he touched my boobs. He cut off my tights." She sniffles. "He had me pinned against the wall, he was gonna-" She can't even finish what she was saying because she starts sobbing again, this time laying her head on my chest. "You... you stopped him, you saved me," she chokes out.

"Winter, I'm so sorry he touched you and I wasn't there for you like I should have been. I will never forgive myself for that. I'm thankful I got to you in time before he went further. But you... don't be sorry. You did nothing wrong, baby girl." I pause pushing her hair away from her face. "You are perfect, you're not broken. I'm here and I'm not going anywhere." I kiss her forehead and she looks up at me.

"Thank you." She looks into my eyes, her bottom lip quivering. Tears stream down her face and I just can't get over how beautiful she is. I can't believe anyone would want to hurt her. She's never had someone to depend on and protect her, and I want to be that person she can count on.

"Don't thank me. I'm sorry I wasn't there when you needed me." I pause, the guilt setting in. I feel like shit that she even had to go through that with Preston, again.

"Carsten, you did. You saved me. Don't beat yourself up over it. Please," she says, putting her hand on my face, I look down at her. Her beautiful honey-brown eyes filled with unshed tears. I reach my thumb under, ready to catch whatever falls. I want to kiss her but I'm afraid to push her after what she just went through, right as I'm about to she tilts her head up and kisses me, softly, slowly. "I love you, Carsten," she says as she pulls away.

"I love you, so much, Snowflake." And I kiss her again. This time she swipes her tongue against my lips, and I open for her, giving her what she needs. I'm afraid to do too much so I let her lead, showing me what she wants. She turns her body to where she's straddling my lap in the front seat, and she deepens the kiss. After kissing for a few minutes, I pull away.

"Let me take you home, Snowflake," I say, giving her one last slow, passionate kiss.

She pulls away, nodding her head and slowly climbs off my lap back into the passenger seat.

Once I put the car in drive I reach over and put my hand on her thigh, slowly rubbing it to hopefully give her some kind of comfort after the night she just had. Ten minutes later I pull into my driveway and get out of the car, rushing over to her side of the car before she can get out. I open her door and reach down and pick her up, I don't want her walking and I love being close to her.

"I'm going to get my bath ready for you and I'm going to join you in there if you don't mind?" I sort of tell her and ask her at the same time, not wanting to give her a choice because I want to help her relax and bathe her. But I also don't want to push her after tonight.

"Yes, that's fine. I appreciate you caring and taking care of me," she says sniffling still, she finally calmed down some since we drove away. I walk through my front door and slowly set her down, she starts walking towards the kitchen to go upstairs but I stop her, grabbing her hand.

"I will always care for you, Snowflake. I love you; I've never loved anyone the way I love you. I've actually never been in love at all before." I stop thinking of what to say next. "It's true I've never had a girlfriend; I've never even wanted or cared to have one. But now that I have you, I'm afraid to lose you. I don't ever want to be without you."

She looks up at me, new tears in her eyes, I'm hoping good tears. "God Carsten, you're so perfect. I'm afraid to be without you too." She wraps her arms around my waist and rests her head on my chest, right on my heart.

"Do you hear the way my heart is beating right now?" I ask her because it's beating so fast, I'm afraid I might have a heart attack.

She adjusts her head and places it over my heart better and waits for a second. "My god, are you okay?" she asks, sounding concerned.

"More than okay, that's what you do to me every time I'm with you." I laugh for a second and look down at her. "Every time I'm with you I question whether or not I'm dying because my heart always races like that." This time I don't wait for her to respond; I lean down and kiss her. Trying to cheer her up I pick her up and throw her over my shoulder.

"Carsten, you're crazy." She starts laughing. "Put me down before I hurt you from you carrying me like this all the time." She shrieks as I start climbing the stairs.

"Shut up, you're not going to hurt me." I smack her ass. "Carstennnn, stop it." She's giggling.

"You love it, or you wouldn't be giggling like a little kid." I tell her because it's true every time I do this it has her giggling like crazy and smiling.

"I might love it, but you are aware I can walk right?" She pauses for a second. "I think you've carried me to your room way more than I've walked."

"That was my plan, for you to enjoy me carrying you while I get to enjoy the view of your ass while I carry you." I say squeezing her ass with both hands.

"Hey, don't drop me." She squeals as I grab her ass.

"I would never, I didn't let you fall off your roof, did I?" I question because that should be enough proof that she should trust my ability to hold her and grab her ass at the same time.

"That is true, you did a great job warming up my boobs that day against your sexy muscular chest." She wiggles her eyebrows as I slowly set her back down on the ground.

"I'm hurt... is that all I was to you that day?" I put my hand to my chest in shock. "A heater... I didn't save your life... just warmed up those... mmm..." I can't help but groan. "You know what, get your ass over here... I need to remind myself what it felt like to have your tits against my chest." I pause for a minute. "If... if that's ok after umm..." she cuts me off.

"It's more than ok. I only want the memory of your hands on me and your body against mine to be something that I think about. Not him. I want you to help me erase him from this night, from my memories and from taking over my thoughts." She takes her shirt off as she walks towards me, and my dick instantly gets hard. God, I never thought someone could turn me on so much all the time. I feel like I could die a happy man sleeping with her every day for the rest of my life. Just that thought alone scares me to think I finally found someone I want to spend every day with, and I'd never get sick of her.

I take my shirt off and pick her up right under her ass pushing my hard dick against her stomach to show her how much she turns me on. Then I lower her slowly onto my bed, for once in my life I don't want to fuck her, especially after what she went through tonight. I'm going to show her how much I love her and make love to her. I lower my mouth to hers kissing her deeply, passionately, taking my time exploring her mouth with mine, I'm not rushing. I have all day to take my time to explore her.

I pull away from the kiss and start kissing down her jaw to her neck, trailing kisses down to her breast until I get to her nipples, I hover my mouth over her nipple and stick my tongue out teasing and slowly licking feeling it harden under my tongue. "Ohhh god." She moans underneath me and then I suck her nipple into my mouth groaning against it. God this woman is perfect.

I suck and gently bite her nipple before slowly trailing over to the next one and doing the same thing. Taking my time, exploring. Memorizing the way her body reacts to everything I do so I can remember the next time I make love to her. I'll remember exactly how to please her. I suck on her nipple one last time before I pull away and she groans. "Please Carsten, I need you."

"I know, Snowflake. I'm just getting started, baby girl. Just relax." I trail kisses and lick my way down her body. Goose bumps spreading across her smooth skin. My dick is so hard it hurts but it's worth it to listen to her moans mixed with torture and pleasure. I stop right when I get to her pussy, throwing her legs over my shoulders, and holding her thighs in place. I start kissing my way down until I get to her clit, kissing it gently before I slowly stick my tongue out, swirling it on the spot I know she loves.

"Fuck Carsten, please don't stop." I place my lips around her clit before I suck on it, pulling on it just enough to tease her and get her closer to the edge. Then I stop and she groans "Carsten, please, I'm so close." She says breathlessly. She sticks her hips up a little to show me she wants more. I lick my way down her slit and stick my tongue inside her.

"Mmm." I growl against her. "You taste so fuuucking good, Snowflake." I lick my way back up, her body shaking now. I know she's getting closer, so I bring my hand up and slide two fingers inside her, curling them up and start pumping them in and out of her, while working my fingertips up and down. I place my mouth back over her clit and start sucking on it and that sends her over the edge, her pussy clamps down on my fingers, squeezing them. I wish it was my cock, but I need to be patient, this is about her not me. I suck on her clit and pump my fingers until her body goes limp. I slowly pull my fingers out of her, licking her to taste her one last time before pulling away. I get up on my knees and look at my cum covered fingers. "God, I can't wait to taste this." I stick them in my mouth one finger at a time, slowly cleaning them off and savoring the way she tastes. "I could lick your pussy every day, Snowflake." I smile down at her, her eyes heavy.

"I won't complain," she says, giving a sleepy laugh.

"I'm not done with you yet, baby girl. After this we'll take a bath then sleep." I come back down for a kiss, moving my hands down and gently spreading her legs. I grip her hips, adjusting them, raising them up with my one hand, I take my cock in my other hand and slowly glide into her pussy. "Fuckk." I hiss in a breath, her pussy feeling amazing making it hard to not go fast. "Goddamn, baby girl. Your pussy feels so good," I groan into her ear while slowly sliding in and out of her.

"Oh god, Carsten." She moans, turning her head, biting into my neck. I grab her hands, lacing our fingers together, pinning them down on each side of her head and thrust into her slowly. I lean down and gently kiss her, and nibble on her lower lip. I pull away again trailing slow soft kisses down to her neck, still taking my time making sure that this is something special for her to remember, especially after tonight.

I suck on her neck, enough to make her moan, but not enough to leave marks—although I wouldn't mind leaving my marks on her, I'll save those for another night. This night is supposed to be special, to show her how much I love her, through our bodies and not words. I readjust myself sliding in her at a deeper angle, her moans driving me crazy. I pick up the pace some going a little faster, but just enough to get her closer. I still want to take my time, enjoying the way her body feels under me, and the way her pussy feels around my cock.

"Carsten, please. I need this." She moans against my lips.

"I know, Snowflake. I know," I say, leaning down to her mouth, pressing my lips against her, swallowing her moans. This time I give her what I know she needs, I pick up the pace pumping into her faster and deeper until she comes undone, her pussy clamping down on my dick sending me over the edge and I cum inside her pussy pushing in deeper each time until her body stops shaking and I collapse onto her, not putting all my weight on her body. I lay my head onto her chest; I haven't bothered pulling out of her yet. I'll worry about that in a minute. Right now, I just want to enjoy the feel of her sweaty body against my own sweaty body and the sound of her heart racing in my ear, knowing that I'm the reason for her heartbeat being out of control.

44

WINTER

We sit there in the hot bath water. I sit between Carsten's legs, my back to his chest as he rubs my body with soap. Tonight was a crazy night and Carsten was just what I needed to help me not become depressed again. I don't know what I would've done if I didn't have Carsten, or what would've happened if he didn't show up in that room. I try to push the thoughts out of my mind, so that way they don't take over like last time. It took me a while to get through that and I'm not ready to fall back into that hole again. It took me forever to climb out of the depression I was in, and the panic attacks I had to deal with. All the sleepless nights and nightmares I had were something I don't wish on anyone.

I turn my body around in the tub to face Carsten and wrap my legs around him, straddling him. "Thank you." I say, looking into his eyes. It's funny how two words can mean so much. He took such a terrible night and turned it into something so meaningful, so special. He helped me erase those nightmares that were trying to take over. I've never had someone care so much about me, or anything that's happened to me. But it feels good to be cared for and to be loved.

"You don't have to thank me Snowflake. You know I'd do anything for you." He leans in, placing his forehead to mine and cups my face placing soft and gentle kisses on my lips. I open mine to invite his tongue, he slowly swipes mine with his before nibbling my lower lip. I let out a quiet moan into his mouth before I pull away.

"What's wrong?" he asks, a worried look on his face.

"Nothing, I just had to stop before I couldn't." I laugh a little. "It's my turn to wash you." I smile at him grabbing the soap. I can at least return the favor for him, even if it's something so simple. He still deserves it. I squeeze the soap onto my hand and set the bottle down, lathering it a little with my other hand before grabbing his shoulders. I decide to massage him along with washing him. I want to make sure I take care of him the way he takes care of me. To show him I love him the way he loves me. As I sit here massaging him, I start to feel nauseous. My nerves getting the best of me from earlier. Maybe constantly pushing the thoughts out of my mind isn't going to be the best way to deal with it. I'm hoping as the week goes it gets easier to deal with. I stop what I'm doing, my hand instantly covering my mouth and practically jump off Carsten and out of the tub, trying not to get water everywhere or slip in the process and rush quickly to the toilet lifting the toilet seat, vomit flying out of my mouth faster than I can open it. Choking on it as it's coming out since I wasn't prepared for it.

Carsten rushes out of the tub behind me making sure all of my hair is still tucked away in the hair tie I put it in so I didn't get my hair wet. He rubs my back until I'm finished puking. He grabs a washcloth from the closet running it under cold water before handing it to me. "Place it on your forehead or the back of your neck, it'll help cool you down."

"Thank you." I manage to say between coughs. Still trying to calm down my anxiety. I lost a lot of weight after this happened the first time from losing my appetite and vomiting every time I ate anything. I hope this isn't going to be the case.

"Are you okay?" He pushes a strand of hair away from my eye.

"I think so. I'm sorry that was so gross." I say, laughing it off to ease his mind.

"Winter, please stop apologizing. Sometimes things happen that you can't control. I'm not worried about me, what about you?" He smirks.

"Yeah, I feel a little better. My stomach is still a little queasy, but I think I just need some sleep now," I say, smiling over at him.

"Let's get you dried off then." He grabs a towel from his cabinet and walks back over to me, wrapping it around me and then walks back and grabs two more towels. He stands in front of me and wraps one towel around his waist and then kneels in front of me and starts drying my legs off with the other towel. He looks up at me smiling as he's kneeling in front of me. "Don't worry I'm not gonna try anything, I was just thinking... I don't think anything you do will gross me out, ever." He grabs my hand and kisses it.

"I hope not, because that was gross. I wasn't expecting it, or I would have warned you." I laugh. As he's drying off my legs my anxiety starts acting up again, my body is slightly shaky, my heart racing. It's all making me nauseous. I rush back over to the toilet, lifting the seat and vomiting so quickly it almost comes out of my nose.

"Are you okay babe?" Carsten asks, rushing up behind me making sure my hair is out of the way again.

"Yeah, I'll be fine." I grab some toilet paper, wiping my mouth. "I went through this before, the last time this happened with Preston. I could barely keep food down... it was like that for months, so I wouldn't be surprised if it happened again," I say frowning a little, tears filling my eyes.

"Come here, Snowflake." He sits down on the floor and pulls me onto his lap. I lay my head on his chest, and he continues to dry me off. "I'll take care of you, no matter what. You just relax." He takes his time drying me off and when he's done, he helps me get dressed. "Let's order some pizza, does that sound good to you?" he asks, wrapping his arms around my waist from behind and resting his chin on my shoulder.

"Yeah, actually... that does sound good. I'll get my purse to give you money." I'm about to move to get up off his lap to stand up when he stops me.

"You're not giving me money, it's not necessary. I just told you that I'll take care of you Snowflake. Let me take care of you." He sighs. "When you're with me you pay for nothing, do you understand?" He smiles at me, a kind loving smile.

"Carsten, I can pay for things too you know." I glare at him making him chuckle as I do. Apparently, I need to work on my dirty looks that I give him.

"I don't want anything adding to your stress or anxiety, so if it is something I can do to help you, please don't fight me." He kisses my cheek, then starts trailing gentle kisses down to my neck. I turn my head to face him, pressing my lips to his. I kiss him with need, because right now I need him. His touch, his warm body against mine. To make me feel safe.

"Can we go sit down while you order the pizza? I'm really tired," I ask, pulling away from his kiss. My body is sore from fighting off Preston, just trying to push him off me and trying to pull away from his hold, took a lot out of me.

"Of course we can. I just need to get dressed first." Heas he looks down. I just realized he's still standing in his towel. He's done nothing but take care of me since we got home, it feels so good to feel this loved for once.

"Sorry, I've been so caught up in my own stress I didn't realize you weren't dressed," I say, placing my hand over my face.

He comes up to me and places his finger under my chin, lifting my head to look up at him. "I'm going to keep telling you this, please stop apologizing, right now... all I care about is you. I could walk around naked for the rest of the day and not care, as long as you're okay and being taken care of." He leans down taking my mouth in his not even waiting before his tongue slides between my lips, a soft moan escapes my lips that I can't control. This man knows exactly what he's doing and how to light my body up and make it come alive.

I never thought one person could turn me on so much, all the time. He instantly makes me wet and every time I look at him, I'm ready to go. I wrap my arms around his neck allowing him to deepen the kiss. I can feel his hard cock pressing against the towel wrapped around his waist and my thighs tighten together, my panties growing wet. I reach down, loosening his towel and feel it drop at my feet. I take my hand, wrapping it around the base of his cock and slowly move my hand up and down. He groans, his head slowly falling back and rolling to the side. Before he gives me a look like he's about to eat me alive. I stand on my tip toes and start kissing him again as starts sliding his hand down to my waist band, but I push it away. This isn't about me right now; I want to please him. He deserves this, especially after everything he's done for me tonight. This is about his pleasure, about me making him feel. Because I love knowing I can please him and drive him crazy.

I pull away from his kiss and start leaving kisses on his jaw, slowly moving down his neck, I tighten my hand on his cock pumping my hand a little faster now. "Fucckk," He growls, throwing his head back again. It's one of the sexiest things I think a man can do, give into the pleasure and show you that he's all yours in the moment. I start licking down his chest, leaving soft kisses and sucking along the way. Until I'm right above his cock. I slowly get down on my knees, looking up at him, his eyes heavy and filled with desire as he lifts his head and looks down at me. I love looking at him from this angle, it makes me feel like I'm in control. I love seeing him so vulnerable. His chest is moving up and down from breathing so fast, it would be alarming if I wasn't about to suck his cock.

"God, Snowflake, you look so fucking sexy like that." He groans. I open my mouth and suck just the tip in, enough for him to throw his head back and let out a husky growl. I pull away long enough to wet my lips and then quickly take him back in my mouth as far as I can take him, hitting the back of my throat. I swallow against his cock, knowing the feel of that drives him crazy. "Goddamn, Winter." The way he says my name in a tortured moan. My pussy is so wet, my underwear soaked. I tighten my thighs together again to calm down the ache. I tighten my hand, pumping faster as I suck and swirl my tongue. I stare up at him, the sexy look on his face making my pussy throb. He's getting close, I can tell by the way his hips start thrusting to meet my movements. He grips the back of my head with one hand tightening his hold on my hair and I stop moving and pull away.

I look up at him. "Fuck my mouth, Carsten, please. I want to feel you take control. I want you to cum down my throat." He lets out another tortured growl.

"Fuck, you're gonna make me cum without even being in your mouth." He says breathlessly. Without waiting another second, I wrap my mouth around his hard cock and breath through my nose. He grips the back of my head, his movements deep and slow at first. He hits the back of my throat with each thrust, fitting almost all his thick, long length in my mouth. He picks up the pace, forcing drool out of my mouth as it starts running down my chin. "Shittt, I'm getting close." He hisses and starts pumping faster. I suction my mouth around him tighter and swirl my tongue with each thrust. "I'm gonna cum." He thrusts in one last time hitting the back of my throat, his warmth spilling down my throat, and I swallow every last drop. Moaning in the process, I'm so turned on. My pussy is aching to be fucked.

He picks me up off the ground, taking me over to his bed and throws me down on it. Not saying anything, just the sound of our heavy breathing filling the room. He then flips me over onto my stomach pulling my ass up in the air, and thrusts inside me. "Oh goddd," I moan out, turning my head to the side to look back at him.

"Fucking shit, baby girl," he says in a husky voice. "Your pussy is so wet and ready for me Snowflake." He thrusts inside me in one quick thrust groaning out as he does. He starts thrusting in and out of me quickly, his cock feels amazing sliding in and out of me, as he stretches me, making me feel so full as my walls stretch to make room for him. Goosebumps spread throughout my body creating a chill of pleasure. He grips my hips pulling my ass up more shoving his cock in deeper and it sends me over the edge.

"Fuck, Carsten." I moan his name as my pussy clamps down on his cock, squeezing it tight, making him groan out.

"Goddamnnn." He pants, breathing heavily. His body comes down across my body. His chest to my back, holding me close as he finishes pumping inside me thrusting in one last time as he cums inside my pussy. "Fuck, Winter." He leans down kissing my cheek as we both collapse onto the bed "I could get used to this." He chuckles.

"What do you mean?" I ask trying to catch my breath.

"You. Having you every day. Whenever I want." He pauses, looking over at me. "For the rest of our lives." And for some reason it makes me blush.

"I'm glad I'm not the only one who feels that way. I couldn't imagine being with anyone else now that I've been with you." I lean in giving him a quick, soft kiss, then pull away.

"I'm going to marry you one day, Snowflake," he says, squeezing my hand smiling at me.

"I won't tell you no either." I giggle, feeling like a kid. I've never talked to anyone about marrying them before, so the fact that he brought it up sends butterflies straight to my stomach. Which isn't anything new with him since being around him has butterflies swarming in my stomach all the time.

We lay there in silence looking at each other. The sound of silence messing with my thoughts, as my anxiety starts to take over again. Suddenly I feel nauseous. I sit up quickly, putting my hand over my mouth and run straight to the bathroom, vomit flying out so quickly I get half of it on the floor this time, thankfully it's not a lot to clean up. Carsten rushes in behind me. "What's going on babe, talk to me. Tell me what I can do." He sounds panicked as he pushes my hair away from my face, again.

"I think it's just my anxiety. Unless I'm getting sick. I've been working so much at the diner; my body is exhausted." He looks at me frowning and feels my forehead.

"You do feel a little warmer than usual, but that could be from the sex too." He laughs. "Let's get you some food and see if that helps, but I'm gonna need you to like hide yourself so I can stop touching you long enough to order it." He wiggles his eyebrows. "Or we're never going to eat... at least you won't, but I have your pussy to eat whenever I get hungry, and the rest of this sexy body to snack on. He winks at me walking out of the bathroom where I stand there blushing, my jaw drops.

"Did he really just say that to me?" I mumble to myself as I walk over to the sink to rinse out my mouth.

I spent the rest of the evening sick, in and out of the bathroom puking, and if I wasn't puking, I was passed out in Carsten's bed. Each time I got up he was right there with me holding my hair back.

45

CARSTEN

THE NEXT DAY I FINALLY HEAD INTO THE TATTOO SHOP AFTER my uncle came back from vacation for a couple weeks. Every year he closes his shop down for a month to take the time off with his family. I text Winter to see if she wants to come in and work on a tattoo while I'm here since I'm not busy today.

Me
how u feelin snowflake?

Winter
Better, must've been a bug

Me
good, u busy?

Winter
nope. Just bored

Me
good come up to my uncles shop. Lets tattoo you

Winter
Really!!??!!??? Yes please!

Me
can you be here in a half hour?

> **Winter**
> i can be there in ten lol but yes see u then

> **Me**
> come whenever i'm not busy. Love you snowflake

> **Winter**
> see you soon. Love you handsome devil

"Welcome to Crazy's what can we do for you today." I hear my Uncle Kane ask from the front desk.

"Umm hi, I'm here for Carsten. I'm uhh, his girlfriend." You hear Winter say and just hearing her say girlfriend brings the cheesiest fucking smile to my face.

"Oh hey, you must be Winter?" he asks her, and you can hear her laugh nervously. Besides my mom and brother, she hasn't met any of my other family members yet.

"Yep, that's me." She sounds nervous, I should probably go out there before he starts asking her too many questions.

"I'm Carsten's uncle, Kane, but you can obviously just call me Kane." I see him shaking her hand as I walk to the front from the back hallway.

"It's nice to meet you." She has a big smile on her face. As she's blushing, she probably thinks he's hot, a lot of the female customers who come in here flirt with him. I don't blame her if she does, he's a decent looking guy for being a man in his early forties. I look a lot like him, except his hair is darker. Kane is my dad's brother, he stuck around and helped my mom raise us, they never dated but he helped out after my dad left us. So, he was kind of like a dad to Chase and I. We just never called him Dad; he didn't expect us too either.

"Hey, Snowflake," I say, walking up to her and leaning down to kiss her.

"Hey, babe," she says standing on her tiptoes to reach me.

"Still feeling better? I don't want to tattoo you if you're still feeling sick." I need to make sure she's okay. One because last night I was really fucking worried about her and because I don't want her passing out on me during her tattoo from puking so much yesterday.

"Yeah, I haven't puked since this morning before leaving your house. But I haven't eaten much today. Haven't had an appetite." She holds her stomach as she says it.

"Is your stomach okay?" I'm worried it could be something serious.

"Oh yeah, I guess I just put my hand there out of habit, I was holding my stomach all night from when it was hurting and being nauseous." She sighs like she's relieved it's not hurting anymore.

"Okay good, I was beginning to worry about you Snowflake." I lean down and kiss her again.

"Hmm," my uncle says, interrupting our kiss, crossing his arms and rubbing his beard while looking back and forth between the both of us.

"What's wrong?" I turn towards him, raising an eyebrow.

"Well–" He pauses. "I know it's not really any of my business but you sure you're not pregnant sweetheart?" He gives a concerned look.

"Ohh um... I umm." She blushes.

"She's on the pill," I say it for her since he doesn't really know her. I don't think she feels comfortable discussing our sex life with him like that.

"Well, there's always a possibility that she can still get pregnant on the pill. Maybe you guys should go across the parking lot first and get a test before you tattoo her." He stuffs his hand in his pocket and grabs some cash handing it over to me as I give him a confused look.

"I'll even pay for it since I'm the one having you go and get one."

"You don't have to give me money," I wave my hand at him. "I'm an adult. This is my girlfriend and our situation. I'd never make you pay for something like that." I look over at Winter. "What do you say? Are you willing to take one so I can tattoo you? Just in case?" I ask, a little worried but not trying to show her because I don't want to stress her out. "Let's step outside and talk about it, Snowflake." I take her hand in mine, lacing our fingers together and gently squeeze it.

"Wait," my uncle says to us. "I'm sorry for putting my nose in your business the first time I meet your girlfriend. I honestly don't know what I was thinking."

"No, it's totally okay. I'm really glad you said something. That thought would've never crossed my mind," Winter says to him with a slight smile on her face.

"Well, I appreciate you being the one to tell me that." He starts walking away then stops turning back. "I guess let me know if you guys need someone to talk to or whatever, I'll be in my office drawing up some tattoos."

We get outside and Winter starts crying. "That thought never crossed my mind, I'm so sorry, Carsten. First Brynn messes with you telling you she's pregnant when she wasn't and now, I might possibly be pregnant." She's sobbing and I step closer to her cupping her face.

"Listen to me, we will figure this out together, pregnant or not. I love you; I'm not going anywhere. And if you are pregnant then I will love you and I will love the baby just as much as I love you." I lean down pressing my lips to her, swiping my tongue against her mouth, she opens, and I slide my tongue against hers, kissing her passionately before pulling away "Let's go get a test baby girl, we will be okay. I promise."

"I love you, Carsten." She sniffles wiping her tears away.

"I love you my little Snowflake." I gently kiss her before taking her hand and heading to the store across the parking lot.

After we come back from the store, she heads to the bathroom to take the test.

"Can you come in here with me?" she asks looking down. "I mean, if you're comfortable with it. I'm scared." She's biting her lower lip, tears in her eyes.

"Of course, Snowflake." I take her hand and walk into the bathroom with her. She places the test on the bathroom counter then she undoes her pants, pulling down her underwear and sits down. I hand her the test because I don't want to feel like I'm not doing anything, and I stand by the door so I'm not in her space. She places the test back on the counter after peeing on it and pulls her pants back up. When she's done washing her hands she walks over to me, crying while hugging me.

"I'm so sorry. I understand if you don't want to stay together if I am pregnant," she says, crying into my chest.

I reach down and lift her chin with my fingers. "Winter, I already told you how I felt, please don't be sorry. You aren't to blame, if anything we both are. Will we be shocked and scared if you are pregnant? Most likely yes, but that doesn't mean I'm running. I wouldn't run out on this baby like my dad ran out on me and my brother." He smirks a little. "And I wouldn't run out of you baby girl. You're mine for forever, I'm too obsessed to lose you."

"Thank you. I love you for forever Carsten," she whispers. "I'm ready to look at the test." She looks up at me, suddenly pale. "Can you grab it please, I don't think I can be the one to look at it," she says, her hands shaking.

"Okay, I'll grab it for you." I walk over to the counter and slowly grab the test. "Do you want me to give it to you or just tell you what it says?" I ask, not sure.

"Just tell me, two lines means it's positive, one line is negative," she says, her voice shaky.

"It's negative. I only see one line, Snowflake," I say, letting out the breath I didn't realize I was holding.

"It is?" she says rushing over grabbing the test. Looking at it, seeing it's negative, she wraps her arms around my neck hugging me, jumping up into my arms. I catch her lifting her by her ass, holding her tightly against me. "Oh my god, Carsten. I was so scared."

"It's okay, Winter. We have nothing to worry about now, just breathe baby girl, breathe," I tell her, rubbing her back while holding her closely.

"Did you really mean what you said?" She looks up at me in my arms.

"Winter, I have no reason to lie to you. I would never lie to you, I'm not just going to tell you something and not mean it, okay gorgeous?" I try to say in as gentle of a tone as I can, so she doesn't think I'm mad at her or something.

"I'm sorry I shouldn't have even asked you that. I trust you, that wasn't the reasoning behind the question. I was just surprised is all, that you weren't afraid to jump into the role of a parent so quickly and so early in our relationship." I cut her off, I can tell she's nervously rambling.

"Winter, I would never let you do something like that alone, and I'd never be afraid to jump into anything, as long as I was doing it with you." I lean down and kiss her passionately showing her my love through a kiss instead of words.

"How about that tattoo now?" I ask her, trying to take her mind off the scare she just had. Although I would have been fine with her being pregnant, I feel a little relieved at the moment.

We walk out of the bathroom at the same time my uncle walks out of his office. "The test was negative." I tell him, feeling a little sad for some reason giving him the news. Now that I said it out loud again it feels different, and I think I might be a little sad that she's not carrying my baby. I'm not sure if I'm ready to be a parent, but the fact that it was a possibility that was taken away as quickly as it was there, kinda sucked. I guess when it's meant to be it'll happen. I just don't want it to be with anyone else besides Winter.

46

WINTER

The next day I wake up in Carsten's bed, my hand and arm sore from being tattooed all evening. I walk into his bathroom looking at the half sleeve of roses that starts on my hand and stops at my elbow Carsten tattooed on me last night. They're so beautiful. I stand there and stare at them a little longer before washing it with antibacterial soap and warm water. After patting it dry with paper towels I walk out of the bathroom and walk straight into a shirtless Carsten.

"Holy shit." I gasp practically falling backwards.

Carsten sticks his arm out wrapping it around me, stopping me from falling. He pulls my chest to his, a sexy grin on his face. "Hello, gorgeous." He leans down giving me soft, slow kisses. "How's your arm and hand feeling?"

"It feels swollen, at least I think it is but it's hard to tell and it feels a little sore. Other than that, it feels pretty good. I can't wait to see it when it's fully healed." I smile down at it. "It's absolutely beautiful, I'm obsessed with these roses. I appreciate you doing it."

"No need to thank me, Snowflake. I'm happy I had the chance to tattoo you, to put something permanent on your body," he says, leaning down and kissing my forehead.

"Well, your work is amazing, I just wish you would have let me pay you." I scrunch my face up at him.

"I already told you, I have quite a few ways you can repay me." He gives a sexy laugh.

"Listen, sir." The words leaving my lips making him growl out as he pushes his body into mine, showing me that he's already rock hard for me. "I told you; sex is not a form of payment." I shake my head laughing, typical man.

He crosses his arms and pouts. "That's not fair. That's all I asked for." He stomps his foot just like a child as he tries to hide his laughter. I roll my eyes sarcastically. "I know babe, I was messing with you. I just don't want you to pay me. Look at it as a gift."

"Anyway, I have to head over to my house to shower and get ready for work. I have to work a double at the diner today if you want to head up for my lunch break, you don't have to be a stalker anymore and sit there for both my shifts." I smile at him.

"I already told you, the food is good, so I don't mind, but the view is my favorite." He winks at me. "Do you have to leave me though?" He says with a sad look on his face. "Weren't you feeling sick again last night?" He looks at me with concern.

"Yeah, but I think it's from my period. I'm supposed to be starting it soon, I usually feel sick before I start it." I shrug it off like it's no big deal because it's something I'm used to happening.

"See, more of a reason to stay home," he says rubbing his thumb against my cheek.

"I'm sure Lisa would understand that your boyfriend is needy and needs you to stay home with me. I would tell you to tell her what else we'd be doing but I don't think she'd appreciate that part." He wiggles his eyebrows with a sexy grin on his face.

"I can't, I have to go to work. I need to help pay my dad's bills, so I need the money." I sigh looking up at him.

"You should get ready here, we can shower together." He leans down and kisses me, then slowly lifts my shirt over my head, leaving me completely naked since I didn't put any underwear back on.

"Mmm." He groans, looking down at my body. "You look absolutely delicious." He picks me up and pins me against the wall and starts biting and sucking on my neck. He trails his way down to my nipples, sucking one into his mouth. He reaches down and spreads my legs a little further, then wraps one of his arms around my waist, taking his other hand he grabs his cock and gently glides it into my pussy, pushing it in as far as he can. "Goddamn," he growls leaning into my ear.

"Mhmm." I moan out, it's all I can manage to say because his cock feels so good inside me. He starts pumping in and out of me, sending chills through my body, making me shiver. "God, Carsten." I moan breathlessly as he thrusts back inside me.

"Fuck baby girl, your pussy feels so good." He moans into my ear, breathing heavily as he pumps in and out of me harder this time, getting me closer to the edge, goose bumps break out across my skin, my legs start shaking.

"Fuck Carsten, I'm getting close." He takes my hands, pinning them above my head, and intertwining our fingers together. I wrap my legs tighter around his waist, pushing my body into his meeting his thrusts. I place my lips against his licking and biting his bottom lip. Sucking it into my mouth.

"Fucking shit, Snowflake." He moans out. "I don't know how much longer I'm going to last; your pussy feels too good."

"It's okay." I breathe out. "I... I'm cuming... Oh goddd," I moan into his mouth kissing him, wanting this closeness with him. He lets go of my hands and I wrap my arms around his neck while he grips my hips, thrusting into me one last time before cuming inside me.

"Shit, Snowflake." He pants. "I love you so fucking much," he says, kissing me then resting his forehead against mine.

"I love you, Carsten." He pulls out of me, then slowly places me onto the ground. "I need to head home and shower now, since someone had to distract me." I give a pretend glare while looking for my shirt on the ground. "Have you seen my shirt? I don't know where you put it when you took it off of me." I stand there hugging myself because I'm cold.

"Here you go, baby girl." He grabs it from the chair in his room and stretches the neck of the t-shirt open while he gently slides it over my head. He helps me into the rest of the shirt pulling it down my body and checking to make sure it covers my butt. I love that he takes the time to help me get dressed. He truly is the sweetest even if he looks a bit rough on the outside.

"Thank you, I won't have time to shower with you now because you took up all of my free time, sir." He groans smacking my ass.

"What did I tell you about calling me sir. If we didn't just finish, I'd go at it again." Is that a threat? Is he threatening me with sex even though we just finished?

"If I didn't have to go to work, I'd take you up on that offer, I'll make it up to you I promise," I say winking at him.

"Don't tempt me, all I have to do is call Lisa and she will allow it, she loves me." he says laughing while pulling his boxers up his body. "Can you let me know when you make it to work at least?" he asks, rubbing his thumb up and down my cheek.

"Of course. I'll even text you during my free time." He pulls me in, kissing me on the lips, then pulls away.

"I'll be there for both your breaks, if that's okay?" he asks giving me his cheesy smile that I love.

"Of course it is, I'm sure Stacey will love to see you too." I laugh as he rolls his eyes.

"Man, fuck Stacey. I don't like her," he says scrunching his eyebrows. I laugh at him because I don't really like her either, but I put up with her.

I walk into the diner and through the back room to my locker to put on my apron. As I'm putting my apron on, I start feeling weird as my heart starts racing, I start to feel a little sweaty and nauseous too.

"Fucking anxiety," I mumble to myself.

"You okay dear?" I turn around and see Lisa standing there with a box in her hands.

"Yeah, I had a stomach bug two days ago, and I was feeling better yesterday, just no appetite, now today I'm feeling..." and I stop talking, putting my hand over my mouth and rushing to the bathroom in the break room, not even able to shut the door because it comes out so quickly, I practically choke on it. I start sweating more, my whole body feeling like it's on fire for a minute. Lisa comes rushing up behind me checking on me and making sure there's no hair in my face.

"Oh my, are you sure you're better? If you need to, you can take the day off," she says rubbing my back as I dry heave over the toilet.

"I just-" I stop talking, vomiting again right over the toilet, thankful it's not as intense this time. Holding my stomach, I stand there bent at the waist, still over the toilet, waiting for the nausea to subside.

After a few minutes it finally goes away, I stand up and walk over to the sink to rinse out my mouth and wash my hands. I dry my hands off, turning around Lisa is standing in the doorway, a concerned look on her face. "You don't look so good, dear." She crosses her arms, leaning against the doorway.

"I feel a lot better now. I think I just need something to drink, and I'll be good to go for my shift." I sigh, smiling.

"I'll get you something. Just take a seat and I'll be right back," she says, walking out of the break room and heading towards the kitchen of the diner.

I sit down and text Carsten to let him know, because now I'm worried that something is wrong.

Me
hey babe, i puked at work :(

Carsten
shit

Carsten
r u ok?

Carsten
Do u need me to bring anything?

He brings a smile to my face sitting there, I love how caring he is.

Me
no i'm ok, Lisa helped me

Me
i'm just worried, ya know?

Carsten
want me to take u to urgent care between ur
shifts?

Carsten
i'd be more than happy to

Me
i'm not sure, u think they'd be able to figure
it out?

Carsten
worth a try, if not i can take u to emergency
tonight

Me
ok, see u on my break

Carsten
love you snowflake

Me
love you handsome devil

"Here you go sweetie. Are you sure you'll be fine working?" she asks, handing me a glass of water and a straw.

"I'll let you know if I'm not, but I'd really like to stay if you're okay with it. Please? I can't afford to miss a day," I ask. I can't afford to not work right now, especially since taking on my dad's payments while he's in rehab.

"That's fine sweetie, as long as you're feeling better, I don't want to push you." She places her hand on my shoulder still looking concerned.

"Yeah, I feel fine now. I just don't know what's wrong. I thought it was a stomach bug, I'm not pregnant-" She cuts me off.

"Wait, you thought you were pregnant?" Her look concerned again, but not judging.

"Well, the thought never crossed my mind until Carsten's uncle asked if I was. So, then we went and bought a test, and I was negative." I look up at her a little confused.

"Well, did you try taking another test? It's possible it was too early and that's why it was negative," she says, sitting down next to me.

"I actually didn't know that was possible." I sigh a little "So no I didn't think to take another test," I say, placing my elbows on my knees and my hands over my face.

"It's none of my business, but maybe you should take another test. I was about to go take a break; I can go get you one if you'd like." She rubs my back.

"Would you care? Because now I'm going to be paranoid about it and it'll be on my mind the whole night." I look over at her. "Or if you don't want to go, I can run really quick or ask Carsten to bring one up." I don't want her to think she has to do it for me, so I make sure to put the other two options out there just in case.

"Of course not, I'll be back in about twenty minutes. If you feel up to it you can work your section, if not I'll let Craig and Stacey know and they can split yours." She smiles, standing up.

"It's okay, I'll need something to distract me until you're back." I laugh and then sigh. "It's been a rough week, so work is best for me right now. I'll be out there in a minute." I grab my apron from my locker and tie it around my waist. Then I head out to go take care of my tables until Lisa comes back.

Lisa comes back about a half hour later calling me to the break room. "Here you go sweetie. Do you want me to wait with you while you take it?" She hands me the box. I try to give her the cash for it but she refuses to take it and I know she's just going to fight me. I'll pay her back one day for it.

"If you don't mind, I don't want to be alone. Carsten won't be here for another hour, and I don't want to wait that long. My anxiety is getting to me and it's driving me crazy." I let out a breath, my hands starting to shake from my nerves.

"Winter, I'm here for you. You will be okay, no matter what the test results are, okay?" she says, rubbing my back. "I'll be right out here."

I head into the bathroom, set the test down on the counter and sit down on the toilet. I pee on the test and set it back down, pull up my pants and wash my hands. I open the bathroom door and walk over to Lisa holding the test in my shaking hand. Tears in my eyes. I hold the test out to her as the tears fall down my cheeks. "Oh, sweetie." She walks up to me and hugs me. I told you it would be okay, and it will." She squeezes me tightly.

"I feel like I'm going to be sick," I say running over to the bathroom again, vomiting into the toilet.

"This is normal, you're not sick honey, it's from being pregnant. It's what they call morning sickness. It can happen any time of the day though." She rubs my back as she talks to me, her soothing voice helping to calm my terrible anxiety.

"Well, this fucking sucks." I wipe my mouth with paper towels. "What am I going to do, what am I going to tell Carsten." I start crying.

"I know how Carsten is, he's going to do the right thing. He will be ok with this too." She pulls away from the hug. "He loves you. I've never seen him act like this around any girl before and I've known him a long time." She squeezes my shoulders.

"I'm just scared. Having a baby wasn't something I pictured for myself right now, I don't even know the first thing about taking care of a baby."

"It's okay, Winter. Just breathe. You don't have to figure that all out right now." She puts her hands down at her sides. "Right now, I want you to just go home and take care of yourself and talk to Carsten. You don't need to be stressed at work right now," She walks over to my locker, opening it for me.

"Are you kicking me out?" I laugh as I wipe at my tears. Because that's what it feels like.

"I think so, but if I don't you and I both know you'll try and stay and right now you don't need the stress of being here, you have enough stress going on."

"Thank you, Lisa. I don't know what I would have done without you right now," I say, giving her one last hug before taking off my apron and putting it into my locker.

I grab my purse and keys and head out to the front, looking down to avoid eye contact. I don't want them looking at me and asking why I've been crying or if I'm ok. I just need to get out of here and head home. I grab my phone to text Carsten to let him know I'm coming home.

Me
hey i'm leaving work.

Carsten
still feeling sick?

Me
yeah, you home?

Carsten
yep, just got in from the tattoo shop

Me
ok, care if i come over?

Carsten
of course not, can't wait

Carsten
i miss you

Me
miss you

Carsten
everything ok

Me
i'll see you in 10 , love you

Carsten
ok snowflake, love you. Hope you're okay

I place my phone down and put the car in drive, heading home. Emerald is at work so thankfully when I get there to change, I won't have to talk to her just yet. I need to tell Carsten first and I know if I end up running into her, I'd turn into a blubbering mess and end up telling her first.

I go up into my room and change into sweatpants and a T-shirt, grabbing a hoodie since it's still cold. I grab my purse, looking down to make sure the pregnancy test is still in there for me to show Carsten. I'm not sure how else to tell him so I think I'll just show him the test.

I walk down my stairs and out the front door, grabbing my keys before locking the door and walk over to Carsten's. Tears start to form in my eyes, I'm shaking again and it's not from how cold I am. I feel like I'm going to puke as I ring his doorbell. I try turning the handle, but it's locked. I run down the front steps and start puking into the snowy grass. "Winter? Oh my god, are you okay?" I hear Carsten running down the stairs and then his footsteps on the side-walk. He's right behind me holding my hair that's falling into my face and wrapping his other arm around my body to help hold me up. I stand there dry heaving, struggling to keep myself from puking again but it's too late. Before I can even get a good breath in, I'm puking again. It's so intense it's hurting my stomach muscles. By the time I'm done puking I'm sweating, which is funny since it's freezing outside.

"Are you okay, baby girl?" I look over to a shirtless and barefoot Carsten, standing in gray sweatpants that hang low on his hips. His muscular chest turning me on. What the hell is wrong with me, I was just vomiting in the snow and now I'm about to jump his bones.

"Yeah. I'm so sorry for puking in your grass." I wipe my mouth with the back of my hand.

"Please, don't apologize. Let's get inside, it's freezing and you're shivering," he says, rubbing my arms. I look over at his body and it instantly makes my thighs tighten. God he's so sexy.

"You're worried about me, you're practically naked right now and it's very distracting." I laugh looking him up and down. Seriously, what is my problem?

"Sorry, I can be fully naked if you'd like." He wiggles his eyebrows and I blush. "Sorry, that's not appropriate right now, let's get you inside."

"Alright, we need to talk too when we get to your room," I say, hoping he just assumes he knows what I'm going to tell him.

"Is everything okay? You're not breaking up with me, are you?" He gives me a worried, sad look. Breaking my heart.

"Hell no, I would never break up with you. I love you too much for that." I pause. "But we can talk about it in your room, right now outside isn't the place I want to talk. It's too cold."

"Yeah, tell that to my half naked body." He laughs covering his nipples with his hands. We walk into his house and up his stairs to his room. I place my purse down, secretly grabbing the pregnancy test from it and placing it in my hoodie pocket so he can't see it yet and I walk over to his bed.

"Do you want to sit down next to me, or do you want to stand?" I ask, cause I'm not sure what he's in the mood for.

"Either is fine, but I missed you, so I'll sit next to you." He comes over and sits by me "What's wrong, Snowflake? You're making me nervous. I feel like you're about to tell me you don't love me anymore or something." He looks so sad, and it breaks my fucking heart seeing him like this. Thank god I love him and I'd never do anything to hurt him and see him this way.

"No, that's definitely not it. I promise." I pause taking the test out of my hoodie pocket. "I'm pregnant." His head jerks up looking from me to the test.

"I... wait what?" He looks again from me to the test grabbing it from my hands.

"I wasn't feeling good at work and when I mentioned to Lisa about taking a test the other day, she told me it could be too early for it to be positive, and she went on her break and bought me another pregnancy test." I let out the breath I've been holding, feeling a little better that I at least told him. "I wanted you to be there, but I couldn't wait for my break. I'm so sorry I took it without you." Now the tears are falling that I didn't even know were forming in my eyes. "That's why I've been sick. Lisa said it's called morning sickness, that it's completely normal. I'm so sorry that it's positive." I'm sobbing now, I feel like I'm about to start hyperventilating.

He cups my face and kisses me. "I love you, Winter." He kisses me again. "Stop saying you're sorry." He gives me a serious look and then a kind smile.

"But I don't want you to think I did this on purpose or like I'm trying to be like Brynn," I say, looking down.

He lifts my chin with his fingers. "You are nothing like Brynn. Don't ever compare yourself to her again, do you understand me?" He gives me another serious look. "Also, shut up. I know you didn't do this on purpose. Like I said before, this is something we both did, not just you." He pauses, like he's thinking. "I already told you I'm not going anywhere. You mean everything to me and I love you."

"I love you, Carsten. I'm scared. I have no idea how to take care of a baby," I say, my voice shaking and my bottom lip trembling.

"We will figure this out together, I promise you." He kisses me again.

"Plus, I'm sure my mom would love to help us out and teach us what we need to know about taking care of a baby." Then he stops talking and smiles for a minute. "Babe, we are both adults, this may not have been something we planned but doesn't mean we can't be excited about it, ya know?"

I sigh. "I know. I mean I know I'll be excited after the shock wears off, but right now I'm terrified."

"Don't be." He slowly kisses me. "I'll be right here with you every step of the way. I promise." He gives me a big cheesy grin sticking out his pinky and interlocking it with mine. He stands up from his bed and stands in front of me, putting my legs between his and gently pushes me back to where I'm lying on the bed, then he slowly gets on top of me straddling my waist and leans down and kisses me desperately, cupping my face with one hand while resting his other hand next to my head on the mattress. He deepens the kiss, swiping his tongue against mine before he pulls away and starts tugging on my hoodie, pulling it over my head. He does the same with my T-shirt, leaving me in nothing but my sweatpants. He leans back down pressing his lips to mine before trailing kisses down my neck to my breasts, he swipes his tongue across my nipple, before sucking it into his mouth, then trails kisses over to my other nipple and does the same.

"Oh goddd," I moan out. "Carsten, please," I say breathlessly.

"I know, baby girl," he groans against my nipple, sending chills down my body. "Don't you worry, I'm gonna take my time pleasing you." He licks and sucks his way down my stomach stopping right before my throbbing pussy.

"No, please." It comes out a breathy moan, not sure why I'm stopping him other than the fact that I want the release now, I don't want to be teased. He stops, looking up at me with a confused look on his face.

"Is everything okay?" He raises an eyebrow as his eyes meet mine.

"Yes, I just, I need to feel you inside me. I don't want you to take your time, please." I say blushing. Now I feel stupid, but I'm so worked up, I want him now.

"Snowflake, just relax. I promise I'm gonna make you feel good." He wraps his arms around my thighs and buries his face into my pussy, spreading my thighs far apart and holding me in place with his hands. He places his lips around my clit and starts sucking on it, softly and slowly, teasing me with just enough to make me cry out, but not enough to get me close yet. He stops sucking then swirls his tongue around my clit before sliding his tongue down my pussy, then sticking it inside me. "Mmm." He growls, the vibration turning me on even more.

"Oh fucckk." I moan. I'm so turned on, my body feeling like it could explode.

"Your pussy tastes so good," he mumbles against me before sticking his tongue back inside me. He slides his tongue back up to my clit and thrusts his finger inside me, then slowly adds another one, making me cry out again from how intense the pleasure is. My pussy is so wet I can feel the wetness dripping from me as he pleasures me with his tongue in the most delicious ways. Making my hips move automatically as my body thrusts against him. He' devouring me like a popsicle that he can't lick up fast enough. My moans fill the room along with his groans that only add to my pleasure. He starts pumping his fingers in and out of me faster, curling them up as he does. Hitting that spot inside me that makes my toes curl and my body finally explodes, my pussy squeezing his fingers, his tongue licking my clit.

My body finally relaxes, and he gets up and climbs to his knees. He crawls up on top of me, his body hovering over mine then his lips crash down against my lips, his mouth pushing into mine, I can taste myself on his tongue, and feel my wetness on his cum covered lips. He pushes his arm under my back, wrapping it around my waist and pulls me on top of him "I want you to fuck me Snowflake, ride my cock baby girl." He places me on top of him over his hard cock. "I want to watch your tits bounce as you fuck me." I give him a sexy smile, his words turning me on.

I can feel myself growing wet again, and it's not from the orgasm

I just had. He does that to me, his words make my thighs tighten and my pussy throb, like it's the first time I've heard him talk like this. "Yes, sir." My chest rising, my breathing growing heavy.

"Goddamn." He growls and then I grip his cock and slowly slide down onto it, my pussy tightening around him. "Fuck, baby girl." He moans out as I sink all the way down onto him. I place my hands next to his head on each side and slowly start moving my body up and down. I lean down and kiss him, while rotating my hips and moving up and down on his dick. I pull away, sitting up grinding my pussy into him, picking up the pace lifting up and sliding back down, he reaches up, grabbing onto my nipples, gently pulling me down by them, making me cry out in a breathy moan, he presses his lips to mine devouring my lips with his, moaning into my mouth, pushing up into me meeting my movements, his cock filling me completely with each thrust.

"I want to feel you cum all over my cock baby girl," he groans out.

"Mmm my god," I moan, his words getting me worked up even more, getting me closer to my orgasm. "Yes... sir." I pant, barely able to get the words out but I know how much those words get him going and turn him on and that's what I want to do. I want to feel him lose control because of me. I want to be the only one responsible for making him feel this good.

47

CARSTEN

I TURN OVER IN MY BED, THE SUN SHINING THROUGH THE blinds that I forgot to shut the night before. After Winter and I had sex last night we both passed out, so I never had the chance to shut them, I don't even think we ate dinner. I grab my phone from my nightstand to check the time and to see that it's ten in the morning. I've got a long day ahead of me that I'm not looking forward to. I have to go and do a couple tattoos at Crazy's and then I have to go work at the bar at five-thirty with my mom and Chase for country night. That seems to be our busiest weeknight.

I look over to see a naked Winter laying on her stomach, her legs out of the blanket, along with her breasts, her nipples hard from the fan blowing next to her. I scoot closer to her in the bed, spooning her with my naked body, bringing my arm up around her waist, poking her ass with my hard cock. I lightly squeeze her boob while pinching her nipple. "Mmm," she moans out in her sleep. I lean over and start kissing her neck, while lightly sucking on it making her stir in her sleep even more. "Hmm, Carsten, I'm sleepy." She whines, letting out a slight moan.

She rolls over, snuggling her face into my chest. "I didn't sleep well last night." She starts stretching, pushing her body into mine, making my dick even harder than it already was. "I was up puking half the night." I pull her closer to me.

"I'm sorry, Snowflake. Are you okay now?" I ask, feeling bad that she didn't wake me up.

"I still feel nauseous, but the puking stopped around six this morning." She yawns as she finishes her sentence.

"Why didn't you wake me up? I could've helped you somehow or held your hair back." I place my finger under her chin lifting her head up so she's looking at me.

"I felt bad waking you up. You looked like you were in a pretty deep sleep, so I didn't want to." She gives me a tired smile. "I just took care of it myself; I figured if I needed you then I'd wake you. I was up like every hour. I wasn't about to wake you up that much." She stops for a second, thinking. "Plus, you have to work both jobs today, I didn't want you to be tired."

"Aren't you working a double today?" I ask her with a concerned look on my face. I don't know much about pregnancy, but I know it makes you tired and I don't want her over doing it, especially since she hasn't been to a doctor yet. We don't even know how the baby is doing.

"I was, but Lisa doesn't want me over doing it, especially in the first trimester, so she is only scheduling me from one until eight tonight instead of one in the afternoon until one in the morning." She stretches as she yawns again. My poor girl, I wish there was something I could do to help her feel better.

"Good, I don't want you to overwork yourself either. I can help you out with whatever you need. Please take care of you for yourself and our baby." I smile at her. Our baby, it still hasn't fully sunk in yet. It's only been a day so I'm not sure when something like that actually sinks in or how long it takes. But I'm not worried about it anymore.

"Our baby." She giggles. "I need to call my doctor to set up an appointment. I honestly have no idea how any of this stuff works. I feel so lost." She looks sad as she talks, I'm sure she feels so lost without her mom or even a parent to turn to.

"Well, I wanted to talk to you. How about tonight we meet at the bar and tell my mom. We can tell our friends too if you want to hang out with them." I feel like telling our friends will be the best thing. Especially for Winter that way she can have more people to support her during her pregnancy.

"We can do that. It makes me nervous thinking about telling your mom." She pauses. "I don't really know her like you do obviously. But do you think she's going to be upset?" She nervously bites her lip as she stares at me, waiting for an answer as I try to think of how my mom would react. I honestly have never had to think about how my mom would react the day I told her I got someone pregnant because I never thought I'd have to worry about it. I always used protection when I slept around so something like that never crossed my mind. But now that the day is finally here. I think she'll be happy, shocked maybe, but happy and excited.

"Hell no, she always said how we better make her a grandma one day. She never said when but I'm sure she's going to be very excited about it." I smile down at her, hoping I'm going to be right. The last thing I want is for my mom to be mad at me.

"Do you want to tell them all to meet there at ten-thirty, so that way I have time to go home and change before driving up there?" She rolls onto her back looking up at the ceiling. I drape my arm over her, rubbing the skin right between her breasts with my thumb.

"I'll come pick you up, that way we can drive back home together, and you won't have to worry about driving. I'm sure you'll be tired."

"Home." She looks over at me, smiling. I've been calling it home a lot lately without even realizing it. But to me wherever she is, is home. I don't care if we haven't been together long. When you know that that person is the one, then you know, no matter how long it's been.

I look over at her, staring into her eyes. "You are my home, Snowflake. I don't want to be anywhere you're not."

"You're my home too, Carsten." I lean in and kiss her, not even letting her finish what she was going to say. She opens her lips for me immediately and I deepen the kiss. I fill her tongue with mine needing to taste her, all of her, any way that I can. To feel close to her on a different level. "I love you." She whispers against my lips before coming back in to kiss me. Swiping her tongue against mine.

"I love you, gorgeous." I kiss her lips hungrily, like she's the only thing I need to survive. I get on top of her, spreading her legs and adjusting her body at the right angle to slide my cock right into her, making love to her again. Making it about more than just fucking her. I take my time, gliding my cock in deep with each thrust, making her moan out in tortured pleasure with every slow thrust. Her words and throaty moans mixed together, her breathing heavy, gasping for air after each pump.

I growl against her lips, her pussy feeling so good, it's hard to last long. "Goddamn, baby girl. I love the way your pussy feels on my cock." I groan out against her neck, I press her body into mine, feeling her sweaty skin slip against mine as I thrust into her, her body meeting mine with each movement.

"God, Carsten, you feel so amazing," she moans into my ear, in a sexy, breathy moan, making it even harder to hold back with each thrust. I reach down to massage her clit, hoping to get her there before I finish without her. "Don't stop, please don't stop." She groans against my lips. Her breathing heavier than it was before, her legs shaking. I know she's getting close. I pick up the pace thrusting into her faster, lifting her hips to get into her pussy deeper. Her pussy clamps down, tightening around me, pulling my cum from my cock as we both climax together.

I finish my shift at Crazy's tattoos and head to my car to sit for a minute and text Winter I haven't talked to her since this morning and I miss her.

> **Me**
> miss u snowflake

Winter
miss u too, my stomach has been cramping
all day

> **Me**
> are u ok, do u need me to do something?

Winter
I think I'm fine right now, I'll let you know if that
changes

> **Me**
> please do, don't hesitate to ask for help

Winter
thank u, how was work?

> **Me**
> just finished at Crazys taking a 10 min break then
> headed to Black Velvet
>
> How's work for you?

Winter
i'm sure ur tired. It's been busy, haven't had a
minute to stop

> **Me**
> maybe that's why you're cramping? Maybe ask
> Lisa if you can take a 5 and sit

Winter
I'm going on break in 10 so I'll sit then

> **Me**
> please make sure you do baby girl I worry
> about u

Winter
I will handsome don't worry

Me
love you Snowflake

Winter
Love you, handsome devil

I pull out of the parking lot at Crazy's and head to Black Velvet. Tonight is country night so it's going to be busy, which I'm ready for. I'd rather be busy than slow. Plus, the tips are always great.

Pulling into the parking lot of Black Velvet I end up parking the same time my mom is getting out of her car. "Hey, Mom." I walk towards her, giving her a hug. It's been a few days since I've seen her.

"How's my boy doing?" She reaches her arms out, wrapping them around me and hugs me. "How's Winter? I haven't seen her in a few days." She gives me a big smile. Weird, I feel like she knows something is up, although no one knows Winter is pregnant besides me. Well, and Winter of course.

"I'm doing good, just been busy at Uncle Kane's shop tattooing. I tattooed Winter as well, finished her sleeve and her hand, it looks awesome-" She cuts me off before I can finish which I guess is for the best. I don't like keeping things from my mom, so if I don't have to answer how she is then I'm not keeping anything from her.

"What?? That's so exciting, I'm sure she looks beautiful with it. I can't wait to see it!" She claps her hands together in excitement.

"Well, she will be here tonight, so you'll get to see it." I say holding the door open for her to walk into the bar.

Chase is already here setting things up and he gives us an annoyed look. "Let me guess, Mom was holding you up in the parking lot, talking your ear off?" He rolls his eyes, laughing.

"Hey, that's not nice." She's laughing too. "I just like to check in and catch up with my boys, there's nothing wrong with that," she says defensively.

"Ya, ya," Chase says, coming up behind her and patting her on the back. "It's ok, this just explains why you're always late for everything, especially if people are involved." He's laughing now, walking away.

"So rude." She sticks her middle finger up at him. I love the relationship we have with our mom, she's like a friend most of the time, but puts her foot down when she needs to, which is rare. Especially now that we're older.

We opened the bar about an hour ago and it's already busy, a lot busier than it normally is since line dancing doesn't start until ten-thirty. I walk into the back room to run to my office real quick and I check my phone on the way to see I have four texts from Winter, which instantly makes me nervous, especially since she's pregnant.

> **Winter**
> I think I need to go to the emergency room

> **Winter**
> i went to the bathroom and there's blood

> **Winter**
> Carsten, I'm scared can you please text me back

> **Winter**
> I'm gonna give it a few more minutes before I
> drive myself. I just figured you'd want to go with
> me so I'm trying to wait but I'm scared :(

My stomach drops and my heart is in my throat feeling like it's about to burst. Instead of texting her back I rush to my office and call her so it's quieter and I can hear her better.

"Hey, Snowflake, are you okay?" I ask trying to calm my nerves.

"I'm not sure." She's crying and I instantly rush down the hall to my mom to let her know I have to leave. This is a little more important right now than work.

"Hold on, Snowflake." I tell her before she continues talking.

Thankfully my mom's office door is open, and I run right in. "Mom, I hate to do this, but I need to leave, it's an emergency," I say, getting ready to turn around and rush out the door.

"What do you mean? What's going on?" she asks frantically rushing over to me looking me up and down to make sure I'm okay.

I move my phone from my ear and put it on speaker phone. "Winter, I have you on speaker phone. I need to tell my mom, maybe she can give us some advice," I say nervously, my hands shaking.

"Ok," she says, sniffling. You can hear she's trying not to freak out, which I wouldn't blame her if she was.

I look over at my mom and take a deep breath to calm myself down some before talking. "Mom, Winter is pregnant," I say, but before I can continue, she's squealing with excitement.

"Oh my god, honey!! Congratulations, I'm gonna be a grandma?" She claps her hands together again, bouncing up and down. It makes me happy to see this is her reaction. I just hope everything is okay with the baby, I'd hate to give her the news that she's going to be a grandma and take it away all in the same day.

"That's the thing, Winter said she's bleeding, I need to go with her to the emergency room." I say in a hurry, trying to show that I need to go.

"Calm down honey, sometimes bleeding can be normal. So, both of you try to calm down so that way you don't put any more stress on your baby." She stops for a second, giving me a worried smile. "Plus, I need you to get you both there safe, if you're all worked up and stressed that might not happen," she says squeezing my arm.

"Okay, Mom," I say, trying to calm down some.

"Just take a couple deep breaths Carsten, you guys will be ok." She's trying to hide the worried look on her face, which is why I wish I didn't have to say anything because I didn't want to excite her to turn around and worry her.

"I'll keep you updated, thanks Mom. I love you," I say, running out of her office and back to mine to grab my keys and rush out the back door.

"Winter, are you still there?" She hasn't said anything, and I don't hear sniffling anymore so now I'm worried something more serious has happened.

"Ye... yeah, I-" she lets out a breath, it sounds like she's been holding and takes a deep breath in. "I'm just scared. I don't want to lose the baby." She's sobbing now.

"I'm on my way, baby girl. I'll be there as quickly as I can. Get ready and I'll honk when I'm there."

She takes another deep breath before responding. "Alright, be careful please."

"I will Snowflake. I love you."

"Love you, Carsten." The way she says it breaks my heart. I wish I was already by her to comfort her.

About an hour later we're back in a room waiting for the doctor to come in with an ultrasound machine, all of her blood work came back fine, and her HCG levels are all where they need to be. Let's just hope everything is still good with the baby.

The doctor comes in pushing a cart in front of him with what I'm assuming is the ultrasound machine.

"Hi guys, I'm Dr. Smith, I'll be doing your ultrasound today. I hear you have had some bleeding?" He says, looking from me to Winter.

"Yeah, I was fine this morning, then I went to work, and I was cramping the whole time. They felt like period cramps, but then when I went to the bathroom there was blood in my underwear and on the toilet paper." The tears start falling from her eyes again.

"Alright, well I'm gonna have you lay down flat, put your feet in the stirrups and scoot your bottom all the way to the end up the of the table," he says, putting what looks like a condom on the end of this weird wand thing and some liquid stuff that looks like it could be lube. Maybe Winter knows what all of this stuff is but I'm clueless and not really in the mood to ask a bunch of questions that aren't related to the baby. "This is going to be cold, and you might feel some pressure while I move the wand around to see the baby." He pauses, sticking the wand between her legs. "Sometimes bleeding can be normal, depending on how far along you are. Sometimes it can just be from your cervix being irritated from something as well.

Have you guys had intercourse at all today or the last few days?" he asks, looking over at us while moving the wand around.

"Um, this morning. We did before I went to work." She bites her bottom lip nervously.

"Well, that could very well be where the bleeding is coming from. I don't see any blood on the ultrasound or in either of the sacs that the babies are in," he says, moving the wand again.

"Wait... babies?" My eyes go wide as I look from Winter to the doctor. My stomach just fell through my ass at this point. Am I hearing things?

"Yes, your babies look healthy actually, I don't see any blood inside, it must've been irritation to the cervix." He shifts the wand again. "Here, let me turn this up so we can hear baby A's heartbeat." Then I could hear a muffled sound almost like a static and then I hear what sounds like a really fast heartbeat. "Good, baby A's heart rate is at 146 beats per minute, now let's shift over to baby B's heart rate," he says, still not answering my very fucking confused question.

"So um, I'm sorry if I'm misunderstanding," Winter says, glancing from me to the doctor. "But um, why do you keep saying babies and Baby A and Baby B?" she asks, wiping the tears from her face that are slowly starting to dry up.

"Oh, you didn't know?" he says, looking at us shocked. "You guys are having twins, fraternal twins to be exact. I'm so sorry, I thought you guys knew prior to coming in here." He looks over at us then back at the ultrasound screen. "Baby B's heart rate is perfect too, it's at 148 beats per minute." He turns the screen for us to look and points. "This sac right here this little thing you see flickering on Baby A is their heart, and then this is its little body. You are currently 9 weeks and 3 days." He shifts the wand over to the right some. "This one right here is Baby B, you can see the little flicker on the screen as well, that's their heart."

Winter and I both sit there in shock... twins... fucking twins?? I can't believe it. Not only did I knock her up, but I knocked her up with two fucking babies.

"Wow." Winter pushes her hair out of her face as she's looking over at the ultrasound machine. "This is all... wow. I'm just shocked. I had no idea we were having twins." Tears form in her eyes again and I'm not sure if they're good or bad tears.

"Look at how perfect they are." The tears fall from her eyes down her cheeks, and she looks over at me then back to Dr. Smith. "So, is everything okay? Do you know where the bleeding came from?" she asks with a concerned look on her face again, she seemed happy for a minute like she forgot we came here for an emergency, now she looks scared again.

"Yes, everything is perfect. I would say the bleeding could have been irritation to your cervix from intercourse. I would refrain from doing any sexual activity for at least two days to be safe. then if anything happens after the two days I would come back to emergency or if you can see your OB, they usually try to get you in right away for urgent situations like this."

"Thank you so much for all this information, I feel so much better. But wow..." Winter looks over at me. "I can't believe we're having twins!" She laughs a nervous laugh. You can tell she's unsure how to feel but I'm sure it'll take some time for the both of us to get used to the news of just being pregnant, now we have to get used to the news of having twins.

"Well, I will leave you two. Congratulations on your babies. I would definitely call and schedule a follow up with your doctor. That way you can start being seen regularly, in the meantime, you need to start taking prenatal vitamins and drink a lot of water," he says. "Also, get as much rest as you can, you don't want to overwork yourself." He starts walking towards the door. "Do you guys have any other questions?"

"Umm, I think I'm good," Winter says, looking over at me.

"I'm good too, thank you so much for everything." I smile, still looking at the ultrasound screen.

"Oh wait, before I forget." He walks back over and then you hear something printing "Here is the ultrasound pictures. I even marked on there Baby A and Baby B for you guys." He smiles as he walks out of the room.

We decide after the appointment to still go back up to Black Velvet to inform my mom about everything and to fill our friends in on the fact that Winter is pregnant and having twins. Holy fuck I still can't believe it.

"Twins." I squeeze Winter's hand as I talk to my mom in her office.

"Wait, what?" Her mouth falls open not sure if it's a look of confusion or disbelief on her face.

"Yep. That was our reaction too. Everything was fine, my cervix was most likely just irritated. That's where the blood was coming from," Winter says to my mom, smiling at her facial expression. "But yeah, we went there thinking one baby and here we are having twins, fraternal twins. I'm 9 weeks and 3 days." Winter places her hand on her forehead like she's still in shock herself.

"Holy shit. This is so exciting! Carsten, you guys are having two babies, my baby is having two babies of his own!" She practically shouts in excitement from her office.

"Shhh Mom. No one else knows yet. We plan on telling everyone when we go out there." I place my finger over my lips to "shh" her.

"Oh, sorry." She covers her mouth and laughs with excitement then rushes over to hug the both of us, practically throwing herself on us in the process.

"Woah, Mom. Watch Winter please, she's supposed to take it easy for a few days." I hold my arm around Winter's waist to help her keep her body balanced.

"I'm so sorry. I didn't mean to knock into you guys, this is just so exciting. Congratulations you two. I will help with anything I can." Her body slightly bounces up and down as the excitement pours out of her. I feel relieved that Winter is okay, and our babies are okay. And I'm happy that my mom is as excited as she is. I knew she would be though.

"Thank you so much," Winter says with tears in her eyes and a smile on her face. "Man, I don't know what's wrong with me. I'm happy but I'm crying." She laughs as she wipes her fresh, falling tears from her reddened cheeks.

"It's the hormones dear, they'll definitely have you all over the place. You'll be okay though." My mom tells her, gently squeezing her arm. "Now head out there and tell your friends, you guys they're gonna be so happy for you." She smiles at us with tears in her eyes from excitement.

We walk out from the back room and see everyone is outside on the patio drinking. That will be the first thing they question is why we aren't drinking. I decided to quit with Winter, she obviously quit, due to being pregnant, so I'll quit with her. I need to chill on drinking for a while anyways, focus on myself, Winter, and now our babies. We walk outside together, holding hands as all our friends greet us.

"What the hell happened man we were slammed after you left where'd you go?" Chase asks since I didn't fill him in on what happened either.

"Yeah, you guys told us to meet you here at ten-thirty and you both were gone. Let me guess, you guys were in your office again?" Creedence asks, wiggling his eyebrows at us and smiling.

"Well, actually we have something to tell you guys." Winter says and everyone stops talking.

"Did you guys go and get married or something?" Chase asks sarcastically.

"That's actually not a bad idea, huh Snowflake?" I ask, wrapping my arms around her waist, standing behind her.

"No, that wasn't it." Winter shakes her head, laughing at him. Leave it to Chase, he always has the craziest things to say. He's the biggest smart ass out of all our friends.

"Well, then what is it?" Emerald raises one eyebrow and crossing her arms impatiently, she's the most impatient woman I've ever met.

Winter looks up at me nodding her head, giving me the okay to go ahead and tell them. I let out a deep breath, not sure why I'm nervous to tell our friends. Other than them possibly judging us or having negative things to say, they should all actually be pretty supportive of the both of us and the twins.

"Winter and I are having a baby…" I pause, not used to the baby being more than one. "Well, babies, actually." My smile grows as I say the words out loud again, reality of me being a dad very slowly sinking in. Actually, relieved we told our friends. Months ago, I never would've thought I'd be where I am now, in a relationship, or even in love for that matter.

"Holy shit," Chase says with a big smile on his face. "I'm gonna be an uncle?" he practically shouts out.

"Oh my god!! Are you shitting me, twins? You guys are having babies? I'm gonna be an aunt?" Emerald shrieks. Her and Winter have been best friends for so long, she's automatically promoted to being their aunt.

"Hell yeah, congrats guys! I get to be an uncle too, if my girl… I mean if Emerald gets to be their aunt I want to be an uncle," Creedence says, trying to hide the fact that he and Emerald are dating. Not sure why he's hiding it, maybe he thinks we'll be upset.

"Congrats man, do I get to be an uncle too?" Axton says, with a cheesy ass grin on his face.

"Thanks guys, yes you guys can be their uncles. Well, Chase doesn't have a choice, but you other two get to be their uncles," I say, smiling like an idiot. I never thought I'd be standing here discussing babies with my friends.

"What about me guys?" Emerald says with a pout on her face and crossing her arms again.

"Don't worry, you're my best friend, of course you get to be their auntie." She runs over and hugs Winter and then turns to hug me.

"This is such a surprise; I wasn't expecting you guys to tell us that at all but I'm so happy for you guys!" Emerald starts clapping her hands together and jumping up and down in excitement. Similar to how my mom reacted.

"Tell me about it. We weren't expecting them to tell us there were two babies in my stomach when they did the ultrasound, then the doctor thought we already knew so it was an even bigger shock, he just kept talking about baby A, baby B and it wasn't even registering." Winter stops talking for a second and looks up at me.

"I'm still in shock but I wouldn't want to do this with anyone else," I say leaning and down, giving her a soft, slow kiss on the lips before pulling away and kissing her forehead. "I love you," I whisper down in her ear then I hug her a little tighter.

"I love you, Carsten." She turns her head up at me and whispers back.

48

CARSTEN

I TURN OVER IN MY BED, THE SUN SHINING THROUGH THE blinds that I forgot to shut the night before. After Winter and I had sex last night we both passed out, so I never had the chance to shut them, I don't even think we ate dinner. I grab my phone from my nightstand to check the time and to see that it's ten in the morning. I've got a long day ahead of me that I'm not looking forward to. I have to go and do a couple tattoos at Crazy's and then I have to go work at the bar at five-thirty with my mom and Chase for country night. That seems to be our busiest weeknight.

I look over to see a naked Winter laying on her stomach, her legs out of the blanket, along with her breasts, her nipples hard from the fan blowing next to her. I scoot closer to her in the bed, spooning her with my naked body, bringing my arm up around her waist, poking her ass with my hard cock. I lightly squeeze her boob while pinching her nipple. "Mmm," she moans out in her sleep. I lean over and start kissing her neck, while lightly sucking on it making her stir in her sleep even more. "Hmm, Carsten, I'm sleepy." She whines, letting out a slight moan.

She rolls over, snuggling her face into my chest. "I didn't sleep well last night." She starts stretching, pushing her body into mine, making my dick even harder than it already was. "I was up puking half the night." I pull her closer to me.

"I'm sorry, Snowflake. Are you okay now?" I ask, feeling bad that she didn't wake me up.

"I still feel nauseous, but the puking stopped around six this morning." She yawns as she finishes her sentence.

"Why didn't you wake me up? I could've helped you somehow or held your hair back." I place my finger under her chin lifting her head up so she's looking at me.

"I felt bad waking you up. You looked like you were in a pretty deep sleep, so I didn't want to." She gives me a tired smile. "I just took care of it myself; I figured if I needed you then I'd wake you. I was up like every hour. I wasn't about to wake you up that much." She stops for a second, thinking. "Plus, you have to work both jobs today, I didn't want you to be tired."

"Aren't you working a double today?" I ask her with a concerned look on my face. I don't know much about pregnancy, but I know it makes you tired and I don't want her over doing it, especially since she hasn't been to a doctor yet. We don't even know how the baby is doing.

"I was, but Lisa doesn't want me over doing it, especially in the first trimester, so she is only scheduling me from one until eight tonight instead of one in the afternoon until one in the morning." She stretches as she yawns again. My poor girl, I wish there was something I could do to help her feel better.

"Good, I don't want you to overwork yourself either. I can help you out with whatever you need. Please take care of you for yourself and our baby." I smile at her. Our baby, it still hasn't fully sunk in yet. It's only been a day so I'm not sure when something like that actually sinks in or how long it takes. But I'm not worried about it anymore.

"Our baby." She giggles. "I need to call my doctor to set up an appointment. I honestly have no idea how any of this stuff works. I feel so lost." She looks sad as she talks, I'm sure she feels so lost without her mom or even a parent to turn to.

"Well, I wanted to talk to you. How about tonight we meet at the bar and tell my mom. We can tell our friends too if you want to hang out with them." I feel like telling our friends will be the best thing. Especially for Winter that way she can have more people to support her during her pregnancy.

"We can do that. It makes me nervous thinking about telling your mom." She pauses. "I don't really know her like you do obviously. But do you think she's going to be upset?" She nervously bites her lip as she stares at me, waiting for an answer as I try to think of how my mom would react. I honestly have never had to think about how my mom would react the day I told her I got someone pregnant because I never thought I'd have to worry about it. I always used protection when I slept around so something like that never crossed my mind. But now that the day is finally here. I think she'll be happy, shocked maybe, but happy and excited.

"Hell no, she always said how we better make her a grandma one day. She never said when but I'm sure she's going to be very excited about it." I smile down at her, hoping I'm going to be right. The last thing I want is for my mom to be mad at me.

"Do you want to tell them all to meet there at ten-thirty, so that way I have time to go home and change before driving up there?" She rolls onto her back looking up at the ceiling. I drape my arm over her, rubbing the skin right between her breasts with my thumb.

"I'll come pick you up, that way we can drive back home together, and you won't have to worry about driving. I'm sure you'll be tired."

"Home." She looks over at me, smiling. I've been calling it home a lot lately without even realizing it. But to me wherever she is, is home. I don't care if we haven't been together long. When you know that that person is the one, then you know, no matter how long it's been.

I look over at her, staring into her eyes. "You are my home, Snowflake. I don't want to be anywhere you're not."

"You're my home too, Carsten." I lean in and kiss her, not even letting her finish what she was going to say. She opens her lips for me immediately and I deepen the kiss. I fill her tongue with mine needing to taste her, all of her, any way that I can. To feel close to her on a different level. "I love you." She whispers against my lips before coming back in to kiss me. Swiping her tongue against mine.

"I love you, gorgeous." I kiss her lips hungrily, like she's the only thing I need to survive. I get on top of her, spreading her legs and adjusting her body at the right angle to slide my cock right into her, making love to her again. Making it about more than just fucking her. I take my time, gliding my cock in deep with each thrust, making her moan out in tortured pleasure with every slow thrust. Her words and throaty moans mixed together, her breathing heavy, gasping for air after each pump.

I growl against her lips, her pussy feeling so good, it's hard to last long. "Goddamn, baby girl. I love the way your pussy feels on my cock." I groan out against her neck, I press her body into mine, feeling her sweaty skin slip against mine as I thrust into her, her body meeting mine with each movement.

"God, Carsten, you feel so amazing," she moans into my ear, in a sexy, breathy moan, making it even harder to hold back with each thrust. I reach down to massage her clit, hoping to get her there before I finish without her. "Don't stop, please don't stop." She groans against my lips. Her breathing heavier than it was before, her legs shaking. I know she's getting close. I pick up the pace thrusting into her faster, lifting her hips to get into her pussy deeper. Her pussy clamps down, tightening around me, pulling my cum from my cock as we both climax together.

I finish my shift at Crazy's tattoos and head to my car to sit for a minute and text Winter I haven't talked to her since this morning and I miss her.

Me
miss u snowflake

Winter
miss u too, my stomach has been cramping
all day

Me
are u ok, do u need me to do something?

Winter
I think I'm fine right now, I'll let you know if that
changes

Me
please do, don't hesitate to ask for help

Winter
thank u, how was work?

Me
just finished at Crazys taking a 10 min break then
headed to Black Velvet

How's work for you?

Winter
i'm sure ur tired. It's been busy, haven't had a
minute to stop

Me
maybe that's why you're cramping? Maybe ask
Lisa if you can take a 5 and sit

Winter
I'm going on break in 10 so I'll sit then

Me
please make sure you do baby girl I worry
about u

Winter
I will handsome don't worry

Me
love you Snowflake

Winter
Love you, handsome devil

I pull out of the parking lot at Crazy's and head to Black Velvet. Tonight is country night so it's going to be busy, which I'm ready for. I'd rather be busy than slow. Plus, the tips are always great.

Pulling into the parking lot of Black Velvet I end up parking the same time my mom is getting out of her car. "Hey, Mom." I walk towards her, giving her a hug. It's been a few days since I've seen her.

"How's my boy doing?" She reaches her arms out, wrapping them around me and hugs me. "How's Winter? I haven't seen her in a few days." She gives me a big smile. Weird, I feel like she knows something is up, although no one knows Winter is pregnant besides me. Well, and Winter of course.

"I'm doing good, just been busy at Uncle Kane's shop tattooing. I tattooed Winter as well, finished her sleeve and her hand, it looks awesome-" She cuts me off before I can finish which I guess is for the best. I don't like keeping things from my mom, so if I don't have to answer how she is then I'm not keeping anything from her.

"What?? That's so exciting, I'm sure she looks beautiful with it. I can't wait to see it!" She claps her hands together in excitement.

"Well, she will be here tonight, so you'll get to see it." I say holding the door open for her to walk into the bar.

Chase is already here setting things up and he gives us an annoyed look. "Let me guess, Mom was holding you up in the parking lot, talking your ear off?" He rolls his eyes, laughing.

"Hey, that's not nice." She's laughing too. "I just like to check in and catch up with my boys, there's nothing wrong with that," she says defensively.

"Ya, ya," Chase says, coming up behind her and patting her on the back. "It's ok, this just explains why you're always late for everything, especially if people are involved." He's laughing now, walking away.

"So rude." She sticks her middle finger up at him. I love the relationship we have with our mom, she's like a friend most of the time, but puts her foot down when she needs to, which is rare. Especially now that we're older.

We opened the bar about an hour ago and it's already busy, a lot busier than it normally is since line dancing doesn't start until ten-thirty. I walk into the back room to run to my office real quick and I check my phone on the way to see I have four texts from Winter, which instantly makes me nervous, especially since she's pregnant.

> **Winter**
> I think I need to go to the emergency room

> **Winter**
> i went to the bathroom and there's blood

> **Winter**
> Carsten, I'm scared can you please text me back

> **Winter**
> I'm gonna give it a few more minutes before I
> drive myself. I just figured you'd want to go with
> me so I'm trying to wait but I'm scared :(

My stomach drops and my heart is in my throat feeling like it's about to burst. Instead of texting her back I rush to my office and call her so it's quieter and I can hear her better.

"Hey, Snowflake, are you okay?" I ask trying to calm my nerves.

"I'm not sure." She's crying and I instantly rush down the hall to my mom to let her know I have to leave. This is a little more important right now than work.

"Hold on, Snowflake." I tell her before she continues talking.

Thankfully my mom's office door is open, and I run right in. "Mom, I hate to do this, but I need to leave, it's an emergency," I say, getting ready to turn around and rush out the door.

"What do you mean? What's going on?" she asks frantically rushing over to me looking me up and down to make sure I'm okay.

I move my phone from my ear and put it on speaker phone. "Winter, I have you on speaker phone. I need to tell my mom, maybe she can give us some advice," I say nervously, my hands shaking.

"Ok," she says, sniffling. You can hear she's trying not to freak out, which I wouldn't blame her if she was.

I look over at my mom and take a deep breath to calm myself down some before talking. "Mom, Winter is pregnant," I say, but before I can continue, she's squealing with excitement.

"Oh my god, honey!! Congratulations, I'm gonna be a grandma?" She claps her hands together again, bouncing up and down. It makes me happy to see this is her reaction. I just hope everything is okay with the baby, I'd hate to give her the news that she's going to be a grandma and take it away all in the same day.

"That's the thing, Winter said she's bleeding, I need to go with her to the emergency room." I say in a hurry, trying to show that I need to go.

"Calm down honey, sometimes bleeding can be normal. So, both of you try to calm down so that way you don't put any more stress on your baby." She stops for a second, giving me a worried smile. "Plus, I need you to get you both there safe, if you're all worked up and stressed that might not happen," she says squeezing my arm.

"Okay, Mom," I say, trying to calm down some.

"Just take a couple deep breaths Carsten, you guys will be ok." She's trying to hide the worried look on her face, which is why I wish I didn't have to say anything because I didn't want to excite her to turn around and worry her.

"I'll keep you updated, thanks Mom. I love you," I say, running out of her office and back to mine to grab my keys and rush out the back door.

"Winter, are you still there?" She hasn't said anything, and I don't hear sniffling anymore so now I'm worried something more serious has happened.

"Ye... yeah, I-" she lets out a breath, it sounds like she's been holding and takes a deep breath in. "I'm just scared. I don't want to lose the baby." She's sobbing now.

"I'm on my way, baby girl. I'll be there as quickly as I can. Get ready and I'll honk when I'm there."

She takes another deep breath before responding. "Alright, be careful please."

"I will Snowflake. I love you."

"Love you, Carsten." The way she says it breaks my heart. I wish I was already by her to comfort her.

About an hour later we're back in a room waiting for the doctor to come in with an ultrasound machine, all of her blood work came back fine, and her HCG levels are all where they need to be. Let's just hope everything is still good with the baby.

The doctor comes in pushing a cart in front of him with what I'm assuming is the ultrasound machine.

"Hi guys, I'm Dr. Smith, I'll be doing your ultrasound today. I hear you have had some bleeding?" He says, looking from me to Winter.

"Yeah, I was fine this morning, then I went to work, and I was cramping the whole time. They felt like period cramps, but then when I went to the bathroom there was blood in my underwear and on the toilet paper." The tears start falling from her eyes again.

"Alright, well I'm gonna have you lay down flat, put your feet in the stirrups and scoot your bottom all the way to the end up the of the table," he says, putting what looks like a condom on the end of this weird wand thing and some liquid stuff that looks like it could be lube. Maybe Winter knows what all of this stuff is but I'm clueless and not really in the mood to ask a bunch of questions that aren't related to the baby. "This is going to be cold, and you might feel some pressure while I move the wand around to see the baby." He pauses, sticking the wand between her legs. "Sometimes bleeding can be normal, depending on how far along you are. Sometimes it can just be from your cervix being irritated from something as well.

Have you guys had intercourse at all today or the last few days?" he asks, looking over at us while moving the wand around.

"Um, this morning. We did before I went to work." She bites her bottom lip nervously.

"Well, that could very well be where the bleeding is coming from. I don't see any blood on the ultrasound or in either of the sacs that the babies are in," he says, moving the wand again.

"Wait... babies?" My eyes go wide as I look from Winter to the doctor. My stomach just fell through my ass at this point. Am I hearing things?

"Yes, your babies look healthy actually, I don't see any blood inside, it must've been irritation to the cervix." He shifts the wand again. "Here, let me turn this up so we can hear baby A's heartbeat." Then I could hear a muffled sound almost like a static and then I hear what sounds like a really fast heartbeat. "Good, baby A's heart rate is at 146 beats per minute, now let's shift over to baby B's heart rate," he says, still not answering my very fucking confused question.

"So um, I'm sorry if I'm misunderstanding," Winter says, glancing from me to the doctor. "But um, why do you keep saying babies and Baby A and Baby B?" she asks, wiping the tears from her face that are slowly starting to dry up.

"Oh, you didn't know?" he says, looking at us shocked. "You guys are having twins, fraternal twins to be exact. I'm so sorry, I thought you guys knew prior to coming in here." He looks over at us then back at the ultrasound screen. "Baby B's heart rate is perfect too, it's at 148 beats per minute." He turns the screen for us to look and points. "This sac right here this little thing you see flickering on Baby A is their heart, and then this is its little body. You are currently 9 weeks and 3 days." He shifts the wand over to the right some. "This one right here is Baby B, you can see the little flicker on the screen as well, that's their heart."

Winter and I both sit there in shock... twins... fucking twins?? I can't believe it. Not only did I knock her up, but I knocked her up with two fucking babies.

"Wow." Winter pushes her hair out of her face as she's looking over at the ultrasound machine. "This is all… wow. I'm just shocked. I had no idea we were having twins." Tears form in her eyes again and I'm not sure if they're good or bad tears.

"Look at how perfect they are." The tears fall from her eyes down her cheeks, and she looks over at me then back to Dr. Smith. "So, is everything okay? Do you know where the bleeding came from?" she asks with a concerned look on her face again, she seemed happy for a minute like she forgot we came here for an emergency, now she looks scared again.

"Yes, everything is perfect. I would say the bleeding could have been irritation to your cervix from intercourse. I would refrain from doing any sexual activity for at least two days to be safe. then if anything happens after the two days I would come back to emergency or if you can see your OB, they usually try to get you in right away for urgent situations like this."

"Thank you so much for all this information, I feel so much better. But wow…" Winter looks over at me. "I can't believe we're having twins!" She laughs a nervous laugh. You can tell she's unsure how to feel but I'm sure it'll take some time for the both of us to get used to the news of just being pregnant, now we have to get used to the news of having twins.

"Well, I will leave you two. Congratulations on your babies. I would definitely call and schedule a follow up with your doctor. That way you can start being seen regularly, in the meantime, you need to start taking prenatal vitamins and drink a lot of water," he says. "Also, get as much rest as you can, you don't want to overwork yourself." He starts walking towards the door. "Do you guys have any other questions?"

"Umm, I think I'm good," Winter says, looking over at me.

"I'm good too, thank you so much for everything." I smile, still looking at the ultrasound screen.

"Oh wait, before I forget." He walks back over and then you hear something printing "Here is the ultrasound pictures. I even marked on there Baby A and Baby B for you guys." He smiles as he walks out of the room.

We decide after the appointment to still go back up to Black Velvet to inform my mom about everything and to fill our friends in on the fact that Winter is pregnant and having twins. Holy fuck I still can't believe it.

"Twins." I squeeze Winter's hand as I talk to my mom in her office.

"Wait, what?" Her mouth falls open not sure if it's a look of confusion or disbelief on her face.

"Yep. That was our reaction too. Everything was fine, my cervix was most likely just irritated. That's where the blood was coming from," Winter says to my mom, smiling at her facial expression. "But yeah, we went there thinking one baby and here we are having twins, fraternal twins. I'm 9 weeks and 3 days." Winter places her hand on her forehead like she's still in shock herself.

"Holy shit. This is so exciting! Carsten, you guys are having two babies, my baby is having two babies of his own!" She practically shouts in excitement from her office.

"Shhh Mom. No one else knows yet. We plan on telling everyone when we go out there." I place my finger over my lips to "shh" her.

"Oh, sorry." She covers her mouth and laughs with excitement then rushes over to hug the both of us, practically throwing herself on us in the process.

"Woah, Mom. Watch Winter please, she's supposed to take it easy for a few days." I hold my arm around Winter's waist to help her keep her body balanced.

"I'm so sorry. I didn't mean to knock into you guys, this is just so exciting. Congratulations you two. I will help with anything I can." Her body slightly bounces up and down as the excitement pours out of her. I feel relieved that Winter is okay, and our babies are okay. And I'm happy that my mom is as excited as she is. I knew she would be though.

"Thank you so much," Winter says with tears in her eyes and a smile on her face. "Man, I don't know what's wrong with me. I'm happy but I'm crying." She laughs as she wipes her fresh, falling tears from her reddened cheeks.

"It's the hormones dear, they'll definitely have you all over the place. You'll be okay though." My mom tells her, gently squeezing her arm. "Now head out there and tell your friends, you guys they're gonna be so happy for you." She smiles at us with tears in her eyes from excitement.

We walk out from the back room and see everyone is outside on the patio drinking. That will be the first thing they question is why we aren't drinking. I decided to quit with Winter, she obviously quit, due to being pregnant, so I'll quit with her. I need to chill on drinking for a while anyways, focus on myself, Winter, and now our babies. We walk outside together, holding hands as all our friends greet us.

"What the hell happened man we were slammed after you left where'd you go?" Chase asks since I didn't fill him in on what happened either.

"Yeah, you guys told us to meet you here at ten-thirty and you both were gone. Let me guess, you guys were in your office again?" Creedence asks, wiggling his eyebrows at us and smiling.

"Well, actually we have something to tell you guys." Winter says and everyone stops talking.

"Did you guys go and get married or something?" Chase asks sarcastically.

"That's actually not a bad idea, huh Snowflake?" I ask, wrapping my arms around her waist, standing behind her.

"No, that wasn't it." Winter shakes her head, laughing at him. Leave it to Chase, he always has the craziest things to say. He's the biggest smart ass out of all our friends.

"Well, then what is it?" Emerald raises one eyebrow and crossing her arms impatiently, she's the most impatient woman I've ever met.

Winter looks up at me nodding her head, giving me the okay to go ahead and tell them. I let out a deep breath, not sure why I'm nervous to tell our friends. Other than them possibly judging us or having negative things to say, they should all actually be pretty supportive of the both of us and the twins.

"Winter and I are having a baby..." I pause, not used to the baby being more than one. "Well, babies, actually." My smile grows as I say the words out loud again, reality of me being a dad very slowly sinking in. Actually, relieved we told our friends. Months ago, I never would've thought I'd be where I am now, in a relationship, or even in love for that matter.

"Holy shit," Chase says with a big smile on his face. "I'm gonna be an uncle?" he practically shouts out.

"Oh my god!! Are you shitting me, twins? You guys are having babies? I'm gonna be an aunt?" Emerald shrieks. Her and Winter have been best friends for so long, she's automatically promoted to being their aunt.

"Hell yeah, congrats guys! I get to be an uncle too, if my girl... I mean if Emerald gets to be their aunt I want to be an uncle," Creedence says, trying to hide the fact that he and Emerald are dating. Not sure why he's hiding it, maybe he thinks we'll be upset.

"Congrats man, do I get to be an uncle too?" Axton says, with a cheesy ass grin on his face.

"Thanks guys, yes you guys can be their uncles. Well, Chase doesn't have a choice, but you other two get to be their uncles," I say, smiling like an idiot. I never thought I'd be standing here discussing babies with my friends.

"What about me guys?" Emerald says with a pout on her face and crossing her arms again.

"Don't worry, you're my best friend, of course you get to be their auntie." She runs over and hugs Winter and then turns to hug me.

"This is such a surprise; I wasn't expecting you guys to tell us that at all but I'm so happy for you guys!" Emerald starts clapping her hands together and jumping up and down in excitement. Similar to how my mom reacted.

"Tell me about it. We weren't expecting them to tell us there were two babies in my stomach when they did the ultrasound, then the doctor thought we already knew so it was an even bigger shock, he just kept talking about baby A, baby B and it wasn't even registering." Winter stops talking for a second and looks up at me.

"I'm still in shock but I wouldn't want to do this with anyone else," I say leaning and down, giving her a soft, slow kiss on the lips before pulling away and kissing her forehead. "I love you," I whisper down in her ear then I hug her a little tighter.

"I love you, Carsten." She turns her head up at me and whispers back.

49

WINTER

I STAND UP AND ADJUST MY DRESS, FIXING IT AT MY WAIST, and then putting my boobs back in my bra. I walk over to the mirror and fix my hair that somehow got messed up in the process. As I'm fixing my hair the doorbell rings. I glance out the back door to see Carsten is back outside, so I'll have to get it. I figured we'd have early guests, but I didn't think this early. I double check my hair and makeup, making sure everything looks ok and it doesn't look like we just had sex and walk over to the door.

I open the door to see its Presley, Carsten's mom, and Chase. Thank God, I'm sure they'll be able to help us finish decorating. Everyone will be here in about a half hour. It feels like time is dragging. I'm so excited to find out the sex of the babies. I feel like I've waited for forever to get to this part of my pregnancy. I open the door and am automatically greeted with a hug. Presley rushes to me wrapping her arms around me.

"Is it okay if I rub your belly, I'd love to say hi to my grandbabies.?" she asks, looking down at it. It's gotten so huge this past week, I don't see how my body will be able to stretch anymore, and I still have hopefully four months left, if the twins make it full term.

"Presley, I told you, you don't have to ask. These are your grandbabies, rub away." I point down at my stomach, still sad that I can't see my feet. It's been a while.

"Well, I don't want to touch you without asking. It's your body not mine," she says, smiling as she places both hands on each side of my stomach.

"Excuse me, Mom, I am standing here. Can I at least get in the doorway and say hi to my future sister." Chase tries to squeeze past us as he says it, making me realize that we really are blocking the doorway. Future sister, I like the sound of that. I've never had any siblings, so it'll be nice gaining him as a brother one day. IF Carsten ever pops the question. I've been patiently waiting, but I know he's waiting for the perfect time and doesn't want to rush because I'm pregnant. He doesn't want me or anyone else to think that just because we're having a baby that that's the only *reason* he wants to marry me.

"Hi, Chase," I say, reaching over to hug him while their mom still rubs my stomach, now talking to it. She wants the twins to feel comfortable around her, so she wants them to recognize her voice when they're born. It's so sweet how much she cares about them already and how helpful she's been.

"Hey, how are you and my niece and nephew doing?" He's convinced I'm having one of each, that way they both can give Carsten hell and that way Chase can spoil them both equally with girly things and all things boys. These babies, whatever their sex is, they're going to be so spoiled, and I love that they have so many people who love them already.

"You crack me up. What if they're both girls, or both boys?" I ask, smiling over at him.

"Either way, Carsten will be fucked with karma. But hopefully you'll get their good side." He reaches his hand out handing me two gift bags.

"Why did you get gifts? We told you guys no gifts just show up." I say, shaking my head at them. See what I mean? Spoiled. At this rate

I won't even need a baby shower if everyone keeps buying stuff for them every time we see them.

We already have two swings, two highchairs and a bunch of gender-neutral clothes until we find out what we are having, because everyone keeps buying us gifts. We are very lucky and so are these babies.

"You know we can't come here empty handed, plus what kind of grandma would I be if I showed up empty handed?" Presley asks, picking her bags up off the ground that I didn't even see her put down.

"Yes, you guys can come empty handed." Carsten walks in the back door shaking his head at the bags I'm holding and that his mom has in her hands.

"Thank you, guys, we really appreciate it, and our spoiled little babies will love it." I want them to know that I'm thankful for them and for the gifts.

"Yes, thank you, Mom. Thank you, dick cheese." Carsten laughs.

"Welcome, barf breath," Chase says back to him.

My face turns up in disgust. "Ew, barf breath, couldn't have called him anything else that wouldn't gross a pregnant woman out." I throw my head back laughing, because sometimes I just can't believe the things they call each other.

"Sorry, Winter. For you I will think of different things that aren't as gross to call him for the rest of your pregnancy." Chase places his hand on his chin like he's thinking.

"Thank you." I laugh again.

"Sorry, babe. I started it, you can punish me later for it." Carsten says, kissing me on the cheek and wiggling his eyebrows as he pulls away.

"Alright, alright, I don't want to hear about your sex life, Carten." Presley says, putting her hand partially on her forehead and eye while shaking her head at him.

"Sorry, Ma, sometimes I forget that you're my mom and not one of my friends, so I gotta remember what I say when I'm around you." Carsten leans in hugging her with a big smile on his face.

"Well, I'm happy you think of me as more of a friend than just your mom." She giggles a little in excitement like this is news to her. But I think she just loves how much her boys love her, and I do too. It's sweet to see how much they both adore their mom.

"It's true, Mom. We both feel that way too," Chase says to her, agreeing with Carsten.

She gets an even bigger smile on her face then pouts. "Stop it you guys, you're going to make me cry."

"Sorry, Mom." They both say in unison then look over at each other and laugh. These two are so much alike sometimes it's scary.

"It's okay, you just gotta be careful. I'm becoming even more emotional in my old age." She's holding her hand over her heart shaking her head, joking around and being dramatic.

"Oh yeah, so old in your young age of forty-one. Here's a confidence booster, you're gonna be a young grandma at least." He gives her a big cheesy smile, looks like he's trying to get brownie points.

"That is true." She smiles at him. "Now, what can we help with and when I say we I mean Chase because I'm going to keep Winter company while you boys do the hard work for her." She says, placing her hands on her hips.

"Actually, everything is done," Carsten says, looking around. "We just need to set out another pile of napkins and plates on the patio that's it." He walks over to the counter in the kitchen to grab the napkins and plates then runs out the back door towards the patio. As we're walking through the house the doorbell rings again.

"I'll go grab that for you guys," Chase says, walking back down the hall to where we just came from.

"Thank you, Chase." I call out behind him as he walks away.

I walk out to the backyard to sit on the swing and wait for our guests, my body is tired, and my back is starting to hurt. I should have listened to Carsten but because I'm stubborn and used to doing things for myself it's hard to just give in and let someone do things for me. That's one thing that will take some getting used the longer we're together.

After all the guests arrive everyone keeps asking when we're doing the gender reveal. We we're going to wait until everyone was done eating but I guess they're just as impatient as we are.

"Does everyone want us to do the reveal now? Or do you guys want to wait to eat?" Carsten asks everyone. There's about twenty people here between our close friends, his mom, brother, and two uncles; they're all the important people in our lives.

I hold my stomach with both hands while blinking back tears. I don't want to cry right now. I've already cried alone, so many times, afraid to really let go because I feel like once I really start crying and break down, I'm not going to be able to stop. I'm looking down so no one can see the tears in my eyes or the sad look on my face. There's a heaviness in my chest that hurts no matter how much time passes, like a hole in my heart that's always empty. I'm just missing two people. My only family. My dad being in rehab, I'm not sure if he would even care. But most of all, I miss my mom. I know she'd be just as happy as Carsten's mom. Which is one reason I'm so thankful for her, besides how loving she's been towards me and the babies, she's like how my mom was and how my mom would be if she were still alive.

"You okay baby girl?" Carsten comes up to me rubbing my stomach and lifting my chin with his other hand to have me look him in the eye. His look is instantly worried when he sees the tears streaming down my face. "Snowflake, are you okay? Are the babies okay?" he asks in a panic, alerting everyone, which I was hoping to avoid—the attention. But I know he didn't mean to, he's just worried about me and the babies.

"Yeah," I whisper, clearing my throat. "Just wish my parents, especially my mom, could be here is all." He instantly wraps his arms around me, swallowing me with his body around mine. Just shows how tiny I am compared to his large, muscular frame.

"I'm so sorry, Snowflake. I wish there was something I could do to take your pain, besides my family is your family, baby girl. My mom is your mom now. I wish I could do more."

"Thank you." I lean up standing on my tiptoes. I don't know what else to say, his words have me choked up even more, and like I said I'm afraid if I let go, I won't be able to stop. I've been keeping these feelings bottled up for so long that I'm afraid once I open up it'll be a waterfall and not even I will know how to stop them from flowing. I wipe away my tears and take a deep breath trying to focus on the positive and all the people here with us today to celebrate our babies.

"Who's ready to find out what we're having?" I ask trying to hide the stuffiness in my voice from crying.

"Hell yeah," Chase shouts. "Let's do this shit!" He throws his hands up cheering as everyone else shouts along with him.

"Alright, do you want baby A or Baby B?" Carsten asks, me holding the balloons that contain the colored confetti. We had to put them in boxes so we wouldn't be tempted to pop them before everyone got here, out of sight out of mind kind of thing, because we both knew if they sat there this whole time in front of us one of us would've convinced the other to pop them.

"Oooh, I'll take baby A, I wanna know what that little booger is, they keep me up all night with how active they've been." I laugh, reaching my hand out to grab the string so it doesn't fly away.

"Good, maybe baby B will be a boy and be like his daddy, nice and calm." He laughs, knowing even he's not being serious, there's been nothing calm about him his whole life.

"Riggghhhtttt," Chase drags out obnoxiously, even he understood the sarcasm in the situation.

We both stand next to each other holding our balloons. Carsten leans down and gives me a long passionate kiss, which causes our friends to cheer like the smartasses that they are.

"Okay guys, let's count down from three, Carsten," I say looking over at him, my heart racing, I feel like I could puke from excitement.

"Three." I start.

"Two." He says, looking down at me with the cutest, happiest smile I've ever seen on his face.

"One," we both say at the same time, both of us pop our balloons.

"Oh my gosh!" I jump up and down holding my stomach the same time Carsten lifts me into his arms.

"Holy shit, I can't believe it," Carsten says, spinning me around in his arms.

50

WINTER

SIX MONTHS LATER

WE PUT THE TWINS IN THEIR CAR SEATS AND HEAD TO THE cars. I'm carrying one baby, and a diaper bag and Carsten is carrying the other baby along with their diaper bag. We put them in the back seat of the car. Carsten comes around opening the passenger side of the car for me and shutting the door once I get in, he's still such a gentleman when it comes to certain things, like holding doors open, opening the car door, walking on the outside of the parking lot or sidewalk, and keeping me and the babies on the inside to block us from cars. It makes me fall even more in love with him every time.

I buckle my seatbelt after looking at the twins one last time to make sure they were still sleeping before we head off. We have about an hour drive, and it makes it easier when they're sleeping, especially at this age when they don't sleep as much as they did as newborns, at least our twins don't sleep as much as they did as newborns. At three and a half months old sleep isn't something they're fond of, which is why we're exhausted all the time. But we love it.

I take a deep breath in and breathe out slowly, my nerves starting to kick in. Carsten reaches over gripping my thigh with his right hand, his left hand on the steering wheel. I place my hand on his and he reaches his thumb up rubbing my pinky. He looks over at me, giving me a reassuring smile.

"Everything is gonna be okay, I promise," he says, squeezing my thigh again.

"I know it's just... it's been a while, ya know?" I say feeling nauseous from how nervous I am.

He turns his car around in our driveway before pulling out onto the road, being extra cautious every time we drive with the twins. It's funny how things change, he used to watch the road for cops so he could speed to wherever he needed to be, now he watches the road for other asshole drivers, to make sure nothing happens while we're driving with or without the twins.

The whole car ride we stay quiet. Carsten is focused on the drive, nervous himself for his own reasons. This is a first for him, he's never met my dad before. Yep, my dad gets out of rehab today and we're on our way to pick him up. He'll be meeting Carsten and the twins for the first time; he doesn't even know he's a grandpa. Hopefully they'll be something to keep him motivated to stay sober, since it didn't work with me, maybe they'll be lucky and get the sober version of him.

I stay quiet throughout the whole car ride, lost in my thoughts and nervous about how everything will go once we see him. Will he be happy, is he going to be a happy sober person or will he be angry. I haven't talked to him since the day I dropped him off, he had told me and the rehab facility that he didn't want any phone calls the whole time he's in there because he wanted to focus on fixing himself, so it's been a year and two full months since I've talked to my dad.

We pull into the parking lot of the rehab center and pull into a parking spot. My nerves are getting the best of me. I feel like I'm going to puke so I close my eyes and take a deep breath. My dad said he would meet us outside, he couldn't wait any longer to get out of that place, but I still want to greet him outside of the car and get a feel for things.

Carsten reaches over and grabs my hand, squeezing it. "You ok, Snowflake?" His voice laced with concern.

I clear my throat. "Yeah, it's just been over a year since I've seen him, ya know? I have no idea what to expect, who to expect. I don't think I ever remember a time where he wasn't sober, if I'm not mistaken, he's been a drunk my whole life." I sigh, removing my hand from Carsten's and placing them over my face. "I'm just afraid that once he's out he'll go right back to it and then I'll lose my dad before I get the chance to even really know him and that the babies will lose their grandfather. I don't want them developing a relationship with him for it to be ripped away by alcohol." I let out the breath I was holding, afraid I'll puke if I stop taking deep breaths.

One of the twins starts crying so I get out and grab them from their car seat. As I turn around, I see my dad walking towards our car.

"Shit, he's coming, Carsten." Carsten gets out of the car and rushes over to my side wrapping his arm around me.

"It's going to be okay, Snowflake." He squeezes my arm with his hand that's wrapped around me.

"Winter?" my dad says, it sounds like a question. Maybe I look different from the last time I saw him. Besides having the twins nothing has changed about me. Maybe being sober he doesn't remember what I look like.

"Hi, Dad," I say, as tears fill my eyes. I'm trying to blink them away but I'm not having any luck.

He rushes over to me, opening his arms. Carsten drops his arm around me so my dad can give me a better hug and I give the baby to Carsten for a minute.

"Oh god, Winter, you look so beautiful. So much has changed about you in the time I've been gone, I can't wait to catch up," he says sounding like a new man, but I'm still afraid to get too excited.

"It has, but Dad-" I pull away, looking him over, the tears falling down my cheeks that I was trying to hold back. "You look so good. I'm proud of you. Thank you." I pause for a second. "Thank you for doing this."

"Winter, please don't thank me. I should be thanking you for opening my eyes to how terrible of a person I was to you. I wish I could take it all back." He hugs me again, tears in his eyes. "I'm so sorry," he says, squeezing me tight.

"It's okay, Dad. Just focus on taking care of you now." I pull away from his hug again, smiling at him.

"I have someone I want you to meet."

"Alright." He stops, looking over at Carsten.

"This is my boyfriend, Carsten. Carsten, this is my father, Jim Vega," I say nervously.

Carsten reaches out his hand and shakes my dad's hand. "Nice to meet you, sir. I'm Carsten Hatcher," Carsten says, you can hear the nerves in the tone of his voice.

"Please, call me Jim. It's so nice to meet you," he says with a gentle smile. He looks over at the baby Carsten is handing me. "Who might this be?" he says looking down.

"Dad." I clear my throat, trying to control my emotions. "This is... your granddaughter." I pause for a second, blinking back tears. "Amelia."

"My... my granddaughter... you had a baby?"

I cut him off. "Actually, twins." I laugh.

"Wow, congratu..." He pauses, finally registering what I said.

"Amelia?" He stops, clearing his throat as his eyes fill with tears again. "Amelia... like your..." He loses it, tears stream down his face as he is struggling to get the words out. "Like your mother," he chokes out and I lose it.

I'm sobbing. "Yes... yes Dad, like Mom," I say, barely able to talk between sobs. I look over at Carsten who has tears in his eyes now. I knew this moment would be emotional, but damn, I could've never been prepared for all the emotions I'm feeling in this moment.

"Your mom would be so proud of you, Snow," he says. His bottom lip quivering. "Can... Can I hold her?" he asks, his arms reaching out to her.

"Of course," I say, handing her to him. I at least know I can trust that he's sober and able to hold her. I look over and Carsten is coming around the car with the other twin that woke up from their nap. "Dad, this is your grandson, Axel." I smile, looking at my son and my daughter. "They're fraternal twins." I chuckle. Some days it's still hard to believe that we had twins.

"Wow, Snow. I can't believe you guys had twins." He's still crying, but it's calmed down some since it started.

"Congratulations you guys. Winter, I'm so proud of you, for... for everything." He's getting choked up again. "I know I haven't been the best dad to you, but I promise I'm working on it, and I promise to be there for you guys and the twins." He looks up at me, looking me in the eyes. "And I promise to stay sober for all of you guys." He reaches in, still holding Amelia and hugs me.

"I love you, Winter," he says, which I feel like is the first time I've ever heard him tell me that.

"I love you too, Dad," I say, crying again. Damn since having kids I've become an over emotional mess and I hate it. I cry over everything now, so does Carsten.

"Thank you, guys, for coming to get me," he says, patting Carsten on the shoulder and smiling over at me.

"No problem, sir. We're happy to help," Carsten says. "I mean, Jim. No problem, Jim." They both laugh and it makes me smile. I'm hoping they'll get along and we can all develop a good relationship together.

"Are you hungry, Dad?" I ask, looking at the time on my phone. It's about three in the afternoon, but I'm starving. I couldn't eat lunch due to my nerves going crazy.

"Actually, yeah, I'm starving. Whatcha got in mind?" he says, looking back and forth at us.

"Let's go get some food, we'll find a restaurant on the way home,"

I say, placing Amelia back in her car seat. Carsten walks around putting Axel back in his and I get into the back seat to sit in the third row of the SUV so my dad and Carsten can sit in the front together. Hopefully they'll get to know each other a little better.

51

CARSTEN

After we ate dinner, we dropped Jim back off at his house. He couldn't wait to get home and be in his own bed. While he was in rehab, Winter and I went over there and did a deep cleaning, even hired a cleaning company to help while we removed all the hidden alcohol that he had missed and most likely forgotten about, that way he had nothing to tempt him if he did find anything hidden. Now we're home sitting in the living room with the twins, enjoying each other's company.

I never thought I'd see the day where I'd be in a relationship, and be this happy with one woman, who gave me the most amazing children. The one woman that I want to spend the rest of my life with. Or that I'd be sitting here on the living room floor watching my gorgeous girlfriend play with our daughter while our son sleeps in my arms. That this would be what made my life complete, to have a family to love and protect.

The first day I laid eyes on Winter I just knew she'd be the one I'd be breathing in for the rest of my life. Tomorrow is the day, probably the most important day, next to the birth of our children, that I ask her to be my wife and spend the rest of her life with me, with us, and to hopefully grow our family one day. There's a beautiful white gold, pear shaped diamond ring, with diamonds surrounding it, that I have hidden from her in my dresser drawer, that I've had for months just waiting for the perfect opportunity and I think I'm just going to say fuck it and go for it. I can't wait anymore. I'm ready to move onto the next chapter in our relationship. I picked a pear-shaped diamond due to its uniqueness, it reminded me of her, of my Snowflake, not due to the shape but because of the beauty of how unique the ring is. Tomorrow is the day I'll ask her to be my wife, to spend her life with me, our lives together with our babies, and however many children we have in the future. Forever.

52

WINTER

Carsten has been acting a little strange today. He was up all night, not even because of the twins, they've been sleeping through the night. But he wouldn't tell me why. I walk out to the kitchen with the twins to breakfast.

"Aww, Carsten, this is so sweet," I say, stopping right at the counter covered with all my favorite breakfast dishes. Bacon, eggs, sausage, pancakes, hash browns, toast. It's simple but it's my favorite. I smile over at him. "What's the special occasion, you were up all night, now you're making my favorite breakfast. Not that you don't ever make breakfast, but I feel like something is going on, did I forget our anniversary or something?" I'm now paranoid that I'm forgetting something.

"Nope, but I do need you to run into the living room really quickly please?"

"Okay, what do you need me to grab?" I ask, confused since he just told me to go there but didn't tell me to grab anything.

"I'll let you know when you get there," he says winking at me, every time he winks, he makes me weak in the knees, and gives me butterflies in my stomach, making me feel like a kid with my first crush all over again.

Now I'm even more confused. I feel like I missed something, a birthday or our anniversary, anything that's important enough to surprise me with all of this. I push my confusion aside for a minute and head towards the living room, slowly, because I'm afraid something or someone is going to jump out at me.

"Carsten, if someone scares me, I'm going to kick your ass," I yell at him, because I know he's not following me. Walking down the hall I hold the twins close because if I'm scared, I don't want to scare them. I should've given Axel and Amelia to Carsten before coming in here. "Right guys, I should've given you guys to Daddy huh?" I look down and back and forth at them as they smile and giggle at me. At least someone is happy about this situation. "Holy... shit... Carsten? What is this?" I ask, looking around at all the flower petals on the ground, the heart shaped balloons floating around the living room, there's a large blanket on the ground with pictures of the twins, and us with the twins that was made with a small box sitting on it. I set the twins down in their Pack 'n Play so I can get a better look at everything, but when I turn around this time Carsten is on one knee, kneeling on the blanket. My hands automatically cover my mouth with shock as tears form in my eyes. I had no idea this is what he was going to do with all of this set up.

"Carsten, are you messing with me right now?" I ask my hands shaking as I finally start crying. He winks at me, and gives me his devilish grin that I love so much and shakes his head no.

"Winter, my gorgeous, unique snowflake..."

"Carsten, I don't mean to cut you off, but please, please tell me this is really happening. I feel like I'm gonna pass out." I'm giggling and crying. The giggling is something I do when I'm nervous and not sure what's going on.

"Don't worry, baby girl. I promise you; this is really happening. Come sit down in front of me so you don't hurt yourself." He chuckles a little and pats the ground in front of him on the blanket. I come over and sit down because I truly feel like my knees aren't going to hold me up any longer. I've been waiting for this moment my whole life. What girl hasn't really. He clears his throat; you can tell he's nervous as well.

"Winter, you are my forever, my home, my person, my rock, I can't see doing this life, for the rest of my life, without you by my side. I know things haven't always been perfect, but I love our imperfect life that we make perfect together. I love you with everything I have, and I never want to be without you. Winter, my gorgeous snowflake. Will you make me the happiest man ever and be my wife?"

He grabs my shaking hand with his and places the most beautiful pear-shaped diamond ring on my ring finger. And the tears start falling faster. I never thought about the type of ring that I would want when I was married. I just figured the man who wanted to marry me would know, I mean I've always been drawn to unique diamonds and this one is absolutely gorgeous.

"God, I love you so much Carsten. Yes… of course I'll marry you." I reach over hugging him and scoot to sit onto his lap. He wraps his strong arms around my waist squeezing me tight, and I feel at peace. Whenever I'm in his arms he makes me feel safe, and at peace. Like all my worries just went away, and that was another reason I knew he was the one.

"Thank god, I knew you'd say yeah, but a little part of me had all the what if's running through my mind of what if she didn't want to marry me." He cups my face, kissing me passionately, then swipes his tongue across, licking my lips. I open immediately and he deepens the kiss, I moan into his mouth, because he always gets me worked up. But then pull away because Amelia and Axel are still awake and right there in the living room with us.

"I'm so glad you didn't make me wait until we were done eating before telling me to come in here," I say, looking down at my hand for what seems like the hundredth time in ten minutes.

"Oh yeah, I forgot about the food. Let's go eat," he says, standing up and grabbing my hand to help me up. I stand up on my tiptoes and kiss him again. I could never get enough of him, and I'll never get tired of kissing him.

Later that night I walked out of our sleeping twins' room to go find my future husband. I turn around after shutting their door and walk right into something hard. "Holy shit Carsten, why are you always scaring me and why am I always running into you," I whisper yell.

He reaches down putting his fingers over my mouth like he's telling me to 'shhh' and picks me up, throwing me over his shoulder. He turns around smacking my ass lightly, so it doesn't make too much noise and I giggle in excitement. He walks into our bedroom and lightly throws me on to the bed, and climbs on top of me, his lips instantly crashing into mine as he tugs at my shirt to pull it over my head, then pulls away from our kiss as he tugs my pants and panties off, going down right along with them. "Damn, I can see how wet you are for me baby girl. I can't wait to taste you," he says, coming down to kiss me again. He swipes his tongue and I immediately open my lips for him, allowing him to deepen the kiss. I moan into his mouth, already turned on and ready to go. I start bucking my hips impatiently waiting for what I want, needing to feel him inside me. "Not yet, Snowflake, be patient baby girl," is all he says as he starts trailing kisses down my neck, biting and sucking along the way.

Goosebumps break out across my skin causing a chill to shoot down my spine, my body trembles. He slowly starts licking his way down my collarbone until he gets to my nipple and sucks it into his mouth making me cry out from how good it feels. "Mmm, baby girl," he groans against my nipple before slowly moving over to the other one. He licks his way down my stomach and stops right before my pussy. I lay there patiently waiting for him to make his next move, but I know he loves to tease me, he pushes my legs open one at a time and then gently licks his way down my slit sticking his tongue inside me, making my hips jerk up pushing my pussy into his face. "Mmm, I love when you do that," he moans against my pussy, the vibrations getting me more worked up.

"Carsten, please, I want you to fuck me."

"I just need to taste you a little longer, I wanna feel you cum all over my mouth baby girl." He shoves his face back between my legs, sucking and licking my clit. He sticks two fingers inside me and pumps them in and out quickly, getting me so close to the edge, my body starts shaking. He places his tongue against my clit, swirling it on my favorite spot and I lose control. My pussy clamping down on his fingers, throbbing as he moans into me. My body goes limp, and he quickly pulls away, licking what's left of me off his lips. "God, I can't get enough of you." I smile at him, he's so sexy, his muscular tattooed arms the way they flex as his body moves is enough to get me going in itself. He leans down and kisses me before flipping me over onto my stomach and pulling my ass into the air, before sliding his cock against my wet entrance and shoving himself deep inside me making me cry out in a tortured pleasure.

"Fuck, Carsten. You feel too fucking good," I moan into the mattress as I shift my head to look back at him. He throws his head back moaning out.

"Fuckkk, your pussy is amazing, Snowflake," he grunts out pumping into me hard and deep, already getting me close to another orgasm.

"I'm already close, baby girl," he says, grunting and thrusting as deep as he can.

"Me too. Cum in my pussy, Carsten," I say panting and he growls from my words.

"Don't you worry, baby girl. I'm going to fill that pussy of yours with all of my cum." He thrusts into me, and I meet his thrusts with mine, both of us breathing hard.

"I'm... I'm gonna." I can't even get the words out. It's so intense.

"That's it, cum all over my cock Snowflake, cum with me baby girl." My pussy tightens around him again as I cry out into the mattress, quieting my moans so I don't wake the twins. He pumps into me one last time, my body going lax and his falling gently onto mine. He rolls off me laying down next to me, I roll onto my back scooting closer to him. I lay my head on his chest, and he wraps his arm around me. He takes his other hand putting it on my chin lifting my head, then he leans down to kiss me, soft gentle kisses before he pulls away and goes back to snuggling me. I lay there, content with a smile on my face.

I can't believe I get to marry my best friend. Who would have thought walking into Black Velvet to line dance and watching this sexy man and his panty dropping smile behind a bar, that he would've been the one I wanted to spend the rest of my life with. I knew I'd give him a chance if the opportunity was there, but I had no idea that that opportunity would turn into more. I glance up at Carsten who is now sleeping and then I look down at my ring, tears in my eyes... again. Then I look over at a picture of our babies on my nightstand. My life is perfect, and I wouldn't ask for it to be any other way. I feel like the luckiest girl in the world, because I get to live this life with them, for the rest of my life, forever.

ACKNOWLEDGMENTS

To think that I finally took one of my dreams and made it come true is completely mind blowing to me. I can't believe I finished writing something I didn't think I was good enough to write and am FINALLY publishing. After this long, emotional journey to think it's over, I get to share my passion with everyone makes me so happy.

First I'd like to thank my husband, Michael and my sister, Danielle for encouraging me to say fuck it and go for it. To follow my dreams that I WAS good enough, and to push all my fears aside. To my sister Danielle, thank you so much for being there for me through this whole process, for being my go to when I needed to make sure things sounded good, for being one of my beta readers and for telling me to keep pushing through when I felt like giving up.I appreciate you more than you know and thank you.

To my husband Michael, my real life happy ending. Thank you for always standing by my side and never letting me give up even when I doubted myself. Thank you for being there through all my tears, and drying them or comforting me when I felt like doubt had won and I wanted to give up. You always reminded me things would be okay and get better. Thank you for putting up with my busy days of writing and for listening to my ideas and me randomly reading you parts of my book to make sure they sounded good. I appreciate you for everything you've done, more than you know, thank you and I love you so much.

To my children, Nolan, Elliana, Dahlia and Cooper, you guys were amazing through this whole process, even on days that were hard on both of us. You guys always hugged me when I needed the extra love or helped change my mood when I was getting discouraged or frustrated. Thank you guys for all of your excitement and support through my journey. I love you guys so much!

To everyone else who told me they were proud of me for following my dreams, and for actually going through with this thank you and I appreciate you. If it weren't for all of you guys I wouldn't be writing this today.

To my beta readers and all of my arc readers, I appreciate each and everyone one of you for taking the time to read something I WROTE... holy crap. It's still seems so crazy that I wrote a book.

To Erica, with Logophile Editing.Thank you so much for working with me, for always answering my millions of questions. For your help with guiding me through this whole process and always being there when I needed you. For all your hard work and time that you put into editing and proofing and everything you did for me that involved me and my book and for your help with making my dream a reality, thank you so, so much I appreciate you more than you will ever know. I look forward to working with you for future books.

To Kate, with Kate Decided To Design. Thank you so much for working with me as well and for always being there to answer my never ending questions, for your help as well with guiding me through this process and for always reassuring me things would be okay when I was stressed out talking to you. Thank you for taking my vision and turning it into my beautiful cover and capturing everything that I didn't even know I was looking for, and for everything else you've done for me that involved helping with my book. Also thank you so much for all your hard work

And time that you put into helping make my dream a reality. Thank you so, so much I appreciate you more than you will ever know. I look forward to working with you for future books.

To Jen and Megan at Grey's Promotions, thank you so much for all your hard work with everything you guys did for getting my arcs and graphics out there, for answering my millions of questions and for all your hard work you put into helping me with everything else for my book. I appreciate you guys.

To my current and future smut loving readers...Thank you for taking the time to read my book, I appreciate you more than you know. I hope you stick around to follow me on my journey with my next book in the Courtlynd Series. I love all of you guys!

ABOUT THE AUTHOR

Christina Maria lives in Cleveland, Ohio with her husband Michael, their four kids and two black cats, Bear and Pixie. Before becoming a stay at home mom, she worked at a salon as a licensed hair stylist for almost eleven years. Christina has always loved reading and getting lost in a good book. Along with writing, for as long as she can remember she has always loved anything that told a story or using her imagination to write her own story. She remembers writing stories on her computer or in notebooks as a little girl. It has always been a dream of hers to write a book of her own one day, after taking a four year break on a book she started writing she finally picked it back up and decided to turn it into her dream of being a first time Indie Author on her very first Dark Romance book, Breathing You In.

CONTENT WARNING

- Alcohol abuse by family member
- Physical abuse done to main character, by family member
- Sexual assault done to main character, not done by another main character
- Anxiety and Panic attacks
- Pregnancy loss scare

www.ingramcontent.com/pod-product-compliance
Lightning Source LLC
Chambersburg PA
CBHW071919150726
47999CB00001B/35